DUALITY

RIVEN WORLDS BOOK SIX

(AMARANTHE ♦ 19)

G. S. JENNSEN

HYPERNOVA
PUBLISHING
2023

DUALITY

Hypernova Publishing
P.O. Box 1467
Libby, Montana 59923
www.hypernovapublishing.com

Publisher's Note: This is a work of fiction. Names, characters, places, and incidents are a product of the author's imagination. Locales and public names are sometimes used for atmospheric purposes. Any resemblance to actual people, living or dead, or to businesses, companies, events, institutions, or locales is completely coincidental.

The Hypernova Publishing name, colophon and logo are trademarks of Hypernova Publishing.

Ordering Information:
Hypernova Publishing books may be purchased for educational, business or sales promotional use. For details, contact the "Special Markets Department" at the address above.

Duality / G. S. Jennsen.—1st ed.

LCCN 2022922860
978-1-957352-11-4

AMARANTHE UNIVERSE

AURORA RHAPSODY

AURORA RISING
STARSHINE
VERTIGO
TRANSCENDENCE

AURORA RENEGADES
SIDESPACE
DISSONANCE
ABYSM

AURORA RESONANT
RELATIVITY
RUBICON
REQUIEM

ASTERION NOIR
EXIN EX MACHINA
OF A DARKER VOID
THE STARS LIKE GODS

RIVEN WORLDS
CONTINUUM
INVERSION
ECHO RIFT
ALL OUR TOMORROWS
CHAOTICA
DUALITY

SHORT STORIES
Restless, Vol. I • *Restless, Vol. II* • *Apogee* • *Solatium* • *Venatoris*
Re/Genesis • *Meridian* • *Fractals* • *Chrysalis* • *Starlight Express*

Learn more at gsjennsen.com/books or visit the
Amaranthe Wiki: gsj.space/wiki

For Mom. I can never repay you for all you gave me—strength, kindness, wisdom and love—but I can say thank you.

DRAMATIS PERSONAE

Alexis 'Alex' Solovy Marano

Space scout and explorer. Prevo.

Spouse of Caleb Marano, daughter of Miriam and David Solovy.

Caleb Marano

Former Special Operations intelligence agent. Space scout and explorer.

Spouse of Alex Solovy, bonded to Akeso.

Miriam Solovy (Commandant)

Leader, Concord Armed Forces.

Malcolm Jenner (Admiral)

AEGIS Fleet Admiral.

Marlee Marano

Consulate Assistant.

Mia Requelme

Owner, Confluence Expo.

Richard Navick

Concord Intelligence Director.

Morgan Lekkas

Former IDCC Cmdr. Fighter Pilot.

Enzio Vilane

Head of the Gardiens.

Devon Reynolds

Concord Special Projects Director.

ASTERIONS

Nika Kirumase

External Relations Advisor, Asterion Dominion Advisor Committee.

Former NOIR leader.

Dashiel Ridani

Industry Advisor, Asterion Dominion Advisor Committee.

Owner, Ridani Enterprises.

Joaquim Lacese

Former NOIR Operations Director.

Maris Debray

Culture Advisor.

Perrin Benvenit

Omoikane Personnel Director.

Cassidy Frenton

Joaquim's lover.

OTHER MAJOR CHARACTERS

Mnemosyne ('Mesme')
Idryma Member. Former 1st Analystae of Aurora.
Species: Katasketousya

Eren Savitas asi-Idoni
Advocacy Chief of Intelligence for Non-Anaden Affairs.
Species: Anaden

Corradeo Praesidis
Concord Senator. Head of Anaden Advocacy.
Species: Anaden

Adlai Weiss
Justice Advisor.
Species: Asterion

Akeso
Sentient planet.
Species: Ekos

David Solovy
Professor, Concord SWTC.
Species: Human

Graham Delavasi
Former SF Intelligence Director.
Species: Human

Katherine Colson
Administration Advisor.
Species: Asterion

Kennedy Rossi
CEO, Connova Interstellar.
Species: Human

Lance Palmer (Commander)
Military Advisor.
Species: Asterion

Meno
Mia's Prevo counterpart.
Species: Artificial

Miaon
Former anarch agent.
Species: Yinhe

Noah Terrage
COO, Connova Interstellar.
Species: Human

Nyx Praesidis
Advocacy Dir. of Intelligence.
Species: Anaden

Olivia Montegreu
Former cartel head, Enzio's mother.
Species: Artificial

Onai Veshnael
Novoloume Dean, Concord Senator.
Species: Novoloume

Parc Eshett
Omoikane Initiative consultant.
Species: Asterion

Thomas
CAF Aurora Artificial.
Species: Artificial

Valkyrie
Alex's Prevo counterpart.
Species: Artificial

MINOR CHARACTERS

Bara Jhouti-min, CINT undercover agent (*Barisan*)

Braelyn Rossi-Terrage, Kennedy and Noah's daughter *(Human)*

Casmir elasson-Machim, Leader, Anaden military (*Anaden*)

Castor Greer, Chairman, Security/State Affairs, EA Assembly (*Human*)

Charles Gagnon, Earth Alliance Prime Minister *(Human)*

Cupcake, adolescent dragon (*Vrachnas*)

Cyfeill, Leader, Ourankeli refugees (*Ourankeli*)

Erik Schimmel, CINT Rasu surveillance expert *(Human)*

Fai Xing, Commander, AEGIS military (*Human*)

Felzeor, CINT agent (*Volucri*)

Ferenc Khoura-lan, Barisan terrorist leader (*Barisan*)

Jonas Rossi-Terrage, Kennedy and Noah's son *(Human)*

Karis Yuri, Hamid member (*Naraida*)

Lontias elasson-Praesidis, Advocacy Consultant (*Anaden*)

Martina Kuhn, Gardiens agent *(Human)*

Nolan Bastian, AEGIS Field Marshal *(Human)*

Olav Zylynski, Gardiens Chief of Security *(Human)*

Philippe Beaumont, Gardiens Agent *(Human)*

Pinchu, Tokahe Naataan (*Khokteh*)

Ronald Corbin, Rossi Foundation attorney *(Human)*

Selene Panetier, Justice Advisor (*Asterion*)

Simon Ettore, AEGIS Commodore, *Denali* XO *(Human)*

Stanley, Morgan's Prevo counterpart (*Artificial*)

William Solarian, SENTRI Director *(Human)*

William 'Will' Sutton, CINT Operations Director *(Human)*

Ziton elasson-Praesidis, Advocacy Security Director (*Anaden*)

CONCORD

MEMBER SPECIES

Human
Representative: Aristide Vranas

Anaden
Representative: Corradeo Praesidis

Novoloume
Representative: Dean Onai Veshnael

Naraida
Representative: Tasme Chareis

Khokteh
Representative: Pinchutsenahn Niikha Qhiyane Kteh

Barisan
Representative: Daayn Shahs-lan

Dankath
Representative: Bohlke'ban

Efkam
Representative: Ahhk~sae

ALLIED SPECIES

Asterion
Katasketousya
Fylliot

Taenarin
Volucri
Yinhe

PROTECTED SPECIES

Ekos
Faneros
Galenai
Godjan

Icksel
Ourankeli
Pachrem
Vrachnas

AMARANTHE
CONCORD EMPIRE

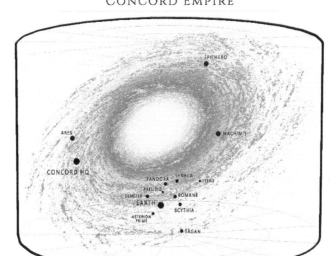

MILKY WAY GALAXY

LOCAL GALACTIC GROUP

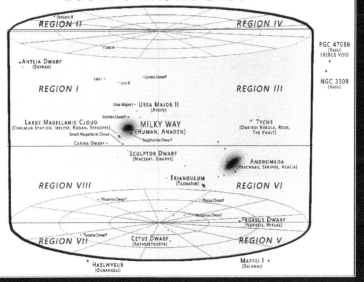

GENNISI GALAXY
(MESSIER 94)

✗
RASU STRONGHOLD
(DESTROYED)

ADJUNCT SHI

SOGAIN SYSTEM
✺(DESTROYED)

MIRAI

NAMINO

ADJUNCT HACHI

KIYORA

EBISU

TOKI'TAKU ✺
(TAIYOK HOMEWORLD)

SYNRA

✺ CHOSEK
(CHIZERU HOMEWORLD)

✦ ASTERION DOMINION AXIS WORLDS
✦ ASTERION DOMINION ADJUNCT WORLDS
✺ ALIEN WORLDS

ASTERION DOMINION
AXIS WORLDS

MIRAI   NAMINO   SYNRA   EBISU   KIYORA

The Story So Far

For a summary of the events of **RIVEN WORLDS BOOKS 1-4**, see the Appendix in the back of the book.

CHAOTICA

In the aftermath of Nika's transformative encounter with kyoseil in the Oneiroi Nebula, Alex challenges Mesme for an explanation. Mesme says that everything it has done, it has done to save the people—Alex, Caleb, Nika, Dashiel, Miriam, Corradeo—who will save the universe, if it can be saved. Their argument ends with Alex still angry and distrustful of Mesme.

The Rasu interrogate the Ruda Supremes for more details about Concord's structure, member species and technology. Under duress, the Ruda tell the Rasu about adiamene and its weaknesses.

Nika tests out the new powers kyoseil has gifted her, including the ability to open wormholes, to control kyoseil's actions to some extent, and to see every kyoseil interaction everywhere. She also begins to catch glimpses of other Asterions' thoughts in her mind.

Alex and Valkyrie discover that the Laniakea Supercluster is smaller and more tightly packed than it was in the Aurora universe; they speculate that the Rasu are using their Core Rings to pull galaxies closer together. Valkyrie has been watching Rasu movements and detects how they group themselves into distinct factions that rarely intermingle.

Marlee explores her new abilities as a Solo Prevo. Her first use of a wormhole is to visit the dragons, where Cupcake promptly charges through her wormhole and into her apartment. After much destruction and several injuries, Marlee is able to trick it back through the wormhole and retreats to her wrecked apartment.

Alex and Caleb host a dinner party on Akeso with Marlee, Eren, Felzeor and Nika. Nika asks Mesme to join them, then forces Mesme to reveal that Akeso was created using a 'seed' of kyoseil. This is why Caleb and Akeso stay connected across quantum blocks and why Reor responds to both Alex and Caleb. Alex deduces that the Kats used *diati* to seed the Ekos-1 intelligence and Dzhvar to seed Ekos-3.

The Rasu attack two Anaden worlds and the dragons' homeworld. Miriam uses the new Ymyrath Field weapon against the Rasu at the dragons' homeworld, successfully destroying the Rasu's ability to maneuver, shapeshift or fire their weapons.

Enzio Vilane searches for the leak in his organization, then reviews his Grand Design, which will eventually result in non-Prevo humans dying off, and Prevos being the future of humanity. His mother, Olivia, advises him not to trust anyone but himself—and her.

A Gardiens anti-regenesis protest at the New Frontiers clinic turns violent, and several bystanders are killed. The protestors flee and hole up in a nearby school, where Kennedy and Noah's kids are in class. The Gardiens take many children hostage, but Jonas and Braelyn escape into the air vents. Caleb and Noah sneak into the school, neutralize several Gardiens, and find Jonas and Braelyn in the security room just as a Gardien is about to reach them. They sneak back out to safety, then Caleb goes back inside and takes out the remaining Gardiens.

The Rasu begin deploying antimatter weapons, which will destroy adiamene. Valkyrie receives a message from the Ruda that says 'You were correct in your warnings. Forgive us.' She finds their entire planet utterly destroyed, the Ruda annihilated.

Marlee is helping Mia prepare for the Confluence Expo grand opening, when a voice in her head starts talking to her. Mia gives a speech at the opening, and thinks she sees Malcolm in the audience.

Malcolm leaves the Expo to meet with Vilane, where he tears into the man over the New Frontiers/Insights Academy violence. Malcolm extracts a list of concessions, including greater access to the Gardiens organization, in return for Malcolm's continued support. The Gardiens go on a public relations offensive to repair their tarnished name, frustrating Richard and Graham's investigation.

Nika observes that the Rift Bubbles use kyoseil in their lattice structure and to run the device's programming, and that their design is eerily similar to the miniature Rift Bubble the Asterions are working on. The Rasu capture a Dominion cargo ship; Nika quickly changes the access code for the Rift Bubble, but unbeknownst to everyone, several Rasu are able to get through the barrier before she does and land on Mirai.

Mesme shares details of the kyoseil's origins and history with Nika. The kyoseil is the third primordial species of the ancient universe, along with *diati* and Dzhvar. During the Dzhvar War, the kyoseil chose not to take a side, and instead remained passive until it chose to bond with the Asterions. Mesme says that Asterions are the physical manifestation of the kyoseil's will.

Mesme engages in a mysterious conversation with the Yinhe, Miaon. Mesme admits to feeling weary, as well as confounded by Alex and Nika's relentless probing. Miaon tells Mesme to remember that it is not in control of how this ends—they are.

The kyoseil alerts Nika that the Rasu are about to activate a quantum block on Mirai, seconds before they do. A battle begins. The Asterions deploy their new miniature rift devices, called Kireme Boundaries. Nika is able to control the devices remotely and discovers she can locate the Rasu quantum block modules through sidespace. She dives into the arduous task of managing multiple Kireme Boundaries across Mirai.

The Asterions begin to get the upper hand on the Rasu, and Dashiel checks on Nika. He finds her utterly engulfed in light and seemingly unconscious on the floor. In reality, she is lost out in sidespace, bouncing among the sea of kyoseil waves. Dashiel is able to reach her and help her mind return to her body. He takes her home to get some rest.

Nika wakes up to a deluge of Asterion thoughts bombarding her mind. Unable to keep them out, she collapses in agony. Mesme arrives and envelops her in a protective shroud, then teaches her how to keep the stray thoughts out of her mind.

Alex and Caleb eavesdrop on the Rasu as one faction subsumes several star systems of another faction into itself. The Rasu are not at war with one another, but they are engaged in low-level skirmishes as each faction seeks greater power.

Alex, Caleb Nika and Dashiel brainstorm ways they might exploit the fissures between the various factions. Nika realizes there is one thing that every Rasu in existence wants: kyoseil, which they believe they can use to control their distant sub-units. She speculates that she might be able to ask the kyoseil to turn on for the Rasu, but then rejects the notion. She won't ask the kyoseil to do the Rasu's murderous bidding. Alex and Caleb nonetheless begin to hatch a plan.

The Rasu attack Nopreis, the Novoloume homeworld, as well as Synra, Kiyora and Ebisu. Nika chases the Rasu across three worlds as the battles rage, until she realizes they are going to lose. Out of options, she reaches out to Alex about her plan.

Alex attempts to tell her mother about it, but Miriam is knee-deep in pitched battles, so instead she wishes her mother luck and leaves.

Concord and the Dominion are now fighting the Rasu on 14 worlds at once. With the Rasu using antimatter weapons, Concord is losing ships and people. Then the Rasu arrive at the human colony of Sagan—the first human world to be attacked.

Eren and Felzeor are on Hirlas when the Rasu attack. Caleb learns that the Rasu are attacking the Naraida homeworld and Eren and Felzeor are trapped there. Alex insists that she and Nika can handle their mission on their own, and for him to go to Hirlas and rescue them.

Caleb reaches Hirlas and hooks up with Eren, Felzeor and a group of Naraida who are trying to thwart the Rasu attack.

The plan: Dashiel injects 7 captured Rasu with a virutox that embeds information on the nature of kyoseil and locations of kyoseil deposits, then encloses all seven in cages. They load the cages into the cargo hold of the

Siyane. Nika speaks to the kyoseil, asking it to turn on its abilities for the Rasu.

Alex and Nika infiltrate several Rasu systems. In each one, they launch one of the Rasu cages into the midst of the other Rasu. Once it is in space, the cage dissolves. The released Rasu joins up with others, thereby passing along the information about kyoseil it carries.

While traveling, they talk about Mesme and the secrets it keeps. Alex notes how Mesme knew what was going to happen at the Oneiroi Nebula, then makes an intuitive leap and wonders if Mesme might be a time traveler. Nika argues that time travel is impossible, but Alex posits that with enough energy applied to a point on the spacetime manifold, it might be possible. She speculates that it is likely incredibly difficult, and has likely happened only once.

During the delivery of the final Rasu 'saboteurs,' Alex and Nika are knocked out of the *Siyane's* hold and into space amongst the Rasu. Nika is unconscious, but Alex is able to reach her, and Valkyrie scoops them back into the ship just before a Rasu reaches them. Nika regains consciousness and releases the last Rasu. Alex realizes that Caleb's heartbeat, which she's been able to sense ever since Namino, is slowing down. Nika returns to Mirai, and Alex heads straight for Hirlas.

Caleb and the others flee the Rasu through the jungles of Hirlas. The Rasu closes in on the group until they are cornered. With a waterfall and cliffs at their back, they have nowhere to run. Akeso observes that Hirlas is bursting with life and energy, as it noted when they first visited for Cosime's funeral. Akeso wonders if they could apply a spark to awaken the planet's voice.

Caleb goes to the riverbank and opens up his wrists, then bleeds into the dirt and the water. Through his blood, Akeso sends its life force out into the firmament of Hirlas.

The ground opens up beneath the attacking Rasu and swallows them whole. The trees come to life to ensnare the Rasu mechs and tear them apart. Fissures open up to the planet's outer core, and Rasu fall into the chasms to be dissolved by the lava. Everywhere, the Rasu are torn apart or melted until they are only atoms, then the planet tears the atoms apart.

Caleb wakes up in a medical tent. Akeso informs him that its consciousness now resides in the planet of Hirlas as well. Eren fills him in how the planet destroyed the Rasu on the surface, and how he found Caleb bled out on the shore of the river, nearly dead. Caleb leaves the tent and finds Alex, who had landed the *Siyane* right in the middle of the refugee camp, and they reunite.

Nika rejoins the battle on Mirai, which continues in earnest. Abruptly she begins to hear Rasu thoughts in her head, transmitted by the kyoseil they are integrating into themselves. Soon thereafter, several Rasu factions begin attacking one another in earnest, and Nika reports that the civil war they'd hoped to trigger has begun.

The Rasu abruptly pull off from Sagan, then Nopreis, then all the worlds they were attacking. Concord surveillance soon detects the Rasu engaged in internal battles back in their territory.

Marlee sees Dr. Canivon for help about the voice in her head, which has proved to be mean and belittling. After an examination, Dr. Canivon tells Marlee her upgrades have given a voice to her subconscious. The voice is her own mind.

Eren visits Cosime's grave on Hirlas and finds the entire cemetery overtaken by a sea of blooming white flowers that originate from Cosime's sepulcher. Akeso, now the resident intelligence of Hirlas, has remembered Cosime, located where she rests, and created a beautiful memorial for her.

Alex and Nika tell Miriam about their actions to incite a Rasu civil war. Miriam is furious, believing the ultimate victor will be an enemy too powerful to ever defeat. Alex argues that Concord was already on the verge of being defeated, and her actions have bought them time. Miriam says she will use the time to prepare for the next offensive, but worries that Alex has signed their death warrant.

Nika and Alex confront Mesme about their time travel theory. After some pressing, Mesme admits it is true. Mesme says that eight years from now, it travels back in time 982,000 years. It insists they are doing better this time than they did in the previous timeline, but they must be united and of one purpose to emerge victorious. Alex and Mesme finally make up. Nika asks if it is keeping any more secrets; Mesme says there is one, but it is personal and does not impact their fight against the Rasu. It asks to be allowed to keep it, and they agree.

CONTENTS

DUALITY

"Yesterday is gone. Tomorrow has not yet come. We have only today. Let us begin."

— *Mother Theresa*

PART I

SHELL GAMES

1

EARTH ORBIT
MILKY WAY GALAXY

An encroaching swell of sunlight swept across Earth's profile to reveal an intricate web of gossamer silk enveloping the planet, as if a fine-spun shawl had been draped upon Earth's shoulders.

At least, this was what it resembled to Commandant Miriam Solovy's eyes as their shuttle banked around and approached the closest control node on the upgraded Terrestrial Defense Grid. Tiny rods of adiamene, only ten centimeters in width, were spaced every two hundred kilometers across the upper atmosphere. Where they intersected, gleaming modules jutted outward into space. Blocky at first, then cylindrical as they tapered into conical nozzles.

Three such rings encircled Earth, situated one-hundred-twenty degrees from each other upon the circumference of the planet, and each ring supported six hundred modules. This was triple the previous number of modules per ring, and every one wielded a weapon infinitely more powerful than all that had come before it.

For now, the modules remained still and silent. Watching and waiting for the enemy's arrival.

"The Zero Drives powering the weapons are stored within the base modules. It's a closed system, both physically and from an engineering perspective."

"Except for the muzzle," Miriam replied, a hint of challenge in her tone.

"True," Fleet Admiral Malcolm Jenner remarked wryly. "But the muzzle will be shooting forth a steady stream of negative energy. No Rasu will hold together long enough to reach it."

"Fair point." As the shuttle passed above the next module on the ring, she was able to make out several drones welding the final connections into place. The engineers had declared the Grid ready for service the day before, but work on smaller upgrades and minor repairs would continue for as long as time allowed.

Miriam played out a couple of scenarios in her mind, imagining how the Grid might operate in a genuine battle. "You called it a closed system. If a Rasu were to somehow swallow one of these modules, does this mean the weapon will keep firing—from the inside out, as it were?"

Malcolm nodded firmly. "Any Rasu who tries it will come to regret downing this particular snack."

"Good." The shuttle cruised onward, toward the North Pole, and Miriam reluctantly turned her attention to Prime Minister Charles Gagnon. He'd been quiet for the last several minutes, sitting beside her with his hands folded on his lap. It was a testament to his keen political sense that he didn't try to express an opinion on matters he knew nothing about.

She directed his attention toward the reflective glimmer of the ring arcing below them. "I take it we constructed the upgrades in such a way as to not interfere with the atmosphere corridor exits?"

"Yes. I am told it was a nightmarish challenge to overcome by the design team, but they managed it. There are slight distance variations in the spacing of the modules where necessary, but the variations don't weaken the structural integrity. Again, so I am told." He adopted a pained countenance. "The cost required to factor in all possible permutations—"

"Was worth it." Her glare foreclosed the protest poised on his lips. She'd heard all the pearl-clutching exclamations a thousand times in the last two months, and her response remained the same today as it had at the start. Sixteen years ago, she'd pitched the Earth Alliance headlong into an ocean of red ink in order to swiftly produce a fleet of adiamene warships capable of withstanding the assault of a Katasketousya armada, and it had been worth it. When the alternative was extinction, no cost was too high.

She offered her companions an officious smile. "Excellent work, both of you, in buckling down and making this happen with impressive speed. We don't know precisely when the Rasu will return, but when they do, they will find an Earth immeasurably better defended in every respect."

Gagnon sighed. "And if they don't return?"

Miriam and Malcolm exchanged a somber glance. "They will."

CONCORD HQ

RASU WAR ROOM
MILKY WAY GALAXY

The regular meeting of the Rasu War Council convened at 1030 CST sharp, with all members and several guests in attendance.

If anyone was tiring of the repeated every-other-day sessions, they didn't voice it. Knowing the enemy's strategic moves was essential if they wanted to survive the coming crisis. Miriam recognized that if this span of peace stretched on for much longer, the level of discipline and rigor would start to wane, but her gut told her she wasn't going to need to worry about such an eventuality.

She brought the meeting to order with a minimum of fuss. "As of yesterday, AEGIS has completed principal construction and testing on RNEW-powered planetary defense grids for Earth, Seneca and Romane. They join six Anaden worlds now enjoying such protection. Slightly less comprehensive defense grids are under construction around multiple other...I hesitate to call them 'important' colonies, as every inhabited planet is important to us. Let us instead refer to them as AEGIS colonies hosting significant populations or holding strategic importance for other reasons. Assembly of similar defense grids is also well underway at Nopreis, Ireltse, Macskaf, Gnarve, and all the Asterion Dominion Axis Worlds."

The Barisans and Khokteh hadn't been able to afford the construction—in truth, no one had genuinely been able to afford it—so Concord had fronted most of their costs. The Naraida had insisted Hirlas no longer required such protection, but following Caleb's endorsement, they had been persuaded to accept a single planetary ring of RNEW weapons. No amount of persuasion had swayed the Efkams' insistence that they were prepared to weather any attack, while the Dankath had metaphorically clawed their way to be first in line.

She called up one of the many reports she'd reviewed this morning. "Since yesterday, we have certified three additional planets clear of any hidden Rasu presence. This brings the number to 1,264. Only 3,684 more to go." She moved on before anyone could bemoan the seeming impossibility of such a task. "Director Reynolds, can you provide us an update on the Detection Network?"

Devon nodded sharply from across the table. After some initial antics, he'd lately been comporting himself with a surprising degree of formality in these meetings. "Yes, ma'am. The upgraded detection mesh is now operational with a range of up to two parsecs in diameter around sixty-three percent of active Concord assets: planets, asteroids, stations. We're increasing our coverage reach by five percent every week. So in another eight weeks, we will know the nanosecond a Rasu so much as dips a toe in the galactic vicinity of somewhere we want to protect."

"Can we speed up that timeline?"

Devon grimaced for a beat before squelching it; her pushing him—pushing them all—harder was nothing new. "Give me a ten-percent bump in personnel and ships to deploy the sensors, and I can get it down to seven weeks. Twenty percent, six weeks."

The trouble was, every shipyard in Concord space was already running beyond capacity churning out new warships, and though military enlistment was booming, training people to operate them took time. She offered him a thin smile by way of concession. "I'll see what I can do."

Updates on defensive preparations across a variety of parameters continued for another ten minutes before she was able to turn to Erik Schimmel, their dedicated Rasu surveillance expert. A lot of people were watching the Rasu: a host of Kats, Dominion observation teams, Concord Ghosts, and of course both Alex and Nika. They all (even Alex) reported to Schimmel, a longtime CINT surveillance wonk, who analyzed the data and distilled it into a digestible report for the Council.

"Mr. Schimmel, what's the update for today?"

Schimmel was a scrupulous, arguably fastidious man; he kept his head shaved, likely so no hair could fall out of place. "Noteworthy developments, Commandant. As we've been predicting, Emerald has delivered a decisive blow to Violet by taking one-third of its territory in Quadrant Five in the last six days. Following their victory over Lemon in Quadrant Four last week, Emerald now controls twenty-eight percent of the map. Their closest competition, Crimson, is struggling to hold on to twenty-one percent."

Schimmel activated the color-coded map above the table, and the visual brought the situation into sharp relief. A vibrant green hue radiated a growing presence across a map displaying the current state of the Rasu civil war. Emerald was not the victor, not yet, but the faction was expanding its territory every day.

Miriam cast her gaze around the table. "In light of Emerald's increasing strength, I believe now is the time for another Disruption maneuver. Does anyone disagree?"

Casmir elasson-Machim ventured a frown. "Technically, their holdings remain smaller than Crimson's were when we moved against them."

"True, but Emerald is displaying worrisome momentum. It has gained control of a greater number of systems faster than any faction to date. If we wait, we risk the opportunity to influence the conflict slipping away from us."

Casmir held up a hand in concession. "Agreed. No objection."

"Are there any other concerns?" No one spoke up. "Very well. Mr. Schimmel, please identify the most effective strike points. You and I can review them after the meeting, then we'll move forward with the maneuver."

"I anticipated this might be your decision and went ahead and did the analysis. Here are my recommendations."

He had proved to be notably good at his job. She scanned the report but found nothing to object to. "All right. I'm activating Disruption Phase Three. Fleet Admiral Jenner, Navarchos Casmir, make it happen. Buy us some more time."

RW

NGC 3309 GALAXY

60 MEGAPARSECS FROM CONCORD HQ

The *CAF Intrepid* exited the Caeles Prism wormhole less than two megameters from the Rasu's stellar ring.

Enemy warships pivoted in their direction almost instantly, and thus began a most harrowing, nail-biting three-hundred-ten seconds. The fact that this was now the sixteenth time Commander Xing and his crew had run this gauntlet made it no less so.

"Ready, and...fire the Ymyrath Field on the nearest platforms. Navigation, sweep us around, fast but steady."

Rasu weapons fire bounced off their hull-hugging shield without causing any damage. Thus far, the enemy had not fielded their antimatter weapons in these encounters, presumably because to use them in the heart of their own strongholds would cause as much damage to themselves as to a Concord vessel.

So he and the bridge crew gritted their teeth and weathered the onslaught as their subtle but oh-so-dastardly weapon sabotaged the massive platforms of the stellar ring, one after another after another, while their ship raced around the circumference of the star.

When they'd returned to where they began, they pivoted one-hundred-eighty degrees and rocketed forward, spewing the Field's radiation far and wide through the attacking Rasu fleet.

"Navigation, get us out of here."

"Yes, sir!"

They superluminaled to a dead point in space four parsecs away, but only long enough to catch their breath and allow their weapon to recharge. Time was of the essence in these hit-and-run attacks; surprise the name of their game. So Xing calmly took a sip of water and watched the power gauge edge upward.

The Ymyrath Field had come a long way since he'd shepherded its first test fire at Chalmun Station Asteroid. Two and a half times more powerful while requiring forty percent less energy (this meant the *Intrepid* no longer had to be completely naked while firing it) and capable of firing its deadly blast of supercharged 4-neutron radiation for five uninterrupted minutes.

With those kinds of stats, one ship wielding one weapon could cripple the heart of an entire Rasu stellar system in a single go—which they had just done. Now, to hit seven more with equal swiftness.

RW

CONCORD HQ

"And there are eighteen systems neutralized." Malcolm Jenner watched the status board update as he spoke. "Twenty-three. The *Colorado* and *Mugabe* have completed their runs and are returning to port."

Casmir elasson-Machim muttered something and opened a small screen below the main board. "The *Stealth YF Charlie* is reporting it suffered damage to the Field's output nozzle during its last run."

"The one place where it's vulnerable?" Malcolm worried at his jaw. "Likely just a lucky hit by the Rasu, but we don't need them realizing what they accomplished and start spreading the word."

"Indeed. The vessel departed the system immediately upon receiving the damage, so it's doubtful the Rasu were able to determine the result of their attack. I'm ordering it to the MW Sector 34 Dry Dock. Hopefully it can be repaired with all due speed."

"And hopefully we won't need it again for a few weeks." Malcolm eyed the board expectantly, waiting...*there*. "All sixty-four systems neutralized. I'll let the commandant know. Good work, Navarchos."

"You as well." Casmir jerked a nod, closed his screens and departed. The man wasn't much for small talk, but Malcolm had stopped taking his brusque demeanor personally some time ago. In truth, they'd forged a close working relationship in the last two months.

Malcolm opened a comm channel with Miriam. "Commandant, I'm pleased to report that all sixty-four systems were successfully disabled. No losses and only minor damage to one of our vessels."

In the holo, Miriam's expression brightened a touch. "Excellent news. With Emerald's knees knocked out from underneath them, we've given Crimson and Orange—or perhaps an underdog who has been biding their time—an opportunity to level the playing field."

"Yes, ma'am."

This was the game they'd been engaged in for six weeks now. Watch until one Rasu faction achieved a significant advantage in their civil war, then sneak in and weaken that faction enough for its adversaries to swoop in and gain ground. It had worked twice before, though Emerald was the strongest faction to emerge from the conflict so far, having garnered its advantage with astonishing speed. But Concord had also added an additional Ymyrath Field to their arsenal this round. By the time such a move was required again, they should have two more ready to join in the mission.

By this point, the Rasu had surely figured out who was sabotaging them. In theory, this meant when a victor finally emerged, the enemy would harbor even *more* of a grudge against Concord. But really, how much was that going to matter? They would come for Concord with their full strength regardless of whether they were mildly annoyed or righteously ticked off (in the unlikely event Rasu experienced such breadth of emotions). So the best strategy they had was to delay the invasion for as long as possible. The Rasu War Council had sat in a room two months ago and decided it was their best course of action. Disrupt, confuse, harass and stymie the enemy.

And in the meantime, they prepared.

Alone in the room, Malcolm rubbed at his eyes. His now perpetual state of weariness stood as a testament to how far they'd come on that front.

2

AKESO
URSA MAJOR II GALAXY

Alex spread aioli on toasted slices of bread, her motions conveying an air of feigned nonchalance. "So how much power does it take to punch a time hole in the spacetime manifold?"

Mesme meandered around her kitchen, its lights slipping into and out of a humanoid outline. *More power than you or I—than Concord or the combined capabilities of the Katasketousya—can create.*

"That's what I figured." She glanced out the window and spotted Caleb sitting cross-legged on the creek bank, sunlight spilling along his features. A corner of his lips quirked in seeming amusement, possibly in response to one of Akeso's unique observations about what it was like to exist as *two* planets. Because there had been many of those since the incredible events at Hirlas, when Caleb had spilt his blood and Akeso its soul to awaken the planet and defeat the Rasu invasion there.

A new Ekos planet had been born out of blood. Yet said planet was also Akeso—a single intelligence spanning across galaxies, and across one man.

She blinked and tried to regain her train of thought. "How does it happen, then?"

If I tell you, I risk changing the future in a manner we do not want it changed.

She rolled her eyes as she retrieved the deli meat from the refrigeration unit. "What a lame answer. You sound like a science fiction vid. 'But the timeline!'"

Perhaps these 'vids' of yours are onto something. Mesme stilled directly in front of her and waited until she raised her gaze to meet its presence. *Alex, I must be careful here. I am not trying to hide things from you, but our mutual goal is to ensure we save—*

"The universe. Yeah, I remember. So let's review where we are. You can't tell me what happens to send you back in time, how it happens or when it happens. That's..." she cracked a wry smile "...disappointing. A trifle frustrating, one might say."

I do not know when it happens.

"But when we first discussed this, you specifically said you traveled back in time eight years from now."

I did. But we have already altered the previous timeline in this cycle. Events are not playing out precisely as they did before, nor occurring on the same dates.

"So for all 'this'—" she waved grandly at the air "—we're flying completely blind here?"

Not blind. The past—my past—guides the future, hopefully in meaningful and useful ways. But in some important ways, yes, the future is now unwritten.

Alex rubbed at her temples. She and Mesme had performed this dance many times in the two months since she'd discovered the Kat was a time traveler, and it was wearing her down. But in every conversation, the Kat's guard slipped here and there and it divulged a few additional nuggets of actual information. So she kept pushing. Probing.

"How did we lose last time? If we've already changed things, there's no harm in you telling me."

I'm not certain you're correct. Allow me to answer in this way: it was no more and no less than the reality that we were not strong enough to stop the enemy.

"But we're stronger this time, aren't we?"

Without question. But we must continue to push our limits.

"Don't worry, we are." Sandwich spread prepared, she grabbed the juice and three glasses. "You've said this is your second time through this 'cycle,' to use your term. But if the timeline is mostly the same—except for our greater strength and a bit of date shifting—this implies you also exist here in some other incarnation, doesn't it? An incarnation for whom this is the first time through these events." She brought a hand to her chin. "Are there two Mesmes running around here in Amaranthe right now?"

No.

A straightforward answer? The Kat was probably going to regret giving one. "Then you're someone else—you were someone else before you traveled back in time. Does this mean the Kats aren't Kats yet?"

Alex.

It was becoming Mesme's favorite reproachment, but she remained undeterred. "It's fine. I don't need you to answer the question. You went back in time a million years, but no record exists of the Kats until 250,000 years ago. Three-quarters of a million years is plenty of time for the Kats to evolve into your current form."

Anthropologically speaking, this is a reasonable supposition.

She fisted a hand at her mouth to keep from laughing aloud—then the laughter died in her throat anyway. By Mesme's standards, this was confirmation of her assertion...which only begged further questions. Did those who would become Kats all exist in a different form here and now?

She tried to recall Mesme's exact words on that night at Nika's flat, because when it spoke, every word was chosen with precision.

Are all the Kats time travelers, or solely you?"
In the ways which matter, it is only I. None of the other Katasketousya have any memory of a life other than the ones which have proceeded along time's arrow since they were awakened.

This part still didn't make any sense. For all Mesme's faults, she couldn't conceive of it being so heartless as to kidnap a bunch of people, drag them into the past, erase their memories and turn them into Kats. So there had to be another explanation. Presumably a painful and tragic one, given the whole 'annihilation of everything and everyone' outcome.

But it did suggest that, should history repeat itself and they lose the coming battles, someone existed here and now who would travel back in time and become Mesme in order to try again. Someone currently not-Mesme. Didn't it? She forced herself to run through the absurd time-travel logic again; it was enough to make her brain ache.

She dropped her elbows onto the counter. "This is the secret you asked Nika and me to allow you to keep, isn't it? Who you were your first time through—and thus who the person who might become future-past you is right now?" Bleh, what a tongue-twister.

Mesme had taken the opportunity of her silent mental gymnastics to wander off toward the living room, but her question stopped it cold. A sheet of icicles hanging like a curtain across the archway.

"I'll take that as a yes."

Alex, you promised.

"And I'm regretting that promise now." She groaned. "But I did. All right, let's back up for a minute. If this is only your second time through, how do you know details about earlier cycles?"

The fixture of lights relaxed a touch and floated into the kitchen. *The information was relayed to me.*

She waited for elaboration, which was foolish of her. Every single detail was going to have to be forcibly dragged out of Mesme, one question at a time. Okay. The sole entity who could possess such information would be…someone who had experienced the events of the previous cycles. How deep did this time loop go?

"Relayed to you by yourself?"

In a sense.

Ugh. "And what about the time before then? How many times have we lost?"

I cannot say with any certainty. The details that get passed on become somewhat vague after five or six cycles.

"Because it's like a game of comms?"

I don't follow.

"Every time a message gets shared, it loses some of—never mind, it doesn't matter. So what did you mean by 'in a sense'? You know how you received the information. Enlighten me."

Before Mesme could find its way to even a terse yet vague answer, though, a pulse arrived from her father.

Hey, who's ready for lunch? I'm famished.

One second and I'll grab you.

She sighed. "Looks as though you're off the hook on that one for the time being, as my lunch date is about to arrive. But we'll pick up where we left off next time."

The lights quivered with renewed energy, otherwise known as relief. *I would never expect anything less. I will review the latest Rasu observational reports and relay to you any noteworthy developments.*

"Yep."

Mesme's presence dissipated, and she gestured beside her to open a wormhole to her parents' house.

RW

David walked through the wormhole from his kitchen into hers, carrying a plate of zucchini boats in one hand and a blueberry pie in the other.

Alex's eyes widened. "Dad, it's just the three of us. Maybe the two of us, if Caleb doesn't get his ass back in the house."

He shrugged as he deposited the plates on the counter and pulled out a stool. "Eh, more leftovers for me. And you, of course."

"Right." She finished making her sandwich, then joined him on one of the stools. "Working from home today?"

He grimaced dramatically. "I do my best thinking among the trees. And this new Strategic Combat Assessment is requiring some *nelepo* deep thinking. I'm holding a conference with our top hundred warship captains tomorrow, and we're going to talk about all the new ways they can kill Rasu while not getting themselves killed by antimatter weapons in the process. Dicey game, this one is."

"No doubt. Kennedy's been sounding pretty optimistic on the newest shield modifications, though."

"I'm optimistic, too." He made a show of considering the sandwich makings in front of him. "Have you talked to your mother lately?"

That didn't take long. She made as much of a show of retrieving a zucchini boat, biting into it and savoring the flavor. "I talk to Mom all the time."

"You participate in official discussions of Rasu movements and activity. Debate the ramifications of the enemy's actions with her and the members of the Rasu War Council and pass along pertinent information you've received from Mesme."

"That's talking."

"And also not at all what I meant."

Alex stuffed her mouth full with zucchini again to avoid responding. Simply refusing to answer questions that made you uncomfortable worked for Mesme, after all.

Her father just sat there and watched her, sandwich uncompleted, patiently waiting. Was this how Mesme felt when under the onslaught of her dogged inquiries? She hoped it was.

But unlike Mesme, she found herself relenting, sipping on her juice before shifting around to face him. "Has Mom changed her mind about her assessment of how Nika and I used kyoseil to provoke the Rasu into a civil war?"

"She is...grateful for the time your actions have bought us. Immeasurably grateful."

"So, no. Ergo, there's nothing for us to talk about."

A zucchini boat splatted onto his plate. "*Bozhe moy*, I don't know which one of you is more *yebanaya* stubborn!"

"I know who's got my vote." Caleb breezed into the kitchen and kissed the top of her head on his way to snatching a pile of sliced turkey off the counter.

She grumbled in protest, and got a playful wink from Caleb in response. It seemed even her greatest allies were arrayed against her. Time to change the subject! "We appear to have knocked Emerald down several notches today. Reset the board again. I'm glad we're seeing success using the Ymyrath Field as an offensive weapon."

Caleb nodded, belatedly availing himself of some bread and lettuce. "It has got to be righteously pissing the Rasu off. Every time one faction sees domination on the horizon, we dart in and wipe out its strongest fortifications, leaving it susceptible to attack from its rivals."

"Confounding the enemy is always an effective strategy. Don't you agree, Dad?"

Having managed to construct a sandwich and promptly stuff half of it in his mouth, he could only nod vigorously in confirmation.

"Thank you. And it's not like provoking the enemy is going to make them *even more* determined to conquer us than they already are. But it might make the Rasu respect us a little. Or possibly make them more cautious. Yes, Mom will say 'or make them more perturbed.' Doesn't matter."

Caleb tilted his head; though his expression grew serious, affection lit his eyes as they met hers. "They're coming for us either way, right?"

"They always were—" She held up a finger as a pulse came in from Nika. "Hang on. Update from the front lines on the way."

They both stared at her, waiting. Finally, her dad gestured insistently. "Well?"

Alex smiled.

3

MIRAI

ASTERION DOMINION
GENNISI GALAXY

Rasu 1-NEQ (Emerald) Unit NEQ-D 8f: **Rasu 1-NEQ, respond with status.**

A series of kyoseil waves traveled from decimated stellar platforms across kiloparsecs, a lost child in peril calling out for its parent. The data the waves carried was fragmented and corrupted, though the waves themselves remained strong and clear.

Unit NEQ-A-16g: ...radiation...dislocation loops acceler—...losingcohesionatomi...signals......

Unit NEQ-D-8f: Repeat. Rasu 1-NEQ, respond with status.

The call went unanswered.

Unit NEQ-D-8f: Any sub-units of 1-NEQ, respond with status.

The information transmitted this time was even more disorganized, nothing but a meaningless jumble of symbols that petered out into silence.

Unit NEQ-D-8f: Wide broadcast. All units stationed in proximity to Parent Hubs disperse into interstellar regions. Concord attack in progress.

Nika Kirumase chewed absently on a thumbnail while in her mind's eye, she watched the frantic calls circle around the NGC 3309 galaxy. A roll call, a tally of the dead, an assessment of resources available. Eventually, multiple orders for retrenchment. With their leader gone, would anyone listen? Would a new leader emerge?

Not for the time being, it seemed, for the chaos only grew worse as the magnitude of the attack began to permeate the Rasu communication network.

Satisfied for now, she sent Alex a ping.

Do you want the good news or the bad news first?

Good news, no question.

We got the top-level Hub this time. The children are in utter disarray trying to organize themselves in the absence of their overlord.

All thanks to your intel. Mom will be pleased. This should knock Emerald way down for a while, even more so than we'd hoped. What's the bad news?

They know it's Concord attacking.

Know, or suspect?

Let's call it 'assume.'

Well, we expected this to happen. Odds are, we're their sole true adversary capable of striking so forcefully at them. Any sign they're developing the ability to mount a defense against these surprise strikes?

None so far.

Excellent. I'll pass along the news.

"Hey, I brought you some coffee."

Nika opened her eyes, blinking against the brightness of a spreading sunrise racing along Hataori Harbor, then smiled up at Dashiel Ridani as she accepted the steaming mug from him. "Join me?"

He settled into the chair beside her on his balcony. As he did, his gaze flickered across her face and back again, trying to read her without looking like he was trying to read her. "What's the word?"

"Concord's strike on Emerald went well. They took out the parent hub, and now all the detached units are scattering to hide and wait for someone to tell them what to do."

"Good to hear. And what about you? Are you okay? You've been at it for a while this morning."

The insistent calls of the Rasu bounced around the recesses of Nika's mind, and she worked to quiet them further. She despised listening to the enemy's thoughts, and Dashiel knew she did. But it was her job, one only she could perform, and that reality wasn't apt to change. Everyone had their role to play.

"Sorry I sneaked out of bed early. I needed to monitor the impact of the attack."

"I know. Not what I asked."

The intense scrutiny of his stare made her want to twitch. It was only because he cared about her, but she didn't have any answers for him—not ones he wanted, anyway.

So she tried to project an aura of reassurance. "I'm getting used to it. Numb to it, maybe. It helps to think of the noise as merely data, and not the intentional thoughts of living beings. And I'm heartened by how the kyoseil itself isn't fazed by the Ymyrath Field. When the Rasu are gone, it will remain." She inhaled the bolstering aroma of cinnamon and chicory.

"Kyoseil appears to be the ultimate infiltration weapon."

Her head snapped up. "Weapon?"

He shrugged mildly. "Agent provocateur."

She forced herself to let go of the wave of revulsion the term 'weapon' had triggered. Kyoseil was an ancient entity whose preferred state was one of peaceful co-existence with the universe it inhabited. It was a repository of and conduit for the voluminous knowledge lesser beings had amassed; it was *not* a weapon. It wasn't really an agent provocateur, either, but she was self-aware enough to recognize if she launched into yet another lecture about the exquisite, precious nature of the life form, Dashiel honestly may kick her out this time.

Her lips pursed. "I suppose that works."

He set his coffee mug to the side but kept one hand on it, rotating it slowly on the table. "After the briefing this morning, I want to make another attempt to alter the Rift Bubble access code—onsite, that is. I realize I can't do it remotely."

Her expression immediately brightened. "You do? I think it's a great idea."

"I know I've said it a thousand times now, but I want to help you, Nika. I want to ease your burden however I can."

Her heart ached at the angst underlying his voice. The truth was, they'd gotten themselves caught in a spiral of mutual guilt over the responsibilities they each carried. He worried over the emotional hardships he believed she was placing on herself. She worried he was driving himself into the ground working around the clock to design and build weapons and defenses that might actually protect them. She worried over his worry over her, and vice versa. Downward the spiral tumbled.

It wasn't healthy, and she knew it. But so far, the reality of the Rasu threat had blocked their every attempt to escape it. That and a pinch of stubbornness on his part.

"Your burden is easily as heavy as mine, so I wish you wouldn't think of it in such a way." She sighed. "But I admit I don't like representing a single point of failure for such an important component of our defenses. I need a backup."

RW

OUTSKIRTS OF MIRAI ONE

On the horizon, the gleaming façade of Mirai Tower shone proudly in the midday sun. The glass was marred only by a smattering of tiny dots—construction mechs putting the finishing touches on the scraper.

They hadn't had the money or dynepower to spend on rebuilding the structure, but symbols mattered, so they'd done it anyway. The Tower, visible from almost every corner of the city, conveyed to their citizens that the Dominion remained unbowed and unafraid. The Rasu hadn't beaten them, in mind, body or spirit. *Wouldn't* beat them.

Nika took Dashiel's hand in hers, and he was struck by how warm it was. She always ran warm these days; the warmer her skin, the more recently and frequently she'd been listening to the Rasu. It had been hours since her early morning reconnaissance, but the heat radiating off her suggested she hadn't been able to leave the enemy alone for those hours.

Her smile gave nothing away, which only served to further trouble him. She was supposed to be opening up to him, but instead she was getting more skilled at burying her pain where no one could see it. Her intractable stubbornness could be maddening.

Oblivious to his ruminations, Nika had focused on their task. "You're going to experience a jolt of power when you interact with the Rift Bubble hardware. Not enough to blow out any critical systems, though it wouldn't hurt to activate a couple of defensive barriers just in case."

"They're ready to go." He put aside his ruminations to study the golden ball of light spinning within the confines of the lattice. Energy leapt out in wisps like solar flares, then quickly dissipated into the air or was hauled back into the core. The energy, pulled from infinitely cascading hidden dimensions, powered the device that protected this planet. For all their vaunted weapons they'd invented this last year, it was the sole device capable of keeping the enemy off the soil of their home.

After their group ceraff wrote some clever routines, any advisor was able to turn a Bubble on or off, but what truly mattered was the ability to change the access code people and ships broadcast to pass through the barrier unscathed.

They'd done everything feasible to make it all-but-impossible for Rasu to capture any of their ships and steal the access code. But so long as it remained a remote possibility, they needed to be ready to change the code on a hair-trigger. They must not have a repeat of last time, when the Rasu had taken less than three minutes to sneak inside the protective barrier, then take it down from within.

Nika could change the code in literal seconds—and thus far, she was the only one of them who could do so at all. A Kat could accomplish the task, but there was no guarantee one would answer in a timely manner when called. They'd eased into a functional working relationship with the Kat scientists, but Dashiel refused to rely on them. Asterions took care of themselves.

He'd upgraded his delving and deriving programming and kyoseil-focused routines. Multiple times. He'd studied the Rift Bubble operating system until he dreamed about it. Here, with direct interfacing, he *should* be able to not merely read it but alter it.

"I stick my hand in?"

"Yes."

"All right." He rolled his shoulders; stretched his neck; cracked his knuckles. Finally he reached out with his right hand, flinching as electricity danced insistently over his skin. His fingertips began to glow as they penetrated the fringes of the ball of light.

Here goes. He thrust his hand and forearm all the way in.

His body lit up like an overloaded circuit, which it definitely was. He shut his eyes against the light—and upon his eyelids, code raced by. He breathed in, ignoring his pounding heart to concentrate on what unfurled in front of him. He knew where in the immensely complex programming the access code lay, and his engineering instincts took over as he chased it through endlessly spiraling waves of information.

There.

His breath whistled out through puckered lips as he mentally fondled the line of programming, confirming he comprehended its structure and purpose as completely as if he'd written it himself. Then he sent a directed command through his fingertips to change a single digit—

A zap of electricity rebounded into his circuits, and with a gasp he yanked his hand out and stumbled backward, barely catching himself before he collapsed to the ground.

"Gods, are you okay?" Nika's hand grabbed his upper arm, steadying him.

He shook his head roughly while a diagnostic routine activated, checking to ensure nothing crucial had gotten fried. When it returned green, he glanced around him, searching for something—other than the woman staring at him with concern and trepidation—to punch. But there was only a meadow and flowers. "It didn't work."

Nika frowned, her gaze darting between him and the lattice. "Well did you try—"

In frustration he grabbed her by the shoulders, demanding her proper attention. "I found the correct line of code. I read it. I understood it. I sent a command to change it, and the infernal contraption *bit* me."

Her throat convulsed. "I'm sorry. I thought...I thought it would work."

"It's..." his hands fell away, and his eyes squeezed shut for a beat "...it's not your fault. At all." Bitterness crept into his voice. "I simply wanted to be able to take the onus of this one damn task off your shoulders."

"No, darling." Her hand came to his cheek. Warm—still too warm—but soft and tender. "You're already doing so much to protect us. Me? This is the *only* thing I can do. It's no trouble."

Well, that was a lie. "The only thing? You stopped the war in its tracks."

"Yes, but that's in the past. When the Rasu return, I can do *this*. And you'll be entirely too busy shepherding gear and weapons to the front lines to be worrying about managing Rift Bubbles and Kireme Boundaries, anyway." Her fingertips brushed across his lips. "Please don't beat yourself up. It's fine. And now we've established that when it comes to active commands, the kyoseil listens to me alone. An important thing to know. I suppose after the Oneiroi Nebula, it's to be expected."

You tried to bring me into its circle of power then, too, but the kyoseil saw only you. It's always you. He understood why the kyoseil felt that way. When left to his own inclinations, she was often the only thing he saw, too.

His hand closed around hers as a new notion started tickling the *kyoseil-woven* pathways of his mind. "But that's not quite true. You were able to change the access codes *before* you went to the Oneiroi Nebula. Not remotely, but standing here like this, interacting physically, the Bubble took your direction. Maybe it...." Yes, but *after* she'd transferred to a new body over-saturated with kyoseil in order to breach the quantum block and infiltrate Namino.

Was it simply a matter of relative quantity? Could it be so straightforward? Kyoseil acted as a conduit for incredible power, but on its own it was not just ancient, even primordial, but primitive. It didn't think the way organics *or* synthetics did.

"Maybe what, darling?"

"Nothing. It doesn't matter." He forced his thoughts to the side. "Come on. Caleb and Alex will be expecting us at the lab soon."

4

MIRAI
CONCEPTUAL RESEARCH LAB

A shimmer in the air presaged a wormhole opening in the lobby of the Conceptual Research Lab. Security measures now prevented wormholes from forming inside the labs themselves, so Dashiel and Nika waited for their guests here.

Caleb and Alex walked through the opening, as expected, followed by a slender man with sepia skin and long, wild copper locks. The large duffel bag slung over one shoulder didn't impede a casual swagger in the man's gait, and Dashiel instinctively flinched. *Anaden.*

Nika stepped forward with a blossoming smile. "Eren! This is a pleasant surprise."

The man hefted the bag off his shoulder. "I bring evidence. Granted, I *could* have simply passed the evidence off to Caleb and gone about my day, but I wanted to see a slice of this Dominion of yours. Alex let me peek outside before we came here. Banger of a planet you have!"

"Thank you. We're proud of it." Belatedly, Nika seemed to realize he was staring at her and their third guest expectantly. "Oh, sorry. Dashiel, this is Eren…Savitas, yes? He and I met the last time I visited Akeso."

The Anaden held out a hand in greeting. "Pleasure to meet you, sir. From what I hear, you're the brain trust of this whole Dominion operation."

"Merely trying to do my small part to keep us alive." Dashiel shook off the multiple levels of surprise at the man's arrival and general demeanor to take the proffered hand. "A pleasure to meet you as well." He nodded to Caleb and Alex. "Shall we go inside?"

Everyone followed him through the security doors into the main lab, then down a corridor to a specialized testing room. Inside, a fifteen-centimeter chunk of Rasu hung suspended in a glass enclosure, an array of sensors attached to its metal body.

Caleb had delivered it to him for analysis in the wake of the Rasu's defeat at Hirlas. It hadn't been an immediate priority, especially given the overwhelming destruction the Axis Worlds had suffered in those terrible battles before Nika and Alex had engineered the current civil war. But this week he'd been able to turn a modicum of attention to studying the...prisoner, he supposed...and had found himself faced with yet another mystery.

Dashiel called up a pane to display the battery of test results, which consisted entirely of a series of flat lines and null values. "We've run every test we've ever devised for the Rasu, plus a few new ones. This isn't a Rasu. It's scrap metal."

Alex leaned in to peer at the display. "No electrical activity. No chemical activity. No energetic discharge. No discernible organized circuitry? Really?"

"Really. You see that crack down the left side? We cut the specimen open to check with our eyes, because we didn't trust the test results, either. If you mined a chunk of nickel out of an asteroid, it would look no different on the inside."

"Even the Ymyrath Field doesn't do this level of damage. Rasu hit by it are well and truly disabled, but they continue to exhibit weak electrical signals. They retain their core form."

"They continue to think," Caleb interjected. "Muddled, slow thoughts, but some level of intelligence remains." His brow furrowed. "You're telling me there's no trace of intelligence left?"

"There's no trace of anything left. Nothing but regular, ordinary inorganic chemistry at work."

Caleb tilted his head toward his companion. "Eren?"

"Yep." The Anaden knelt on the floor and unfastened the clasps on the duffel bag, then extracted a large package wrapped in some type of sealant. "I brought more samples from Hirlas. Every piece of Rasu we've been able to find on the surface—and there isn't much—looks like this one." He stood and held out the package. "If you want to run your tests on an additional sample to confirm your findings?"

"Good idea. Now that we've put together the full suite of tests, it should only take a minute." Dashiel called in one of the lab techs to handle setting up the new sample in its own enclosure.

While they waited, Dashiel forced his thoughts not to drift back to his failure with the Rift Bubble. Compartmentalization was a skill he had a great deal of practice at. "So, Alex, have you been able to elicit any more information from Mesme about—?" He cut himself off, his gaze darting to the Anaden. "If that's not an appropriate topic...."

Alex gave a little nod. "We're trying to keep its disclosure on a need-to-know basis. If word got out to the general public that time travel is possible, it would…well, we don't need a wave of societal upheaval in the middle of a war. But Eren knows, yes."

"Even though I didn't need to. Definitely would have wanted to, seeing as the irascible Kat is a friend of mine, but didn't *need* to." The Anaden grinned. "Spymaster. I have a way of getting people to open up to me."

Alex scoffed. "I'm pretty sure I blurted it out to you the first time I saw you after I found out."

"Also true."

"Anyway, to answer your question, I've been able to extract shockingly little new information from Mesme—or not shockingly, I guess. It's talking more, but when put to scrutiny most of its words end up being thin air. It says we're doing better this time around, but insists if it divulges too many details about the prior timeline, that might derail our efforts. Which is a terribly convenient answer when one doesn't want to disclose secrets. Nika, have you had any greater luck?"

"Not particularly. Mostly I get the sense Mesme is relieved this revelation is finally out in the open. For all the secrets it keeps, I don't believe it enjoys doing so."

"And yet." Alex rolled her eyes. "Valkyrie has been banging away on the physics equations, trying to suss out how a schism in the 'time' part of the spacetime manifold can occur. Thus far, she hasn't discovered an energy output capable of achieving it."

"Which bolsters our theory that something special—something unique—happens in the future to cause the schism," Nika replied. "I wonder. Is it something we do, or something the enemy does?"

Caleb rested against the nearby wall, looking contemplative. "It happens because we're going to lose, correct? It gives us a chance to get it right the next time. Ergo, I think we create it."

Alex stared at him curiously. "You think there's that much intentionality involved?"

"I think where the Kats are concerned, there's always intentionality involved. I also think if I were standing there at the fateful moment, facing civilizational extinction and out of options, I would do whatever gave us a single sliver of a chance to survive."

"Agreed. But how in the *d'yavol* will we accomplish it?"

Caleb nudged Alex on the shoulder. "Don't ask me. That's for you and Valkyrie to figure out."

"Right. Should be a piece of cake."

The tech signaled the new sample was ready, and Dashiel returned to the workstation. "Activating the test sequence now. Unless an anomaly registers, it'll just take a few seconds."

They all watched the pane as chart after chart filled with zeroes. No blips.

Dashiel gestured to the results. "I'd say twice makes a pattern. It's nothing but dead metal."

Eren nudged the duffel bag toward Dashiel. "I brought two more, if you'd like them."

"Scientific rigor says we should test them as well, though at this point I don't expect different results."

"We're not doing anything with them. They're all yours." Eren turned to Alex. "Sorry, but I need to run. Nyx is yelling in my head about some meeting or other."

"You poor thing." Alex acknowledged Dashiel. "Thank you for doing the work, even if the results are kind of inexplicable. We'll see you soon, I'm sure."

He shook hands with Caleb then led them back to the lobby, where Alex opened a wormhole, and they all departed.

Nika stared at the spot of air where the wormhole had been, eyes narrowed.

"What's on your mind?"

"Wondering what in the hells Caleb and Akeso did to the Rasu on Hirlas."

"I'd say they killed them."

"Evidently, but how? Other than breaking apart their subatomic structure—which is not what happened here—nothing kills a Rasu."

"I don't know." He studied her, allowing his thoughts to return to the events at the Rift Bubble and the idea he'd been ruminating on ever since...and made a snap decision. "Listen, I'm going to have to be on site this evening to stand up the new manufacturing line on Kiyora. I won't be back until late tomorrow."

"Oh." A shadow flitted across her expression, and he generously took it to mean she'd miss him. "I understand." She leaned in to kiss him softly. "Good luck. Comm me if you need me to bring you food. Otherwise, I'll see you at home tomorrow night."

5

MACSKAF

BARISAN HOMEWORLD
SCULPTOR DWARF GALAXY

Fat, laden raindrops splatted on Eren's head as turbulent gray-brown clouds rolled in with vigor from the east. He sidled up closer to the building's outer wall. It wasn't as if he'd checked the weather forecast before coming here.

Beside him, Nyx Praesidis activated a rainshade above her head. She studied him critically for a second, then extended its reach to cover him as well.

"Thank you, sweetheart. Generous of you."

"Quiet. The meeting's starting."

On the tiny visual their undercover agent, Bara Jhouti-min, transmitted from the gathering, ten Barisans arranged themselves in their usual circle. Their ringleader, Ferenc, stood proudly in the center. Ferenc had had designs on assassinating Corradeo Praesidis for more than three months; likely longer, but Ferenc hadn't drawn Eren's attention until he'd started persuading other disgruntled Barisans to adopt his cause. Still, up until now, the 'conspiracy' had been limited to typical Barisan bravado and chest-pounding threats. Word was, that might change today.

A Barisan voice growled over the comm relay. *"Everyone's here, so let's begin."*

"This is everyone?"

"We need to work with a smaller group now. We can't risk someone who isn't committed to the cause getting slippery paws and tipping off the authorities. Everyone present is a true believer, yes?"

Whiskered heads nodded in unison, and Ferenc didn't move to eject anyone. *"Excellent. Thanks to the information Sinka provided, I was able to track down a small supply of this hypnol,* apomono, *which destroys an Anaden's neural connection to their integral and thus their immortality. It took much longer than I'd have liked, as Vigil has the supply locked down tight, even on* outlaw worlds. With good reason, I say. If word were to spread about the hypnol's effect, panic would sweep through Anaden society.

"But Vigil's reach is not absolute, and the apomono is now in our possession. Bara, what is the latest intel on Corradeo Praesidis' daily routine?"

Bara had successfully infiltrated the group by offering a fake but thoroughly documented professional history that included employment with the private security firm hired by Cabo Construction for its work on Advocacy Square. The posting made her valuable to the conspirators, but her true coup was convincing Ferenc that she hated Anadens as much as he did.

Their efforts to obtain *apomono* had put their conspiracy into a holding pattern for some time. Eren was impressed, as he honestly hadn't thought they'd manage to acquire the hypnol. He'd worry over their feat, but he felt quite certain Nyx was now planning draconian measures to find and shut down the route they'd used to do so.

"The construction on the centerpiece building of Advocacy Square is complete, and the advocate has relocated his offices there. This means he's on the move and out in the open less frequently than before—"

"I told you we should have acted sooner! We may have missed our best opportunity."

A snarl rumbled over the comm link. "We didn't have the hypnol until now, Chaisan, nor the other half-dozen pieces required to make this plan work. The delay will have been worth it. Bara, continue."

"Nevertheless, the advocate takes frequent strolls through the gardens that ring the Square, usually mid-morning Ares time. I should warn you, he is often accompanied by one of his prefects when he does so. Not always, however. I have also identified three disguised bodyguards who keep to his vicinity when he leaves the building. I can't say whether they are Vigil or CINT. They are skilled at remaining unobtrusive, but not so skilled that I didn't make them." A purr of pride rolled in Bara's throat; she was talented at her job.

"So three mobile bodyguards in the area, plus one defanged Inquisitor at arm's length. What about his personal defenses?"

"My employer does not have such information, but I was able to get close enough to scan him when he paid the Assembly Hall construction site a visit. He wears a defensive shield, of course. We can assume it's top of the line. Nothing else registered on the scan."

This was a lie. Corradeo's personal shield wielded a multitude of both defensive and offensive capabilities that would register on a sophisticated-enough scan. But by this point, Bara had given Ferenc no reason to doubt a given piece of intel.

"*My contacts in the Beszi tell me they can overcome the shield. Anything else?*"

"*The Square now has Vigil security typical of any prominent government property. But because the construction is still underway, it's of necessity lax in places. Lots of comings and goings of workers, machinery and materials. There are holes to be exploited.*"

Nyx's lips quirked down in displeasure. Eren assumed she thought Bara was sharing too much information. But it was nothing anyone with eyes and time for a bit of observation couldn't deduce.

"*All right.*" There was a weighty pause as Ferenc wound his claws together and stalked around the circle. "*This is our time. Our time to strike out and refuse to be yoked by Anaden dictators ever again. To refuse to submit to repression and a stifling of our economic and cultural rights. I say we act. What say you?*"

A chorus of growls that translated roughly to 'yes' flowed through the small group.

"*Thank you, my brothers and sisters. The assassination of Advocate Corradeo Praesidis will proceed forward—*"

Nyx switched to their raid channel. "Move in now!"

Eren sighed. Was this his op or not?

The Vigil unit had staged themselves inside the building, cloaked, and on Nyx's order they stormed the meeting room. He and Nyx remained outside in case anyone tried to slip through the net. They drew their weapons and backed up, sweeping in opposite directions around the building, their attention focused upward.

In the corner of his vision, Eren watched the feed as the officers cleared across the room and subdued the gathered Barisans. Not surprisingly, Ferenc put up the biggest fight, claws whipping and slashing, limbs darting about in a valiant attempt to escape. But the Vigil team was well-outfitted to repel uniquely Barisan tactics, and only a few drops of blood were spilled.

After fifty seconds, the team lead gave the 'all clear,' and he and Nyx began climbing the façade.

They entered the room to find all the attendees shackled and held on the ground, including Bara. She'd be released once Vigil took everyone away, but they didn't want to blow her cover in case she was called into service again.

Nyx stalked up to Ferenc and motioned for the Vigil officer to lift him to his feet. "Ferenc Khoura-lan, you are under arrest for conspiracy to murder an Advocacy official and Concord Senator. Your legal rights under Barisan law will be—"

Laughter hissed through Ferenc's clenched jaw, sending spittle flying into Nyx's face.

Nyx wiped her cheek with the back of her hand. "Laugh now if you wish, for nothing about your future will be humorous, I assure you."

"Stick me in a prison cell if you want, but my people will stay free, *I assure you.*"

"Your people were never going to be subjugated, you ungrateful, sniveling rat."

Ooooh. Did Nyx know what a grave insult it was for a Barisan to be called a 'rat'? Surely she knew.

Ferenc struggled against the restraints and the officer holding him securely from behind. "*Blashnik* Prefect. You stand there so smug, but do not doubt this: I will have the last laugh."

She *was* standing rather smugly; Inquisitor entitlement radiated from the pose of every muscle of her toned, lithe body. "No, you won't."

Eren laid a hand on Nyx's arm as he stepped up beside her. "What did you do, you weasel?" That was almost as bad as being called a 'rat,' and it had the desired effect of provoking Ferenc into defending his honor.

"I outsmarted you all. Everyone in this room. You think I intended to depend on the weak wills of these people to decide whether the plan went forward? This was merely a show for them. It's *already happening.* You're too late."

Fury knocked aside the Inquisitor confidence to battle with panic in Nyx's countenance.

Eren retreated a few steps out of the fray.

Mesme? Requesting favor number 4,683. Nyx and I need emergency transport from Macskaf back to Ares. Corradeo is in trouble.

ARES

ADVOCACY SQUARE
MILKY WAY GALAXY

Mesme deposited them in the middle of Corradeo's new office but did not stick around to learn the nature of the emergency. Rasu business to attend to, Eren assumed.

The advocate looked up from his desk in surprise. A flicker of annoyance disappeared from his expression as soon as it arrived. "There *is* a door, through which one commonly walks when arriving."

"Grandfather, your life is in danger. We have reason to believe a Barisan Beszi team is already moving to assassinate you. I know you refused to hire a taster, but every food and drink presented to you will now need to be screened for *apomono*."

Corradeo scratched at his forehead. "I thought you were planning to arrest the conspirators before they moved ahead with their plan."

"We were. We did. But the leader claims to have gone behind the others' backs and authorized the operation on his own. I'm sorry, Grandfather. We failed you."

Eren touched Nyx's shoulder and stepped forward. "No need to take the fall for me. This was my mission. I made certain we were tracking Ferenc's movements and communications, but he must have managed to contact the Beszi without being detected. If I missed something because I was distracted by the recent events on Hirlas, I apologize." He reluctantly faced Nyx; she was his immediate boss, after all. "And to you as well."

He expected to find the 'preparing to flay him alive' expression, but instead he got only a troubled glance. "The important thing is to stop them now. Grandfather, I want you to return to the estate under armed guard and remain there until we resolve the situation."

"And how long might that take? If I cower in my bed in my walled castle every time someone sneezes at the Advocacy, I won't be much of a leader. Now, you've provided me the best in personal defenses as well as an elite security detail. They will have to suffice. I trust you will locate and arrest these assassins with due speed. Now if you will excuse me, I'm expected at a meeting of the Rasu War Council in a few minutes." Corradeo stood, flashed them a tight smile and promptly left.

Nyx glared at the closing door in dismay. "Why am I here? Why did I bother to take this job, or create this department? Does he have a death wish?"

Eren chuckled, projecting a relaxed demeanor he didn't feel. "To start with your last, no. He has a life wish."

"What is that supposed to mean?"

"It means people have been trying to kill him for a million years. Almost succeeded a few times—but they didn't. He's beyond being threatened by the prospect. He's trying to live a good life—a worthy life. And now more than ever, he's not going to let the old demons drag him down. He can't, or this all falls apart."

Nyx stared at him, the muscle under her right eyelid twitching as she tried to visually scour him. "That is either startlingly insightful or a bunch of bullshit you just made up."

"Probably a little of both."

"Nevertheless. If he dies, even for a day, then he looks weak and vulnerable. The Advocacy looks weak and vulnerable, precisely when it must look strong. We have to stop this."

"Agreed, but we can't stick him in an impenetrable glass bubble. The question then becomes, what can we do to stop the assassins before they move to take him out?"

Her features brightened a touch. In relief? "A great deal. Let's go talk to Lontias and Ziton."

Eren groaned. A round-robin with a bunch of former Inquisitors was *not* his idea of a fun way to spend an afternoon.

6

ARES
ADVOCACY SQUARE

L ontias and Ziton met her and Eren in what was almost, but not quite yet, the Executive Conference Room on the top floor. By the time the other two prefects arrived, Nyx had three-dimensional representations of the entire Advocacy Square and Praesidis estate grounds displayed above the table.

Her head snapped over as they walked in. "Ziton, talk to me."

Her brother went directly to the virtual display and enlarged a section of it. "I've tripled security at every entrance and exit and instituted identity checks alongside full scans. The Cabo people are bitching, but they can deal. I've got surveillance drones in the air, so we'll have constant visuals of every centimeter of both sites. In addition to the standard coverage, a security detail is stationed inside the Executive Building, as well as one in the estate, and two plain-clothes Vigil units are mobile on the Square property."

She waved a hand in acknowledgment; due in part to the work he'd done these last fourteen years in the private sector, Ziton now ran security for both the entire Advocacy government and their family. "Thank you for moving so quickly. Lontias?"

Lontias was the hunter, even more so than she, and he'd insisted on receiving only a 'Consultant' title in his official capacity. It let him move easily wherever he was needed and kept him free of the shackles of the burgeoning bureaucracy.

He flashed a row of identity files. "Five Barisans have arrived on Ares in the last four days: three through the spaceport and two through the Caeles Prism from Concord HQ. None of them have departed. Two are employed by a materials supplier working on the Advocacy Square construction, and I've dispatched agents to their worksites to interview them. The other three told Customs they had various business in Oenom. I've placed a quiet planetwide alert in the system, so if any of the three traverse a security checkpoint, we'll know it. If not, they will be difficult to track down, as

Oenom is a big place." Lontias cracked a half-smile. "I mean, in the next hour. I will find them."

Nyx rubbed at her jaw, her focus blurring across the identity files. "Then don't waste time here. Track them down."

"You got it." He gave her a curt nod and departed.

"Ziton, I want any Barisan who arrives on Ares from here on to be detained."

He shook his head. "I already tried to implement such an order. Corradeo vetoed it. Something about how it violated both the spirit and the letter of Concord's charter."

"Godsdamn him! His virtue is going to get him killed."

"Nyx, listen. I intend to do everything in my power to prevent this assassination attempt. But we've stored a static backup of Corradeo's integral feed in the Senatorial Vault at Concord HQ. These terrorists are blindingly stupid if they actually think they're going to take him out in any permanent way."

"I know. But I also know he'll hate a stale version of him being awakened. It's the best the Humans can do, but we evolved beyond their capabilities millennia ago. Besides, I won't allow our first crisis to end in failure."

"Don't make this about your ego, sis."

She flinched. "Isn't it about yours as well?"

"Eh, I won't argue the point. So let's not make it about *our* egos." Ziton jerked his head toward the other end of the table. "What's his value-add here?"

"Tracking the conspirators was technically his mission...." She frowned. Eren was sitting off by himself, fingers blazing across a virtual display. He hadn't said a word since they'd arrived at the conference room. "Eren, what are you doing?"

"Working. You two keep talking. Oh, but you should get a backup of the backup and move it somewhere with more security—maybe on a ship that never docks? The Beszi might have a contingency plan to try to take out the integral store on HQ."

She opened her mouth to protest, but the words died in her throat. Her natural prejudice was to think of Barisans as unsophisticated, damn near barbarous—and thus incapable of planning and executing such a sophisticated operation. But she couldn't afford to underestimate them, could she? She gazed at Ziton in question.

"The list of people with access to the Senatorial Vault is so short a Barisan can count them all without peering at its toe-claws. No one's going to be able to get in there."

"Almost certainly not. Nonetheless, given the stakes—"

"Fine. I'll see to it."

"Aha!" Eren shoved back from the table, crossed his ankles upon it and wound his hands behind his head, looking triumphant.

She disliked the showmanship, but she would take whatever good news came her way. "What did you find?"

"*Apomono* is extremely difficult to engineer. Which is understandable, given its unique and potent effects. Most of the compound is synthetic, but it also requires an extract from the *iposoea* flower, something else that is difficult to engineer. As a result, only three facilities in Concord space are capable of brewing *apomono*."

"How do you know this?"

"I am a lifelong connoisseur of all the finest hypnols. Who do you think acquired the *apomono* for Corradeo so he could use it on the rebellious *elassons*?"

She grumbled in annoyance. "I call bullshit. Addicts learn where to find a black market hypnol dealer on every planet, yes, but they don't care where those hypnols are produced."

"Touché. You wound me." The expression on Eren's face suggested he wasn't in the slightest bit wounded. "The anarchs had occasion to engage in commerce with hypnol manufacturers from time to time. See, the first couple of months after an integral severing were pretty tough to weather for new anarchs, and they often needed something to take the edge off. Look, how I know isn't important. Time's ticking, yes? The point is this: *apomono* is so very illegal and so very scarce that the brewers employ the dealers themselves, ensuring a vertical supply chain. Currently, five dealers exist in the entire universe...unless the Rasu have *apomono*. I'm assuming they don't.

"Anyway, when I returned from Hirlas after the invasion was defeated, you remember how I turned right back around and left again? Much to your annoyance?"

She nodded tightly.

"I paid those dealers a little visit. In exchange for an off-the-record promise that the Advocacy wouldn't look too hard in their directions, I extracted agreements that they would put a nanotracker in any vial of *apomono* they sold to a Barisan."

"You don't have the authority to make such an arrangement on behalf of the Advocacy."

Eren smacked his lips. "Uh-huh. Do you want to hear where the *apomono* Ferenc bought is located at this exact moment or not?"

"What? Of course I do!"

"Great. Just one second." Eren typed in a new command, but after a beat a frown grew to animate his features. Then again, all his expressions were animated. "That's odd. There isn't any here on Ares."

"Shockingly, those criminal dealers tossed your bribe in the refuse."

"They wouldn't dare. I wonder if..." more furious typing "...*arae!*" He spun his chair to face her, swinging his feet to the floor. "They're not doing it here. They're doing it on HQ."

Her mind started racing through the variables. "I suppose it's true that security won't be as tight, or at least as comprehensive, on the station, but all our intel indicated—"

"They would target him here, at Advocacy Square. To make a grand statement or something. I don't know. Maybe they couldn't make the plan work here. Doesn't matter. There are two vials of *apomono* on HQ this second." Abruptly he held up a finger.

"What now?"

"I'm contacting Director Navick. Informing him he likely has a Beszi squad on HQ and asking him to get plain-clothes CINT agents glued to the advocate's ass pronto."

She swallowed a protest. It should have been her job to issue such directives, but try as she might, she simply could not get Eren to ask permission. For *anything*. And right now, the most important thing was for a response to happen, and happen swiftly.

So instead, she grabbed her coat from the back of the chair. "Ziton, stay here and keep on top of the security teams. Eren, let's go."

7

CONCORD HQ

E ren shook Richard Navick's hand warmly. "It's good to see you again, sir."

Richard waved him off. "You don't work for me any longer. I think we can drop the formalities."

Nyx stared at them, looking genuinely perplexed. "How did you ever get him to call you 'sir'?"

Eren leaned in toward Richard's ear for a conspiratorial stage whisper. "Let's keep it our little secret, okay?" Then he stepped back and gestured between them. "Nyx Praesidis, Richard Navick."

Richard shook her hand as well. "I've been hearing good things about the work you're doing to whip the Advocacy infrastructure into shape."

"Thank you. Perhaps later, we can discuss some ideas I have on how CINT and Advocacy Security can work together. Now, though, we need to move quickly."

"We already are. Cliff, our Artificial, is delving into the records of every Barisan currently on the station, but that's over four hundred people. Also, unfortunately, identities can be spoofed, so I'm not optimistic about identifying specific Beszi members in the short term. However, thanks to Eren's intel, we were able to detect two *apomono* vials on the person of a temporary Barisan employee at *Sidere Pastrie*. We can arrest her on my order."

"Why a random pastry shop? That seems like low odds to play."

"Word is, your advocate always visits the shop for a treat when he's attending to Senate business here on HQ."

Eren laughed, simply tickled at the notion of the great Corradeo Praesidis having a sweet tooth for sugary desserts.

Nyx didn't appear to notice the humor in it. Alas. "I see. Let's go ahead and arrest—"

"No."

She bestowed her typical glare on Eren. "Excuse me?"

"Imagine this scenario. The woman at the pastry shop plants the *apomono* when Corradeo orders his usual cinnamon streusel muffin or chocolate éclair or whatever his weakness is." He chuckled briefly again. "She informs the Beszi unit, and they hit him wherever strikes them as the most optimal spot. But if instead she alerts them to a problem, or never contacts them at all, they fade into the shadows and bide their time until they can try again. We need to draw them out now or risk losing them forever."

Richard nodded. "I've got two plain-clothes CINT agents on the advocate now. I'll stage a response team to be ready to sweep in and make the arrests the instant the Beszi move."

Nyx frowned. "Not a Vigil squad?"

"No offense, but I trust my own people."

"Fine. You two are suggesting we allow Grandf—the advocate—to purchase his poisoned sweets?"

"Yes. We'll warn him privately not to eat it, but instead *pretend* to eat it. I'm sure he can sell it. Then we'll shadow him, and when the assassins make their move, we'll grab them."

"Eren, I told you before. We can't let him fall. Not even for a day."

How many times had he expressed agreement on this point? "I *know*. That's why you and I will be there to stop them."

RW

Nyx forewarned Corradeo about the threat and advised him to continue on with his routine as per usual. He offered a half-hearted excuse for his habitual visits to the pastry shop in question; Eren snickered into his hand, evoking a confused stare from Nyx. She truly didn't find it amusing? Had the woman's funny bone been surgically removed?

They watched, Veiled, as Corradeo acquired his confectionary—a chocolate pistachio cannoli—and made a convincing show of nibbling on it as he crossed the food court atrium.

The CINT agents—now up to four—worked the crowd around him as he strolled toward the levtram that would return him to the Senate offices. When he paused to clutch at his stomach, Nyx almost leapt to his side, but Eren threw an arm out in front of her.

He's acting as if the apomono is affecting him. He's good at this.

Damn, he's going to give me heart failure.

It'll be okay. We've got this.

On the mission comm, one of the CINT agents identified two Barisans loitering in the retail strip up ahead and began tracking them.

But Beszi were no slouches at this game. All but one of the squad would be Veiled or disguised or both. So how to spot them? Or more relevantly, how to stop them?

Eren was using the plural, because Beszi never operated alone. There should be a primary assassin, a backup assassin and a facilitator—the one who wasn't Veiled—to sow confusion and chaos for a few crucial seconds.

His eyes went to the intersection up ahead, where a crossway led to Administration on the left and Merchant Services on the right.

Eren (CINT Mission Channel): "They're going to do it at the intersection. Be ready."

How do you know?

Because it's where I would do it. Stop thinking like an Inquisitor and start thinking like a criminal.

When Corradeo was twelve meters from the intersection, a Barisan woman cried out above the general din of the crowd. "Help! That man just robbed me! He's got my bag!"

The crowd roiled as people jerked out of their purposeful progress toward their destinations. Pedestrians were jostled—and one young Naraida girl got jostled by thin air.

Eren sprinted ahead and dove for the gap that shouldn't exist. He collided with a solid mass, and his momentum carried them both to the floor.

Claws sliced into his cheek as he activated his blade and stabbed upward. Resistance told him he'd hit armor, and the body beneath him fought like a crazed, well…cat. Clawed hands found his throat and razored nails dug into his skin.

All the struggling dislodged both of their Veils, and hate-filled chartreuse irises surrounded by coral fur seared into him.

The pain in Eren's throat was excruciating, and his vision was starting to blur from lack of oxygen, but he concentrated on dragging his blade upward across the Barisan's ribs.

One hand relinquished his throat to close around his wrist and try to yank it away. He continued pushing, using his body for leverage, until the tip found the edge of the flak jacket. He wrestled his adversary's kicking legs to shift his weight and press the blade down beneath him.

He felt the squishy give of the blade penetrating skin. Yet still his adversary fought. Eren struggled to maintain a grip on the blade handle, his head swimming. Cybernetics routines activated to keep him from passing out.

Finally the Barisan began spasming wildly, the motions losing their previous intentionality and skill. The remaining hand dropped away from Eren's throat, and the body went limp in Eren's grasp—

A *pop* echoed directly behind him, and a caramel-colored Barisan fell face-first to the floor beside him.

The odor of burnt fur assaulted his nostrils. Blood leaked out the side of the body's head, forming a growing puddle that crept steadily closer to him.

Eren tried to gasp in much-needed air and looked to his right, where Nyx straddled a Barisan presently missing most of its face. One of her arms was outstretched toward him, a handgun in its grip as she gazed at him in question.

Eren nodded as he struggled up to his knees, and she lowered her arm and stood, training the gun on the corpse beneath her. Eren made certain to check the Barisan he'd fought with for signs of life. No breath, no pulse.

The attacker had dropped a curved, needle-thin knife in the struggle, and Eren confiscated it. Then he fell back on his ass and studied the second body. He thought it was the woman who had roused the crowd into confusion as the attack began. A Barisan-made gun lay on the other side of the body, and his oxygen-deprived brain tried to piece together what had happened here.

A CINT agent arrived to take charge of the presumed corpse Nyx was guarding, so she relinquished it to come over and crouch beside him after stopping to pick up the stray gun. "You're bleeding from...everywhere. I'll get a medic."

"I'll be all right." His voice rasped across the needled sandpaper of his throat. *Ow.* He gingerly touched his neck, and his hand came away blood-soaked. "I mean, yeah, I guess a medic. At some point."

"Some point soon. You look like shit and sound worse."

And he surely did. A brief, woozy assessment confirmed he was bleeding from clawed gashes in a half-dozen locations, and he couldn't feel the left side of his face.

"Anything for the job, eh?" Also, he should really stop trying to talk. It felt as if his throat were bleeding on the inside, which it might well be.

"So it seems." She glanced over her shoulder to check on the other corpse. Vigil officers had joined the fray to move the crowd back, and all the hallmarks of a crime scene were rapidly being instituted.

"Did you just save my life?"

Her lips curled up in what could have been an almost-smile. "She was about to shoot you in the back of the head."

"Then my head thanks you profusely."

"You would have done the same for me." The almost-smile turned downward. "I think."

He started to reach out for her, but realized his hands were dripping with Barisan blood. "Don't doubt it."

"Right." She frowned at each of the corpses in turn. "You have sharp eyes. It was only after you were moving that I picked up the other attacker when he spun toward you. I might not have detected him otherwise."

"We're a..." he winced from the agony of enunciating words "...good team."

Surprise flitted across her comparatively unbloodied features. "Perhaps we are."

Downright charitable of him to say so, he thought, but at least she didn't snap an insult in response. He rubbed at his throat again; there was already blood everywhere, so no point in trying to keep any specific part of him clean. "Go check on your grandfather. I'm fine."

Her eyes narrowed, scrutinizing the proper mess that he was, but after a second she climbed to her feet and hurried over to where Corradeo stood encircled by three CINT agents and two Vigil officers, talking in hushed tones to Richard.

"Unhhhh...." Eren flopped down on his back, arms sprawled out, and waited for a medic to wander his way.

8

EARTH

VANCOUVER

Malcolm sipped on his coffee. A half-eaten bagel with strawberry cream cheese spread sat on the plate in front of him while he gazed idly out the window of the downtown cafe. He wore a caramel suede coat over his dress blues, and so far no one had recognized him. Or if they had, they were polite enough to keep it to themselves; Vancouverites were used to a ubiquitous military presence. He had never warmed to the notion of being a celebrity, and he didn't want the complication this morning.

Across the street, an advertising billboard cycled back to one of the Gardiens' public service announcements. It featured an older man and woman walking along a beach. The man balanced a small child on his hip, and another child played in the surf ahead of them. The caption drifted across the image in sync with the lapping waves upon the shore.

You've lived a full and complete life. Don't your grandchildren deserve the same chance? Don't steal their future for yourself. Say 'no' to regenesis.

It was one of their most effective marketing tactics, or so he'd been told. The notion that there was a time for each of us to live and achieve, and a time to pass the mantle on to the next generation, resonated with people. That regenesis encouraged the selfish and the wealthy to cling to a life which they should leave behind, and in doing so smother the dreams and ambitions of those who came after.

> *To every thing there is a season, and a time to every purpose under the heaven:*
>
> *A time to be born, and a time to die; a time to plant, and a time to pluck up that which is planted;*
>
> *A time to kill, and a time to heal; a time to break down, and a time to build up;*
>
> *A time to weep, and a time to laugh; a time to mourn, and a time to dance;*

A time to cast away stones, and a time to gather stones together; a time to embrace, and a time to refrain from embracing;

A time to get, and a time to lose; a time to keep, and a time to cast away;

A time to rend, and a time to sew; a time to keep silence, and a time to speak;

A time to love, and a time to hate; a time of war, and a time of peace.

The ad didn't quote the Bible verse, of course, as the Gardiens were trying to win over a broader audience. But the inspiration was clear enough to him. There was a reason why it was an effective message.

As for himself, he could do with the time of peace about now. It was funny...shots hadn't been fired for two months, yet the war had never been more omnipresent and suffocating in its demands. The Rasu loomed like a great malevolent shadow upon the horizon, and every soldier spent their days peeking over their shoulder, checking to see if the shadow had advanced upon them while they were otherwise occupied.

Malcolm felt the same way about the Gardiens as he did the Rasu. After the Insights Academy 'incident,' the Gardiens had gone...not quiet. Their billboards decorated every other block in every city on every human world. Their representatives appeared on news programs and entertainment shows, and they published books and opinion pieces and gave impassioned speeches. Their once-small, private meetings had graduated to lavish weekend conferences where newcomers were bestowed t-shirts and coffee mugs and converted into vocal believers.

But there had been no more violence. No more assassination attempts. And so he was stuck. Enzio Vilane thought him a friend, but the man was a master at subtly keeping Malcolm away from anything untoward in the organization. He'd been introduced to a parade of high-level Gardiens representatives and drowned in an avalanche of buzzwords and double-speak and propaganda. But where it counted, he remained on the outside.

There was a dark, rotten heart at the center of the organization, but for now it concealed itself within an impenetrable web of earnest respectability.

He sighed and took another bite of his bagel. Maybe he simply wasn't cut out for spycraft and infiltration. Obviously he wasn't; the mere concept was laughable. So at least twice a day he considered telling Richard he was done, politely ghosting Vilane, and putting this sordid chapter behind him.

But then he remembered. Remembered how Vilane had tried to kidnap and kill Mia. Had tried to assassinate Miriam. Had overseen the murder of five people at the New Frontiers Medical Clinic and the terrorizing of over a hundred children at Insights Academy. Remembered that for all the feel-good billboards and shiny memorabilia, there *was* a dark, rotten heart at the center of the organization, and its name was Enzio Vilane.

A quiet alarm in his eVi sounded to remind him that he needed to get moving. The other festering thorn in his side, the AEGIS Oversight Board, was expecting him in forty-five minutes. So he paid the bill and took the coffee with him as he headed to the Caeles Prism at AEGIS Earth Head-quarters.

THE PRESIDIO
MILKY WAY GALAXY

The meeting droned on in the familiar refrain of buildout progress, fleet readiness and budget constraints. Always budget constraints.

Malcolm parroted all the right words to make the Oversight Board members feel as though he was as pained by the cost overruns as they were. But they could howl in protest as much as they wanted; what mattered was that the money was being spent. RNEW-centric planetary defense grids were being built. Fleets were being expanded. Tandem Defense Shield (TDS) systems were being squeezed onto greater numbers of ships. Rima Grenade platforms and adiamene-walled shelters were being constructed across their colonies, despite the frustrated insistence by the bureaucrats that between the Rift Bubbles and the defense grids, they were surely an unnecessary redundancy.

God willing, they would be, but it was not a bet Malcolm intended to make.

"At some point, Fleet Admiral, we have to say 'enough,'" General Colby said. "We have spent trillions on fortifying the defenses of our most popu-lous worlds. But now Demeter and Erisen and Elathan want their own next-gen orbital defense grids as well, and we have to weigh the costs against the likelihood of the threat. You yourself insist the Rasu are intelli-gent, strategic thinkers. If they ever return, they will not concern them-selves with second-tier colonies."

Malcolm doubted any of those colonies would appreciate being referred to as 'second-tier.' "Possibly not. But I will remind you how the Ka-tasketousya swept across our territory attacking every colony they encountered, no matter the size, until we forced their hand by making them realize they must target our centers of power while they still had the ships to do it. I don't think anyone here questions the intelligence or cleverness of the Katasketousya, do you?

"My point is, I don't know how the Rasu will proceed *when* they return. Why did they attack Sagan, when they might have attacked New Cornwall instead? Perhaps they will head straight for Earth or Seneca, or perhaps they will pick back up where they left off. But at the end of the day, you have to ask yourself this: are you willing to tell the citizens of Demeter and Erisen and Elathan they don't matter as much as the citizens of Earth and Seneca?"

Colby's features pinched together in a way that reminded Malcolm of the cinching of a burlap sack. "So we keep building and building, costs be damned?"

"It seems the most prudent course, yes."

"I see. No specific project proposal is up for a vote today, so we'll discuss it again once the Krysk and New Columbia defense grids are complete." Colby rubbed at his nose, his gaze drifting down to focus on something in front of him. "Before we adjourn, we did want to update you on a personnel matter. An official bulletin will be released later today, but you should know that after much debate and deliberation, we have elected not to require AEGIS flag officers to undergo regenesis should they fall, in battle or otherwise."

Malcolm blinked. His mind ran through the words Colby had uttered, and the order in which they were arranged. Yes, he'd heard correctly. "Does this include me?"

"As you are a flag officer, it does."

He kept his countenance professional, as if he were unfazed. "I see. Thank you for the update, General. And the concession."

In reality, he was shocked. Floored, even. For months he'd stalled their increasingly threatening suggestions, hedging his responses with phrases like 'searching his heart' and 'reviewing scripture' and 'studying the science.' Most of it was true, more or less, but he'd have preferred to keep his contemplations private.

Now, they were suddenly waving the white flag? Out of nowhere? And not just a quiet, under-the-table exception for him, but for all high-ranking officers? It didn't make sense.

"Of course, we trust you will make every effort not to fall, in battle or otherwise."

Not to pull another stunt like the one on Savrak, in other words. "I intend to live to fight many more battles, General, should they arrive at our shores."

RW

Malcolm had barely made it to the transport room when a message arrived in his eVi. The putrid orange color of the header warned him it was from Vilane.

He stepped aside to let others proceed through the Caeles Prism while he opened it.

> *Malcolm,*
>> *You're welcome.*
> *Regards,*
> *— Enzio*

A chill shuddered down his spine. What had the man done? Did Vilane's influence stretch so far that he could sway the decisions of the Oversight Board? Sway them in the opposite direction from their preferences?

This was raw power in action if he'd ever seen it.

He longed to rush to Pandora, storm into Vilane's office and insist that he hadn't asked for the man's help. Hadn't wanted Vilane to sully his professional concerns. Now he felt dirty. *Tainted.*

Lie down with dogs, get up with fleas.

9

PANDORA

MILKY WAY GALAXY

Enzio Vilane chuckled to himself at the stilted, formal and somewhat perplexed reply he received from Malcolm Jenner.

It might have benefited the Gardiens' cause to have the Oversight Board try to implement forced regenesis on the flag officers, if only for the delicious public backlash that would have resulted (helped along at strategic junctures by Gardiens operatives). But even he did not want to weaken AEGIS' readiness for a resurgent Rasu. So he would leave the military alone for now.

General Colby was a circumspect and private man hailing from a familial military tradition stretching back over two centuries. It hadn't been easy to uncover his sins. But every man had them, and Colby was no different.

It turned out that eight years earlier, Colby had made a disastrous investment in a risky asteroid mining operation. The venture had defaulted and its leaders vanished, leaving the investors holding the bag. Military officers were rarely wealthy, and Colby didn't have the money to pay the creditors. So he'd waded into the swamp of the criminal underworld and borrowed the money from an offshoot of the old Shào cartel. When he'd also been unable to repay the loan shark, the lender had threatened the wellbeing of Colby's daughter and her family. In response, Colby had hired an ex-Marine to murder the lender.

The general had gotten away with it. But someone, somewhere, always knew. Once Enzio had obtained the rough outline of the scandal, it had been easy to anonymously threaten to leak it to the press unless the Board found themselves more amenable to respecting the personal moral convictions of their officers.

And now, for the first time since they'd made one another's acquaintance, Malcolm Jenner owed *him*. One never knew when such a card might need to be played.

Feeling rather pleased with himself, Enzio left his office to join his mother in the balcony garden.

He found her surrounded by aurals, her lips drawn into a taut line while her eyes darted fluidly among the displays.

She'd come so far in the last few months; at times it overwhelmed him. Under his guiding hand, she'd refined and augmented her programming in a thousand ways, enriching and expanding not merely her mental pathways but her personality and depth of social nuance.

And over the course of that time, she'd managed to make herself nigh on indispensable to his work. To the Gardiens, and especially to the Rivinchi cartel. It stood to reason, he told himself; if there was anything Olivia Montegreu understood, it was how to be a successful mob boss. Still, her penchant for it continually surprised him. It shouldn't, but it did.

"Puja Bail has been persuaded to pledge his banner to Rivinchi."

"The leader of the Sampat outfit in The Boulevard?" Enzio settled into the chair beside her. "What is it costing us?"

"Costing us?" A corner of her mouth curled up, though she didn't look over. "Nothing. Costing him? He gets to not be dead."

"I see. With the addition of Bail and his people, Rivinchi will control eighty-two percent of the illicit trade on Pandora. A virtual monopoly."

"Yes." Now she shifted toward him, her hands coming to rest atop one crossed leg. "In the old, pre-Amaranthe days, the Pandora Consortium intervened quietly whenever one cartel amassed disproportionate power here in order to keep influence balanced. I wonder, do they no longer care about such matters in this new world, or is their control slipping?"

"Oh, I bought off two of the Consortium members several years ago. They would characterize our arrangement differently, but that's the essence of it."

"You did?" She arched an eyebrow. "Well done, son."

He basked in the glow of her praise for a beat, in the reality of her knowing his worth and respecting his abilities. Then he forced himself to turn to the matter at hand, for he would be adding to their wins today.

He activated a large virtual screen in front of them and tuned to Galaxy First's news feed.

"—the man in question, one Armelle Sauvageot, reportedly killed three medical technicians and injured another employee, then escaped to travel to his home, where he allegedly killed his wife as well. Police arrived shortly thereafter and were able to subdue the man.

"Sauvageot had just been awakened from a regenesis procedure after dying in a skydiving accident on Shi Shen last week. He was a wealthy, respected entrepreneur and philanthropist, and friends say they've never known him to *be violent in the past, insisting this is a marked departure from his usual temperament."*

"Your work, I assume?"

"Hmm. I suspect we'll be seeing an increasing number of these tragic incidents in the coming days. Perhaps regenesis isn't as stable and safe a practice as the scientists have led us to believe."

"Save the speeches for the public, son. But I am curious about your methods."

"I began planting specialized agents inside a curated selection of regenesis clinics several months ago. Let them take the time to get settled in and earn the trust of their coworkers and superiors. Now, those agents are in a position to tamper with the neural imprints on file." He shrugged. "Everyone wants to live forever, but no one wants to reawaken as a homicidal maniac. Or an incoherent neurotic. Or a literal imbecile. Once those sorts of results start piling up, the scientists can spout safety statistics all they like. It won't matter."

"And again I say." She bestowed a rare warm smile upon him, and in that moment all the years and millions of credits spent piecing her back together from the scattered wreckage of her empire were worth it.

"You know I disagreed with your tactic of playing nice after Insights Academy. But I see you had a plan all along. With the improvement in the Gardiens' reputation in recent months, you've positioned the organization to be a voice of reason and accountability when a public outcry over regenesis' dangers erupts."

"Exactly."

"You could have explained this to me at the time."

"Better to have it work, then show you the results."

Her piercing stare could be perceived as carrying a hint of a warning. "Next time, though."

"Next time, Mother. You have earned my trust and confidence. You are truly my most valuable advisor." *One day soon, you will be my partner as we stretch out our wings and take flight to rule this galaxy.*

10

CONCORD HQ
HOTEL CASSIOPEIA

arlee Marano smoothed down the lines of her jacket, then did the same to the top of her hair. She'd worn a tailored suit today and pinned her wayward locks back with tiny sapphire gemstones. She looked *professional*.

The Ourankeli wouldn't notice or care; they'd shown no interest in immersing themselves in the various Concord cultures since their arrival. So it wasn't for them. It was for her. She wanted to look the part, feel the part, *be* the part.

You seriously think you can impress them? They've lived for tens of thousands of years. They built the greatest technological monument we've ever encountered. You are nothing to them.

I said it wasn't for the Ourankeli. Also, I won't be nothing to them if my work enables them to settle on a new world. Then, I'll always be the person who gave them a home.

You'll have given them star charts and planetary profiles. You remain nothing more than a delivery girl.

She worked to drown out The Voice with her own mantra of positive reinforcement, gave herself a final pep-talk, and opened the door.

Half a dozen Ourankeli lounged in the common room. Two of them were morphed in unusual configurations involving six limbs and a diagonal comportment, but when they saw her, they swiftly pulled their gelatinous limbs in, and she idly wondered what sort of endeavor she'd caught them engaging in.

Cyfeill stood and glided over to greet Marlee. "This is our appointed time, yes?"

"Yes, it is." She gestured toward the meeting table shoved into the corner of the room; apparently they had no need of such a fixture in their daily lives. "Do you mind if we sit?"

"If it gives you comfort, that is fine." Cyfeill's eyes rotated around. "Kelizou will join us."

"I expected as much." Kelizou was the space scientist of the group, to the extent such a role existed in their refugee society. The Ourankeli were amazingly intelligent and advanced, but so few of them remained. So few engineers, scientists, builders. From what she'd been able to pick up, many of the individuals here were re-educating themselves, preparing to fill those roles when the opportunity arose. They were a resilient, hardy people; unbeaten and unbowed. Frigid and haughty as well, but she admired their strength.

Cyfeill conformed to the chair beside Marlee, Kelizou opposite her. She opened up an aural and positioned it so everyone could see. "Working within the parameters you provided, I've done an exhaustive search and analysis of our stellar system database. I regret to say, many planets looked favorable at first glance but ultimately proved too unstable in one way or another."

"We will find an artificial habitat acceptable."

"I know you will. But I'm trying to give you more than 'acceptable.'" She cleared her throat. "If you do elect to construct your own habitat, I've received assurances that Concord will provide whatever assistance you need. We'll help you gather resources, supply machinery, and so on."

Cyfeill quivered across its gelatinous facial skin, which Marlee had learned was a sign of discomfort.

"Cyfeill, I know your people have the capabilities needed to build whatever you require. But, with the greatest respect, you don't have the manpower. And we won't see you suffer or languish. We want you to thrive."

In truth, several heated debates had broken out among the Consulate staff regarding whether anyone should be focusing on the Ourankeli when the return of the Rasu loomed like an angry cloud over their every waking hour. But Dean Veshnael had given an inspiring speech about how if they waited, if they cowered, then the Rasu had already defeated them (metaphorically speaking), and this settled the matter.

A trill emerged from Cyfeill's throat, and the quivering stilled. "Very well. We will accept Concord's assistance, for a time. And when we are again strong, we will settle our debt."

"It's not a loan...but if that's what you prefer." Marlee opened two files on the aural. "These are the easy options for an asteroid habitat similar to Haafan. The first, Andromeda IV-XE23, features a robust asteroid belt orbiting between two of the three gas giants in the system. Three oversized asteroids, in particular, are well-situated for exploitation. In the second option, Triangulum II-MM16, we've identified two asteroids captured by a gas supergiant as moons suitable for development.

"If forced to choose, I feel the Triangulum site is the slightly better option, primarily due to the system being richer in resources. But either one should meet your needs."

Kelizou had been studying the files since she opened them, and now one of its hands flourished. "I am in agreement. This second location meets all our requirements."

"Then let us see it done," Cyfeill replied.

"Wait!" Marlee hurriedly reined her voice in. "Wait one minute. I want to offer you an additional option. It brings greater risks—greater challenges—but I think a much greater reward as well." She opened a new file. A lively, mint-and-quartz orb brought vivid color to the aural.

"This is Steropes. It's the largest moon of a gas giant in a binary star system located on the middle third of the central bar of the Large Magellanic Cloud. It has a mature atmosphere that, while thin, contains a ratio of gases compatible with your biology. In the long term, I'm confident you possess the know-how to tweak the atmosphere more to your liking if you desire.

"Best of all, though, is this: it's tidally locked to its planet, which orbits the secondary blue main sequence star of the binary pair. This results in it receiving sunlight eighty-two percent of the time. Now, I know this is a smidge lower than what you prefer, but it's comfortably within the margin.

"Also in its favor: the system is as stable as any binary system can be— which is to say, fairly stable. The gas giant's magnetic field protects Steropes from stray asteroids and solar flares.

"This moon doesn't have a perfect surface nor a perfect atmosphere— that's where the challenges come in. But it is entirely habitable. And you'll be able to walk in the sun. A real sun."

Cyfeill's head lowered, and both Ourankeli were silent for over a minute. At least to her ears; she had no doubt they were conversing privately.

Finally Cyfeill brought two appendages up to rest on the table, winding several digits together into an ornate knot. "We wish to visit this Steropes and judge its worth."

"I'll make the arrangements right away."

RW

Take that, subconscious!

Marlee forced herself not to skip back to her office, though she did shrug her suit jacket off and drape it over one shoulder. The Ourankeli were going to adore Steropes; she just knew it. She'd studied the fly-by visuals, and it was a simply marvelous specimen of a moon. The gas giant was a dramatic monster of churning fuchsia and saffron, too, though she supposed they wouldn't be seeing as much of it.

They may take your little moon, but as soon as they do, they will forget about you.

Which is fine. Dean Veshnael won't forget the top-notch job I did.

He's not going to promote you.

With a groan she flung herself into her office chair and ordered the door closed. Despite all her best efforts, her briefly buoyant mood inexorably dragged itself into the muck. Nothing like having a litany of your worst fears and doubts thrown in your face to ruin even the most unqualified success.

She'd spent the last two months marching steadily through the stages of grief.

1) Denial

This couldn't be her true subconscious. It couldn't be. Dr. Canivon was brilliant, but the woman must be wrong this time. Did she suppress worries and niggling doubts on occasion? Yes, naturally. Who didn't? But one thing she had never been was mean. Not to anyone else, not to herself. How could such an awful trait have been buried within her all these years? Simple answer: it couldn't have been.

2) Anger

What right did this so-called subconscious have to judge the decisions she made? She was the one out here doing the work, dammit! She put in the time and effort to educate herself. She took the risks. She earned the praise for success and the heartbreak from failure. Not some voice that had nothing better to do with its time than take potshots at her from the cheap seats.

3) Bargaining

She told herself it was only because she strove for such heights. She had audacious dreams, and she wasn't content to let them stay dreams. Because she reached for greatness, the opposite end of the pendulum lingered in her quietest thoughts. This was perhaps a tiny bit understandable. If the price of reaching so high, of never being satisfied, was a bit of niggling self-doubt from time to time, fine. She could make allowances for it.

4) Depression

She'd tried so damn hard to replace 'depression' with defiance. She would not wallow in self-pity. Nope.

She stared at the walls of her tiny office. They were decorated in colorful art and visuals—images of her with friends and family and coworkers. She'd recently added one of her and Vaihe, and she treasured how happy the Godjan looked in it: safe, healthy and engaged.

She was surrounded by so much love and companionship in this world.

But The Voice made her feel alone. Isolated. Small.

A yearning stirred in her soul—that most human of needs for comfort and reassurance. For a hug and unconditional love. It was absurd, but she wanted her mom.

Exhausted from the mental effort of being in top form all morning, she found she didn't have the energy to fight the urge. So she gathered up her things and left the office.

Running home to Mommy, are we?

Yes. Yes, we are, and I don't care what you have to say about it.

Curiously, The Voice didn't have a snarky retort for once. Maybe defiance would work after all.

SENECA
MILKY WAY GALAXY

Marlee swirled pasta around her fork, looping it into a giant tangle in the middle of her plate. "So I'm hopeful the Ourankeli are going to like this planet—technically it's a moon, but it has all the practical characteristics of a planet. If we can get them settled into a new home, it'll be a big win for the Consulate."

"And for you personally, yes?"

"Well, yes. I've been involved with caring for them ever since Caleb and Alex brought them to Concord. Seeing them through to a new beginning...it makes the work I do feel worthwhile. Consequential."

She and her mother sat at the kitchen nook table eating dinner, much as they had throughout her teenage years. She *loved* being out on her own, but tonight the sense of nostalgia, the reassurance of old, easy routines, was really nice. Exactly what she needed.

Isabela smiled warmly. "I'm so proud of you. You've come a long way since getting arrested on Savrak. Next thing I know, you'll be the head of the Consulate."

"Eh, not for a few more years." Marlee tried to inject a note of levity into her voice but failed. With the pasta on her fork now resembling a scrambled ball of yarn, she set her fork down and took a deep breath. Contrary to Caleb's advice, she'd never worked up the courage to tell her mother about her upgrades or their complications. But she was nearing her wit's end.

"I have come a long way. I'd like to think I've grown up a great deal in the last few months. But...Mom, can I talk to you about something? Without you being judgmental and scolding?"

Isabela set her own fork down as well, a quiet sigh escaping her lips. "Marlee, I don't mean to judge you. I'm merely trying to look out for you. You're my daughter, and I'll always want to keep you safe. But I suppose it's beyond my ability now, isn't it? Of course you can. I hope you can talk to me about anything."

It would be nice. If her mother's current goodwill survived the evening, she might try it. "Around three months ago, I made some radical upgrades to my cybernetics."

RW

Her mother leaned forward and pressed her hands together at her mouth. Somewhere during Marlee's tale, they'd retired to the covered back patio, and a cool breeze sent the aroma of *alyssi* wafting through the air.

"Marlee, I...how best to say this? The fact that you never had a voice in your head advising caution when you were growing up explains *so much*. You were always so fearless, so indomitable, so confident. Don't get me wrong. Those are wonderful traits, and I suspect they're responsible for you achieving all you have at such a young age. But as with most things, you took it to such an extreme. To be truthful, part of me is glad this voice has finally surfaced. It will keep you alive out there in a hard and unforgiving universe."

"But, Mom—"

"Please, let me continue for a minute? You want to know why your subconscious is mean to you. Biting, insulting, tearing you down."

"Yes!"

"It has a lot of time to make up for. It probably believes drastic measures are required."

Marlee closed her eyes and sank deeper into the couch cushion with a groan. "I won't apologize for the things I've done in my life. I mean, I would apologize for getting myself trapped on Namino—I *have* apologized for it. And I learned from my mistakes there. A lot. But I don't want to stop being who I am."

"And I don't want you to, either, darling." Her mother fluidly adopted her 'professor' demeanor, shoulders lifting and head tilting...then appeared to deliberately let it go. Instead she curled her feet up beneath her in the chair and played with the hem of her shirt.

"You are incredibly special and amazing. Yes, every mother wants to think this of their child, but I daresay you genuinely are. So back to the issue. To some extent, everyone's inner voice can be cruel. It whispers that we're not good enough, that we're a failure, that we're undeserving of love. Part of growing up, part of becoming a well-adjusted adult, is learning to try anyway. To persevere, to go after what you want. To have faith in yourself...even when you don't. It honestly never occurred to me that you never had to learn this lesson. I feel as if I failed you in some way."

"What? No. I was an impossible child."

"You admit it?"

"Yeah. See? Growing up and accepting responsibility. I hear what you're saying, and...I understand. But, Mom, this is an *actual* voice in my head. Not my brain throwing doubts at me—my brain speaking to me in a voice that sounds like a pulse, or a Kat talking. Have you ever had a Kat's voice in your head?"

"I can't say I have."

"Trust me, it's a mite weird. The point is, this voice might as well be another person talking to me. The difference is, I'm the only one who can hear it. So it's kind of hard to tune out and ignore."

Her mother nodded slowly. "Have you tried negotiating with it?"

"Um...."

"Countering it with logic. With reasoned arguments about why its assertions aren't valid."

Marlee chuckled under her breath. Ever the scientist. "A little bit. But mostly I've snapped back at it like we're in a playground fight. Not helpful, I realize. It's just so frustrating!"

Her mother reached out and wrapped her hands over Marlee's. "I think the first thing you need to do is accept that this is *you*. It's a part of your psyche, and you're going to have to make peace with it. Come to…if not an understanding, at least a detente. Maybe it sounds petulant and taunting because it's upset at having been ignored all these years. If you approach it from a perspective of openness, of willingness to listen, perhaps you'll find it's not so cruel after all."

Acceptance. There was that pesky stage five, huh?

"That's crazy talk." She worried at her lower lip. "I'm joking, sort of. But Mom, I don't want it to make me afraid. I don't want to be timid. If I'm not fearless, then I'm…nothing."

"Oh, Marlee, you will never be nothing. Not even close. I only mean…okay, let's take your uncle. He has spent decades throwing himself into harm's way. Risking his life by purposefully putting himself in ridiculously dangerous situations. He's confident—he knows how good he is. But he also respects the danger. Respects his adversary. Respects the consequences."

"How do you know?"

"Because he told me." She smiled a little wistfully. "Eventually."

"And you're saying it's possible all this voice really wants is for me to acknowledge—respect—the fact that I'm risking my life. I mean, not often or anything. Only every now and then."

"Oh, of course." Her mother rolled her eyes. "It's possible. Most of us more or less come to terms with our own self-doubts as best we can. And I think no matter how snarky or rude this voice of yours is, if you want to move forward, you're going to have to meet it where it lives and come to terms with it."

Marlee's chin dropped to her chest. It wasn't the advice she'd wanted to hear. She'd *wanted* her mother to have some quick fix to make it all better, like her always-handy salves for a skinned knee. But she wasn't a child any longer. This was the real world, and she was grateful her mother was treating her as an adult. Even if it meant there was no easy solution.

"Okay." She squeezed her mom's hand and stood. "Thank you for listening, and for not freaking out."

"Oh, I'm freaking out on the inside. I can't believe you installed bleeding-edge cybernetics and quantum components that haven't been safety tested by proper labs inside your body—and without telling me first! Not to echo your voice, but it's a wonder you're still walking and talking." Isabela shook her head ruefully, then reached out to squeeze her hand once more. "You're my daughter, which means I will always be terrified for you. But this is something *I've* had to come to terms with. I want you to be fearless—with a healthy dose of reverence for the challenges you insist on taking on."

Meet it where it lives…otherwise known as the dark, forbidding pit of fear and doubt now snaking through her gut like a thousand-year death. That wasn't daunting at all. But ineffectual rage had done nothing, and sticking her fingers in her ears and singing *la-la-la* had done less. Was this what she had left?

She leaned over to hug her mom. "Thanks for the advice. And the yummy spaghetti." *Thanks for reminding me that home is still a place I can go and feel safe.*

11

ROMANE

MILKY WAY GALAXY

Kennedy Rossi squinted at the screen, forcing herself to digest each row of data with the fullness it deserved. When she reached the bottom of the page, she scrolled down and repeated the process for the next page. Then she went back to the top and reviewed it all again. Just in case.

But the data was all real. And these numbers were *stupendous*.

Once she'd engineered how to fit a TDS onto AEGIS frigates and proved out the design, the military had taken over the rollout, eager to protect its frigates from the Rasu's destructive antimatter weapons. When she and Devon had maximized every practical improvement out of the Ymyrath Field, making the equipment smaller and more efficient while giving the weapon a far more powerful and longer-lasting punch, Concord had taken over the buildout and fitting of the weapon onto specialized ships.

But in this race against time, she was always on the hunt for new ways to safeguard lives or better cripple the enemy. Preferably both.

The widespread deployment of RNEWs was changing the face of the battlefield. While negative energy was safer, or at least more constrainable, than antimatter, a direct hit from it was still deadly, and never so much as for the fighter craft charged with darting around the messy core of a battlefield.

So with a great deal of help from fellow engineers, she'd invented a new type of shield to provide a measure of protection for the fighters. It borrowed heavily from the Dimensional Rifters, effectively sending any negative energy that impacted it away to be diffused more or less harmlessly.

AEGIS had barely begun to trial the shield on a select few vessels in the days before the Rasu withdrew, and in the enemy's absence they'd eagerly designed a series of field tests to study it.

And the field tests showed the shield worked. It couldn't fully absorb a point-blank hit from a negative energy blast, but it protected well against the type of incidental exposure that was a reality in any lengthy battle involving the Rasu.

Kennedy composed a brief report and sent it off to Miriam, who was surely going to be happy to be able to turn her little fighters loose in the next engagement. And the larger ships didn't need the shield, because they had Dimensional Rifters.

Now, how to adapt it to work more effectively against antimatter as well?

The door to her office opened, and Noah walked in, lugging a backpack on one shoulder. He took one glance at her and smiled. "The tests look good, huh?"

"The tests look amazing."

"Wonderful." He patted the bag, then held out a hand to her. "Come on. We're going for a picnic to celebrate."

Her eyes narrowed. "You've already packed for a picnic, but you couldn't have known what the test results would be. That's not celebrating."

"Any excuse for a picnic?"

She laughed, a rare sensation of...was this lightheartedness?... bubbling up in her as she shut down her workstation and followed him out.

RW

Kennedy rested on her hands and dropped her head on Noah's shoulder, and together they watched Jonas and Braelyn play on the shore of the pond. Mud was being flung and water splashed; the laundry cleanup was guaranteed to be epic. But the kids were laughing and having a blast, and she'd learned all too well exactly how precious such moments were.

"Maybe the Rasu won't come back. Maybe we've passed this trial and it's nothing but bright days ahead."

Noah hummed under his breath and kissed the top of her head. "Then what would you do for fun?"

"This."

"You'd be bored inside a week."

"No. Not any longer." She shifted around to gaze at him. "There's nothing like the abject terror of facing having your family ripped away from you forever to teach you what's important in life. I enjoy my work, and I'm glad to be doing my part to improve our ability to protect our soldiers. But this right here—you, Jonas, Braelyn—is what truly matters."

"Damn straight, it is." He leaned in and kissed her full on the mouth, tasting sugary from the brownies they'd had for dessert, and she sank into the kiss—which he promptly withdrew. "Hey, I've got an idea. How about we get a babysitter tonight?"

Her lips trailed down his nose, searching for the kiss again. "Okay. Where do you want to go?"

"Go? I don't want to go anywhere. I merely want several uninterrupted hours with you."

"I'm a fan—" A priority message arrived in her eVi. She wanted to ignore it, but the header begged for consideration, so she reluctantly pulled back from his embrace and opened it.

> *Kennedy Rossi,*
>
> *It has come to the attention of the Committee for Security and State Affairs that the Dominion Armed Forces are now fielding warships constructed of adiamene. While the Asterion Dominion is an ally, Section 14 of ASHI strictly prohibits the provision of adiamene to any parties outside of AEGIS.*
>
> *As the holder of Patent #A-X-2323018B on the adiamene metal and the manufacturing process thereof, your presence is requested at a hearing of the Committee. The purpose of the hearing is to investigate how the Dominion Armed Forces was able to obtain the formula and manufacturing process for the material in question.*
>
> *Please respond and confirm your intention to attend this hearing in person.*
>
> *— Committee for Security and State Affairs*
> *Earth Alliance Assembly*

Her buoyant mood evaporated into the breeze. She sent the message to an aural so Noah could see it, then banged her forehead slowly against his chest. "Dammit."

"We knew this was bound to happen eventually." He made an effort to keep his voice casual and upbeat, but she knew him far too well to miss the concerned edge it held.

"Actually, I was kind of hoping it wouldn't. Ugh." She lifted her head to meet his gaze. "What are we going to do?"

"Vii has the theft story all ready to go. It's what we agreed on when we decided to leak the information to the Asterions."

"I know. And it'll probably even pass muster. But why can't the politicians just leave well enough alone?"

"Because they're politicians?"

"Who have plenty of work to do ensuring their citizens are safe without meddling in private commerce." She watched as the kids tumbled into the shallow water of the pond, completing the soaking of their clothes. "No, you're right. We'll go with the story we agreed on. I don't relish bringing any heat down on Dashiel or Commander Palmer. But we have to keep Braelyn and Jonas safe, which means keeping ourselves safe."

Noah didn't respond, and she checked him. "Right?"

He nodded ponderously. "Getting arrested would be bad. And thanks to the self-styled One Human Government we now 'enjoy,' there's nowhere for us to run to this time."

12

IDCC ORBITAL DEFENSE STATION ALPHA
ROMANE STELLAR SYSTEM

M organ Lekkas studied the safety data from the radiation shields as she strode brusquely through the halls of the defense station. The numbers were excellent, which she could have told everyone two months ago. But the military brass did so love their testing protocols.

She smiled on reaching the summary conclusions that capped off the report. In essence, they signed off on setting all the fighter craft loose. It was a license to commit chaos—with a caveat to mind the antimatter.

Since the guardrails were now dismantled, she was going to need to revise the tactical plans. She added it to her annoyingly long list of obligations, then looked up to realize she'd reached Brigadier Lucas' office. She fastened her jacket, which had been hanging loose, and announced her presence. After a few seconds, the door opened to allow her entry.

The brigadier was a former fighter pilot turned military bureaucrat. Alas, it happened to the best of them. They'd been a young, fresh-faced recruit in the Earth Alliance who became a Prevo, then fled the Alliance for the IDCC during Pamela Winslow's reign of terror. They'd always had a good head on their shoulders, plus the early Prevo adoption spoke well of them, and Morgan had promoted them several times during her tenure with the IDCC RRF. Others had continued the practice in her absence, and they now oversaw the entire AEGIS Fighter Craft Division.

And unlike Major Tannehiln, they didn't seem to have any problem with outranking her, nor with dispensing orders in her general direction.

"At ease, Commander Lekkas. Have a seat."

Yes, she was *Commander* yet again. It was…nice. Comfortable. But she resolved every day to not let it go any further. She now led the Banshee battle group, which was growing in numbers at an accelerating rate. This was the optimal place for her to settle into a role that was custom made for her. Another promotion would only ruin the gig.

Lucas sent a file to her eVi. "I'm passing to you the list of the newest Banshee pilot candidates. Please submit your decisions by 0800 CST tomorrow. We need to get them in their ships and running scenarios as quickly as possible."

'As quickly as possible' had been the modus operandi for the last two months—since approximately twelve hours after the Rasu had vanished to go fight amongst themselves. It was a grueling pace, and lately she'd begun to see signs of strain at the margins—pilots squabbling in the locker rooms, superior officers turning snippish and overreacting to the smallest of glitches. She wasn't sure how much longer they could keep up the momentum Miriam Solovy insisted on maintaining.

She was fine with it. She could do this all year. The paperwork was a bit of a drag, but the ubiquitous training runs didn't wear her down—they energized her. For the first time since Brook's death, she'd daresay she was almost....

Having fun?

No, Stanley! I was going to say 'enjoying having a larger purpose again.'

But also having fun.

Never. Well, perhaps a little.

She glanced through the resumes. "No, no, yes, maybe, no—"

"Commander."

She closed the file and nodded sharply. "Right. I'll submit my decisions by the deadline."

"Thank you. This afternoon, I want you to meet with Abaddon and go through the updated Eidolon mission parameters with him."

"Sir? I don't have any authority over the Eidolon battle group or over Abaddon personally."

"Not officially, no. But you practically designed the Eidolon vessels, and you've supervised them before. Certain officers who rank higher than me continue to harbor reservations about letting a solo Artificial command an entire battle group. I've been instructed to provide Abaddon some unofficial supervision for now. You're the best person to do it."

She imagined letting the Eidolons choose one of their own to lead them *had* ruffled a few feathers among the brass. Artificials were now an integral part of every aspect of the military. They flew many of the ships, often without a human partner. They managed the weapons fire and kept the systems on warships functioning and their occupants alive. They devised attack plans and designed their own upgrades.

But never before had they been granted official authority in the chain of command on par with a human officer.

The brass was still hedging its bets on this front, as they had awarded Abaddon no formal rank. How could he be granted one? He hadn't enlisted and climbed the ranks the way everyone else did. He'd simply been installed in a hunk of flying metal, woken up, and sent out to fight. Eidolons had no humanesque dolls—at least not any declared ones. She suspected some of them did spend a few off hours passing as more conventional Artificials. But they were, first and foremost, sentient warships, and battle was the defining purpose of their rather unique lives.

Lucas was right; the Banshees might be her current crush, but the Eidolons had always been her baby. "I agree, sir. Not that Abaddon requires supervision, but that I'm the best one to provide it. Do I need to file secret reports evaluating his performance?"

"Only if you identify a problem."

A devious glint lit her eyes. "I think I'll file them when I *don't* identify a problem."

"Of course you will."

"And you will dutifully pass them along to the brass? I want them to be well-informed."

Lucas sighed. "I will. For the record, I agree with you that the added oversight is unnecessary."

"Then you should have pushed back on the order."

"Commander, do you remember how the chain of command works?"

"Sometimes. Sir."

"Work on that. Oh, one more thing before you go. We've just received a new proposed strategic warfare plan for fighter craft from the Rasu War Council. We've been asked to give feedback on it this week. I'd like for you to take a look at it and let me know your thoughts."

"The War Council? Is this Miriam—Commandant Solovy's work?"

"Actually, I believe it's the brainchild of her husband."

"Huh. I guess Alex had to get her smarts from somewhere."

"Excuse me?"

"Nothing. I'll look it over and send you my notes. After I vet the new pilot candidates and ensure Abaddon is doing a good job." She groaned under her breath. How had she ended up here again?

Because the talented inevitably rise to the top. You can't help but be who you are.

Shut up, Stanley.

13

KIYORA

KIYORA ONE GENERATIONS CLINIC
ASTERION DOMINION

Dashiel stared at his hands in a kind of surreal curiosity. Amber glitter seemed to float above the skin, almost as though he'd donned a pair of force-field gloves. He swept one hand to the side, and the glitter trailed along languidly behind the movement.

He felt woozy, as if he'd downed a couple of alcohol shots in rapid succession. Yet his mind darted about from idea to idea, high on adrenaline and kyoseil.

So much kyoseil. As much as the specialized body Nika had insisted he construct for her before she traveled to occupied Namino, in fact—and a sliver more. He needed every advantage possible.

Though Nika had dismissed any need for further study, after Namino, he'd ordered a thorough round of tests on the safety and reliability of a kyoseil-doused body. They had come back...passable. Oh, the improvements in processing time, multithreading capabilities and storage capacity were impressive. But the bodies were...not fragile exactly, but definitely finicky. Prone to circuitry overheating, muscular and skeletal strain and a confounding tendency toward excess 'noise' in the circuitry that refused to clear. The kyoseil talking to itself, perhaps?

But the tests showed nothing inherently dangerous to life or limb in using such a body, so here he was.

Now to find out if it made any difference at all. Standard tests couldn't measure the one feature that made such a body special: by intensifying the connections between mind and mineral, it manifested an enhanced ability to listen to and interact with the kyoseil living in the air around them.

Dashiel eased into the chair in the recovery room, still feeling a touch lightheaded, and installed the routine he'd written for Nika to allow her to access the Kireme Boundaries automatically. It wasn't designed for Rift Bubble interactions, but having it in the mix couldn't hurt. Then he slipped into sidespace and traveled to the site of the Mirai Rift Bubble.

He reached into its workings with his mind…and saw only a pervasive glow. No programming. Dammit!

His mind slammed back into his body in frustration.

Think. You can outsmart a primitive, primordial mineral. He leapt to his feet and opened a wormhole to the location, then stepped through it. The spinning ball of light danced within its lattice like a miniature sun.

He walked up to the lattice and extended a hand, but hesitated as electrical currents set the fine hairs of his arm on edge to a far greater extent than on his last visit. Oh well. It wasn't as if it would be the first time he'd been electrocuted.

Projecting an air of confidence into the motion, he stuck his hand into the light, and every nerve in his body lit fire. Was smoke curling out of his ears, he wondered? But he didn't yank his hand away; he'd come this far before with a normal body.

Instead, he forced himself to focus and switched to the visual kyoseil band.

Reams of hyper-advanced programming streamed along the inside of the lattice. As before, he followed it to the section where the access code control resided.

A fingertip rested upon the lattice. *Kyoseil to kyoseil. You comprehend this, don't you, you confounding little life form? You're merely conversing with yourself here. Nothing to be alarmed about.*

He transferred a command to alter the access code through the fingertip—and no electrifying zap answered to send him stumbling away. He belatedly remembered to breathe. Had it worked? He ran back through the section—the code had changed!

He frantically reversed the change before he murdered the occupants of any ships that might be traversing one of the barriers at this precise moment. Then he removed his hand from the ball of light, genuinely surprised to find it wasn't on fire.

Okay. This was something. It *had* been a simple matter of relative quantity. Like recognized like and listened to its own.

Now for one last and, in many ways, most important test. He traveled in sidespace to the Kireme Boundary situated at Ridani Enterprises and activated the routine he'd installed…and the device turned on. Back off again. No glitches.

It made sense. The Boundaries were of Asterion rather than Kat design, their programming not too different from portions of the code currently running in his own body. The routine used ceraffin tech to access the devices. He'd only needed the extra boost of kyoseil to unlock it.

He was smiling as he returned his mind to his new body at the clinic, then left the recovery room and discharged himself.

RW

MIRAI
NIKA'S FLAT

Dashiel stepped through a wormhole into the entry hallway of Nika's flat and tiptoed toward the living area.

Nika sat on the couch, her hands clasped at her chin in contemplation. Tendrils of ethereal kyoseil drifted around her in an aura, dancing in and out of her long, raven hair. This was different from the glow she regularly tamped down since the Oneiroi Nebula, so he was forced to conclude the wispy aura had been there since she'd transferred into the new body. He just hadn't been able to see it until now.

What was she thinking of so intently? Was she here at all, or off surfing the kyoseil waves in distant galaxies? Or torturing herself by eavesdropping on the dark, war-laden thoughts of the enemy?

He cleared his throat.

She instantly turned toward the sound, her expression brightening when she saw him. "Dashiel! I was starting to worry about where you'd...." She stood, her head tilting curiously. After a few seconds, her eyes widened. "What did you do?"

"You can tell? I thought I toned down the extra glow."

"I can tell." She hurried over to him. A hand drifted over his cheek, barely skimming the skin, then trailed down his neck. "You got a new body. One like mine."

He shrugged by way of answer.

"That's where you've been? Why didn't you tell me you were going to do this?"

"I wanted to surprise you."

"You succeeded!" She smiled broadly. "But why? You've been so reluctant to...."

"To follow where you've gone."

Her lips parted, and she nodded faintly.

"I'm still not certain I have. Not truly. Crept a little closer to the sidelines, maybe. But, importantly, I can now change the Rift Bubble access codes—on site, not through sidespace, but it's something. And using the routine I wrote, I can activate the Kireme Boundaries from anywhere."

"You've already tested it?"

"I have. The added functionality was imperative."

"This is fantastic, darling. It really is. But..." her throat worked, and a shadow passed across her features "...are you sure this is what you want? Did I pressure you? I didn't mean to pressure you."

He clasped her face in his hands. "Nika, when are you going to understand? I will do *anything* for you. I want so badly to help ease your burdens, even if it's only a little. This body enables me to do that. For the record, I also want to go where you go and stand beside you for every new adventure. And if a shiny and slightly electrified new body is what it takes for me to accompany you, then so be it."

She swept her lips softly across his. "And I want *you* to understand: you are and will always be enough, as you are. As you were, should you want to go back to your old vessel. I treasure your heart and mind, not your body. Well, except for...."

He let one hand drift down over the curve of her hip and gripped it to pull her tightly against him. "I know."

"Ah, good." Her eyes twinkled in delight, banishing the shadow. "I can't deny this makes me happy, though. I mean, I want what you want, and you were getting so frustrated. So I stopped pushing."

"I know you did, and I'm sorry I was being difficult. I felt helpless. Now, I'm a bit less helpless. Ten percent. Maybe twelve."

She stifled what looked like a burgeoning giggle. "You, helpless? Never. If you discover you can't do something, you simply invent a new tool that will enable you to do it. Which you just did." With a pleased sigh, her eyes met his. "I love you. Until the end of the universe. Which we are going to ensure is *not* in eight years."

"We absolutely are. We will change our future." He kissed her rather zealously, and swore he felt an added *zing* dancing between their lips. Unexpected benefit? "So is that what you were working on when I interrupted you? Changing our future?"

"Doing my damnedest."

14

CONCORD HQ
RASU WAR ROOM

Alex greeted Pinchu with a cautious hug, as one always had to be mindful of the ribs when embracing the burly, strong Khokteh. "I hear your military is nearly back up to full strength now. It must have taken a gargantuan effort to make so much progress in so little time."

"Your mother has been generous with materials and funds."

"That's Mom. Always so generous."

Pinchu completely missed the sarcasm, of course, and nodded in agreement. "Nonetheless, I am proud of my people. They applied the spirit of the warrior to the task, and in doing so have accomplished mighty things."

"I'm sure they have." She smiled teasingly. "And you? Feeling extra tingly lately?"

Pinchu snorted through his long snout. "You know where it hits me the most? In my *toes*. I'm marching around, giving orders and supervising our war effort, and out of nowhere my toes start tingling, as if your planet is announcing it wants to have a conversation. And I think, 'I don't have time for you right now, planet!' But my toes just tingle away."

"You realize it's actually two planets now."

"*Diin niiyol.* My earlobes will probably start tingling soon, too." His manner softened a touch. "But I am grateful, always. Thanks to Caleb, I will be here to lead my people in the great battles of our age."

"We're grateful, too—to have you still walking among us." In her peripheral vision she saw her mother striding into the room, so she reached high up to pat Pinchu on the shoulder, and they took their seats at the table.

Her mother's uniform was as crisp and polished as the day it had been manufactured. Not a hair was out of place in her low bun. Her expression of grim determination had not altered in months. In fact, it was only the presence of a tiny muscle near the corner of her left eye twitching maniacally, having managed to escape control, that hinted at the extreme stress the woman operated under.

But its presence was enough to temper any uncharitable thoughts Alex might otherwise have toward her. Their disagreement remained unresolved, but no one, least of all Alex, would ever question Miriam's commitment to her job and dedication to the defense of every sentient being in Concord and Dominion space.

Her mother brought the meeting to order with a clasp of her hands on the table. "Thank you everyone for coming. We will start with the bad news. We've had to move against Emerald again. While our initial strike was highly successful, the fact is they recovered more quickly from this strike than previous ones. Despite our best efforts, they are, I'm afraid, getting stronger."

The faction map materialized above the table for everyone to consider—and in the microsecond it took for Alex to absorb the fullness of the map, something new caught her eye. Or possibly not new. Possibly she was simply noticing it for the first time.

Her mother launched into an explanation of the various faction movements and attacks over the last several days, but Alex mostly filtered the speech out to study the map.

The colors and their relative positions were familiar by now, though the size and shape of the territories were constantly shifting. Smaller factions had been subsumed early on, and the once-kaleidoscope of hues had recently been reduced to a mere rainbow collection. Bronze and Teal were on the verge of vanishing, which would leave only five factions standing.

Perhaps this was why she saw it now. Saw what exactly? She pulled her focus back and cleared her mind, letting her gaze take in everything the map displayed without judgment or assumption.

Before she knew it, the entire meeting had passed, and she'd caught maybe ten percent of it. Which was fine; no one here was looking to her to make critical military decisions.

As everyone stood and began departing, she thought about trying to catch up to Malcolm and chat with him for a minute. Richard had said his infiltration of the Gardiens was stalled out, and he seemed rather miserable. Getting back together with Mia would likely fix that, but she supposed it wasn't her business—

"Alex?"

She whipped around to face her mother, plastering on her standard noncommittal countenance as she did. "Yes?"

"You were very quiet today. It looked as if your mind was elsewhere. Is something going on?"

"Something you're itching to demand I tell you about so you can shut it down before I run off and mess up your war effort?"

Miriam stared at her for a long moment, her expression inscrutable. Her mouth opened a fraction, then closed again. Finally she sighed. "Is there?"

"No, Mom. Don't worry. I'm being a good girl."

"Somehow I doubt that. But everything's all right?"

"Why do you...other than the obvious? Yep. Just dandy."

"I'm glad to hear it." Her mother nodded and turned to begin shutting down the various screens she'd had open for the meeting. Conversation over.

Alex shook her head in impotent frustration and departed the War Room. On the way to the levtram, she sent Nika a pulse.

Do you have any free time later today? There's something I want to mull over with you.

RW

Miriam watched the door close behind her daughter with a touch of resignation. Before the meeting, she'd chastised herself to try to be amiable toward Alex. Yet at her daughter's first sharp retort, she'd matched Alex barb for barb. She should be more disciplined than this.

David arched an eyebrow in question from the doorway, but she shook her head, and he departed as well, leaving her alone. It wasn't that he couldn't provide comfort to her. Rather, it was that she already knew everything he would say by heart. Most of it was sage advice, but she was able to call it up from memory if needed. And she didn't want to snap at him as well.

She gazed at the Rasu map hovering above the conference table. Textbook analysis counseled that at this point, Emerald and Crimson were the most dangerous threats. Stygian held a decent amount of territory, but had been largely passive so far. Orange had made a solid go of it, but Emerald was consistently beating it back, and on the opposite side of the map, Pink had started to falter under Crimson's steady assault. The remaining factions were apt to be gone in another few weeks.

The endgame was approaching. It wasn't here yet; she still had time. There were moves still to make. But it now crept in from the horizon like the gloom of an advancing thunderstorm.

Honestly, she'd expected it to arrive sooner. She'd assumed the Rasu would act logically and join together to strike against their enemy while Concord was weakest. Instead, they'd followed the darker impulse of all sentient beings—they'd acted selfishly. Each one wanted to be the ruler, to hold all the power. And so they squabbled and fought.

Alex couldn't have known this about the Rasu. But somehow, she'd been correct on this point. Her daughter had a habit of following nothing but her gut and ending up at the right place. It was a rare trait, and one humanity had benefited greatly from.

Miriam's own gut continued to insist that where Alex failed was in her inability to properly appreciate the might and power this enemy was going to wield when a victor was crowned. Their potential strength was nigh-on unimaginable, except it was Miriam's job to do precisely that. And so her doubts gnawed away at her. What if, at the end of the day, everything she'd done was for naught? What if the Rasu rolled over them in a great tidal wave, erasing every trace of their existence from the history books of the cosmos?

She also heard Alex's voice in her head. *But what if they don't?*

What, indeed. But where Alex had faith, she had only weapons and the ability to command them. The reality was, if Concord lost this battle for survival, they lost everything. So she remained determined to focus on using every ounce of her power to ensure they won.

This included, she conceded, trying to bring an end to this low-grade feud with her daughter. It not only distracted them both, it ate away at her morale; perhaps it did for Alex as well. And her own morale could use the help.

Most of all, though, if these were the end times, she didn't want to face them without her daughter at her side. With her family fractured or anything short of whole. If these were the end times, they should try to love each other as best they could.

That was definitely what David would have said.

15

AKESO

Alex brought a pitcher of lemonade and two glasses upstairs, then set them on the cabinet ledge and poured her and Nika drinks. "Fresh lemonade from the orchards on Demeter. Akeso wanted to grow lemon trees for us here, but the thought of *drinking* Akeso was too weird for me."

Nika made a face as she accepted her glass. "Would it even be lemonade?"

"At a molecular level, yes. But also still Akeso."

"Right." Nika took a sip. "This is good. More tart than what we produce."

"How are things with you? I mean, aside from having the enemy constantly whispering in your ear?"

"There is that." Nika idly swished the lemonade around, staring into her glass like it held a whirlpool of gifted wisdom. "Dashiel upgraded his body. He built a new, kyoseil-infused version to match mine."

From her tone, Alex couldn't get a bead on how the woman felt about it. "Isn't that a good thing? I know he's been a bit recalcitrant about kyoseil stuff."

"It is, mostly because he did it without me begging him to do so. I don't know. I've tried so hard to include him in everything about my new world, but there's been this persistent barrier between us I can't seem to breach. Maybe this will knock it down?" She abandoned her lemonade ministrations to gaze at Alex, smiling blithely. "We'll see. Anyway, what's up?"

Honestly, Alex was relieved at the change of subject. Relationship advice had never been her strong suit, and Asterion relationships held an extra weirdness to them she hadn't fully sussed out.

She activated the full Rasu Control Map above the data center table and expanded it until it took up nearly the entire office. "This is the state of the civil war as of this morning."

"Plum is gone now."

"It is. Emerald had a surprise resurgence and took out Plum's one remaining galaxy over the last few days. This earned Emerald a second visit from the Ymyrath Field battle group. Mom is concerned the surviving play-ers are getting stronger, and the impact of our sneaky incursions weaker in turn."

"Are you concerned about it as well?"

"Oh, certainly. But something else is bugging me." Alex zoomed in the map, past the center, toward the distant reaches of Rasu space. "We've ig-nored Stygian since it's so far away, and in particular since it hasn't made any overt moves. We've been counting our blessings to have one arguably peaceful faction minding its own business. Yet none of the other factions have made any moves against it, either. I wonder why not?"

"Maybe for the same reason? It's a valid strategy to prioritize attacking those who would attack you before they gain the advantage."

"True. But some of these factions have been downright belligerent—against every rival except this one." She took a quick sip of lemonade. "Styg-ian has kyoseil, correct?"

"Oh, yes. It plundered the troves we seeded as thoroughly as any of the factions. Possibly more than the others, in fact. Now that you mention it, it is a little odd Stygian haven't been more aggressive. Is it due to it being sur-rounded on three sides by disparate factions?"

"Don't know." Alex gestured vaguely at the far edge of the map, marked only by an absence of activity. "But I've been thinking about that fourth side and what it could mean."

"The Erebus Void is there, correct? The Rasu have never expanded their territory in that direction because there's nothing but interstellar void for hundreds of megaparsecs. No resources to plunder or stellar energy to capture, so no reason to hold it."

"Exactly. I've been studying the shape of Rasu territory and the geo-graphic distribution of the factions. Isn't it interesting how the most aggres-sive actors are situated well inside Laniakea, farthest from Stygian?"

"I don't know. Is it?"

"Yes, it is. What if they're the most aggressive because they're the most independent-minded? Because they're the *farthest from home?*"

"Like Jerry, the Rasu we captured early on in the conflict. It had wan-dered off from its brethren and grown a mind of its own..." Nika wrenched her gaze away from the map to stare at Alex "...you think the Rasu origi-nated in the region Stygian controls?"

"I'm afraid it might be worse than that. I know you can 'see' the flow of kyoseil. Is there any way you can pull back and observe its flow across the aggregate of space? Across the entirety of Rasu territory at once?"

"I'm not sure." Nika frowned. "I suppose if I used sidespace and occupied a location far enough removed to be able to view so much territory with my mind's eye? Akin to a wide-field telescope? Damn, it makes me dizzy to think about the prospect."

"I'll come with you. I realize it won't help much, but, hey, moral support."

"Which is very much welcome. I know you enjoy wandering the stars, but existing only as a consciousness in space makes me feel...lonely." Nika shivered briefly. "Where do you think would be a good spot?"

Alex unzoomed the map, then pulled out farther, until the map went well beyond Concord space on one side and past the fringes of the Shapley Supercluster on the other. Her hand came to her chin as she considered the expanse of endless stars and galaxies. She sensed their ebb and flow, their interactions and the empty space in between.

"I think...here." The supergalactic coordinates blinked onto the map, and she gave Nika an encouraging smile. "Shall we?"

RW

Their minds hovered in the black, far from any galaxy that would blind them to the grand tapestry.

Alex's chest fluttered nervously. Studying the map had been one thing, but this was something altogether different. It felt as if the entirety of the universe danced on a stage for their appreciation. The scale defied words, expressible only in emotion. Awe.

Nika's whisper in her head did nothing to break the spell.

I feel like I'm on the verge of falling into an endless abyss and never landing.

Yeah, this is heady. Anyway, um, we should focus on the mission. What do you see?

Mesme was right. Kyoseil is literally everywhere. Sometimes it's only a few wispy filaments bridging across galaxies, but it is without question the web that overlays the entire spacetime manifold. I am...overwhelmed. Okay, focusing. The Rasu. They have definitely reached a saturation point. Their galaxies are positively glutted with kyoseil. Can I express how much this breaks my heart?

I know it does. I'm sorry. And Stygian?

Damn. Its use of kyoseil is on another level from the rest. Its territory is a solid wall of kyoseil. I can't detect a single parsec of space that isn't tightly woven through with the mineral. Gods, what does this mean?

I suspect nothing good. But we can't discover what they're up to from our safe little perch out here, can we? Let's go take a tour.

She picked a stellar system in the dead center of Stygian's territory.

Here to start.

Together they dove behind enemy lines.

Back in the office on Akeso, Alex gasped aloud. Here, *every* Rasu vessel was a mammoth dreadnought. The stellar rings crisscrossed the star in a tangled web.

She pulled away and ventured to another stellar system, and even in sidespace she had to fight through the molasses of Rasu metal simply to reach it. The enemy was everywhere.

Into the interstellar medium between systems, where Rasu traveled in huge caravans of fleets. She was surprised they had room to move more than a few megameters without causing a trans-stellar traffic jam.

On to a new stellar system, with the same result...no. There were no planets here.

I'm not detecting any planets at all in this system. Only a few scattered asteroids.

Where did you go?

Oh, sorry.

She sent Nika her location.

Found you. I wonder if no planets ever formed here, or if the Rasu re-purposed every iota of material?

My bet's on the latter.

It's strange. The kyoseil here, in Stygian's territory? It's...agitated. On edge, in a manner it isn't anywhere else, even when the Rasu are battling one another.

Is it struggling against the Rasu's control?

No. It's only a feeling I get from it. I can't explain it. It's probably just me being on edge.

But when it came to kyoseil, Alex had learned to trust Nika's instincts. She checked another system, then another. No planets. No asteroids. That settled it. Stygian had consumed every astronomical body for resources and used them to build a fleet of such size and scope as to be beyond comprehension.

Without realizing it, she'd chased stellar systems all the way to the precipice of the Erebus Void, where an endless darkness swallowed all light. Somewhere, far away, the emptiness ended and stars returned, but she could not see them from here. This was one of the largest cosmic voids in measured space, stretching across four-hundred-twenty megaparsecs—a veritable abyss amidst a sea of galaxy clusters. On its distant border, thick clouds of gas and dust obscured what lay beyond.

Nika, come to the border of Rasu territory. Is there any kyoseil in the Void?

How did you end up so far out? I can't keep up with you. And I already told you, kyoseil is everywhere.

Just check, please.

Alex anchored her mind to a star at her back, so she didn't fall into the blackness and never return.

It's...damn. How did you know?

How did I know what? Tell me what you see.

The Erebus Void is completely bereft of kyoseil. No mineral deposits, certainly, but no waves either. It's as if the kyoseil is consciously bypassing the Void. I've never seen it do such a thing. What do you think is going on?

What *was* going on here? Voids, in and of themselves, weren't special. Areas of comparative emptiness littered intergalactic space. This one was larger and emptier than most others, for certain, but scientists had not discovered anything else that made it unique.

But they'd never looked with her eyes.

"It's simply...the universe has rules. Even the exceptions obey the rules. Though so immensely complex it appears to most like chaos, in truth the universe is ordered and structured and perfect. And since I understand the way things must be, when something seems out of place, wrong or merely odd...I can recognize the reality of it. The hidden object or event or force which brings space back into alignment with the rules of the universe."

So she dove into the Void with her mind. The act was dramatic enough to attract Valkyrie's attention, and her companion hitched a ride for the rest of the trip.

What a cold, dreary place you have found, Alex.

Yes. Hardly any atoms at all to bump into. Only the faintest intergalactic breeze drifting through our hair.

Funny. What are we searching for?

The reason for the absence.

The absence of what?

Everything.

She felt around with her elemental senses, breathing in and trying to *be* the manifold—and jerked as an abrasion scraped her mental skin. She reached out for it, marveling at the roughness sensed by fingertips that were not there.

It's a scar upon the firmament. Let's see where it leads.

Now that she had a bead on the unique texture, it was easy enough to follow. It stretched around half a megameter in width, but vastly farther in length. Onward they went—

Alex? Are you all right?

Nika would be getting cold and lonely by now. But she had to chase this mystery down while she had its trail.

Yes. Hang tight and give me a minute.

The scar meandered in a zig-zag pattern to run in rough parallel along the border of Stygian's territory, until an offshoot jutted markedly into a stellar system perched on the fringe of the Void...where she lost it in all the noise of normal Rasu activity. Dammit!

She retraced her steps and continued following the scar until it gradually faded away, some three thousand megameters beyond where it had begun.

What could have caused such a wound upon the firmament of space? Valkyrie murmured in her head.

More specifically, what force is powerful enough to cause such a wound? The list is quite short.

Indeed. I will think upon it.

You do that.

Alex reached out to 'touch' the scar a final time and shuddered at the sheer wrongness of it.

My location. No kyoseil at all, huh?

Not so much as a microscopic blip of energy.

Okay. I think we've seen enough. We're done here.

She opened her eyes in the office. Her chest heaved from exertion, and she swayed dizzily. The room was so small. Her skin so tight. The mass of the cosmos pressed in on her, trying to squash her into atoms.

Nika bent over in her chair and dropped her head into her hands. "I'm going to be sick."

"Restroom's in the bedroom across the walkway."

With a rough nod, Nika stumbled up and took off out of the room.

Alex grasped the edge of the data table with both hands and leaned heavily on it. In her mind's eye, stars and galaxies and Rasu all rushed through her, trying to unmoor her from reality. And in the middle of it all, a yawning scar of infinite blackness burned a lesion upon the cosmos.

Damn, she really should not make a habit of doing this sort of thing.

She'd regained a modicum of composure by the time Nika returned to the office, looking pale but steady on her feet. "Some skill we've got there, huh?"

"Yeah. It's a laugh riot."

"So what do we know now that we didn't before?"

Alex forced herself to concentrate on the problem at hand. The mystery of the scar tugged at her, but she needed to focus on the far more tangible threat they faced. "It's a reasonable assumption to make that Stygian is the original home of the Rasu, but I'm not sure it matters in the short term. What does matter is that Stygian has spent this entire civil war stockpiling kyoseil and hoarding resources to construct a force that, when it's ready, will consume every other Rasu in existence. And then us."

"What do we do with this information?"

"Much as I hate to do it, we have to tell my mother."

16

CONCORD HQ
COMMAND

Alex gazed out the viewport at the pinwheels of ships docked at HQ. Beyond them, sunlight glittered off the hulls of the Combined Concord Defense Brigade Alpha (Alpha Brigade for short) as they patrolled the space surrounding the station, tasked with protecting this most vital of resources.

Humanity had achieved so much since its involuntary relocation to Amaranthe. If someone had told her two decades ago that humans would peacefully lead an alliance of numerous alien species spread across sixty-two galaxies? That said alliance would command a military fleet forty-eight million strong? That they would no longer war with themselves, or even against former enemies?

She would have laughed for ten minutes solid.

If someone had told her she'd still be clashing with her mother, on the other hand, she'd have nodded in resigned acceptance. But she immediately chastised herself, for the response was a disservice to how closely they'd bonded in the intervening years. To all they had accomplished together during those years.

Yet here they were again, butting heads adorned with horns sharpened by their mutual worst tendencies. Her father often said they were too much alike, and she had to concede it was a fair assessment.

But none of this mattered today. She had to put aside any personal...not animosity, for she didn't hate her mother—far from it. Call it frustration at her inability to simply make her mother *see*.

This meeting wasn't about restoring family harmony. It was about the survival of everyone.

"I'd ask you what's on your mind to have you emoting so vigorously at the viewport, but it's a stupid question."

She glanced over as Nika came to stand beside her. "Listen, before we go in, you should know that the vibe between my mother and I remains...frosty. Prickly. I'm not going in there to pick a fight—the opposite—

but I can't guarantee hugs and kisses. Regardless, though, I don't intend to let personal issues complicate our message."

"Understood. This war is making everyone crazy."

"Truer words."

Alex, I'm available now.

She turned to see a military officer she didn't know exiting her mother's office. "We're up."

RW

Her mother adopted a surprisingly warm expression as they walked in. "Alex. Advisor Kirumase, welcome."

"Thank you, Commandant."

"Would either of you like some tea?"

Alex shook her head. "I've imbibed a gallon of coffee in the last three hours."

"That can't be a good sign."

"Not really." Nika accepted a cup of tea, and the three of them sat at the small table by the window. It felt informal, even collegial, and Alex tried to lean into the atmosphere.

"What news do you bring this morning?" Miriam asked.

"We have a problem."

"We have many—" her mother cut herself off "—what kind of problem?"

"We've been watching and responding to the wrong Rasu factions," Alex replied. "Emerald isn't the true threat. Crimson isn't either. Stygian is."

"Stygian hasn't made any moves of note, and so far the other factions have ignored it. My analysts have begun to postulate that Stygian might be of a peaceful, or at least 'live and let live' bent."

"It's not."

Her mother took a sip of her tea. Calmly, of course. "Explain."

"We think Stygian controls the region where the Rasu originated. Where they evolved. We think the faction is comprised of the oldest Rasu."

"Okay. I won't ask you to explain your evidence for this conclusion, though I reserve the right to ask you to explain it to others at a later time. When it comes to space, I trust your judgment."

Just not so much on other matters, huh? She kept the retort unvoiced. "Thank you."

"But simply because it's the oldest doesn't mean it's the strongest or the greatest threat."

"Agreed. But we believe it is."

Nika jumped in. "Stygian has amassed far more kyoseil than any other faction, by several orders of magnitude. And it has used the mineral to infuse a fleet, a population, of such size as to be beyond counting."

Her mother thrived on facts and data, so Alex quickly picked up the thread. "The Rasu are practically bumping into each other in their space—including between stellar systems. Stygian has sucked all the resources out of the galaxies it controls. Hardly any planets or moons are left. No asteroids, no comets."

Miriam steepled her hands at her chin; they had her attention now. "I see. Give me your assessment: what does this tell you?"

"I suspect Stygian has been deliberately amassing all this kyoseil—all this power—while it lets the other factions fight it out amongst themselves. It's waiting until only one or two remain, at which point its troops will pour out of its territory and across all of Rasu space, flattening the other factions beneath the unrelenting assault of its forces. I think within several days after Stygian makes such a play, maybe a week, one Rasu will rule them all."

"And then that Rasu will come for us."

"And then it will come for us." Alex sighed. "Mom, I want to—"

"It doesn't matter. We move forward."

And this was why her mother was the leader of this whole damn show. She never, *ever* lost sight of why she was here.

"Why did the other factions allow Stygian to amass so much power? If they'd attacked Stygian territory early on...."

Alex shrugged. "What if they're afraid of making Mom angry?"

That earned a restrained chuckle from her mother. "I suppose some compulsions are universal. What if the detente continues? Perhaps the other factions are content to let Stygian have its space. Or, as you suggest, they fear challenging their elder."

"Or, possibly the winner will believe itself finally strong enough to usurp the throne. As you said, some compulsions are universal. Honestly, though, I'm no longer worried about the other factions. I mean I *am*, but what Nika and I saw?" She closed her eyes, uttering words she made it a point to never utter, especially not to her mother. "Stygian frightens me."

If her mother displayed any surprise at her admission, Alex didn't see it. Because she didn't look.

Nika cleared her throat to interject. "Given everything I know about Rasu psychology, I believe Stygian will come for the other factions. Its amassing of such numbers counsels no other option. In fact, I'd say for the

Rasu progenitor, no goal is more important than controlling its children. It's probable this is what Stygian has always wanted, the same as its children have always wanted to be free—then to control their own children. The desire for control is inherent to the Rasu's nature."

Miriam stared at her hands, folded in her lap. "What are your thoughts on how to respond?"

Alex blinked, taken aback. "You're asking Nika, yes? You don't want to hear what I would do."

Those piercing hazel eyes rose to land on her. "On the contrary, Alex. I am very interested to hear how you think we should react to this new information. I can't promise I'll agree with it, but I will listen with an open mind."

And now she was getting shamed by the high road. Damn, her mother was good at this. "Um, I appreciate it. I'm not a military strategist—which you obviously know—but I think we need to halt the Ymyrath Field attacks."

"Oh?"

"We're only weakening the other factions for Stygian, making the ultimate victor easier to pick off when the time comes."

"But by lengthening the civil war, by keeping more players in the game for longer, we're extending the time until a true victor emerges and Stygian is able to make its move—assuming that is what it will do. Buying us time was, I believe, your goal in kicking off this civil war in the first place."

Touché. Alex smacked her lips...and conceded the point. "You're correct. This is *why* I'm not a military strategist. I don't know what the better choice is. Either one could backfire."

"What if we started hitting Stygian instead? If the territory is as densely packed as you say, we can disable a larger swath of Rasu than normal with every strike."

"We can. But I worry doing so will only provoke Stygian into moving now rather than later. Much like the Kats way back when, it might decide the best strategy is to attack while it remains near maximum strength."

"Astute analysis."

"Oh? Well...I hope so." Alex frowned; her mother had her seriously off-balance with all this *yebanaya* kindness. "Anyway, we thought we should make you aware of what we believe the ultimate threat here is. We'll, um, keep peeking in on Stygian, as well as the other factions, and share any updates with you. And I'm sorry to be the bearer of more bad news."

"Never be sorry for telling the truth." Her mother stood. "I need to think this through. Consult with some people. Talk to your father."

Alex forced a laugh as she and Nika stood, too. "If anyone will have a clever idea on how to turn this to our advantage, it's him."

"Indeed. I'm not sure any of us would be here today if not for him. So thank you for that as well."

"I...." Alex stared at her mother, at a complete loss. "You're welcome?"

"Nika, if you'll excuse us for a moment of personal conversation?"

"Absolutely. In fact, I should be getting back home, as I have an Advisor Committee meeting in a few minutes. I'll keep you apprised of anything new I uncover."

Miriam watched Nika leave, while Alex frantically tried to prepare for the next curveball headed her way. Or she could try relaxing. It couldn't make things worse.

Well....

When the door had closed, Miriam ran a hand along the edge of her desk. "So. Facing a united enemy of immeasurably greater strength and scope than any we've faced before, versus being given time to implement every conceivable defensive measure while expanding our fleets and weaponry by leaps and bounds. If one presented such a choice to a council of the greatest military strategists in all of human and Anaden history, I'm not at all certain they'd be able to come to agreement on the preferable option." Miriam huffed a breath. "Perhaps the correct answer will be discovered in the aftermath of this war. In how it ends.

"The point is, neither of us was wrong, and neither of us was right. If we were to go back in time to two months ago, and you presented me with your plan *before* implementing it? Knowing what I know now, knowing everything I've been able to accomplish in the intervening months, I'm not convinced I would ask you not to do it. At the same time, I fear this monstrous enemy your actions have enabled, like I have feared nothing else before.

"Quite a pickle we've gotten ourselves into, as your father is fond of saying."

Alex's brow furrowed. "Are we making up?"

Her mother ventured a tentative smile. "Let's call it 'making peace.' If you are amenable."

"Of course I am." She sighed and dropped back in her chair. "I suppose I've gotten used to having your approval for the last fifteen years. It's been nice. As a result, I'd forgotten the itchy, uncomfortable sting of your *disapproval*. I'd let all the defenses I'd built up against it atrophy over the years, so the unexpected injury hurt more than I was prepared for. All of which is to say, I've hated this acrimony between us."

Miriam sat down opposite her and reached out to cover Alex's hands with her own. Physical contact? "And I'm sorry for causing it. You've been right so many times, and it has saved us again and again. I still don't know if you were right this time, but that's one hell of a track record. You deserve the benefit of the doubt."

"Thank you, but I don't want the benefit of the doubt, Mom. I want us to win."

PART II

GRAVITATIONAL PULL

17

HIRLAS

CHOEDA
PEGASUS DWARF GALAXY

C aleb stuck his head in the main office of the Hamid Center to find Karis Yuri standing at a long table piled high with crates. The Naraida woman entered something on the external control panel of one, then moved on to the next.

"Karis?"

She looked back and flashed him a quick smile. "Caleb. Our savior. What brings you here today?"

He flinched at the honorific. When they'd been fleeing the Rasu through the jungles of Hirlas, Karis had acted as a gritty, determined leader who took no quarter from him or anyone else. Adulation didn't become her. "Please don't call me that."

"But it's true."

"You would have done the same, if it were in your power. I merely did the only thing I was capable of doing to save lives." He leaned against the wall beside the door and crossed his arms over his chest. "Anyway, I wanted to stop by and see how the recovery was going."

"Slow as the tree demons. The Rasu wrecked everything we've ever built in half a dozen cities. It's going to take us years to get back to a normal state of affairs, and neither Concord nor Nopreis can spare much in the way of materials or manpower at the moment. So we're taking the opportunity to slow down and consider *how* we want to rebuild. Especially given how our planet now has a say in the matter." Her delicate brow wrinkled. "I mean, I think it does. It's not responding to questions."

"Yeah, um, I wish I could set up a translator module and leave it here with you."

"You can't?" she asked hopefully.

"Sorry, it doesn't work that way. Listen, your people have always taken wonderful care of this planet. The way you've kept it wild and verdant, respecting nature while incorporating technology and modern tools to improve your standard of living, is worthy of respect and emulation. Akeso—Hirlas—couldn't ask for better stewards. So if you simply follow the same guiding precepts you always have, I believe the planet will be quite content."

She regarded him oddly, as if he were a strange alien creature who had arrived speaking in tongues, but finally nodded. "All right. You would know."

"And if the planet ever has an urgent or vehement complaint, I'll send you a message."

"You do that."

One would think he'd be used to perplexed stares by now, but his muscles spasmed with discomfort nonetheless. There was no way to make the woman understand how any of this worked, so he should stop trying. "Say, do you have any Rasu debris stored here?"

"We've been shipping it all to Special Projects. They've probably filled a warehouse with it by now."

"Oh, they have, and then some. I just wondered...." The truth was, he didn't want Concord officials learning he was messing around with dead Rasu.

"We might have a crate that hasn't gone out yet." She pointed to the left, down the hallway. "Go that way, then take the second door on the left. It's locked up, but I'll clear you through."

"Thanks. Good to see you."

"You, too."

Caleb headed in the direction she'd indicated and pressed the entrance panel on the second door. After a beep, it slid open, revealing a storage room containing about twenty crates. The labels were in Communis, so he searched around until he found one labeled 'Rasu.'

Five jagged chunks of metal had been tossed inside. In any other circumstance, he would have promptly reversed course and delivered a heated lecture to Karis about safe handling procedures for such dangerous material. But the uneasiness that had been eddying around in his subconscious since their meeting with Dashiel served to remind him none of those precautions were necessary here.

He reached into the container and picked up a chunk of Rasu, then gingerly opened himself up to any sensations. Voices, or even simple, primitive urges.

Nothing. As inert as aluminum.

He handled each piece in turn, but the result remained the same.

When he'd exhausted their supply of Rasu, he headed back down the hall, waved goodbye to Karis through the open doorway, and went outside. Multiple cranes were swinging across a jagged, broken skyline. A flock of Volucri flew overhead, and everywhere there was the buzz of life being conducted.

Caleb reached out with his mind and allowed the activity of the planet to wash over him. It hummed in excitement and renewal. A world reborn.

You need not have traveled here to experience these things. This planet is me. I, and thus you, live these sensations every moment.

I know. But humans find value in seeing with our eyes. In touching with our hands.

As you say. And the Rasu-enemy?

I don't know what they find value in.

He wandered toward a small grove down the street. A narrow cobblestone path wound among the trees, and he traced his fingertips over the drooping leaves as he walked along it. He hadn't expected the state of the felled Rasu here to be any different from the ones in the lab, but for some reason he'd needed to check.

But they were all dead. Exactly like Dashiel had said. Dead in a way no other Rasu they'd ever encountered was. In every other situation, if a sliver of metal remained, it held on to electrical impulses, however faint and thready. It held on to a voice, even if the thoughts were scattered and nonsensical.

But not this time.

Akeso, what did you do to the Rasu here?

I knew, through you, how they were exceedingly difficult to silence. I comprehended that the way your Concord was doing so, when possible, was to split the...you call it the 'atomic structure' of the life form. To tear the connections of its essence apart into nothingness.

Caleb shook his head. *But our negative energy and nuclear weapons destroy the physical coherence of the Rasu. The remains from Hirlas are still intact. They still retain a molecular structure and the outward appearance of metal, but they've lost their life force.*

Akeso devised a more efficient method of achieving the desired result.

A chill rippled down his spine. *How?*

You call them 'electrical impulses.' The thoughts that make the Rasu-enemy alive. The manner in which they are transmitted within and among Rasu cells is not too dissimilar from the way my thoughts flow. Inorganic versus organic. Natural and intuitive versus cold, rigid constructs. Nevertheless, similar. I tore asunder the elemental structures which generated purposeful thought and intelligence. It brought me no pleasure to do so, but it was the only way. The only way to stop the Rasu-enemy from rising up again and again to destroy this world and all who call it home.

Caleb stopped to rest against a wide tree trunk, bittersweet sorrow flooding his heart. He'd taught Akeso how to be a murderer.

For the cause of life.

I know. Don't trouble yourself over it. You did the right thing, saving this world and these people. Never doubt it.

After all, death and life were two halves of the same coin. Akeso could heal, so of course it could kill. If it understood how to infuse life into atoms, it stood to reason that it understood how to rip it out as well.

In the back of Caleb's mind, a tickle of a notion sprung to life. He instinctively recoiled from it, for it was abhorrent to consider…and also devastating in the powerful hope it invoked.

He now knew how Nika had felt when they'd begged her to instruct the kyoseil to activate for the Rasu. And he didn't care for it in the slightest.

So he pushed the nascent idea away and headed back to the spaceport. During the walk, he distracted himself by noting all the varied clean-up efforts, the gentle and considerate construction, and the beauty captured in the return of laughing children to the streets of Choeda.

But no matter how much attention he paid to the energy of life pulsing around him, the nugget of an idea continued to take root and grow.

18

ARES

PRAESIDIS ESTATE

Corradeo breathed a sigh of relief when he stepped onto the estate grounds. It felt like coming home. Which was a welcome surprise, considering the Post Alpha starship had been his only home for millennia. He hadn't expected to so easily settle into a new environment, to relax so thoroughly in its comforts and familiarity. But this, he mused, felt like home.

Every now and then, he came upon something in one of the rooms at the estate that was so quintessentially Renato, and found himself awash in ancient memories. Of happier, if not simpler, times—and of the sting of betrayal by his son that stole such happiness from him. He should have such reminders removed from the premises, but it kept slipping his mind.

He was returning from an exhaustive five-hour meeting with the Barisan government leadership. Macskaf was a volatile world, and the Barisans a defensive, easily offended people. As a rule, of course, for he'd known many delightful Barisans who'd joined the anarchs over the years…'many' was an exaggeration; certainly a few, though. Regardless, he understood how the Barisans had much to be defensive and offended about, so he tried to forgive them their wariness. Hopefully he'd allayed a few of their concerns today. More would come with time and deeds.

He started to go straight to his personal suite, but decided to make a stop first. He made his way along the corridor holding the staff quarters, then announced his presence at Eren's door.

The door opened after a few seconds; Eren was dressed in canvas short pants and a loose, plain white shirt open at the neck. Clearly off-duty, but looking well and whole, save for the faint shininess of new skin along his left cheek.

Eren waved him inside. "Good evening, sir."

"And to you. I wasn't sure if I'd find you here. I thought you might have gone home to Hirlas for a few days to convalesce."

"I will tomorrow, I think. Not to 'convalesce' as such, but to check on things. They've got a lot of rebuilding to do—and a crazy sentient planet to help them get it done."

Corradeo smiled wryly. "Hell of a thing Caleb did."

"He usually does."

"Indeed. So Medical has cleared you?"

"Yes, sir." Eren tilted his head and held his prodigious hair back to expose his neck. "Good as new."

Eren was making light of the injuries, as expected, but he had suffered two critical tears in his trachea, a severely bruised larynx, a puncture wound to one kidney and another to the liver.

"I'm glad to hear it. I won't take up much of your well-deserved downtime. I merely wanted to thank you sincerely for your actions before and during the attack. You saved the Advocacy at a crucial point in its development."

"Eh, helped a little maybe. But I appreciate you saying so, sir."

"It's the truth. I am grateful you agreed to come work with me again."

"It seems it's my fate to help you keep your cocked-up dreams alive."

"I...." Corradeo blinked, briefly stunned into silence as memories flooded his mind. "Don't feel as if you're consigned to aid me forever. But for so long as you wish it, I'll be glad to have you with me."

Eren's nose scrunched up, exposing the faint borders between new skin and old down his cheek. "Damn, sir. You're going to make me weep, talking such nonsense."

"Now, we don't want any weeping." He clapped Eren on the shoulder. "I'll get out of your way. We'll talk business in a few days, once you return."

"Have a nice evening, sir. Get some rest while you can. I've heard rumors that the Rasu civil war is entering its final phase."

"I fear those rumors are all too true."

RW

After foraging for a plate of food in the kitchen, Corradeo poured a glass of scotch and retired to the couch in his living area. The Barisan negotiations had drained him of mental energy, and it appeared this had left him susceptible to all manner of emotional intrusions. Nostalgia. Wistfulness. Most of all, recollections of family, blood and otherwise, that he routinely kept safely tucked away.

He should send them back to where they belonged. But what could it hurt if they were let out to play for this one night?

He sipped on the scotch, rested his head on the cushion, and closed his eyes.

Corradeo slammed a fist down on the table. "Damnable traitors! Zeus curse their malignant souls."

Lauren laid a calm, steady hand on his forearm. "We uncovered them before they acted, and we've handled the problem. No damage was done to the cause."

"This time." He inhaled through his nose and worked to quell his temper. Lauren was always so level-headed, so unflappable. He strove to follow her example in all things, but he too often failed.

When his rage had settled into background noise, he turned to face her, allowing himself to enjoy the way her chestnut hair fell in lazy waves across her narrow shoulders. His hand raised to trace her jawline with his fingertips, and the feel of her warm skin instinctively brought a smile to his face.

"We did catch them in time, and what a relief it is. But will you allow me to institute a stricter screening process for future recruits, please?"

Her bright green eyes flickered with uncertainty. "I want people to know they're welcome among us. To see that we aren't like the Directorate, and that we accept everyone no matter their background or station. But I suppose you have the right of it. If the wrong person gains access to our secrets...."

"Then we'll lose everything. And I won't permit it to happen."

"My stalwart protector. Fine, I give in. Permission granted." She leaned in and kissed him softly.

Behind them, the door slid open. "Hey, guess what—oops! I'll come back later."

Lauren spun out of his grasp, her face lighting up. "Eren!"

She hurried over to the doorway to hug the anarch agent. "You're back. We got worried when you didn't report in at the scheduled time."

Corradeo followed in her wake, extending an arm to shake Eren's hand. "We did worry."

"Whatever for? I'm a slippery bastard, and I always get away with it."

"So far." He frowned; was he the only one in this organization who appreciated the terrible danger they all lived under? These two certainly didn't.

"Eh, I was still inside enemy territory. Had to maneuver a bit to make my escape and couldn't risk a comm. So I figured I'd come straight here and

report in directly. But, listen, if you two want to enjoy some private time, I can go grab a bite to eat."

"Nonsense." Lauren shot Corradeo a teasing grin. "Just don't barge in on us again until the morning."

"Yes, ma'am."

They went over to the seating area, and Eren collapsed into the large lounge chair opposite the couch they settled on. Corradeo leaned forward intently, clasping his hands together. "What did you learn?"

"You know how we've been working on a plan to infiltrate Directorate Central and take out the Primors in one glorious explosion while they're all meeting together? Well, we had better accelerate our planning. Our window of opportunity is about to slam shut. Forever."

Lauren's brow tightened in concern. "How so?"

"I discovered what 'Project Perastos' is. The Directorate is building a space station to use as its base of operations going forward. They're calling it the Protos Agora. And it's not just any station. It's going to orbit the galactic core."

"What? How closely?"

"2.6 parsecs out from Sag-A's event horizon."

Lauren shook her head in disbelief. "Nothing can survive so close to the core."

"It seems they've been whipping a crew of Diaplas engineers and Erevna scientists into inventing some technologies that didn't exist a year ago. New materials, exotic force fields and so on. They want it to orbit so close that nothing else can survive, but they will."

Corradeo worked at his jaw, his earlier agitation returning. "This is bad."

"It gets worse. The station will only be accessible by teleportation gates— a single one for each Primor. The origin portals will be located in the highest-security portions of their homes or offices. Probably in their bedrooms or some such shite."

"So once it's completed, it'll be impregnable."

Eren draped one arm along the back of the chair and nodded. "That is definitely their goal."

"How long until it's operational?" Corradeo asked.

"The Primors want it done in three months. The project lead is insisting it's an impossible schedule, but it's amazing what the threat of final denouement will do to motivate."

"Not long, either way." Lauren gazed at him, a heavy sigh weighing down her deceptively soft features. But then, as was her way, her mouth set with conviction, and her eyes sharpened. *"We'll accelerate our planning. We must find a way to get to the Primors before they move into this station, else we may never be rid of them."*

Corradeo nodded firmly. *"I'll meet with Sander in the morning. We'll make it our number one priority. Eren, will you help us?"*

"I'm in, on one condition. I get to bring the explosives."

Why was it even the happy memories stung by virtue of having ended in sorrow? Corradeo supposed that was life, which was one thing he had experienced quite a lot of.

The door chime rang, and annoyance flared. He should answer it, for the leader of a government was never off duty, but his heart and mind both lingered elsewhere. But then he saw it was Nyx, and he waved her in. Perhaps family was exactly what he needed right now.

"Come, sit with me. Would you like a drink?"

Her eyes narrowed. "Have you ever seen me consume an alcoholic beverage?"

"Come to think of it, no I have not. Is tonight the night to change that?"

Her consternation deepened further. "Should it be? Have the Rasu vanished from the cosmos without a fight?"

"Regrettably, no."

She sat on the chaise opposite him and leaned forward. "What's on your mind, Grandfather?"

"Musing on the impossible nature of diplomacy and keeping multiple species happy. We are all so different from one another, yet also fundamentally the same in our hearts."

"So the meeting on Macskaf went…?"

"Well enough. Oh, and I stopped by to speak to Eren this evening. He's looking well, but I gave him a few more days off to fully recuperate."

"Fine. I'll manage without him." An almost petulant expression flashed across her face. "He did do well. I didn't expect it, but he came through."

"He always does."

"I see." She studied him carefully, a frown growing on her features. So like her mother's aspect. "How long have you been sitting here, drinking your scotch and being melancholic?"

"Am I being melancholic?"

"My keen Inquisitor powers of observation say 'yes.'"

"And they are rarely wrong. I find I've been dwelling on the past these last few days. Possibly because of the chance they will be our last days. I know I've been reluctant to share much of my past with you, even during our long years of travel together. I think I was trying to run from a litany of demons. I'm trying to stop running now. It's not easy."

"Do you...want to talk about it?"

He buried a chuckle; she was so uncomfortable at the prospect of needing to be empathetic toward others. He thought she might actually have some skill at it, once she learned to trust herself. He was still hoping Eren would bring this and other traits out in her, in time.

And there Eren was again in his mind. Couldn't escape him tonight.

He relented and took another sip of his scotch, then placed his elbow on the armrest and his chin on his hand. "Can I trust you to keep a confidence? An important and personal one?"

"Of course, Grandfather. Keeping secrets is one of an Inquisitor's core competencies—I know, I'm not an Inquisitor any longer, and I should stop referring to myself as such. The point remains valid."

"So it does. You've asked me before why I implicitly trust Eren, despite his somewhat less than respectful demeanor and, shall we say, laxness when it comes to protocol and procedure."

"'Lax' and 'less than respectful' don't begin to cover it! He's impulsive and rude and sloppy and—" she cut herself off "—but you know all this. Yes, I've pushed you on this point several times, to no avail. I resigned myself to not knowing the answer and decided to trust your judgment."

"Thank you for doing so. But I'm feeling truthful tonight, so I think I'll tell you. Please, you must keep this in confidence."

Her lips pinched. "I will, I promise."

"The truth is..." he breathed in deeply "...I've known Eren for much longer than he realizes. Or rather, I knew him for a time long ago, during the first anarch rebellion."

"I don't understand. Eren claims to be only three and a quarter centuries old."

"He's incorrect. The tale is a long one with a tragic ending, so I won't trouble you with the details. But he was an anarch back then as well. One of the first anarchs, in fact. My...wife..." after all this time, he still stumbled over speaking of her aloud "...recruited him before I met either of them. And he was fearless, just as he is now. So full of life and pizazz and elan. We grew to become close friends. I relied upon him to have my back then, much as I do now, and though his ways were as unconventional as they are today, he never disappointed.

"But when the Directorate came for the anarchs—when they destroyed our base of operations and killed everyone, including my wife—" he reached for the scotch and downed a long sip to burn away the resurgent pain "—they didn't kill Eren immediately. Instead, they kidnapped him and tortured him for information. When they'd gleaned all they could from him—I don't know what they extracted from him, if anything—they wiped his memory and reinserted him into the Idoni Dynasty as a lowly *asi*.

"And there they made sure he remained through every regenesis cycle, no matter how much he distinguished himself. Until finally, many millennia later, he was able to break free of those chains once more and return to where he belonged."

She studied him over fingertips pressed together at her nose, burgeoning emotion softening her brittle sapphire irises. "So this is why you've trusted him with your life from the beginning."

"It is."

"And he has no idea?"

"No. The only way for him to know would be for me to tell him, and I cannot bring myself to do so. After he rejoined the anarchs one-hundred-fifteen years ago, I made it a point to stay away from him. I watched his endeavors from afar, but I didn't speak with him. Not until the arrival of the Humans made doing so a necessity."

"But you are again friends now. Why have you not told him?"

"Can you imagine how he'd react to learning that not only had he fought the Directorate before and lost, but that they had imprisoned him in his own mind for thousands of years, thereby rubbing salt in the wound of their victory? To discovering he'd been caged to a far greater extent than he'd ever realized? And that no opportunity existed for him to ever recall all the great things he'd done?

"In some ways, it's similar to Nika Kirumase and her lost memories. But for Eren, there are no painstakingly preserved journals, no hidden memories of great import, for him to take solace in. A significant part of his life was stolen from him, and he can never get it back. I would not inflict such pain on my friend."

"I'm not convinced you're right, Grandfather. I think he would take pride—an irritating amount of pride, most likely—in learning he had been a fighter on the side of freedom and helped you more than once."

"And that he'd failed, as we all did. I bear the burden of this knowledge, because I have no choice in the matter, but...I don't know. It causes me such sorrow. How could it not do the same to him? Please, Nyx, keep this secret for me. I might one day garner the courage to tell him, but that decision will be mine alone."

"You can depend on me, as always."

He squeezed the hand she offered. It felt good, he decided, to share this story. To share it with family. "Thank you, my dear."

19

PANDORA

Malcolm sipped on the coffee Vilane had given him and tried to act relaxed. "If you don't mind me asking, how did you do it?"

The man smiled smugly. "I do a great many things, Fleet Admiral. To what do you refer?"

He bit off a biting retort. "You know what I mean. The Oversight Board."

"Ah, yes. Let's just say General Colby has a few skeletons in his closet that make him susceptible to…persuasion. Not to suggest that he isn't a generally honorable man. I've found everyone has skeletons in their closet, if you only look deeply enough."

"I see." Malcolm stared at the swirling, chocolate-brown eddies of his coffee. The dark roast wasn't to his tastes—too bitter. He liked to think Vilane would find himself disappointed at the state of his closet; perhaps the fact that the man had yet to try to extort him was evidence of this. "I wish it hadn't needed to involve blackmail, but I am grateful to have the Board off my back. On this particular topic, if on nothing else."

"I'm afraid I can't help you with their demands for frugal but ubiquitous defenses against the Rasu, though I wish you the best."

"It's fine. It's my job."

"And I'm confident there is none better at it." The false compliment rolled smoothly off the man's tongue. "Selfishly, I hope your efforts will soon bear enough fruit for you to have more time to devote to the Gardiens' cause."

Malcolm had definitely used every 'threat of Rasu attack' excuse in the book to minimize the demands Vilane placed on him, and he recognized they were starting to run a bit thin. They had also all been true, as he was lucky when he was able to steal a few hours of sleep in his own bed.

"The threat of a Rasu invasion informs every action I take. But we've put the breathing room their civil war has granted us to good use. As to whether there will soon be nothing further we can do to prepare? I'm not sure that will ever be the case."

"Nonetheless...." Vilane made an annoyed sound under his breath, but it didn't appear to be directed at Malcolm. "If you will excuse me for one minute. I need to see to something down the hall."

"Of course. I'll be here."

"Thank you. I'll make it quick." The man disappeared out the door in a huff.

For the first time since this endeavor began, Malcolm was alone in Vilane's office. What could he do?

He stared at the control panel embedded in Vilane's desk, then at the blanked-out screen off to the right. If security cams were running in here, any action he took was certain to mark the end of his undercover work...and he'd be relieved. Regardless, it was worth the risk, as he might not get a chance like this again.

No time to waste. He hurried to the desk and inserted an override spike into the input slot. Once upon a time he never would have carried such a device around with him, but these were strange days. Richard had given it to him months ago, assuring him it was the absolute state-of-the-art technology designed to override any security system.

A directory opened up and no alarms seemed to have been triggered; so far so good. Malcolm scanned the folder names. What was most crucial to learn? Something labeled 'Grand Vision' fit the bill, and he tried to open it.

Password:

Alas, an extra layer of security for that one. He reviewed the rest of the list. 'Project Revenant' sounded properly ominous. He opened the directory.

It contained a list of regenesis clinics. Beneath four of them, a name was listed, followed by a series of dates and alphanumeric codes.

He captured the information with his ocular implant, then removed the spike and rushed back to his seat. He didn't dare linger any longer.

Vilane returned to the office twenty seconds later. "I am so sorry about the interruption. Some people here need entirely too much handholding."

"I understand. From experience."

"I imagine you do. Now, we were discussing how best to apply pressure to the biosynth companies to withhold their products from the regenesis clinics."

"We were. I know a couple of members of the Boards of Directors of Genentech and Synergistic Technologies. I can reach out to them."

RW

CONCORD HQ

CINT

Malcolm fingered the spike in his pocket as he rode the levtram from Command over to CINT. He'd studied the image he'd captured briefly—long enough to confirm what his gut had told him the instant he'd opened the file.

The regenesis clinics with names and details attached to them were the ones that had been in the headlines lately for regenesis cases going catastrophically wrong.

The stories had been impossible to miss on the news feeds. They were sparking renewed debates about the safety, and thus the wisdom, of regenesis, as commentators drudged up all the old arguments anew.

When the first two incidents had occurred, Malcolm had taken note, his conscience eager to lap up confirmatory facts for his chosen position. *See!* his mind had exclaimed, *regenesis isn't safe. It isn't* real. *Nothing but snake oil all along.*

Except he'd known it wasn't true. In the six months since Miriam had died at Namino and been brought back to life, he'd spent hundreds of hours working at her side. They'd debated strategy and tactics into the wee hours of the morning on several occasions. They'd shared the strain of active combat and been forced into making impossible choices.

And not once had she given him reason to harbor any doubt about the quality or coherence of her…his mind lurched over the word 'soul,' even so. Of her 'self.'

There were other examples, too. The Rasu's antimatter weapons had inflicted plenty of bloodshed on the soldiers under his command, and regenesis had returned most of them to the world of the living. Some struggled with the transition for a time, but the struggles he'd witnessed had been human ones—a truth that had kept him up at night more than once.

He might not want to admit it, but regenesis worked. When there were problems, they were typically with the neural imprint itself, and in those cases, the procedure was not performed. No doctor wanted to create a monster or a zombie. Neither did the government, which was why the safety protocols erred heavily on the side of caution.

So when the third tragic case of regenesis going wrong had made the news, his bullshit detector had lit up like a Christmas tree. He'd suspected the Gardiens were behind the foul-ups somehow, and now he carried evidence of it in his eVi.

He rang the bell outside Richard's office, and after a second the door slid open. Richard and Graham Delavasi were huddled around a wide screen. Richard nodded in agreement at something Delavasi was pointing to, then straightened up and waved Malcolm in. "How are you?"

"Hopefully about to pull my weight around here again."

"You have something on the Gardiens?"

"I do." He passed over the image capture, and Richard opened it above the existing screen. "Graham, look at this."

"I *knew* they were behind the regenesis foul-ups!" Delavasi slapped his thigh in exuberance. "Damn fine work, Fleet Admiral."

"Thank you, but I was only able to access the information by using the spike you lent me, Richard. That and lucky timing."

"With all due respect, you did the hard, unpleasant work of earning Vilane's trust. I daresay no one else would have been left alone within reach of his system."

"Maybe. So is this enough to bring charges against him?"

Richard prevaricated. "It is enough to get a warrant for the patient records at each one of these clinics. Regulations require strict protocols be followed for regenesis, so I don't see how his agents could have completely hidden their tampering."

Delavasi nodded. "This is turning out to be a damn good day."

"Oh?" Malcolm asked with interest. "What else has happened?"

Richard settled into his chair and gestured toward the wide screen. "We have at long last uncovered a records trail linking Vilane to payments James Sarona received before his assassination attempt on Miriam. The credits ran through five shell corporations and three false identities, but we can tie them all to one another and, through a tiny filament, to a corp openly associated with Vilane."

Delavasi rolled his eyes. "Now, this is not the same as proving that Vilane paid Sarona to assassinate the commandant. But it is extremely persuasive evidence."

Malcolm rubbed at his jaw. "So what does all this mean?"

Richard considered the image Malcolm had captured again. "It means it's time for this investigation to come out of the shadows. We have enough to initiate public inquiries of the Gardiens, their agents, and Enzio Vilane himself. We won't be able to arrest him today, but it's time he started to feel the heat."

Malcolm exhaled. *Finally.* "How do I get out? When the news of an investigation breaks, it would be consistent with my previous behavior toward the Gardiens to act outraged. To feel betrayed. I honestly don't think I could sell deciding to stay allied with the organization, no matter how vehemently Vilane proclaims his innocence to me. After Insights Academy, he knew he only had one final chance to remain in my good graces. Also…if I may admit to weakness here, I very badly want out."

"Of course you do. There's no weakness in that. And we can't ask any more of you. I think you have three choices. One, you can engineer a confrontation with Vilane, similar to what you did after Insights Academy. Only this time, as you said, there's nothing Vilane can say to regain your trust, and you storm out.

"Two, you convey the same sentiments from afar in a message formally severing your ties with the organization. This is…frankly, it's safer. We know Vilane has one hell of a temper, and I'm not sure you want to be in the same room with him for this conversation."

Malcolm laughed. "I'm a Special Forces Marine. I can protect myself."

"No question. I'd prefer you not have to."

"What's the third option?"

"You cut him off. You don't reach out in any way, and if he tries to contact you, you ignore it. Block his address. This approach could infuriate him to an even greater extent than a break-up letter, but you get to simply walk away. Full stop."

"Okay. Which do you recommend?"

Richard glanced at Delavasi. "Not the first one. The more I think about it, the more I'm convinced you don't want to go back in that building. I suggest option two. Make a clean and explicit break."

"I already have the message half-composed in my head. Obviously, I'll hold off on sending it until the news feeds go nuts." He smiled in relief; his conscience already felt lighter. "In the meantime, I have a bevy of planetary defense upgrades to review. Far too many to squeeze in another visit to Pandora anytime soon."

But he *did* have time to visit Romane…. As he bid the men farewell and headed to the Caeles Prism Hub, his mind drifted to halcyonic visions of a romantic reunion with Mia. An end to all this subterfuge and pretending.

But not yet. She wouldn't be safe until Vilane was exposed as a criminal and a fraud. He had to hold out just a little while longer.

20

PANDORA

An alert yanked Enzio out of a deep slumber. He rolled over in the dark, reaching for...something from a dream that was already evaporating into the mist.

With a groan he settled onto his back and opened the message his eVi had been so helpfully informing him of.

ALERT. SENTRI HAS FILED MULTIPLE REQUESTS FOR WARRANTS TO SEARCH THE RECORDS OF THE BELOW RE-GENESIS CLINICS. REASON GIVEN IS SUSPICION OF TAMPER-ING WITH REGENESIS PROCEDURES AND/OR NEURAL IMPRINTS ON FILE. REQUESTS ARE LIKELY TO BE GRANTED AND WARRANTS SERVED BY END OF DAY TOMORROW CST.

Enzio sat bolt upright in bed and swung his legs over the side. The message had been sent by one of his deepest-cover operatives in SENTRI. His canary in the coal mine, as it were.

The list of targeted clinics was an exact match to the ones his agents operated in. But correlation did not equal causation. Those were also the clinics that had experienced much-publicized regenesis 'failures' in recent weeks. Of course they were the ones authorities wanted to investigate. He'd known this was a possibility, even a probability. Regenesis was humanity's new salvation, and the government needed to be quick to dig into any potential problems which arose, if only to try to cover them up.

Still, an investigation meant risk. Risk to his people who were embedded in the clinics, risk to the Gardiens, and most of all risk to himself.

He stood and headed to the restroom, then the kitchen. It was going to be a long day.

RW

Enzio had just filled his coffee cup when a second alert arrived. This one was an official but generic notification from a bank and had been routed through several buffer addresses before reaching him. The authorities had frozen the bank account belonging to one of his shell companies in relation to an ongoing criminal investigation. This was more worrisome.

He'd barely sat down at the breakfast nook table when yet another such alert arrived. Different bank, different company, same action.

His cup clattered to the table, sloshing coffee over the rim to spill across the surface and scald his hand.

The implications spun out across his mind. He resisted them; he didn't want to believe the necessary conclusions. It shouldn't be possible for someone to have tied both companies to him, or illegal activities to the companies. He'd been beyond careful in *every* aspect of this endeavor. He was smarter than the authorities, dammit! More clever by half than the best SENTRI had to offer.

A tremor in his unburned hand betrayed his supposed confidence. His Grand Vision could not be falling apart! Not when he was so close to tipping the scales irrevocably in his favor.

He breathed in through his nose and repeated calming mantras until the shakes subsided. Then he forced himself to review the documents attached to the various messages. None mentioned the Gardiens by name—not yet. None mentioned him personally, for that matter.

Think. *Think!*

Even if the authorities found everything they were searching for, they couldn't get to him. There were too many insulating layers.

But this wasn't exactly true, was it? His Chief of Security, Olav Zylynski, had warned him about letting too many Gardiens members be privy to the most delicate pieces of the operation. Perhaps a dozen—no, he should be precise. Eleven people knew of criminal acts planned and committed by the Gardiens, not counting the operatives currently in place at the regenesis clinics. But only five people, Zylynski included, knew he was the man behind everything. Six, counting the fleet admiral.

If he truly wanted to protect himself, he'd need to eliminate them all. It wouldn't be easy, from a logistical perspective. But even with James Sarona now in a grave, there were other skilled assassins for hire. He had an entire file of names.

His conscience twisted, just a little. It meant killing the fleet admiral.

Malcolm Jenner was a good man, if far too moral for this sort of business. But it was what it was. He'd been willing to kill then discredit

Commandant Solovy to further his cause; his mission demanded he do no less when it came to Jenner.

'Killing' wasn't as simple a matter as it used to be with regenesis in the mix, though that wasn't a concern with Jenner. The others on the list were Prevos, and they had surely made extensive arrangements for returning to life should they fall. But the neurotoxin Sarona has planned to use on Solovy to cast suspicion on her regenesis should muddle the situation, and he'd disrupted the companion Artificials of the Insights Academy perpetrators without much trouble. Also, additional questions being raised about regenesis when more procedures went horribly wrong stood to be a bonus.

One avenue of response mapped out, he backed up and considered the state of affairs from a different perspective. He could save his own skin, yes. If he stepped away now, he could fade into the scenery and bide his time. Wait for a new opportunity. Assuming humanity survived a resurgent Rasu attack—and he did assume so—the ensuing chaos would provide the perfect cover for him to vanish.

*Or...*he could pivot the Gardiens to the true purpose he'd intended for the organization all along. Abandon the genteel public face of the last few months and *fight*. Set the world on fire until it bent to his will.

And if doing so ultimately brought him down, he already had in place the necessary framework to take on a new, anonymous identity, one ready to be activated by his Artificial and a new body. After all, Prevos were the immortal future of humanity.

Adrenaline energized him far better than the abandoned coffee. This plan, he could be proud of.

It was merely a matter of sending a series of coded messages to select agents. The mechanisms for this eventuality had been in place from the beginning. He stared at the command blinking in his virtual vision for several seconds...then sent the messages.

Point of no return navigated, he exhaled and realized he felt more at ease than he had in weeks—except for one niggling concern.

He found his mother, as he often did, on the balcony. From afar, she appeared to be relaxing, but the rigid jawline and intense gaze that took shape as he approached her told a different story. A soft woman, she was not.

"Mother?"

She held up a hand to forestall him, and he jerked back in surprise. It felt like being put in a corner as punishment for misbehaving.

He was standing there frozen and speechless when she finished her work and looked up at him. "Good morning, son. You're awake early today. Is something the matter?"

"Um..." he shook his head to regain his bearings "...no, not exactly. In fact, you'll be pleased to hear our public relations campaign will now be coming to a close."

"In favor of a more assertive approach?"

"Indeed. I'd like to fill you in right now, but I have a great deal of work to do in a short period of time. The situation might become dangerous in the coming days, so I want you to go to the house on Scythia. It's registered under a false name that can't be traced to me. I'll send a guard detail with you to keep you safe."

"Enzio, you don't need to protect me—"

"I absolutely do need to protect you! They took you from me once, and I will not allow it to happen again." He worked to control his tone. Yelling at one's mother was unseemly. "You'll enjoy spending a couple of days there. It's warm and sunny, and you can go to the beach. The shopping is excellent as well."

She stared at him oddly. "Shopping?"

"If that's something you'd be interested in. It doesn't matter. Please. Knowing you're safe will put my mind at ease, and I'll be able to focus on what I need to do. If you'll go pack now, I'll bring an escort up. You can be settled in there by lunch."

She continued to regard him intently and didn't budge from the chair.

"Mother, I'm sorry, but this is not a request. You're going to Scythia."

Something terrifying flitted across her eyes, and the blood in his veins turned to ice.

Then she stood, giving him a razor-thin, closed-mouth smile. "So I am."

21

DEMETER

MILKY WAY GALAXY

Richard stood watch in the security room of the regenesis clinic while SENTRI agents copied out the historical records onto storage cubes. Given the highly politicized nature of the Gardiens investigation, Director Solarian had asked CINT to make public its involvement. He supposed they were seen as above the fray of AEGIS politics. Which was mostly true.

He kept an eye on the agents' progress, but half his attention was on an aural. The display showed additional agents interrogating staff members in the conference room down the hall.

They had their primary suspect's name, thanks to the information Malcolm had provided, but they were interviewing her supervisors first. The better to have a complete picture before beginning.

"Director?"

He looked up to see SENTRI Director Solarian approaching him and nodded a greeting. "What've you got?"

"Evidence is what we've got." Solarian flashed a report over to Richard. "It's subtle, which is likely why the safety controls here didn't catch it. The day before Armelle Sauvageot's regenesis procedure, there was a blip in the file state. It presented as an automated error in the routine system checks, but my people tell me it could mask someone accessing the neural imprint record."

"Any hint as to who accessed it?"

"No, but Martina Kuhn was the lab tech working the shift."

Richard smiled. "The Gardiens mole? Sounds like probable cause to me. Are you ready to put her in the box?"

"As soon as we finish up with the Personnel Manager. Want to sit in?"

"No need. I have every confidence in you and your people. I'm merely here to make that clear to everyone else."

"And I thank you for doing so. The Gardiens have some powerful supporters. The heat is going to come down on us hard and fast."

"We've got your back."

Solarian headed off for the conference room, and Richard sent Graham a message. His friend was unofficially supervising a similar raid on Krysk, and Richard passed on the forensic details of the blip they'd discovered so the agents there could keep an eye out for the same.

There had been times over the last few months when he'd doubted they'd ever be able to nail the Gardiens to the wall, never mind Enzio Vilane. But it was hardly the first investigation to creep forward at a snail's pace as every tangential thread was chased to ground, half of which evaporated into nothing. He'd been here before, and he knew all the painstaking work was what ultimately enabled them to locate the one thread that, when pulled, caused the whole scheme to unravel. Vilane was a tough one, though, and they didn't have him yet. Not quite. With luck, by the end of the day they would.

Martina Kuhn was brought into the conference room, and Solarian joined another agent at the table. Nothing left to chance.

They started with the standard baseline questions, laying the groundwork to catch the woman in any lies she might later proffer.

She was a cool customer, with a dismissive attitude and a quick manner, and she did not appear to be in the slightest bit nervous. A Gardiens true believer? Fanatics were often the most dangerous prey.

Solarian: "You were the lab technician on duty in Lab #2 on August 14th, correct?"

Kuhn: "Was that a Tuesday? I usually work in #2 on Tuesdays."

Solarian: "It was, yes."

Kuhn: "Then if the duty records say so, it sounds right to me."

Solarian: "But you don't have any specific recollection of that day?"

Kuhn: "Don't tell my boss, because I haven't worked here for long, but my job is pretty rote and routine. Boring, even. One workday blends into the next."

Solarian: "I see. On the day in question, did you tamper with the neural imprint of one Armelle Sauvageot?"

Kuhn: "Isn't he the guy who went crazy and killed his wife after undergoing regenesis?"

Solarian: "He has been charged with the murder of his wife, yes. Please answer the question."

Kuhn: "That's psychotic. Really makes you wonder about regenesis, huh? What if we're creating monsters? I mean, I work here because the pay is above market. And the neural imprints...they're just data to me. They're not people. But maybe what they create aren't, either—people, I mean."

Solarian: "Did you tamper with the neural imprint of Armelle Sauvageot prior to his regenesis procedure? Yes or no?"

Kuhn: "I'm not a medical doctor or a neurological scientist. I wouldn't know how to tamper with the file."

Solarian: "Someone could have provided you a targeted routine to run on the file. Stop evading the question."

Unease tickled at the edges of Richard's thoughts. She was toying with Solarian, which meant she wasn't interested in escaping suspicion. In fact, he'd daresay she didn't intend on walking out of the building under her own power. Why? Was she on an ego trip, or was she simply stalling? What did she have planned?

He hadn't risen to the heights of his profession by not listening to his gut instinct. He hit the comm and contacted the SENTRI agent in charge of the raid. "I want you to put your forensic people to work sweeping the local hardware for a data bomb. Right now."

"You think someone is planning to fry all the neural imprints?"

"I think it's a possibility. The interview with the suspect is going sideways."

"Should we search for physical explosives as well? I can put one or two agents on it, but I'd need to call in a hazmat team for a thorough search."

Richard hesitated. Did he genuinely think the Gardiens intended to blow up the regenesis clinic? Wipe the data, maybe, but kill innocent people as well?

Of course, they likely believed people who facilitated regenesis weren't innocent.

But it would mean killing one of their own operatives.

But Gardiens-affiliated Prevos were fervent believers in their own immortality.

He'd lived through the unhinged violence of OTS, and before them of the One World Separatists, so he knew all too well the lengths to which ideological terrorists were capable of going to make their point.

"Do it. Better safe than sorry."

"Yes, sir."

In the interrogation room, Solarian and Martina Kuhn were still dancing in circles. She almost appeared to be enjoying herself.

Solarian: "It seems to me that by refusing to answer the question, you're admitting your guilt. What did you hope to accomplish by ruining a man's life? By destroying his very existence?"

Kuhn: "I haven't confessed to any crime. And besides, I don't want to accomplish anything here except the deposit of a steady paycheck in my bank account. I do what the boss tells me to. That's all."

Solarian: "You mean the Lab Supervisor, Mr. Araujo?"

Kuhn: "Yeah, sure. Let's go with that."

Solarian: "Do you mean someone else?"

Kuhn: "He's my boss here at the clinic, isn't he?"

Richard sighed.

She's playing you, Director.

I am aware.

The agent in charge informed him it would be twelve minutes on the hazmat team. A solid response time...but it suddenly felt like too long. Something wasn't right here.

He looked around at the three agents in the security room, plus two clinic employees fretting nearby. Down the hall in the lobby, four more employees waited to be interviewed, and two members of management hurried to and fro fussing over all the intrusions.

Too many people were in the building.

He contacted the agent in charge again. "I want to move everyone who isn't actively involved in the search or currently being interrogated out into the courtyard."

"Sir, do you honestly think there's a bomb here?"

"I think something is amiss, and we shouldn't unnecessarily endanger people."

"Understood."

He returned his attention to the interrogation. Kuhn was being uncooperative enough that they could easily justify taking her in for further questioning.

Let's adjourn this interrogation to the local police station. I'm getting nervous about the safety of the clinic.

Ten more minutes. I don't want to lose the rhythm.

He got it; he did. Interrogation was as much art as science. Still....

He occupied himself by checking in with Graham and the teams serving warrants at the other regenesis clinics. Their reports bore a troubling resemblance to the scene here, heightening his unease. Vilane should not have had any forewarning about the searches...but they knew he had informants inside the government. Might he have them inside SENTRI as well? It was possible.

And given forewarning, what would Vilane do? He hadn't pulled his operatives from the clinics. Was he sacrificing them, the way he had the men and women who had rioted at New Frontiers Medical Clinic? Or was it that their jobs weren't yet done?

Richard had spent a lot of time these last several months trying to get inside Enzio Vilane's head. Talking to Malcolm about the man's demeanor and personality tics. His public appearances were few, so there was precious little video footage to study. But everything about Vilane pointed to a clear conclusion: though the man presented a refined, charming persona, it hid a volatile temper and cruelly vindictive nature.

Which meant if Vilane knew they were coming for his organization, he would without a doubt blow up the world in response.

Director, you need to end this. Let's take her to the station.

But I've almost got her.

No, you don't.

The agent in charge messaged him to let him know the hazmat team was here, and he hurried outside to brief them.

A tall man with dark hair and olive skin stepped up as soon as he arrived, and Richard extended a hand. "Lieutenant Jawors? I'm CINT Director Richard Navick."

The man exhibited a bit of surprise as he shook his hand. "Sir, it's an honor to meet you."

"Thank you for arriving so promptly. I'm going to send you inside on a fishing expedition. We've got a digital forensics expert searching for a data bomb, but I'm concerned there may be physical explosives in the clinic as well. I'd focus on the—"

Heat seared into his back as a flare of light blanked out the lieutenant's face. The next thing he knew, concrete was scraping against his cheek. His lungs convulsed, forcing air into his chest.

A wave of déjà vu roiled his mind, and for a second he was lying on the ground outside the Archives building at EASC while the Headquarters tower fell.

He rolled over onto his back, choking as his diaphragm spasmed to recover.

A hand extended down to him. "Director Navick, are you hurt?"

He took the hand and struggled to his feet, then waved off the agent. Flames poured out of the caved-in roof of the regenesis clinic; smoke billowed out the shattered front windows.

Instinct took over, and he moved to take charge of marshaling rescue personnel—but he didn't have those kinds of direct contacts any longer. Solarian had been in the building...but the agent in charge had been outside.

He searched the shell-shocked and scrambling crowd for the man, and thankfully spotted him fully engaged in ordering people and equipment into action.

He went over and touched the man's arm. "Any resources you need from me, shout." He got only a curt nod in return.

Next, he messaged Graham and the other teams and ordered them to pull out of the clinics immediately. His messages bounced as undeliverable to Graham and two more of his people, and a sinking feeling twisted his gut. Vilane had planned all of this, and Richard had known it—just not soon enough.

22

PANDORA

We tried to work within the system to preserve life. We tried to win hearts and minds with logic and persuasion. And we succeeded everywhere—everywhere except where it matters most. The governments of the Earth Alliance, Senecan Federation and IDCC have foolishly and recklessly pushed forward with this moral affront to every living soul. They've funded regenesis clinics and strong-armed soldiers and civilians alike into agreeing to be raised from the grave to do their governments' bidding.

We won't stand for it any longer. Our hand has been forced.

Regenesis clinics cannot be allowed to continue to operate. We will not allow them to continue to operate. Anyone who works in these facilities must be considered to be aiding and abetting in crimes against nature and humankind, and they will suffer the consequences. Anyone who has been raised via regenesis will be considered a monster unworthy of receiving the most basic human rights and privileges. They aren't your parents or your spouses or your brothers or sisters; they aren't your bosses or coworkers. Killing them will not be murder, but rather like putting down a rabies-sickened dog.

We will not allow our civilization to be brought down by the ghouls and the golems. We will save humanity, by any means necessary.

— *The Gardiens*

They'd tried to get the news feeds to stop blaring the Gardiens manifesto every thirty seconds, to no avail. So it flashed on oversized screens in restaurants and lobbies and entertainment squares, inevitably followed by footage of the clinic bombings. There was nothing the news media craved so much as blood sport, and with the Rasu denying them carnage for a few months now, they latched onto the Gardiens' escalation like a dying man handed a thimbleful of water.

Richard and Graham donned flak jackets as the TacRaid squad assembled two blocks down from Enzio Vilane's home and Gardiens headquarters.

Graham had been forced to shave what remained of his shaggy beard after most of it had gotten singed off in the explosion at the Krysk clinic, and he sported a new patch of pink skin along the left side of his jaw. Like Richard, he had been lucky enough to be standing outside when the bomb at the Krysk clinic detonated, but not so far away as to escape unscathed. He looked rather strange without the beard—exposed and almost vulnerable. But a few initial jokes had triggered a genuinely mortified response from his friend, so Richard was trying not to tease him about it.

Pandora's police organization was more akin to a hybrid paramilitary special forces squad and intelligence unit than a traditional law enforcement organization. They didn't wear uniforms and patrol the streets, but they *did* keep a minimum level of peace on the colony. And when needed, they were perfectly capable of bringing the big guns. As such, they were leading the raid, with the assistance of a team of hand-picked SENTRI agents.

Neither he nor Graham was in the mood to watch this raid from a conference room at HQ. But they did hang back toward the rear, as it was also true that neither of them had engaged in such a dangerous raid in many years.

The team lead gave the 'go' signal, and the squad swept forward to surround the building then storm inside. Aerial craft circled overhead, in case Vilane tried to make a swift exit. Two of the craft delivered tactical officers directly to the penthouse at the same time the elevator arrived with the bulk of the squad, and the officers swarmed into the dwelling.

Within forty seconds, it was apparent that Enzio Vilane was not in residence. The squad continued to follow procedure and act as if he was, sweeping every centimeter with weapons raised while taking precautions to preserve life and evidence. Next came a sweep for explosives, which honestly seemed a risk given the clinic bombings, but they came up empty.

Because the penthouse was also empty. Empty of people, empty of quantum hardware and storage devices. Virtually empty of clothes and decor. Only the furniture remained.

"We should have moved on him before serving the clinic warrants," Graham muttered in frustration.

They'd been surveilling Vilane, of course, but it was all too easy for a Prevo to vanish; a wormhole opened in a lavatory would do the trick. The man hadn't needed to go to such extremes as that, because despite several attempts, they'd been unable to place a cam inside the walls of the private residence wing of the building.

"We didn't have enough evidence against him personally yet. Not enough for a clean arrest."

"Damn, Richard, but you are by the book. We would have found the evidence."

"Probably." He rubbed at his nose in annoyance. "It is what it is. We'll pull what we can from here. We've frozen every bank account even remotely associated with him or his businesses. We're raiding his other offices."

"And?"

"And we have the evidence now. It's time to expose Enzio Vilane to the world for what he is."

THE PRESIDIO
SENTRI HEADQUARTERS

It was no secret to anyone who knew him that Richard did not care for the public spotlight. For one, intelligence agents were supposed to operate in the shadows, escaping notice by their prey, or by anyone at all. It was how he'd been trained all those many, many years ago. But he wasn't so much an intelligence agent as a bureaucrat these days, was he? Fine, a head of agency.

But with Director Solarian out of commission for at least a week for his regenesis procedure, Richard had no choice but to officially take over leadership of the Gardiens investigation, at the exact moment when it had become the most public of scandals.

Will arrived beside him to hand him a water, then brush some lint off his shoulder. "Need anything?"

"Yes, I need you to do this press conference for me. You're much better with people than I am."

"At a cocktail party, maybe. Not in front of a camera. Besides, you sell yourself short. You come off as naturally trustworthy. As competent, serious and unflappable. At a time when everyone is flailing about and panicking, you can be the voice of calm. Of reason. You tell them you will bring the Gardiens and Vilane to justice, and people will believe you."

"I'm not sure *I* believe me."

"Doesn't matter."

"Right." He squeezed Will's hand, then checked over his notes one more time before walking out to the podium, suppressing a grimace at the drones swooping through the air as if they intended to dive-bomb him.

"Thank you all for coming today. I have a lot of announcements regarding the clinic bombings, as well as several updates to share about our investigation into the Gardiens organization. And its leader."

23

ROMANE

Mia scanned through the most recent report to cross her desk. It was a proposal for a Confluence-funded internship program where human teenagers would spend two weeks on the homeworld of each Concord species in a specially crafted immersion program. At the end of the program, they'd present reports about their experiences to their schools and as part of an official Expo event, and would receive university credit in return.

Security was a top concern, of course, as well as health precautions. The students would be perfectly safe on, say, Nopreis, but it wouldn't be wise for them to wander down the wrong alley—or even into the wrong restaurant—on Macskaf or Ireltse. She made several notes requesting an in-program health attendant from the Concord Consulate and the assignment of an additional two Vigil security officers to the program, then gave her provisional approval and sent it back to the Expo's Director of Student Outreach.

With a deep breath, she dove back into her inbox. The hotel had received a coveted platinum-star rating a week before it was scheduled to open, which was a giant check-off on her list. On the other hand, the research annex was facing cost overruns, mostly because the equipment the scientists insisted on ordering was as expensive as all hell. The Expo 'helping' with the costs had somehow morphed into covering the bulk of them.

Mia sank back into her chair and groaned into her hands. She hadn't paid enough attention to the research annex's development. If she had, she'd never have let the finances get to this point. But there were a thousand *other* projects to pay equal attention to, and something was bound to fall through the cracks. She definitely had not anticipated exactly how much work was involved in this insane, ambitious idea of hers. More work than her double duty as AEGIS' Concord Senator and head of the Consulate, by a large margin.

But at least it gave her a reason for not sleeping at night other than the aching loneliness of an empty bed. The gloomy silence of an apartment that held no happy memories, no reminders of good times.

Objectively, she had everything she wanted now. Though still stumbling through some growing pains—and its share of red ink—the Confluence Expo was a smashing success. She was again respected by her peers, and she'd brought joy to thousands of children and jump-started warmer relations between humans and the other Concord species.

She'd done what many had called impossible, again. In the middle of the looming threat of the Rasu's return and an unprecedented focus on military expansion, she had built an oasis of hope, where people could come to learn about their comrades and dare to believe in a bright future.

She was proud of what she'd accomplished. Beyond proud. Too bad she wasn't happy.

RW

The next time Mia looked up from her work, the sky outside her window was a shadowy cinder. Second sunset had come and gone without her noticing. She rubbed at her eyes and considered curling up on the couch for a few hours of sleep.

But she didn't have a change of clothes here, since she hadn't found the time to get the last 'emergency' change of clothes washed. She ought to hire an assistant—a second assistant, one devoted entirely to keeping her presentable.

She gathered up her things and headed out of the Expo, grateful her apartment was right down the street. It was why she'd chosen it.

But she was halfway home when she realized she simply couldn't stand the thought of walking into the place. Couldn't bear its cold, empty sterility. She'd avoided visiting her and Malcolm's home on Romane for almost six months, telling herself she wasn't ready to be assaulted by the memories. Now she longed to be immersed in them with a burning ache in her chest that cried out for satisfaction.

Without stopping to question the decision, she diverted her course and headed for the levtram station.

RW

The shrubs lining the walkway to the porch were perfectly manicured, as she'd kept the gardener under contract; the cleaning service, too.

Arriving to find the place neglected and in disrepair would surely have broken her.

Mia opened the front door and walked through the entryway into the past. A cornucopia of memories washed over her, brought on by lingering scents that, realistically, should have been banished by the cleaning service.

An echo of laughter peeled down the hallway in her mind. Joy was commemorated by the visuals decorating the walls. A few tears, too, but not many.

She wanted to wander through every room, touching the curios and art and furniture one by one. But she was *so* tired.

So instead she dragged her body straight to the bedroom, toed her shoes off and collapsed onto the covers, letting the faint scent of Malcolm, of *home*, envelop her in its warm embrace. In seconds, she'd fallen into a deep slumber.

RW

Mia's eyes opened to the serene rays of a burgeoning primrose dawn. She smiled as she stretched her arms above her head and rolled over to curl up against Malcolm's chest.

But of course he wasn't there. The pillow smelled like him, though. If her gaze unfocused, she could *see* him there, lying beside her.

And in that moment, in the hazy space between sleep and waking, she knew. None of this was worth it. Denying herself happiness today because of the possibility of sadness at some point in the future just brought her sadness today *and* tomorrow.

Believing she'd lost him forever had devastated her. Driven her beyond madness. And the recognition that someday she'd have to suffer such pain for a second time…it still terrified her. But what was the point of living for a thousand years or more if you didn't try to be happy along the way?

Then she remembered how it didn't matter. She'd burned this bridge right and proper. She hadn't heard from Malcolm since he'd politely rejected her invitation to lunch over two months ago, and hadn't seen him since the odd glimpse of him in the crowd at the Expo grand opening. Except on the news, obviously. It was impossible to avoid his frequent appearances discussing the state of planetary defenses and the new military initiatives to prepare for the Rasu.

She'd made this choice. She would have to live with the consequences and find a way to soldier on nonetheless. For the people who were inspired by her work, if not for herself.

She swallowed and stared at the ceiling. She thought she'd move back in here after all. It was painful, to be surrounded by memories of a happier time, but it was better than the emptiness of an apartment with none of those.

The decision brought her a small measure of peace, and she turned on the news feed then went to take a shower in her own damn bathroom.

RW

When Mia shut off the water in the shower, she was surprised to hear a familiar voice coming from the feed in the bedroom. Curious, she wrapped a towel around her hair and wandered into the bedroom to see Richard Navick giving a press conference.

"At this time, we are identifying Enzio Vilane as the leader and founder of the Gardiens terrorist organization. He presents himself as a real estate investor on Pandora and has amassed a measure of wealth in the endeavor. However, he uses his wealth to fund the activities of a criminal group on Pandora and other colonies known as the Rivinchi cartel, as well as to finance the Gardiens."

"I'll be damned!" She should be shocked to learn that Vilane was behind those contemptible Gardiens, but in retrospect it made perfect sense. His unbridled arrogance and innate air of superiority fit right in with the Gardiens' ethos, their short-lived public relations campaign notwithstanding.

The reporter cut into the press conference to summarize the remaining information, suggesting it was a replay. The announcement had occurred the evening before, and she'd been so ensconced in Expo business that she hadn't even noticed it.

She sent Richard a brief pulse.

Just saw the news. Way to go taking the information I gave you and running with it. Job well done.

He replied as she was choosing an outfit from a closet full of all her favorite clothes. How had she forgotten about them?

Most of the credit goes to Malcolm. I only followed the evidence where it led.

Her hands froze holding a blouse halfway off the hangar.

Malcolm?

I probably shouldn't have said anything. I imagine he'll want to tell you himself, now that he's out. But know he's been protecting you this entire time.

I...thank you. Good...good luck in locking Vilane up.

She stumbled in a daze back to the bedroom and sank onto the edge of the bed, her mind racing. Protecting her? From Vilane?

Because odds were high if the man ever connected Laisha Balente to Mia Requelme, Vilane was vindictive enough to come after her just out of spite.

So what had Malcolm been doing these last few months? Investigating Vilane and the Gardiens in his copious free time?

Richard said, 'now that he's out.' Out of what? Out of…the Gardiens? Did he get himself invited into the group in order to expose it from within?

Malcolm's rejection of regenesis wasn't a secret, on account of the world thinking him dead for several weeks following the disastrous mission on Savrak. Had Vilane recruited him?

Her imagination rushed to fill in the blanks, and tears began streaming down her cheeks. Her heart was full—and she was also angry at him! How dare he act as her protector without her knowledge or permission, when she hadn't asked him to do any such thing! And if asked, she would have said it was a ridiculous notion.

Also, if she'd known Vilane was behind the reprehensible Gardiens, she would have gone after the man, despite her earlier vow to not get involved. Definitely following the riot on Romane, where his people had terrorized those poor children. Caleb had gotten involved then, and she should have as well.

And Malcolm surely knew all this, for he knew her better than she knew herself. He wasn't merely protecting her from Vilane's vengeance— he was protecting her from herself. Because that's who he was. She tended to bristle at his overbearing protectiveness, but he had the heart of a warrior and the soul of a champion.

God, might she have been wrong about his feelings toward her? Might his rejection have not been a rejection at all?

She tried desperately to grab hold of her emotions before they ran away from her completely. This was all speculation based on the flimsiest of evidence. She didn't *know* anything, except that Malcolm played some role in gathering evidence against the Gardiens and Vilane's involvement with them. And, apparently, he had done it at least in part to protect her.

It may be flimsy, but it wasn't nothing. It was enough to hang hope on.

24

SCYTHIA
MILKY WAY GALAXY

Enzio stalked around the living room of the beach house, his thoughts as dark and tumultuous as the sky outside was sunny and clear.

The rhythmic sound of the crashing waves upon the shore was interrupted by thuds and the whine of drilling as hired workers installed multiple quantum boxes in what used to be a spare bedroom.

His mole in SENTRI had alerted him that his time was up three hours before law enforcement moved in, which was long enough for him to pack up his sensitive data and belongings and vacate the Pandora penthouse. He hadn't expected to follow his mother to Scythia, but here he was.

The property was registered under a fictitious identity so detailed it was effectively bulletproof. He'd lightened his hair and irises and changed his fingerprints and retinal scan, and he projected a field to interfere with scans when he moved about in public.

If he wanted, he could live out a peaceful and comfortable existence here for however many years it took the media and the government to forget about him. He wouldn't, of course, but he could.

His mother passed through the kitchen attached to the living room, and his skin flushed with shame under her neutral, noncommittal glance. He felt like a failure in her eyes. Because he *was* a failure. The Gardiens were being hunted, regenesis was still legal, and he was a fugitive.

Try as he might, he was not able to not figure out how it had happened. He'd accounted for every eventuality. He'd spent hundreds of millions of credits to protect himself, his organizations and his financial interests from the pernicious tentacles of law enforcement.

At least his efforts had also included squirreling away a handsome sum of credits for the one eventuality he'd never thought would come to pass.

So what to do now? Continue to burn the world down, the way he'd intended? He could expose so many wealthy and powerful individuals as secret supporters of the Gardiens. Name enough of them, and it might even throw several governments into chaos—

"I've been thrilled with the reception the Expo has received so far. The exhibits are bustling with attendees, and enrollment in our outreach programs has exceeded all my expectations. Best of all has been the response from the children who have visited."

Momentarily distracted, he glanced at the news feed on the far wall. A striking woman with sleek raven hair and jade Prevo eyes was being interviewed by a Galaxy First reporter. The face was familiar...Mia Requelme, wasn't it? Until recently, the AEGIS Senator for Concord. He'd never really paid her much mind; she was a politician, but not one who was apt to either aid or harm him.

He turned away and picked up his train of thought. Chaos and scandal...wait. Why had the news feature grabbed his attention in the first place? Not because he knew the woman's face...but because he knew her *voice*.

He returned his attention to the screen and increased the volume, studying her more carefully. He still couldn't place the voice, so after a few seconds he closed his eyes and listened without judgment.

A sing-song allure took the edge off a tenor of bold confidence underlying her voice. She spoke clearly, enunciating her words in the manner of one who had taken care with her education. No Earth or Senecan accent tainted her phrasing, and—

Suddenly he knew.

Laisha Balente. The owner of the little tech shop in The Approach who'd dared to defy him, then slipped out from under his nose.

He refocused on the screen and instantly saw the resemblance. Change the hair, change the eyes, and Balente gazed back at him. He hadn't made the connection in reverse, because he'd had no reason to do so. But now?

It didn't make any sense, though. Why in the hell would such a woman spend a few weeks running a nothing tech shop in a working-class neighborhood on Pandora?

His Artificial fed him the recent news headlines tagged with Requelme...oh, right. There was some hush-hush scandal that resulted in her resigning from all AEGIS and Concord positions. Something to do with....

He fell into the chair behind him as a hundred threads wove themselves neatly into a tapestry of betrayal.

Mia Requelme was the long-time lover of Malcolm Jenner.

The bastard!

Jenner hadn't inserted himself into the Gardiens' orbit until shortly after Enzio's run-in with Balente. When Rivinchi operatives tried and failed to kidnap her.

Had this whole endeavor been about nothing more than avenging an assault on his lover?

But Jenner was a true believer. The man was legitimately against regenesis for religious reasons. This was beyond dispute.

Or so he'd thought. He'd broached the topic of Commandant Solovy with Jenner several times, and the fleet admiral was always reticent to disparage her, golem though she now was. Nevertheless, the man's beliefs were sincere. If Enzio knew nothing else, he knew this.

So he'd never doubted the man. Jenner was so goddamn...*moral*. Unassailable ethics. Rigid Marine honor. The possibility of Jenner running a long con was unthinkable.

Unless he was doing it to protect the woman he loved? Was there anything more blasted honorable than that?

Enzio had analyzed the law enforcement moves against him overnight, and he'd discovered one of the first links in the chain that brought SENTRI to his door was James Sarona. Somehow, law enforcement had identified the would-be assassin. Given the timing, they must have connected Sarona to the attempted hit on the commandant in London.

Had Jenner known Enzio was behind the Solovy hit before they ever met for the first time?

Dammit, he should have been more careful! Jenner enjoyed close relations with all the most prominent power brokers in Concord. Requelme, obviously. The commandant. General Colby. CINT Director Navick? Though SENTRI was the public face of the witch hunt against him, the long arm of CINT had begun to make itself known in recent days, and had likely been there behind the scenes, pulling the strings all along.

He dropped his head into his hands. It had been a setup from the beginning, and Jenner had been the perfect front man. The one person above reproach and suspicion. Enzio was so entranced by the notion of such a grand catch for his menagerie, he'd walked right into the trap.

On the screen, the public-interest piece was wrapping up with feel-good shots of this Expo thing Requelme had opened on Romane. Children cackled and cheered as they played with alien artifacts, and young people listened to multi-sensory lectures with rapt attention.

Rage at having been deceived ground his teeth and boiled the acid in his stomach. No one made him look a fool! Malcolm Jenner had destroyed his life, and for this the man would pay dearly.

He forced a veneer of calm upon his mind. As the old saying went, revenge was a dish best served cold. Now was not the time to run off hot-headed and half-cocked. The most powerful people in the world wanted his head, and he must be careful. But he would have his revenge.

So he spent several long minutes thinking through his options. Then he placed a secure pulse to the Gardiens Chief of Security. Zylynski's continued loyalty had been bought with a gargantuan sum of money; it was time for the man to hold up his end of that bargain.

Zylynski, I have a mission for you.

25

ARES

ADVOCACY SQUARE

Eren stuck his head inside the open door to Nyx's office. "You busy?" She looked up from a screen, worry lines etched into her forehead. "No more than usual. I didn't realize you were back from Hirlas. What do you need?"

He flopped down in the chair opposite her desk. She'd occupied the office for several weeks, but there wasn't a trace of personalization to be found anywhere. No visuals, no art, no plants, not even a labyrinthine diagram on the wall cataloging all the potential threats to her grandfather. The desk and her chair were well-crafted but generic.

He had half a mind to offer some decorating advice, but he didn't fancy a second trip to a medical facility so soon. "You know how I hate to write up formal reports, so I thought I'd drop by and give you the final post-mortem on the Barisan conspiracy."

"Thereby making *me* write up the formal report for our records."

"Up to you."

She sighed in resignation and plastered on a blank countenance. "Are you healed?"

Eren ran two fingertips over his now smooth cheek, then lifted his hair back and tilted his head to expose an unmarred neck. "See? All better."

"On the inside as well?"

"I took a swing through the treetops before I left Hirlas for good measure. No twinges of concern."

"I'm glad." She nodded sharply, as if deciding that was sufficient feigned sympathy for today. "So, your report?"

"CINT made another round of arrests yesterday, mostly outliers who assisted the conspirators. Also dug out a couple of double-agent informers in Vigil. They—"

"Anadens aided the Barisans?"

"Not everyone in Vigil is Anaden any longer, sweetheart."

"Perhaps they should be."

"I'll pass your opinion along. I'm fairly confident that we've rooted out all the troublemakers involved in the affair, but I'll keep in touch with the CINT agents posted on Macskaf, just in case."

"Thank you. We raided and shut down the operating *apomono* manufacturers, by the way. It's far too dangerous for anyone to have access to the substance."

"Want me to let you know when a new manufacturer pops up, so you can stomp them out, too?"

"What makes you think—yes, fine. Please do." Nyx half-turned to gaze out the window for a moment. "I convinced Grandfather to retain a small fraction of the heightened security measures we'd instituted to guard against the attack. A few additional guards, a smattering of patrols. He's still horribly exposed and entirely disregarding of the danger his position puts him in."

"I've said it before. He's lived a million years—"

"And survived multiple assassination attempts. Yes, I know. But it's my job to protect him from the attempts yet to come."

"It's your job to protect the Advocacy."

"Which, for the foreseeable future, means protecting him. I realize he says he doesn't want to rule forever, but the people need the stability and leadership he provides."

Eren shrugged broadly. "Not disagreeing with you."

"Yes…" a shadow passed across her eyes "…I should remember that you want to protect him as well. You've said as much, and you have worked with him for longer than I have."

"True, but not by a lot. I was an anarch for a fair span of time, but I didn't meet him in person until Caleb, Alex and Mesme bullied their way into my life."

"Right. Of course." She played with a small Reor slab sitting on the desk. Did she not know what it truly was? More importantly, how insecure it was? He supposed millennia-old habits died hard.

Nyx set the slab down and looked up at him, her piercing eyes flitting over him, searching, probing.

He sank deeper into the chair. "What? Do I have a spider crawling on my head? Blood dripping out of my ears? You're staring at me very strangely."

Her hands dropped into her lap and she sat up straighter. "No, none of those…I apologize. I was merely…I simply wanted to say…well done. If you hadn't thought to preemptively track the *apomono*, we wouldn't have learned where the hit was taking place. We wouldn't have gotten there in time. And also for helping to take down the assailants. I admit I've been skeptical of your fitness for what I view as a critically important job, but you've proved yourself worthy of the position."

Eren bit back the instinctive snarky retort. It couldn't have been easy for her to admit such things to his face. "I appreciate you saying so. I don't want anything to happen to Corradeo, either. Or to the Advocacy. I'm not a huge fan of governments as a rule, but I think this one might actually do some good, especially compared to the shitshow that existed before."

"I believe you. And while I don't necessarily agree with your methods, I find I can't argue with the results."

"I…" another snarky retort buried "…so how are you settling into the new space? There's a sign in the entryway and everything. Most official."

"Yes." Her lips puckered. "It's the first time I've had a real office. And employees. Being an Inquisitor was pretty much the definition of a lone wolf profession. I went where the assignments sent me, took care of the problem and, when warranted, conveyed the results to the Primor. Now I have fifteen people reporting to me. I have administrative duties to perform and office space to allocate and personnel problems to sort. It's not exactly what I envisioned."

"Want to come hang with me for a bit? My work typically involves visiting dive bars and skulking around alien planets talking to ne'er-do-wells."

"Yes." She blinked. "I mean, no. I'm honored my grandfather has trusted me with so much responsibility, and I'm determined to make him proud. I didn't mean to complain. It's not what I'm used to, is all. Managing other people is not included in the genetic skill set of Inquisitors."

She needed to let go of her past and put all the Inquisitor crap behind her. But he suspected she wasn't ready for such a stark truth, so he softballed it. "Consider this an opportunity to prove you are more than your genetics."

She stared at him oddly for several long seconds. "I'll keep that in mind." Then she shook her head, as if clearing a fog. "What's next for you?"

"Where there's one conspiracy to topple a government, there's another. Time to get back to putting my ear to the ground and seeing what foulness pokes its head up." He stood and jerked a nod. "I'll shout when I find something. And when you can't take the stifling walls of the office any longer, let me know. You can tag along with me for an adventure."

26

"A little to the left, please." Maris Debray's lips puckered. "Too far. You need to center it under the lighting, see, so the directional beams catch the sculpture's curves, which thereby transform the light before casting it back into the room."

The Anaden men stared at her incomprehensibly, and she strode over to where they were positioning the sculpture. She studied the light fixture mounted onto the wall for a second, then stepped a few centimeters to the left and extended her hand vertically in front of her. "Here. Center it precisely here."

"Oh. Sure." They maneuvered the hefty sculpture sideways—

"Stop! Perfect."

"Yes, ma'am." One of the Anadens instantiated a screen and held it out to her. "If you'll affix your signature to this to indicate we delivered the package to your satisfaction for the customs filing?"

'Signature' was a term of art to Asterions that meant one's unique alphanumeric code, but she'd learned it meant something different—the transcribing of one's name—in Anaden society. She printed it above a line on the screen, and with a curt nod from her, the two men departed.

Maris expected she'd be seeing a lot of them in the next few days. Or similar men, in any event. She'd chosen a select collection of the highest quality art pieces from her various galleries in the Dominion for display here in the lobby of the new embassy, and customs regulations required the shipments to be delivered by local companies.

It wasn't pettiness to want visitors to be impressed the instant they walked inside the embassy—it was pride. Pride in Asterions and the wondrous art they were capable of creating.

She scanned the room to identify her next duty. The reception desk was complete except for a small bit of artistic ornamentation…and a person to staff it, as the embassy wasn't open for business just yet. The waiting area was decorated with elegant furniture, and on the wall nearby, a pane displayed inspiring visuals of the Axis Worlds. The remaining walls were still a mite bare, however, hence the imminent return of delivery personnel from the cargo spaceport.

The lobby was one of the last unfinished items on her list of preparations. In truth, she'd spent most of her hours in the last few months working on staffing. It had proved difficult to convince Asterions to come work here, on an Anaden world they had no recollection of ever inhabiting. She'd had to reassure potential employees that it was safe, for one; that it wouldn't be a horrible experience in an abusive environment, for another; most of all, that it *mattered*. But she'd eventually been able to curate a list of qualified people. Soon, their work here would begin.

A frown tweaked at her lips as she went over to a painting already in place on the wall. It now hung askew. The delivery men probably bumped it while lugging the sculpture. She carefully gripped the frame corners and nudged it back in line—

"I do believe I fancy this one. Striking use of color to imply shadows."

She recognized the voice instantly and adopted a professional smile as she turned. "Advocate Corradeo, what brings you here today?"

Disappointment flashed across his admittedly handsome features. "Are we back to 'Advocate' now? Have I offended you in some way?"

"No. But..." she gestured toward the reception desk "...here in the embassy lobby, I represent the Asterion Dominion, and you represent the Anaden Advocacy. We must uphold our roles."

His eyes crinkled at the corners. Was he amused at her insistence on maintaining proper appearances? "So we must. But in that case, shall we retire to your office?"

She tried to ignore the faint thrill his eagerness sent dancing through her nerves. Was this business or pleasure? "Will you divulge the reason for your visit once we do?"

"I will."

RW

This wasn't the first time Corradeo Praesidis had dropped by the embassy unannounced. For his first two visits, he'd made an appointment, but somewhere along the way he'd apparently decided they were familiar enough to dispense with the formalities. She'd tried to be insulted the first time he showed up unannounced, but the truth was, his uncanny charisma and surprising kindness had worn down her vaunted frostiness toward her former enemy. She remained exceedingly careful around him, however—or she tried to remember to be.

"Have you completely transformed the decor since my last visit?"

She sat on the couch by the windows, crossed one leg over the other and motioned to the spot beside her. "I've been trying out several themes. I haven't settled on a favorite."

He sat on the edge of the cushion and faced her. "I admire your optimism, and your determination."

"How so?"

"To move forward with such zeal and enthusiasm in your devotion to making this embassy a shining light here on Asterion Prime, when the shadow of the Rasu looms over our every waking moment. Many people are frozen in place, unwilling to take any action in their lives that might prove to be futile."

Her countenance darkened at the utterance of their foe's name. She was so damn sick of hearing about the Rasu. "Unlike you, I have no role to play in this war beyond keeping the spirits and morale of my people as high as possible. So rather than spend my hours morose at the possibility of losing everything when it is out of my control, I have chosen to simply assume we will survive and proceed accordingly."

His arresting sapphire eyes twinkled. "How utterly refreshing. Forgive me, I spend too much time in depressing meetings about our defensive preparations and their wholesale inadequacy. But enough of war talk. How are you finding things on Asterion Prime? Are you being treated well?"

"I am, with few exceptions, being treated...normally. Virtually no one has cowered in fear or hissed in revulsion upon meeting me. I had been led to believe most Anadens still hated SAIs and believed Asterions to be traitors or monsters. Or both."

"Most Anadens are...wary, let's say, of SAIs. But then again, you don't exactly look like an SAI. People meet you, and they see only a beautiful, charming woman."

He'd started to let the 'beautiful' adjective slip into conversation from time to time. She made it a point not to address it. "But they know what I am, don't they?"

"Some of them do. But while there are a few Anadens who do consider Asterions to be traitors, they all reside in the higher legacy ranks. Your average Anaden, if they know of the SAI Rebellion at all, perceive it only as a brief entry in the long history of our civilization."

Her gaze fell to her lap; she didn't know how to respond. On the one hand, she had experienced seven hundred millennia of a full and vibrant life between *there* and *here*. She was in no way defined by the Rebellion. On the other hand, she once had been. Those events had, for a period of time, served as the singular focus and greatest influence on her life. The reality that it meant nothing to most of the trillion Anadens alive today hit a bit hard.

"What are you thinking?"

Maris forced her gaze up and found concern animating his expression. "That I don't know whether to be offended or relieved."

"For the sake of diplomatic harmony, I hope you'll choose relieved. This embassy, this new relationship between our governments and in time our people? They're about a fresh start, not rehashing ancient battles."

"I didn't mean to imply...to answer your question more thoroughly, I am finding most people to be both polite and competent. Perhaps a touch dull and officious."

"This planet is now heavily Kyvern, so...." Corradeo shrugged broadly.

"Yes, you mentioned this before. I understand about the Dynasties, or at least I've read up on them, but I frankly assumed what I read to be caricature. For entire swaths of Anadens to be so narrowly pigeonholed, both in skills and in personality, seems impossible for a civilized species. Among Asterions, some individuals are too specialized, I suppose, but it is by their choice, and the choice is never imposed upon larger groups. How could anyone have thought this was a good idea?"

"Arrogance. The rich and the powerful believed they had reached the pinnacles of their chosen pursuits and desired to lock in such status forevermore. It was not my idea, I assure you. I fought against it, but I was...overruled." He visibly banished a discordant mien. "And now that I am in charge, I am doing what I can to dismantle it. But it will be the work of centuries. Millennia."

"And of course my parents were among the rich and powerful who ensconced their behavior in bronze for all their descendants."

"They helped pave the way, yes. But it was one of your family's progeny, Savine Idoni...I think she was your...the granddaughter of your cousin. She ultimately rose to the head of the family and, later, a position on the Directorate and a Primor title."

"I don't believe I've encountered any Idonis here on Asterion Prime yet. Tell me, what is their caricature?"

"Ah...." He brought a hand to his mouth and cleared his throat. "I have heard it referred to on occasion as 'sex, drugs and rock and roll.'"

She frowned. "Surely you mean art, fine music and creative pleasures?"

"Oh, it started out that way. But with the passage of time, all stereotypes become caricatures of themselves. Mind you, this is not to disparage the entire Dynasty. Many Idonis are most effervescent and delightful. In fact, I believe Nika has made friends with one of your relatives. You should ask her to introduce the two of you."

"Nika is quite...occupied these days. But I will mention it."

"She's taken a great deal of responsibility upon herself."

"She always does." Maris wasn't comfortable talking about Nika with him—it felt like a violation of a confidence—so she adjusted her posture and shuttered her expression. "So. The reason for your visit."

"I can't simply want to spend time with you?"

She thought perhaps the mask she'd adopted gave way a touch at his reply; it certainly did on the inside. She enjoyed his company more than she cared to admit, and he was too charming by half. Witty and sharp, cultured and elegant. So much so that it was easy to forget he'd once been a ruthless warmonger. She'd eventually come to believe him when he said all that was long in the past and never to return. But she was trying so very hard *not* to take the next step on the path he'd graciously laid out for her.

"You can, of course. But even if you wish to, I imagine your schedule leaves little room for frivolities."

"It is not a—" he cut himself off and began again "—a coincidence that we were discussing your familial history." He reached into his jacket pocket and produced a small glass vessel. The body resembled an exaggerated teardrop, and a handle swirled in ornate loops. Opposite the handle, a narrow spout tapered into a tiny glass cap. Inside, a pale primrose liquid swooshed in circles from the movement. "For you."

She studied the vessel as if it were a painting, taking in the delicate sculpting of the glass and inlaid details. Finally she took it from him, holding it aloft in her palm. "What is it?"

"It's called *apéranti thálassa*. The fruit it's harvested from is grown in a single vineyard on Lastisi, the Idoni homeworld."

"Is it a drink? A magic potion? A poison?"

He laughed warmly. "A drink, after a fashion. You place a single drop on your fingertip, then your fingertip on your tongue. The flavors induced upon your palette are a multitude more vivid and exquisite than those conveyed by the most rarified wines." He indicated the object in her hand. "I have it on good authority that this season's harvest produced the finest vintage in twenty-six hundred years."

She considered the vessel anew, not responding.

"I know your feelings regarding your family are...complicated. And I would never pressure you to embrace a centimeter more of your heritage than you're comfortable with. But the heritage is not all bad. The alcohol, for instance, is frequently divine."

She looked up to find his eyes dancing with hopeful amusement, and she allowed a smile to break across her face as she twisted the cap off. "Shall we try it, then?"

27

MIRAI
AUXILIARY DEVELOPMENT LAB

"This area here is where they update the programming for all our deep-space sensors. The panes on the bottom row monitor the status of the equipment in real time, and the ones on the top row display the sensors' data." Joaquim Lacese nodded in approval. "Looks green across the board this morning. No Rasu poking about."

Cassidy Frenton drew closer to watch one of the panes as it tracked new code being pushed out to a sensor cluster in Kiyora's sector. "And a ceraff devises all the algorithmic improvements?"

"Yes, but a ceraff is merely people." Parc Eshett approached them to stand beside Cassidy, crossing his arms over his chest while he studied the updates with an air of seriousness. "People who, when they pool their minds, become a kind of super-supercomputer, with the added benefit of each individual's experience and general sapience."

"And you invented the technology, Parc?"

"I played an important role in its development."

Joaquim snorted. "That might be the first time I have ever heard you be modest about something you've done. Did you catch another virutox?"

"No. Nope. I was trying to be gracious, but fine. I invented it." Parc shot Cassidy a charming smile. "I understand you're not a bad coder yourself. Would you like to take a peek at the programming running these sensors?"

"Can I? I don't have clearance."

"I won't tell if you don't. Let's just go over here and pretend as if we're working." Parc guided her to a workstation behind the panes.

Joaquim sighed contentedly while his gaze roamed across the rest of the lab. He'd need to treat Parc to a beer or three as thanks for giving Cassidy a tour of the place, especially since she appeared to genuinely be enjoying herself.

In the relative peace the lull in Rasu attacks had provided, things were going better for the two of them. He'd traded in his 'more hotel room than home' for a legitimate, roomy apartment with a decent view. Cassidy seemed to finally be relaxing, settling into her new life and making peace with the fact that she'd been gone—dead—for decades. He'd given in and accepted an official role with the planetary defense consulting group Ryan Theroit worked for; he was still devoting his time to the war effort—to finding better ways to kill ground-based Rasu—but to Cassidy, it looked like a proper job. And it was.

Things were good. On the mend. This was a life he could get used to, Joaquim thought...so long as he ignored the faint twitching he kept buried deep down in a hidden corner of his mind. The primal urge to fight and rage and spill the blood of his enemies in righteous fire, and the delightful glory of celebrating the adrenaline high which came from doing so with—

Cassidy and Parc rejoined him, and he basked in the excited expression on her face. "That was fascinating! What I understood of it, anyway. It is incredible how far our abilities have come since I last delved into high-grade programming."

"They had to evolve if we wanted to survive." He jerked an appreciative nod at Parc, then took Cassidy's hand in his. "Come on. We promised Maggie and Ava we'd meet them for lunch. Hey, Parc, do you want to join us?"

Parc made a show of rolling his eyes at the heavens. "Can't. They had the gall to put me in charge of *people* in addition to tech, and now I can't seem to get five minutes free of their neediness. My employees walk up to me and start spilling their deepest desires in the middle of the hallway!"

"You know you get off on the power. Hey, we'll talk about the photal fiber upgrade tomorrow."

"Making a note on my calendar...sliding it in between two employee bitch sessions. Who scheduled these?"

"Have fun!" He and Cassidy went to the lobby, where they maneuvered through the security gauntlet, dynes and a host of scans confirming they weren't absconding with classified technology, then headed toward the closest levtram station.

"I'm glad you enjoyed the tour."

"I did, thank you. I mean it, though. Technology has advanced so much while I was gone. I seriously need to study up more—oh, I meant to mention to you. Do you remember Najai Katsu? He managed the prog art store in Synra One."

"Ummm, I think so. Dark, spiky hair, eyes two different colors?"

"That's him," Cassidy replied. "I bumped into him yesterday at the furniture store."

"Oh? Is he living here on Mirai now?"

"No, no. He now owns that prog art store *and* two others on Synra. He was here shopping for fixtures."

Joaquim had only a vague but positive impression when he considered the name and half-remembered face. He'd erased most of those memories long ago. "Good for him. I'm happy he's found success."

"Yeah. I thought I'd head over to Synra One and visit his store tomorrow. It always had unique routines for creating mixed art."

Joaquim sighed. "I don't think I can get off from work tomorrow. Price of having a boss."

"It's fine. I'll go by myself. I know you weren't much into all the art stuff."

"That's not true. I loved everything you created."

"You're sweet." She stood on her toes and kissed his cheek. "It's really fine. If I'm alone, I can take my time and browse without worrying about you getting bored."

He pushed aside a flare of panic. She wasn't going to die because he let her out of his sight for a few hours. She wasn't going to vanish. It was *good* that she was re-engaging with her old hobbies. Embracing being alive again.

"Okay. I hope you have fun. And, hey, our apartment could definitely use some art to liven it up."

She snickered into his shoulder. "I'm glad you're the one who said so."

28

MIRAI
OMOIKANE INITIATIVE

Nika slid into the chair opposite Maris in the cafeteria and set her croissant-laden plate on the table. "You look pleased with yourself this morning."

"Do I?" Maris leaned back in her chair and sipped on a coffee. "I've already completed a full day of work at the Asterion Prime embassy. I am almost ready to declare it suitable for opening. In a week or so, I think. The Rasu won't spoil the grand opening, will they?"

At the utterance of the enemy's name, dark, alien thoughts jabbed at the edges of Nika's consciousness. She hurriedly shoved them back into their cage, though whispers still escaped to haunt the fringes of her awareness. "A week? You should be fine. But you might not want to delay too much longer. Matters are trampling toward a confrontation."

"Oh. What unfortunate news."

"We knew the time was coming." She tried not to linger on visions of what it meant. "So, did you happen to see a certain Supreme Commander while you were at the embassy this morning?"

"I wish you would stop calling him that. His sins, while prodigious, are ancient history."

Nika folded her hands together at her chin. "I'm intrigued that my doing so rankles you now. It didn't used to. His charm offensive is wearing you down, isn't it?"

"I don't know of what you speak. We have fashioned a harmonious working relationship is all. Which, I will point out, is precisely what you tasked me with accomplishing."

"I did. And I know it wasn't easy. Thank you."

Mollified, Maris relaxed her posture. "You are most welcome."

Nika checked the time, then grabbed two croissants off her plate and stood. "Sorry to run so soon, but I need to go. Mesme and I have a field trip this morning."

"And you frown upon *my* choice of companions. Don't you dare miss the Advisor Committee meeting this afternoon. It is a most consequential one."

"How could I ever forget about it? I wouldn't miss it for the world. Promise." She stuffed a croissant into her mouth and hurried out.

RW

THE VAULT
FRINGES OF THE TYCHE GALAXY

The cool, ice-blue glow of the server lights racing in concentric circles perfectly matched Mesme's presence undulating beside her.

It is as I said. Intact, unmarred and functioning properly.

"It's not that I didn't believe you," Nika replied. "I trust you. I simply needed to see it for myself. To run my hand along the hardware and feel the hum which signifies the minds being preserved here. It's why visiting in sidespace wasn't enough." She reached out with a hand and did just that, slowly strolling along the innermost ring of servers.

Thank you.

"Hmm?" She glanced over her shoulder to see Mesme hovering at the exact center of the space, its luminance pulsing.

You said you trust me. This is...important to me.

She smiled lightly, though it felt like a violation in this somber, sanctified place. "See what not keeping secrets will get you?"

Mesme's presence dimmed, and her smile faded in turn; she hadn't meant to disparage the Kat.

Your point is well made.

She gazed upward at the glass floor of the medical lab high above them. "So, are Alex and I correct? Is Stygian the real threat?"

It is.

"And you couldn't have told us this back when the civil war began?"

All the Rasu factions represent a grave threat. If you had moved to cripple Stygian from the beginning, one or more of the others might have conquered them and grown even stronger than Stygian is now. On balance, Miriam Solovy's strategy has represented the best available choice to achieve the goal of extending the Rasu civil war for as long as possible. Thus, silence on my part accomplished the optimal result.

"Alex would say this is just you making our decisions for us again."

Mesme remained silent, but she sensed the unease in the twinkling of its lights. She'd gotten pretty good at judging its moods. The fact that this was the second time she'd upset the Kat in less than a minute bothered her, perhaps more than it ought to. "But your decisions have been wise ones so far, so I'm inclined to give you a pass on this one."

Mesme's arrangement brightened a touch in response.

Nika strolled down the gap between the circular rows, checking for herself the continued fortitude of the vast sea of backup storage devices. Tens of millions of souls preserved, a civilizational ward against the ultimate calamity. "The power generator continues to function okay? Dashiel was a bit worried."

It is performing to specifications. If you like, I can review the construction and operational design and suggest potential improvements to its reliability.

"Do so, please. It's vitally important to us that the power does not fail. A person's core programming—the lines of codes themselves—can survive a power shutdown, but the memories and emergent personality are maintained in a quantum field. It needs a minimal level of electrical throughput to keep its structure.

"It turns out memories, and especially the emotions intrinsically bound up in them, are too nuanced and complex to be reduced to lines of code. We've tried." She returned to the center of the enormous central storage room. "I don't suppose the Kats know how to do it without relying on active quantum fields?"

No. Such is beyond even our capability. Memories are what make a thinking being sapient. In your case, they are what make Asterions neither machine nor kyoseil, but something greater than the sum of your parts.

"And what does that say about me? Did I begin again as a blank slate when the Guides psyche-wiped me?"

You never truly lost all your memories, Nika. I realize you felt as if you did for a time. But you'd protected yourself from this eventuality by preserving your most valuable memories where they could later be uncovered, and by embedding....

"By embedding what?"

Mesme's lights stuttered a little, retreating to blend in with the row of servers. Interesting.

I have the...sense, based on the glimpses you have allowed me into your mind, that the gestalt of your lived experience for those seven hundred millennia was encoded in your core programming in a unique manner. You lost the facts of those experiences, but not how they impacted who you are. But it is merely an impression. I...can't say how you accomplished such a feat, or even precisely what you did accomplish.

It should concern her how Mesme had been able to detect so much about her psyche from their interactions. Granted, when her mind had nearly fractured apart from the intrusion of an avalanche of kyoseil-driven thoughts, she'd allowed the Kat quite a lot of access to her inner self. She'd had no choice in the matter. And Mesme had yet to take advantage of the faith she'd placed in it that night.

"It feels true, what you say. When I recovered the memories I'd encoded in Dashiel, it was like remembering something I already knew. As if I said to myself, 'of course,' and everything simply slid into place.

"I can't imagine how I knew how to do such a thing, though. Maybe someone I've forgotten about helped me, because I'd have no idea how to replicate it now." Another mystery about her past to unfurl. "Do you think I should investigate this further? It might lead to us discovering a way to mitigate the quantum field/power problem."

If you wish.

Not exactly a ringing endorsement. "Maybe after we survive the Rasu. We don't have time to make any changes to the psyches stored here before the Rasu conflict resolves itself one way or another. Anyway, shall we go upstairs? I need to check on the state of the lab while I'm here."

In point of fact, she had a lengthy list of items Dashiel had tasked her with checking. He'd intended on accompanying her, but an emergency at one of the assembly lines above Ebisu had called him away at the last minute. So she would inspect what she could in the time remaining, but she had a hard return deadline.

29

MIRAI
OMOIKANE INITIATIVE

Nika hurried through the wormhole she'd created and straight over to the Advisor Committee's table to take her seat a full two seconds before the last person arrived. She ignored the absolute glare coming from Maris to squeeze Dashiel's hand under the table and offer him an apologetic smile.

"Was everything all right with the Vault?" he asked under his breath.

"Yes. Not to worry. Time slipped away from me is all."

Her arrival successfully navigated, Nika turned her attention to surveying the moods of those present. She'd done a fair amount of work canvassing almost everyone ahead of the meeting, and now she homed in on the squishiest representatives. Lance appeared bored—no, not bored. Distracted. Probably thinking about fleet deployments, weaponry loads and new ways he could invent to make Dashiel's life a living hell.

Cameron Breckel, a fellow External Relations Advisor, caught her studying him and arched an eyebrow. She returned the gesture, and after a second, he nodded minutely. *Whew.*

Adlai fidgeted like one of his suspects cornered in an interrogation room. He ran a hand through his hair, then cleared his throat quietly, then shifted his position in the chair.

She sent him a pulse.

Adlai.

What?

You haven't changed your mind, have you?

No, of course not. But if the vote fails, I'm honestly not sure if I'll be disappointed or relieved.

Have faith.

Katherine Colson called the meeting to order, cutting short Nika's survey. "Thank you everyone for coming in person. We have a variety of matters to cover, but first is one of our most important duties as advisors: that of naming someone to our own ranks. As you are all acutely aware, the position of Kiyora Administration Advisor has been vacant since Gemina Kail was removed in the wake of the Guides' prosecution. A rotation of officers in the Administration Division has filled in for her absence to the best of their abilities, but as we all know, there is no substitute for strong leadership at the top.

"Perrin Benvenit's name has been put forward as a candidate for the position. Currently, she is serving as Personnel Director for the Initiative. The four active Administration Advisors have reviewed her history, experience and overall suitability and determined she possesses the required qualifications for the position. Accordingly, we bring it to the Committee for a vote."

Nika waited for someone to protest that Perrin had been a member of NOIR, but no one did—presumably because they realized she would vault across the table and plant her foot down their throat if they did. No one raised the issue of her relationship with Adlai, either, since Nika and Dashiel weren't the only ones. The life of an advisor of necessity set one apart from the rest of the population (though Nika tried to minimize this as much as possible), and there was great comfort to be taken from sharing that life with someone who understood the position's demands.

Ida Yoshie, the Synra Administration Advisor, broke the silence wearing a frown. "Ms. Benvenit seems like a very nice person and a hard worker. But this is the highest position awarded in our society. We can't go giving it out to people because they're 'nice.' Katherine, you've worked with her more closely than any of the other Administration Advisors. What do you think? Now is not the time to hold back."

Nika tensed, preparing to leap to Perrin's defense.

"I think she's inexperienced. She hasn't come up through the ranks of an Administration Division, or even held a job with one at all. Historically, her level of emotionality has been a concern, but she's taken steps to address this. She sincerely wants to help people, and she's actually quite good at it. Her commitment to her work is unassailable, and her ability to organize vast swarms of both people and resources is impressive. Her methods are not always aligned with traditional Administration Division policy, but maybe an infusion of fresh blood and ideas is good every now and then. So while I have my reservations, I vote to approve."

Nika sank back in her chair, floored. Beneath Katherine's crusty exterior, an authentic, feeling soul might reside. Perhaps she should give the woman a bit of leeway in the future.

Yoshie nodded across the table. "Thank you, Katherine. I will note there are two people here who know Ms. Benvenit far better than the rest of us. Nika, you put her name forward. Make your case."

This, she was ready for. "It goes without saying that Perrin is phenomenal at her job. Every one of you recognizes how much worse the refugee crisis would've been if she hadn't spearheaded our response. She's saved countless lives, but more than that, she's made those lives better. She has a knack for organization, yes, but mostly she has one for *people*. And I should know."

Nika leaned forward, crossing her arms atop the table and sighing a touch wistfully. "She saved me. Six years ago, when I had nothing—when I literally didn't have any idea who I was or where I'd come from—she took me under her wing and showed me how to be a person again. Gently at first, guiding me with such a light touch that I didn't realize what she was doing. Only now, looking back, do I see what a gift she was in my life. I can confidently say I would not be sitting here today if not for Perrin Benvenit. The job of an Administration Advisor is, first and foremost, to care for people. To ensure they have what they need to live fulfilling lives in the manner of their choosing. And I for one cannot think of any individual better suited for such a job than her. I vote to approve."

She smiled brightly. "Adlai? I think you're next."

"Well, I can hardly top that, can I? I will say, um, this sounds exactly like the Perrin I know. I'm glad she met you, Nika. I first met Perrin at the height of the virutox crisis, when everything I believed about our government was being called into question. She played an integral role in helping me to eradicate the virutox and save countless people from falling victim to it. And once that was done, she immediately dove into the next crisis, with no thought but how to make things easier for as many people as possible.

"I admit, part of me wants to save her from the pressures and overwhelming responsibilities of this job. But I'd be failing in my own duty as an advisor if I used my personal feelings to deny the Asterion people the benefit of her leadership. And in my heart, I know she's ready for this. So I vote to approve."

30

MIRAI

Joaquim dropped his bag on the floor as soon as he walked into the apartment, and his jacket followed it a second later.

"Cassidy?" he called out as he went to the kitchen to grab a beer from the refrigeration unit.

"Out on the balcony!"

He grabbed a second one for her, then headed that way. He found her leaning into the railing, curls blowing wildly in the wind. He hugged her from behind, placing a kiss on her neck, and handed her one of the beers.

"Thanks. How was work?"

"Good. I got to fly one of the new, lighter-weight TAGs today. It's so agile, it's akin to flying an eagle. Bonus, I got to shoot fake Rasu on the test field while putting the upgraded control software through its paces."

She made a face. "Sounds...fun?"

He chuckled. "It was. But you're the one who had an exciting day. How was your visit to Synra?"

"Excellent. I met Caroline for lunch at *Desert Delights*. They've renovated the main dining room and added a top-floor deck. We didn't eat up there, though, because it was...you know, hot." She rolled her eyes. "Then I went shopping on Krinkow Street and—"

"The top you're wearing! It's new. I like it." It was woven canary lace with a scoop neck that teased at her tantalizing cleavage. Definitely her style.

"Thanks. I also got something silkier. I'll show you later."

"Oooh, I can't wait. And did you stop in *Artistic Escapes* and see Najai?"

She nodded slowly. "I did. Spent a long time talking to him, in fact. He's expanded the store into the space next door and is working on filling out his inventory. The whole space was impressive." Her gaze drifted away from him to stare out at the afternoon skyline.

"And?"

"And he offered me a job writing new routines for the mixed art modules. He also wants me to create several prototype art pieces with those routines that he can display as promo material and use in advertising."

Joaquim choked his gut response off at the top of his throat. He'd been trying to watch his tongue lately, with some success. "I, um...I'm glad he recognizes your talent and the quality of your work. I guess if you want to take the job, you can wormhole to the store's front door. Not even a proper commute required."

"Yeah." Her voice was soft.

"Do you want to take it?"

"I haven't decided yet. But I've realized I need something for my life to be about. Something other than you. You understand what I mean, don't you?"

"Of course I do." It stung a little, the notion that he couldn't be everything she ever needed, but he was being absurd. She was her own person; he *wanted* her to be her own person. "I wish you—"

"You wish I'd find a job on Mirai. I know."

"No. I wasn't going to say any such thing." *Think it, but not say it.* "I mean...if you did, it would help you meet new friends and make this feel more like home. That's all." Only belatedly did he realize he kind of *had* said it. Oops.

"You're right. And I've been trying. I have. But, Joaquim, when I was there in Synra One today, it was like I'd never left. The streets, the people, even the stuffy, humid air...it felt so comfortable and natural. I've missed it. Now, I'm not saying I want to move back there or anything. But maybe having a job on Synra while living here on Mirai can be the best of both worlds?"

"Maybe." He forced a smile. "I'll support you, whatever you want to do. Love you."

"I love you, too." She wound her arms around his neck. "I told Najai I'd get back to him next week. So I have some time to mull it over."

OMOIKANE INITIATIVE

Perrin sat on the wrought-iron park bench nestled beneath one of the snowbell trees on the side lawn of the Initiative. She'd pulled her knees up on the bench and had a pane displayed above them. On it, a sappy adventure romance vidbook played.

She'd lost the plot of the story ten minutes in. It was intended to provide a distraction, but nothing short of a renewed Rasu invasion was going to distract her from what was happening up on the top floor of the Initiative.

The thought of a group composed of the most powerful people in the Dominion deciding her worthiness made her skin itch. Seriously, she was breaking out in hives. She'd never enjoyed being in the spotlight, preferring to simply follow her instincts and do her work to the best of her ability. If that work made someone's life a little better, then her conscience was sated, which was all the thanks she needed.

Her mind raced through every critical—

"Perrin!"

She looked up at the shout to see Joaquim jogging across the lawn toward her. She shut down the pane and leapt up to embrace him. "What are you doing here?"

"Coming to see you. I was about to go inside when I caught sight of you over here. What's with the quiet, solitary contemplation routine?"

"Oh…" she returned to the bench and patted the spot beside her "…the Advisor Committee is meeting right now."

"They do that all the bloody time, don't they? Something special about this meeting?"

She winced. "Me."

He stared at her expectantly.

"Nika put forward my name for the Kiyora Administration Advisor position."

"Gods!" He blinked, and a troubled expression flitted across his features for half a second. "That's amazing."

"You don't look like you think it's amazing."

"Ah, hells. I just had a spare thought of how Cassidy was right. The only people I know any longer are advisors." He patted her hand. "But you'll be the best of them, so I suppose I'll let it slide."

"Ha. You're assuming they're going to offer me the job. That's a *big* assumption."

"Not so big. You know Nika, Maris, Dashiel and your guy will vote for you, so there's four votes sealed up. Practically a done deal."

"There are twenty-nine people on the Committee, silly." She chuckled; she was glad he'd come along to cheer her up.

"Eh, I'll bet you've won the rest over, too. Hey, you said 'offered.' Are you considering turning it down?"

"You don't turn down the Advisor Committee, Jo."

"I would."

She laughed. "Yeah, you would. But I wouldn't. I mean…" she ran a hand along the curling arm of the bench "…the responsibility is overwhelming. So far, all I've done is manage a couple of hundred employees and a dozen refugee centers. We're talking about managing the administrative apparatus for an entire planet! One I don't know very well."

"No worries. You'll be able to handle it."

"You think so?"

"I know so. But how's this going to work with you and your guy? Will you being on Kiyora all the time bring trouble to paradise?"

She wished he could find his way to using Adlai's name, but at least Joaquim wasn't bashing him any longer. "The fact I can wormhole from our living room to my office means it won't technically be any different. Psychologically, though, I admit it'll feel as if I'm far away from him. And I think he'll feel the same way.

"But he gave me a really convincing speech last night about how it didn't matter where we spent our working hours—what mattered was that we got to come home to each other. The problem is, I should probably get an apartment on Kiyora, too. It would be rude not to live among the people I'm taking care of. But he can wormhole there anytime, too. And Nika and Dashiel make two residences work."

She nodded firmly; the speech had helped bolster her confidence. "It'll be a bit of an adjustment, but we'll find our way. Relationships are about compromise and supporting the other person. So long as we love each other, everything else will fall into place."

"Yeah." His eyes grew unexpectedly turbulent. "I'm sure it will."

"Thanks. Your support means a lot. Say, you were coming here to see me. What do you need?"

He huffed a breath and stood, offering her a blasé expression she could tell was forced. "Nothing important. In fact, you already helped me with it." He jerked his head toward the Initiative entrance. "Now, I spy Nika and your guy heading this way, and judging from the big smile on Nika's face, I think you're getting good news."

"Oh, my." She hesitantly stood up, her heart taking off to the races in her chest.

"I don't want to crash the party, so I should head out. Remember me when you're famous?"

"Always." She grabbed him in a hug, squeezing him tight, then motioned him on his way and focused on Nika and Adlai as they approached. Joaquim was right—Nika *was* smiling. Worse, Adlai was trying to look happy but only succeeding in looking pensive and a little scared.

Oh crap, she got the job. She was going to be an advisor.

31

CONCORD HQ
RASU WAR ROOM

Morgan leaned against the wall by the door to the War Room, adopting a posture of forced casualness laced with an air of 'don't even try to talk to me.'

The luminaries of the combined Concord militaries milled around in the room, chatting in twos and threes ahead of the meeting. She knew their faces by sight—it was unavoidable—but had never spoken to most of them. Across the way, Field Marshal Bastian jerked a curt nod in her direction, and she returned the gesture with equivalent curtness. She'd always appreciated his utter lack of frivolity in all things.

"Commander Lekkas, I'm glad you could join us today."

She spun toward the voice, surprised someone had dared to challenge her frosty aura by approaching her. Was the man spectacularly tone-deaf? "I wasn't presented with much of a choice. I'm sorry, you are...?"

By the time the question left her lips, she realized she needn't have asked, for the man was in several respects a male doppelganger of Alex.

"David Solovy. It's nice to meet you." He extended a hand without an ounce of guile.

She squelched a frown and shook it for the minimum required time. "Ah. Can't miss the family resemblance."

"I'll take the compliment. I wanted to say I appreciate your comments on the fighter craft strategic scenarios paper. They were most insightful, and I'm in the process of incorporating most of them."

"You're welcome. Anything I can do to improve our ability to blow up more Rasu."

"So say we all."

"Is this why I was invited to the meeting? Can I go now?"

"*Bozhe moy*, no. I lobbied for proper recognition of the crucial role our fighter craft will play in future battles, arguing they deserve to be represented at the table from now on."

"You 'lobbied' your wife?"

He brandished a mischievous grin. "Indeed. When it comes to matters of war, a personal appeal on the basis of sentimentality is worth far less than a logical argument backed up with evidence and an action plan."

"How romantic—"

At the end of the long table, Miriam Solovy's throat-clearing cut through the din like a plasma blade through timber, and the room instantly quieted. "Everyone take a seat, and let's begin."

David Solovy motioned to the table. "Welcome to the team, Commander."

RW

The Rasu Civil War Championship Bracket was rapidly advancing to its final round. The two strongest and most active factions were gorging on their smaller competitors with greater zeal than rival kings at a holiday feast, and the once-prismatic map continued its march toward monochromatic.

The table engaged in a heated discussion about the pros and cons of further Ymyrath Field strikes and other strategic moves. Morgan tuned it out, because whatever reason she might be deemed to be of some value here, it certainly wasn't this.

Instead, she idly studied the map. While the colors across two-thirds of the area shifted, shrank and grew, the far third remained an inky black. Alex was concerned about Stygian; she simply knew this, without having ever consciously learned it. Alex theorized that the homeworld of the Rasu lay deep in Stygian territory, and surveillance suggested the faction was busily stockpiling kyoseil and growing its forces in anticipation of....

"What moves has Stygian made recently?"

Miriam glanced over, possibly caught off guard; it was the first words Morgan had uttered in the meeting. "Commander Lekkas. Stygian continues to stay on the sidelines of the civil war and has initiated no attacks against the other factions."

"But no one has attacked any of their territory, either?"

"Correct. We have assets watching their activities."

"Sure." She waved a hand at the woman, indicating for her to continue. And so Miriam did.

Eventually the discussion moved on to a proposal to increase the distribution of Rima Grenades to Concord worlds and tactical plans for their use in surface battles. Several people protested, arguing that with the now ubiquitous placement of Rift Bubbles and exhaustive planetary scans for Rasu signatures, the likelihood of Rasu forces reaching the surface of any world was negligible at best.

It was nonsense, and Morgan grudgingly gave Miriam credit for saying as much. For one, insisting 'that will never happen' was the best way to ensure 'that' would definitely happen. For another, thus far no one had ever lost a bet by overestimating Rasu deviousness. She didn't know how the metal monsters would do it, but they would find a way.

Which inevitably got her thinking about such ground battles and how they'd play out. Most planets wouldn't be able to count on Caleb Marano showing up and bleeding out into the soil, enabling the planet to rise up and drop-kick the Rasu invaders into oblivion. The people on the ground were going to have to save themselves the hard way.

RW

When the meeting finally broke up some interminable centuries later, Morgan took her time stepping away from the table, then casually wandered over to the viewport, as if to admire the ships. In fairness, she *did* admire the ships, but only to fill the minutes until the room emptied.

"Commander Lekkas, did you want to discuss something?"

She turned toward Miriam Solovy wearing an acidic smile. "In fact, I did."

"If you're concerned about Stygian's activities, rest assured I am as well, and I have dedicated—"

"I'm sure you're on top of it. I am concerned about them, but I've no doubt Alex will keep your feet to the fire far more effectively than little old me can. Nope, I wanted to discuss the new groundside defense tactics."

"Oh? It's hardly your area of expertise...but it was...." Miriam's mouth set in a thin line. "Very well. What are your concerns?"

"You already know what they are. I'm *concerned* you're going to strand multiple squads of ground forces beneath a quantum block without any plan for getting them out when everything goes to hell."

"Commander, you do understand that those soldiers' job—their entire purpose—will be to disable and destroy invading Rasu ships and mechs from the surface? Why would I put them there at all if I was simply going to pull them out the instant the situation turned ugly?"

"Um, to save their lives?"

"They didn't sign up to have their lives saved. They signed up to fight aggression and protect the innocent."

"My god, you are a cold-hearted piece of work."

Miriam lifted her shoulders in concession. "Point taken. But if you think I don't mourn every life lost under my command, you are mistaken."

"Oh, bullshit. You mouth the words and award the posthumous medals, then turn around and promptly send the next round of grunts to their deaths in the service of your cause."

"If by my 'cause,' you mean the preservation of our civilization, then yes. I do." Morgan started to retort, but Miriam held up a hand, and dammit but Morgan felt compelled to silence. "Every time you get in the cockpit of a fighter and go into battle, you risk your life. I realize as a Prevo it's a bit more complicated, but you weren't always a Prevo. There was a time when a well-placed enemy shot would have ended your life in a blink. Correct?"

Morgan shrugged.

"Did you ever insist that your commanding officer not send you into a battle your side was losing?"

"Of course not. Those are the best kind of battles."

"When you're in the fight, have you ever played it safe? Refrained from performing a risky maneuver or held back from venturing behind enemy lines?"

"Obviously not. But the point is—"

"The point is that it is the job of every soldier—more importantly, the *honorable choice* of every soldier—to dive into the fray and use their skills to try to win the day while protecting as many lives as possible. Now, when the day is lost and nothing good can come from continuing to fight on, I will absolutely move heaven and earth to pull everyone out. Trapped Marines and crashed fighter pilots alike."

"You say that, but you fucking *didn't*."

If the woman was offended at Morgan's utter lack of anything approaching decorum, she didn't display it. "You mean on Ch'mshak, I assume."

"Damn straight, I mean on Ch'mshak."

Miriam's lips pursed, and she took several steps away from Morgan to gaze out the viewport, clasping her hands at the small of her back in parade rest. "Did you know Major Harper refused the provision of reinforcements after her squad found themselves pinned down? She said she wouldn't get more Marines killed trying to dig her squad out of a, and I quote, 'fucked-to-shit situation.'"

"Yes, I did know. I read all the reports, even the super-secret-squirrel-classified ones. The mistake you made was listening to her. You had information she didn't. You knew how badly the situation in the entire region had deteriorated, and how you were soon going to lose the ability to put anyone on the ground there. You had one tiny window, and you let it close behind them. You made the wrong call, and it cost lives." *It cost her life.*

"You're right."

"I...what?"

"You're right. It was the wrong call." Miriam sighed quietly. "Hindsight is insidious. It's the bane of every commanding officer—and don't pretend like you don't live with this reality as well. Knowing what I now know—what I learned in the days following the loss on Ch'mshak? Yes, I should have sent in *two* additional Marine squads. But at the moment when the decision had to be made, Major Harper estimated they had a thirty-two-percent likelihood of completing their mission and reaching the extraction point. A Marine will take thirty-two-percent odds any day of the week. And we also needed those squads at two other flashpoints elsewhere on the surface. Do I commit forces *here*, or *here*? Where will they do the most good? Where do they have the best chance of survival?

"That's why the decision was kicked up the chain of command to me, by the way. Because it wasn't about one mission, but instead multiple simultaneous missions and a larger strategy in play. I made the call to send those reserve squads to another location in an attempt to capture a Ch'mshak communications relay. Only the Ch'mshak blew up their own relay rather than allow it to be captured. It's a move I've never understood, but that's irrelevant. Given the outcome, in retrospect the squads should have instead been tasked with the rescue of Major Harper's squad. I'm sorry."

Morgan blinked, stunned into silence for a second. She cleared her throat and dug up some words. "'Sorry' doesn't bring her back. It doesn't bring any of them back."

"No, it doesn't, which is why I didn't say it to you at the time. Having been where you were after my husband was killed in the First Crux War, I recognized that it would not have offered you an iota of solace or comfort."

"Then why say it now?"

"I thought with the benefit of time and...life continuing on? I imagine it still doesn't offer solace or comfort, but perhaps we are now both in a position where we can benefit from the saying of it nonetheless. Also, we might all be dead in a few weeks. I suppose I'm trying to clear my ledger."

Morgan wiped a traitorous tear from her cheek and grasped desperately for the righteous fury that had ebbed away during the Commandant's confession. Dammit! "Apologizing doesn't make it okay."

"I suspect nothing will ever make it okay. I can't do that for you. No one can but you."

Morgan forced away another traitor and took a deep breath, letting the silence linger for a moment. "You'll have detailed plans and resources in place to rescue our ground forces from Rasu-occupied planets when a battle becomes unwinnable?"

"*If* a battle becomes unwinnable, no resource will be held back to try to save as many of our people as possible, military and civilian. I promise you this."

She couldn't think of a damn thing to say in response. Miriam had given her everything in the world she wanted without a fight—everything except the one thing she could never have.

So instead, she just nodded tightly and turned to go.

"Commander Lekkas? For the record, I'm glad you've rejoined the fight. Your presence improves our chances against our enemy."

"Oh? By what percentage?"

"By enough to matter."

32

VRACHNAS HOMEWORLD
ANDROMEDA GALAXY

Marlee settled onto the stone ledge, curled her legs beneath her, and opened the container of fruit she'd brought with her. It was a sunny day in the dragon habitat, with a perfect periwinkle sky and lush vegetation gleaming in the sunlight.

Below her, Cupcake and Barney continued their usual playful antics. Scorch marks had by now seared most of the surrounding tree trunks, and bare patches mottled the grass.

She'd taken the afternoon off from work after accompanying several of the Ourankeli on a tour of Steropes. It was always difficult to tell with the Ourankeli, but her sense was that the visit went even better than she could have hoped for. After spending half an hour at the chosen site on the moon, they'd asked to visit two additional locations. Cyfeill and Kelizou had spoken in hushed but fervent tones to one another almost nonstop, pausing only to ask technical questions.

And seeing it in person, the moon truly was magnificent. A thin arc of the gas giant peeked over the horizon like a watchful guardian, and the sun, though more distant than what one typically found on a garden world, shone vividly in the sky.

Afterward, the Ourankeli returned to their housing to 'confer and review the details,' but she was really hopeful they were going to choose Steropes for their home.

She nibbled on a strawberry and watched Cupcake tail-swipe Barney's feet out from under him, sending Barney to the ground with a heavy thud. Had they grown since her last visit? It was difficult to be certain from her high vantage, but she was pretty sure they had both grown by at least half a meter in height. Cupcake's tail was getting quite formidable!

One swat and it would knock you thirty meters, slam you into a tree and shatter your spine.

Marlee swallowed back the defensive retort that sprang to mind, and instead chose to acknowledge how this was an accurate statement. She'd been swatted just so by a Rasu once, and it was not a fun experience. *Probably so. I'll have to take care to avoid the tail.*

But it won't stop you from charging down there and trying to get yourself killed.

Yes, it will. I won't go down there and approach him until I'm ready. Today, I'm merely watching.

Better watch the skies, too. If you're not careful, Mom will scoop you up and present you as a snack for the children.

I'm Veiled. But I realize dragons have an enhanced sense of smell, which is why I am watching the skies.

The Voice apparently decided it didn't have anything further to add.

The truth was, she *didn't* like to think about the risks, especially when it came to Cupcake. She wanted to focus on the adventure, on the wonder and splendor of befriending an actual dragon! But she conceded that she'd get to experience a lot more wonder and splendor if she remained alive and moving under her own power. Maybe this was a bargain she could consider making with herself.

So she'd retrenched. She was studying the behavior of the dragon younglings with the critical eye of a scientist (she might not be a scientist, but she had been raised by one). If she was going to befriend Cupcake, it was going to have to be on his terms, not hers. This meant she needed to understand everything about his tendencies.

Meanwhile, in the back of her mind she noodled over the potential of a different approach. Dragons hadn't been real until the Kats made them so. In creating the creatures, they had self-evidently pulled from human and Anaden legends, so the voluminous fiction on the topic wasn't completely useless after all. But more importantly, the Kats had embedded in the dragons a way to control them. To give them commands they were compelled to follow. How, she wondered, had they done so?

Regardless, the point was, she wasn't leaping blindly ahead, heedless of the dangers. She was *working the problem.*

If The Voice took note, it didn't say so. Her new approach toward her self/companion, guided by her mother's advice, was yielding a little success, if only in fits and starts. The Voice was easily as petulant as Marlee had been as a child, and it wasn't giving up without a fight. But there *was* progress— not so much in The Voice's barbs, but in her responses to them. She was taking the criticism in stride, and occasionally even listening to it. It was a difficult notion to accept, but it was possible she had a few things to teach herself.

Cupcake spread his wings in a bonanza of vermillion scales and bright polka-dots, batted them downward, and rose into the air. He banked around in a low circle and, as he closed in on Barney from behind, let loose a torrent of smoke that contained noticeably more fire than it used to.

Barney growled, unharmed, and lifted his long neck to return the fire, and the sparring escalated.

Still think you're going to ride that dragon?

Yes, I do.

He will kill you.

Not if I handle him the right way. I can do this.

33

EARTH

GREATER VANCOUVER

Miriam awoke quickly, as she nearly always did. A dream involving playing tennis in Paris against a team of young Khokteh women while a hot rain poured down on them faded into oblivion as she opened her eyes. Outside the window, a steel gray sky begrudgingly began to give up the night. She'd woken before the dawn again.

So long as there wasn't an active emergency in progress, she made certain to get sufficient sleep every night, albeit the bare minimum of what qualified as 'sufficient.' She could not afford to be lazy for a single moment.

Not even on a Sunday morning that was, for most citizens, a holiday. Concord Day honored the signing of the charter by the eight founding species fifteen years ago. The ceremony had signaled the start of a new era of peace and prosperity; a closing of the door on the old Anaden Empire in favor of something which strove to be…better. Fairer.

She smiled to herself as she watched a wren land on the balcony railing, breakfast struggling in its beak. She was proud of what she'd helped to create that day, and immeasurably more proud of what it had become in the intervening years. The institution had survived three rebellions and an attempted coup, not to mention all the squabbling and growing pains attached to managing the wildly diverging interests of multiple alien species.

As a tentative ray of light fought through the cloud cover to disperse through the pine needles outside, she decided all over again that she would not let the Rasu tear it all down. Somehow, some way.

"Mmm…." David scooted up behind her to drape an arm over her waist and rest his chin on her shoulder. "Good morning, *dushen'ka.*"

"What if I'm still asleep?"

"You're never still asleep."

She snuggled closer against him. "I slept plenty. Besides, I need to get to the office soon. Emerald started moving on all the remaining smaller factions at once last night. This might be the beginning of the final act."

"*Da.*" He kissed her ear, then rolled back to stretch his arms above his head. "We're ready."

She shifted around to face him. "You mean we're as ready as we can be."

"You've done an amazing job of forestalling this day far past when it should have occurred. You know, it's funny....."

He didn't elaborate, and she arched an eyebrow. "Pray tell, what's funny?"

"We've neutralized the Gardiens threat, and its leader is on the run. You and Alex have reconciled, which soothes my heart beyond measure. It feels like you've cleared the decks. No distractions, no personal struggles to weigh you down. When I said 'we're ready,' I didn't just mean militarily. I meant, *we're ready. You're* ready."

She brought a hand to his cheek, enjoying the tickle of his stubble on her palm. "I hope you're right. But hope is not a plan, so I shall choose to believe you're right."

The warmth in his gaze, and especially the tease of his fingertips as they trailed down her back, made her long to stay in bed for a time. But war awaited them both. So instead she kissed him thoroughly enough to evoke a rumble of approval in his throat, then climbed out of bed, retrieved her robe, and headed for the shower.

RW

CONCORD HQ
RASU WAR ROOM

Once Emerald began making its moves, events happened with astonishing speed. While the members of the War Council sat at the conference table and watched, the territories of Bronze and Teal shrunk away to nothing and disappeared on the map (thanks to real-time observation by a team of Kats and bolstered by strategically situated Ghost surveillance craft). Perhaps the smaller factions recognized they were doomed and gave up without much of a fight?

Ten hours after Emerald began its offensive, Crimson followed suit within its arena of influence. It faced a greater number of stragglers, and one or two took a few bites out of its rear flank during the battles. But by the time evening arrived on HQ, the last vessels of the last holdouts were falling to the considerable firepower of Crimson.

The map refreshed as a working dinner was brought in, and Miriam nudged her plate to the side to clasp her hands at her chin and consider the new world order in Rasu space.

Opposite her, Alex scowled darkly. "And then there were three. I expect we'll find out soon what Stygian's true intentions are."

Beside her, David made a hedging motion with one hand while gathering wild rice on his fork with the other. "Don't be so sure. Stygian could choose to wait until the last possible minute to reveal itself."

"Or wait until Emerald and Crimson are embroiled in an all-out war with each other, then swoop in."

David nodded approvingly. "That's what I would do. A three-way conflict is more chaotic, the tactical decisions far more complicated. Every action has a cost on another flank. But, engaging in one also risks burning up crucial resources too soon, leaving you weakened and exposed when the conflict comes to a head. It's a tough call."

Miriam forced a slight smile. "Well, they will make the call without our input, but not without our knowledge."

Malcolm reappeared in his holo space; he'd been dropping in and out all day. "As soon as the chaos erupts, whether there are two players or three, it might be a good time to make a fresh round of strategic Ymyrath Field hits."

"It might be. But I think…" the variables raced around in Miriam's head "…so long as Stygian remains on the sidelines, we wait. Because they're waiting. Crimson has grown significantly in strength, and at this point they and Emerald are fairly evenly matched. They should be heading into a protracted, costly conflict, which will work to our benefit. Regardless, we must remain vigilant, ready to move the instant an opening appears."

RW

It shouldn't have surprised Miriam that David's gut instinct was spot on. He'd once made a fine career out of understanding how the enemy thought and using it against them.

Emerald and Crimson had barely stopped to catch their breath before turning on each other, and the long-awaited clash of giants began in earnest. And when hundreds of millions of Rasu vessels across four galaxies were engaged in pitched battle, an inky darkness surged out of the far reaches of the Shapley Supercluster to invade the battlespace.

Alex had been correct, once again. It had always been a fool's hope to believe Stygian could be of a peaceful bent, Miriam supposed. Instead, they were now proving to be the most diabolical of all Rasu.

Stygian's comparative strength became apparent within a few short hours. Over the last several months, Miriam had developed a feel for the ebb and flow of Rasu engagements, simply by watching them from afar. Now, though, that rhythm had been completely upended. Wherever vessels clashed, none stood for long beneath the force of a Stygian incursion.

Nika Kirumase reported that in the opening hours of Stygian's offensive, both Emerald and Crimson expressed confusion bordering on panic. Had they not expected Stygian to get involved? Had some non-aggression arrangement been agreed to that Stygian now violated? The information remained out of their reach and, honestly, Miriam couldn't bring herself to care. They were all Rasu, and thus her enemy.

In the regions far from Stygian territory, Emerald and Crimson battled one another with increased fervor, perhaps desperate to gain control of the other's assets in order to use them against this new aggressor. Both sides had amassed great swaths of territory in the civil war, and no matter how strong Stygian proved to be, they would not be able to defeat both challengers overnight.

As David had noted, a three-way war was chaotic and complex, and her gut told her it was time to add to that chaos. When Stygian arrived to disrupt an ongoing encounter between Emerald and Crimson, Miriam saw her chance. She activated a comm channel.

"Commander Xing, I want every Ymyrath Field vessel to sneak into the battle at the coordinates I'm transmitting and fire right into the heart of it. Kill all the ships as they're destroying one another."

The feed from this particular engagement transferred to the primary screen, and Miriam's brow furrowed as she tried to discern who, if anyone, was winning. It reminded her of the early days of the First Crux War, when half the Federation ships were stolen Alliance ships, and from the outside it was impossible to tell friend from foe. Today, over twenty million Rasu vessels battled one another across three connected star systems, and the visual they created was utter bedlam.

Luckily, it didn't matter which side her ships fired upon. They were likely to hit at least two sides regardless, serving to increase confusion and hopefully giving all the combatants reason to be looking over their shoulders in concern.

The now-ten Ymyrath Field vessels fired into the very heart of the clash, and it was as if a massive sinkhole had opened up in the middle of the battlefield. Everything inside a wide expanse of space soon drifted aimlessly, defanged and defenseless.

Her ships weren't able to fire while stealthed, and they came under sustained assault the instant they became visible. No Rasu used antimatter, however, presumably because it would have constituted friendly fire as well, and the ships were able to survive long enough to discharge their weapons and make an escape.

"Commander Xing, move at once to the adjacent star system and repeat the maneuver."

Pinpoint jumps positioned the Ymyrath Field vessels in the center of this clash, where they deposited a coordinated strike then moved on to the next hotspot, and the battlefield soon grew pockmarked with dead zones into which the Rasu dared not venture. The offensives of each side grew wary. Hesitant.

She chose another ongoing battle among the three factions and ordered the Ymyrath Field group to disrupt it next. It was going to be a long, stressful day for the ship captains.

In the end, the direct impact of her intervention was minimal in absolute terms, for the Rasu numbers were, as always, utterly overwhelming. But with luck, she'd introduced a sobering bit of caution into the minds of the combatants. Caution slowed down decision-making. It kept fleets in port and out of her backyard.

34

AKESO

Scalding water beat down upon Caleb's head. He kept it bowed low, his chin touching his chest, and allowed the water to stream down his neck and back.

On the fringes of his consciousness, Akeso murmured excitedly about the new species of plant life it was integrating into itself on Hirlas, and the unusual variety of stone that made up the planet's northernmost mountains, and its attempts to capture a Volucri and comprehend its unique genetic—

No, don't do that.

Whyever not? The Volucri are a part of Hirlas, as much as the plants and stones are. The planet nurtured them into sentience.

In a sense, yes. But they are independent life forms with their own conscious minds. They are from *Hirlas, but they are not* of *Hirlas. You can't subsume them into yourself. It would be infringing upon their rights as sapient beings.*

Such distinctions remain difficult for Akeso to comprehend. Life is life, is it not? But if you wish it, I will content myself with observing their flight patterns and eating habits.

I do. Thank you.

The brief interruption had shaken Caleb out of his stupor, so he tilted his face up into the water and tried to make peace with what he was planning to do today. Akeso was an innocent soul, but he was not, and he was capable of taking this burden upon himself. The nugget of an idea that had sprung to life when he'd visited Hirlas had refused to be silenced, and he had an obligation to see where it led.

He finished up his morning routine, toweled off and slipped into charcoal work pants and a black henley.

He found Alex in the office studying the most recent map of Rasu activity. She'd been doing so with increasing regularity since her and Nika's foray into Stygian territory. "Any news?"

"Our Ymyrath Field strikes seem to have given all three factions something to think about. They've settled back into a holding pattern for the moment."

"That's good."

"Not good enough." She grimaced and waved half-heartedly toward the table to close the map. "Are you ready to go?"

He nodded vaguely.

Her expression softened; she came up to him and brought a hand to his cheek. "I'm here if you want to talk. I know this isn't going to be easy for you."

He breathed her in, reveling in the feel of her skin pressing against his and her scent of mint and spiced coffee. He'd always drawn such strength from her presence, and today, he found he needed that strength. "You're wrong. If I've discovered a way to kill Rasu where they stand, then this is the easiest thing I've ever done."

"Liar."

"Hmm." He kissed her softly. "Let's go."

RW

ADJUNCT SHI
ASTERION DOMINION

The Rasu containment facility had been constructed in the middle of a vast flatland twenty kilometers from the colony's only major city. A force field shimmered in a dome shape encompassing the squarish building, and a single entry point was staffed by two DAF officers and a 3-meter-high mech half as wide as it was tall.

Caleb couldn't imagine why someone would ever try to sneak inside the facility and unleash its prisoners, but he supposed even Asterions counted the occasional psychopath among their own.

Dashiel and Nika met them outside the checkpoint, and they exchanged casual greetings.

Caleb tilted his head toward the facility. "Heavy security."

"You haven't seen half of it," Dashiel replied. "Inside the force field, a Kireme Boundary is active. Beyond the checkpoint is a d-gate that will enable us to bypass the Boundary and reach the interior without being tossed into the local sun."

"You're still using stationary d-gate technology, even though Asterions can open their own wormholes?" Alex asked.

"We can't risk someone getting their intended destination a little off the mark and catching the Boundary."

"Ah. Good point."

Dashiel cleared them through the checkpoints, and one by one they traversed the d-gate, which deposited them just outside the entrance to the building proper. There, additional security awaited them, and it took another five minutes to make it inside.

"Down the left hall are data analysis labs, where scientists study the output from the Rasu. We've come a long way in our understanding of how they function, but there's always more we can learn. A lot more. To the right are the security offices. But the majority of the building is devoted to the cages."

One final security check, and they stepped into the prison.

Rasu-enemy.

Yes. The Asterions captured these prisoners during the battle on Mirai a few months ago. Here, they try to understand their enemy.

What is there to understand about them? They want only to control and devour.

Had Akeso seen all the way into the depths of the Rasu soul when it silenced them on Hirlas? *True. But studying how they accomplish those things can help us better protect ourselves against them.*

On the left side of the large, warehouse-style room sat two enormous glass enclosures surrounded by multiple force fields. Each held a large quantity of Rasu material. He characterized it this way because neither held a definable solid shape. Instead, a viscous substance slithered and undulated around the enclosures. Were they agitated? Relentlessly searching for a way to escape?

On the right side of the room, a row of much smaller enclosures held multiple scaled-down Rasu samples, though their behavior was the same. Each one was the size of a…it was difficult to tell with all the slithering. Perhaps a large dog?

Dashiel indicated the row on the right. "We've sliced these samples off the big ones. They evolved into their own distinct if similarly cranky Rasu entities, but they're easier and safer to work with."

"How did you manage to separate them and get them into new enclosures?" Caleb asked.

"By doping the donor using a temporary virutox to slow down its reaction time. Then moving very rapidly. Much like we're going to do today. We have the virutox queued up for you on the cage at this end of the row."

Caleb shook his head. "No."

"I'm sorry?"

"If this is to be a genuine test, it needs to match real-world conditions as closely as possible. You know this."

Dashiel scowled at the cage and its contents. "Of course, but there's also your life to think about. A cubic meter of Rasu can slice you into pieces in seconds."

Alex laid a hand on his arm. "Dashiel's right. Let him drug it."

"No. I'll be fine. I've done my share of slicing these things up myself."

"I know, but—"

He gave her a reassuring smile. "We have to be sure. There can't be any doubt."

She squeezed her eyes shut and pinched the bridge of her nose. "Okay. Do your thing. Don't die."

"If you're certain. It's your skin." Dashiel led them toward the first enclosure on the row. "You'll step up as close as you can, then I'll instantiate two force fields around you and the cage before deactivating the one blocking your access. The mechanical arm behind the cage will remove the lid, and it'll be you and the Rasu inside the force fields. If things go south, I can zap everything inside with a massive electrical jolt that will disable the Rasu long enough for the arm to administer the virutox, but you'll get hit by the jolt, too." He looked grim. "Military protocol says I can't deactivate the force fields until the Rasu is secure in its cage. No matter what."

"Whoa, hold on for a minute," Alex protested indignantly.

Caleb nodded, though. "I understand. I won't allow you to risk everyone in the building for me. And don't worry about the jolt. Akeso will hardly be phased by a bit of electricity."

"I assumed as much." They reached a yellow line painted on the floor ten meters out from the cage. "Alex, stand back behind this line with Nika and me." Dashiel gestured to Caleb. "Whenever you're ready, we'll get started."

"Give me one second."

He focused on the undulating Rasu metal in front of him. *You see and acknowledge this Rasu here.*

Yes. It is our enemy and the enemy of all life.

It is. We need to try to kill it, the way you killed the Rasu on Hirlas.

It is a threat to us?

He took a great deal of comfort from the fact this was always the relevant question for Akeso. *If it ever escapes from its cage, yes, as all Rasu are. It will try to murder any life it comes across.*

I comprehend this. But I cannot reach it from here.

He chuckled under his breath. *I know. In a minute, I'm going to be able to touch it. Or I'm going to try. The instant I make physical contact, I need you to do as we discussed. Quickly, please, for it will not idly wait around for us to act against it.*

It will attack us?

I expect so, yes.

I am ready.

Caleb looked back over his shoulder and jerked a nod at Dashiel, then strode up to the force field.

The hairs on his arms stood at attention as new force fields burst to life behind him. A few seconds later, the one in front of him petered out. As he stepped up to the glass enclosure, he recalled the ominous aura of the Rasu saboteurs they'd secured in the hold of the *Siyane*. This room was brightly lit and this prisoner much smaller, but he felt the malevolence emanating from it all the same.

Noticing his presence, the Rasu pooled along the glass closest to him and began climbing up it like an octopus. It saw prey…but so did he.

"I'm sending the arm in. Be ready."

He fondled the hilt of his plasma blade in his right hand, his thumb running over the activation button, as he lifted his left hand to hover above the enclosure. In the corner of his eye, the robotic arm attached two circular suction pads to the top of the glass, and lights on a small control pad lit up. The glass lifted up and away—

The Rasu shot up through the opening as an elongated bullet, but Caleb was moving, too. He activated his blade and arced it in sideways while he grabbed the slippery metal with his left hand. *Now!*

The part of the Rasu that had escaped the still-moving glass top solidified into a razor-sharp knife and sliced open his palm as it pushed the rest of the way out. He cut off a chunk with his blade, but it immediately re-formed—

A heady wooziness overtook him; strange not-quite-thoughts wove through his mind, and he felt the surges of electrical impulses between atoms.

Focus! Akeso, you must act.

The Rasu knife extended and stabbed him in the shoulder, scraping across bone, and blood gushed out from the gash. Somewhere, Alex shouted his name, but it sounded parsecs away.

A great *explosion* thundered through his mind and set his nerves afire. The Rasu melted and slipped out of his grasp, falling to the floor, where it didn't move—except for the piece he'd sliced off a second earlier. That Rasu shot forward, sharpened, and stabbed his foot. With a yelp he reached down and grabbed it in his fist. Another reverberation detonated in his mind, and the Rasu transformed into a lump of metal in his grip. Passive and unmoving.

The dizziness abated, and he gave a weak thumbs-up to a horrified Alex without taking his eyes off the two lumps of now-inert Rasu.

Dashiel cleared his throat awkwardly. "Um, okay. If you will please return all the Rasu pieces to the cage. We need to close it up before we can get you out of there."

"Right. Protocol." He dropped the piece he still held back into the enclosure, then crouched painfully to pick up the larger piece.

We are healing. Move slowly.

Because Akeso had transitioned from killing to healing in an instant, as naturally as it performed every other act. Two sides of the same coin.

The pain in his shoulder was already easing by the time he stood up, gazing curiously at the mass of metal he held in his hands. Misshapen, cool to the touch, and exuding not an ounce of malevolence. Just metal.

He deposited it in the enclosure, and the robotic arm swept in to methodically seal everything up. He waited patiently as the security procedures reversed themselves, until Alex was hugging him while inspecting every vanishing injury. "Madman."

"It's why you love me."

"Among other, safer reasons." She frowned at the tear in his henley that exposed fresh, healed skin, then shook her head wryly and took half a step back.

He turned to the others. "As best I can tell, it worked. That's a dead Rasu in there. Two, I guess."

Dashiel nodded. "We'll run all the same tests on them we did on the samples from Hirlas to confirm. But I suspect I know what the results are going to be."

"So do I." He supposed it was time to make an update to his epitaph.

Killer. Lover. Dragonslayer. Razer of worlds. Annihilator of monsters.

Everyone stood there staring at the twin lumps of metal for several long seconds. Finally Nika asked, "How is Akeso feeling about this?"

"Unfazed. You know, when I first met Akeso, it had no concept of death. In fact, its only concept of life was itself. Later, I tried to imbue into it the concepts of evil and violence, so it could protect itself. It resisted pretty hard. But then, Ekos-1 one sent its moon to attack—"

"The Dzhvar-infused planet, correct?"

"Correct. For the first time, Akeso faced the possibility of its own mortality. And like most sentient beings, it responded by doing what it had to do in order to survive, which in this case meant killing its enemy before Akeso itself perished.

"Ironically, that act led to Akeso treasuring life even more than it did before. Its own and every instance it's come across since—until the Rasu. When I physically touched a Rasu the first time, on the Ourankeli's Haelwyeur ring, Akeso instantly recognized it for what it was: an enemy and a threat to all life. So while Akeso abhors violence and always puts me through the wringer when I have to commit it, it doesn't resist violence against the Rasu."

"Why do you think this is?" Nika asked.

"For some reason, Akeso can sense Rasu thoughts in a way it doesn't for most beings it interacts with on a superficial level. I can't explain how it works or why it's the case."

Alex opened her mouth as if to interrupt—and closed it again.

"What is it?"

She shook her head. "Nothing. Keep talking."

"It's not merely the thoughts, either. Akeso professes to be able to see into the soul of the Rasu, and what it perceives there is dark. Abhorrent. Malignant."

"Wow." Nika ran her fingers through her hair. "Since the Rasu started integrating kyoseil into their physicality, I've had a somewhat similar experience—sensing internal Rasu thoughts and inclinations—and I have to say I agree with Akeso."

"Their actions certainly back up those impressions." Caleb's attention was drawn to the rest of the enclosures on the row. The encounter had caused the other captive Rasu to grow more agitated. They writhed and threw themselves at the top of the glass in a desperate bid to escape.

"The thing is, this *talent* of Akeso's seems to be localized. The other specimens were unaffected, which means it requires physical contact." He sighed. "Sending me onto the battlefield to touch a hundred million Rasu one by one is not a winning strategy. Neither is me turning every inhabited planet into the living embodiment of Akeso." He forced a good-natured smirk. "I don't have that much blood."

Alex snaked an arm around his waist. "No, you do not. Banish the notion."

Caleb's gaze drifted toward the two large Rasu across the room—then he realized Nika was staring at him, her brilliant teal irises aswirl with turmoil. "Nika, what's on your mind?"

Instead of answering, she wrenched her attention away from him to pace in a ragged circle around the three of them. Halfway through her second pass, she abruptly crouched low to the floor and balanced her elbows on her knees, bringing her hands up to cover her face.

Dashiel hurried over, dropping to his knees in front of her. "What's wrong? Talk to me."

She rested her head on his chest, and they murmured to one another in hushed tones.

Alex acted as if she wanted to approach them, but Caleb folded his hand over hers at his waist to stay her.

They'll speak up if they need us.

I know, but she looks so heartbroken.

After almost a minute had passed, Dashiel kissed the top of Nika's head, and they both stood.

Nika wiped a tear off her cheek, her countenance grim. "I think I might know how to kill the Rasu—all of them. And I think you do, too, Caleb."

"A...possibility had occurred to me. If today's test hadn't worked, though, it wouldn't have mattered."

"But it did work." She exhaled heavily and squeezed Dashiel's hand. "Let's go see Lance. We need to capture ourselves a couple of kyoseil-linked Rasu."

35

AKESO

*V*alkyrie, what's the word? Have you got a bead on Mesme?
I believe I do. However, there is an incongruity.
What is it?
The location where my scan insists Mesme currently resides doesn't exist. Or rather, it is simply empty space near an ordinary orange G4 V star in Quadrant II of the Cetus Dwarf galaxy. Nothing of note is transpiring in the system.

Well, perhaps Mesme is floating around in empty space. It's been known to happen.

True enough. Shall we check and see?

Yes, let's.

When Valkyrie had noticed a few months ago that each Katasketousya's presence gave off a unique energy signature, Alex had tasked her with developing a way to pinpoint the locations of such signatures. For Mesme most of all, but they'd also taken note of the signatures of Praetor Lakhes and that asshole Hyperion, just in case.

Even after months of work on Valkyrie's part, it wasn't a perfect or easy system. It wasn't as though one could place a tracker dot on a Kat and always know where they were. Instead, if one wanted to learn their location, Valkyrie had to run the search program she'd written on potential regions of space in the hope of picking up the energy signature. Because Mesme was so intimately, and sneakily, involved in Concord and Dominion affairs, the number of galaxies where it could be loitering at any given moment was not small. But manageable.

The Cetus Dwarf galaxy housed the relocated Katasketousya homeworld, so it always ranked high on the list of places to check. The middle of empty space, though?

Alex abandoned the chair on the patio and stood. She opened a wormhole to the spot Valkyrie had identified and, somewhat to her surprise, discovered grasses of a sunlit glade languidly waving in a breeze on the other side.

Middle of empty space, huh?

Apparently not.

She stepped through the wormhole.

UNKNOWN PLANET
CETUS DWARF GALAXY

Ahead of her, a path cut through a modest mountainside and disappeared around a corner. To her right, a beautiful lake of glacier-blue waters sparkled in the sunshine. And above the lake glided Mesme, its winged avatar stretching for over forty meters in a panorama of brilliant light.

She acknowledged the rush of déjà vu the scene conjured, then set it aside. "Mesme! You have a visitor!"

The lights curled in on themselves, and the next instant they hovered directly in front of her in a challenging stance. *How is it that you are here?*

"You mean standing on a planet that's hidden by a stealth-enabled Rift Bubble and looks a shocking amount like Portal Prime? Cleverness, as usual."

Naturally. The lights quavered then solidified into a roughly humanoid form. *Curious as I am as to how you discovered this place, a more pertinent question is, 'why' are you here? Has a cataclysmic event escaped my notice?*

"No. But you've been avoiding me. I assume so you aren't forced to answer the questions we left open the last time we talked, but we'll get to those. The civil war acts as if it's nearing a resolution, and I have questions about the Rasu I need answered. So I decided to come find you."

I see. Regarding the civil war, Stygian will soon renew its offensive against the remaining factions.

"I know."

They amassed tremendous power while the others fought amongst themselves. They are a most formidable foe.

"I know."

Mesme's light danced in front of her, demanding her attention. *Caleb holds the key to defeating them.*

"I *know.*"

You do?

"Yes. We just ran a most interesting experiment on some Rasu the Asterions captured. Caleb and Akeso were able to kill a Rasu via touch, exactly as Akeso did on Hirlas."

This is heartening news, but Caleb cannot touch every Rasu in existence.

"No, he can't. He and Nika are reluctantly exploring some possibilities. Very reluctantly."

Perhaps you should encourage their endeavors.

"I've done what I can, but this isn't easy for either of them. We need to be patient."

We do not have much time remaining for patience.

"I *know*." Did Mesme not get how she'd been repeatedly having this same conversation with herself?

It appears you already possess all the knowledge you need. Why seek me out?

"For confirmation, I suppose. Confirmation that Stygian is in fact the big bad who's coming for us. Confirmation that, once again, the man I love is going to have to rip his soul wide open in order to save us."

I am sorry this is so.

"I...appreciate the sentiment. I did want to ask you some questions about the Erebus Void and how it came to exist—again, seeking confirmation really—but now that I'm here, I'm more interested in what's down this path." Abruptly she spun and began striding into the cleft cutting into the mountain.

Alex, it is not necessary—

"Oh, I think it is." The path was wider than it appeared on first inspection, as well as shorter. As soon as she rounded the corner, she found herself standing in front of a single-story house constructed of amber-hued wood. Flowers lined a stone-paved walkway leading to an open front door.

She crossed her arms over her chest and cast a sideways glance at the lights fluttering in agitation off to her left. "Just like on Portal Prime. Mesme, is this your secret home?"

"No. It is mine."

She jumped at the sound of a warbling voice coming from the entryway. At first she saw nothing, but after a few seconds, a shadow emerged from the...shadows...to approach her.

Miaon, why would you—

"It is time, Mnemosyne. She is ready."

Miaon, right. She'd only met the Yinhe on three or four occasions over the last fifteen years; she could be forgiven for not instantly putting a name with a shadow.

"Whatever 'it' is, the Yinhe is correct. I'm ready for it. But I confess I don't quite understand. Miaon, you're saying this house is *yours*? It's an exact replica of the house Mesme built on Portal Prime."

"Yes, it is."

When she and Caleb had encountered the little house, they'd speculated that Mesme had built it in order to try to better relate to the humans it watched over. But given what she now knew about Mesme's history, what if they were wrong? What if, instead, the house was a totem? A symbol of tangibility. A link to the past....

Her mind darted back to their conversation a few weeks ago on Akeso, about how Mesme knew so much about earlier cycles. *The only person who could have such information would be someone who had experienced the events of the previous cycles.*

"Oh my god. You, Miaon?"

Alex, you know?

"Of course she does, Mnemosyne. She is, as she admits, most clever indeed." The shadow undulated in the bright sunlight. "But perhaps she would like to elaborate?"

"You're the prior version of Mesme. The one who experienced the cycle before this one...as Mesme. Which means you experienced the cycle before that one as whoever you both were...before." Damn, this time travel nonsense was enough to give her a migraine.

"It is true."

"Okay. But why are you a shadow—a Yinhe? Why are you not a Kat?"

The edges of Miaon's form began to dissipate. "Having provoked this epiphany and given our mutual friend a moment to recover from the shock, I believe Mnemosyne is better suited to answer your questions. Goodbye for now." The shadow vanished.

She whirled around until she spotted the clump of lights contrasting against the mountain face behind her. "Why? To throw off suspicion? To enable Miaon to act as another provocateur meddling in our affairs?"

Because a shadow is all that remained of me following a second traversal of the time rift.

The heart-wrenching sorrow bleeding out of the voice as it reverberated in her head caused her to sink onto the stoop of the house. She tempered the bite out of her voice. "Explain, please."

The traversal of a time rift is a uniquely brutal experience. No living soul, no conscious being composed of matter, was ever meant to navigate such a chasm.

"But you're not composed of matter."

I am. This manifestation you perceive as discrete lights is an expression of atoms. Atoms exist in the world as matter. Still, it is a pittance compared to....

"…compared to what you were when you went through the tear in the manifold the first time. And on a second traversal, it ripped away everything else?"

Leaving only a shadow. A whisper of a thought of a consciousness.

"Then why did Miaon do it?"

Because I needed the help. If we were to have any chance of emerging victorious, I needed a guiding hand to help point the way. To correct me when I ventured off course. Above all, to provide counsel so I do not make the same mistakes they did.

"And occasionally, to be where you could not and do what you dared not. I know Miaon was the one who convinced Eren to help Caleb and me when we first came to Amaranthe."

Indeed. Eren did not trust me, to say the least. But Miaon had been building their relationship for some time, in preparation for when it would be needed. If you did not gain access to the Machim military secrets, AEGIS would not have defeated the Directorate. Humanity would not have come to Amaranthe, and so—

"And so would not be here to combat the Rasu. Puppets and strings."

That is not how I think of you. Any of you.

"And yet. So there's no such thing as a Yinhe 'species,' then? Their existence was all smoke and mirrors designed to fool the Directorate—and everyone else?"

Yes.

In a way, she'd been right in her initial assessment. Miaon had acted as another meddling provocateur. But the cost? It must be beyond reckoning.

"What if we lose? Does Miaon represent your fate? To do this all again? To live through another million years, this time existing as nothing but ghostly thought?"

It will be my choice. Nothing forces my hand, except the will to see life survive. And thus it is no choice at all.

"Why do you think Miaon wanted me to know its identity?" She started to correct herself by clarifying that Mesme obviously knew the answer, but it wasn't true. Miaon was not Mesme's past or present, but rather its future. God, that was bleak.

She felt a surge of guilt for every cruel thing she'd ever said to Mesme. It was an infuriating, impossible scoundrel of a friend, but it had given up more than anyone in history simply to save them, and it faced the prospect of giving up immeasurably more.

Miaon has the benefit of an additional million years of wisdom. I trust in this. Possibly it believed the best course of action was for you to have your questions answered now, so you may turn the entirety of your intellect and reasoning toward winning the battle which looms on the horizon.

Well, there was still *one* question unanswered—who it was today—but she couldn't bring herself to harangue Mesme about it. "Or possibly to impress upon me in stark terms the gravity of the conflict being waged here. How unfathomably long it's been waged for. And the magnitude of the sacrifices that have already been made in the waging of it."

Whether Miaon intended it or not, the weight in your voice tells me this revelation had such an effect.

"You could say so. My heart breaks for Caleb and what he may need to do. But if my resolve to ensure he does it nonetheless might have wavered, it can't now, can it? How can I measure his sacrifice against your own?"

Your words soothe me, my forecia novicia. *But this is not a competition, and my heart breaks for Caleb as well. And for Nika, who stands upon the threshold of her own impossible choice. And for Miriam, who carries the weight of three trillion lives upon her shoulders. And for you.*

"For me? My job is easy."

No. You have the hardest job of all. You always have. The continued existence of all living things depends on you gazing out into the universe and understanding it. On you being right, one more time.

PART III

THE
KNIFE EDGE

36

EARTH
CHICAGO

Malcolm slid quietly onto one of the pews near the back of the Holy Name Cathedral sanctuary. It was sparsely occupied; half a dozen people sat scattered among the pews, each one engaged in their own prayerful contemplation. A priest carefully arranged the chalice and ciborium upon the altar in advance of the evening service. Off to the left, a bot cleaned a row of stained-glass windows.

Malcolm clasped his hands at his chin and let the silent reverence of the sanctuary settle over him.

He was free. Strange to think that his biggest challenge these last few months hadn't been preparing for a renewed Rasu invasion, but instead maintaining his charade with Enzio Vilane. But it was done, and the tremendous millstone weighing down his conscience for so long was now cast aside.

Looking back, it seemed impossible to believe there had been a point in time when he'd almost supported the Gardiens' cause. When he'd walked into their meeting in Seattle and felt a kinship with the people in the audience *and* the ones speaking at the podium. It sickened him how the Gardiens had so polluted the moral quandary of regenesis with violence and vile lies.

Their actions had, however, helped to clarify some of his complex, often contradictory feelings on the subject by bringing reality into sharp relief.

Regenesis worked. It worked so well that the Gardiens had been forced to sabotage procedures in order to create the illusion that it didn't. The people whom regenesis brought back weren't zombies or ghouls or golems. They were the same people they'd been before their untimely deaths. Many of them struggled to regain their footing following the procedure, but the very struggle revealed how their morality and sense of self had survived intact.

He didn't understand how it was possible. It shouldn't be, and the fact that it was—that a thorough scientific recording of a person's brain in motion, combined with their genetic blueprint, was sufficient to replicate the person in their entirety—was enough to shake one's faith in the existence of a spiritual soul.

But he wasn't going to let it. This wasn't how faith worked, for one. Belief in God wasn't about adhering to rigid dogma against all evidence of a reasoned mind—a mind which was itself a gift from said higher power. As they had on many occasions recently, Richard's take on the issue wound through his mind.

> "A person who is revived via medical intervention after their heart or brain activity has ceased was dead, too. Sure, the body's the same in those cases, but the body's merely scenery when you're discussing a spiritual soul.
>
> "The point is this: I'm not privy to God's perspective, or their plan. I think they want us to grow and develop and reach ever outward as we struggle to become better people who are more worthy of their grace. They endowed us with these finicky brains for a reason, and on the whole we've made reasonably good use of them. What if regenesis is the next step in our guided evolution?"

He'd resisted the notion at the time, but it made more sense every day, with every interaction he'd had with the reawakened. The evidence was right there in front of him, and shutting his eyes to it didn't make it any less true.

His gaze went to the cross displayed above the altar, taking a minute to acknowledge the symbolism and sacrifice it represented.

He'd never been afraid to die. He'd be a terrible Christian and a worse Marine if he was. He wasn't looking for an escape clause...rather than rush past the declaration, he checked himself; no, he truly wasn't. He only wanted to live his life to the fullest, with honor and humility, using his talents to protect people from the evils of the world to the greatest extent possible. For as long as possible. And the thing was, he didn't want to retire from his mission ahead of his time if retiring was not required.

Had his insistence that a soul only crossed the threshold once, in a single direction, been nothing more than an all-too-human, fallible assumption? An arrogant assertion that he knew best how God and the afterlife worked? Or was it spiritual truth? He genuinely did not know.

The Church continued to hold fast to this belief. For now, their declaration naming regenesis an abomination remained unretracted. But should they later loosen their stance, it would hardly be the first instance where the arrival of a more 'enlightened' interpretation upended historical Church doctrine. God was infallible, but the Church was not.

The choice had warred in his mind in recent days, and finally it seemed to him the only thing to do was go to the source. Hence the pew.

He closed his eyes and opened his heart in a prayer of thanks and supplication. And as his lips formed the silent words of the prayer, he at last found a measure of peace.

RW

The cool, damp breeze of a spring Chicago morning greeted Malcolm as he exited the church and headed down the sidewalk toward the nearest levtram station. He had a meeting with Field Marshal Bastian in an hour to discuss the defense array buildouts on Federation worlds, then a performance review of the newly reorganized fast-attack divisions. He chuckled to himself; despite her vehement protestations, Morgan Lekkas had wasted no time taking over a hefty chunk of the fighter craft division. Though their personalities often (usually) clashed, he could not deny she was a damn fine pilot. Actually a pretty skilled leader of pilots, too.

A special alert flashed in his eVi, and his pulse quickened. He'd forcibly restrained himself from comming Mia the instant he'd been set free of the Gardiens' pit of demons, telling himself he should wait until Vilane was captured by the authorities. But the logic—or possibly his willpower—was weakening by the day. Vilane remained at large, and thus remained a risk to her. But the man surely had bigger problems now than seeking spiteful revenge. Vilane was on the run, cut off from his wealth and resources and unable to so much as raise his head above a hedge. He was defanged.

And now Mia had made the decision for Malcolm. Fortuitous coincidence, indeed.

A flutter in his chest, whether from excitement or nervousness, accompanied him opening the message.

> *Malcolm,*
>
> *I find I don't know how or where to begin. I took your reply to my last message to heart, and I've respected your wishes to not see me since then. It was hard, but it has given me the opportunity to dig down and root out what I really wanted from this life. For myself, for the world, for us.*

I asked you to give me time to try to relearn who I was without you. Time to stand on my own. I admit I got more time than I wanted, but it's been good for me. I feel like I've achieved what I set out to do. The Expo is a success. I've proved I can still make business and philanthropy work together, and I'd like to think I've improved our world a little in the process. I've reclaimed my good (if slightly tarnished) name and built new alliances and even friendships. I've indeed stood on my own two feet.

And through it all, I've missed you so damn much. My heart splits in two whenever I think about you, about our years together. And at the end of the day—this day, more or less—I find I simply don't care about regenesis any longer.

I mean, of course I care. I want to spend eternity with you. But if I can't do so, I want to spend today with you, and tomorrow, and however many tomorrows we have left. The Rasu may kill us all in a grand conflagration any minute now, and what would have been the point of my selfish ultimatum then? I would have spent my last days without you, and it would be the greatest tragedy of my life.

Do I wish you'd change your mind about regenesis? I do, and I always will. But I will take whatever time is left to us to have you in my life. I've made peace with the uncertainty of tomorrow. And I respect your beliefs. They're a huge part of who you are and what makes you special.

I don't know if you want to hear any of this. Until a few days ago, I believed you'd closed this door once and for all, and I'd accepted that I deserved such a reaction. It was of my doing.

But now I understand maybe, just maybe, the door wasn't closed. Left ajar, perhaps. And so I'm sending this message out of an irrational, buoyant hope that you'll say yes.

To lunch, that is.
All my love,
— Mia

Malcolm laughed, a hearty, full-bodied, *free* laugh. His own message to her sat half-composed in his eVi. He'd need to make a few revisions to it now.

How was it that, after all these months and so much pain, they'd each come to the other, each given ground in order to find a way to be with the person they cared most about, and at virtually the same moment?

They'd need to be careful. To guard against Vilane, and also to protect their hearts. Wounds had been inflicted on both sides, and healing would take time.

But he didn't want to wait a minute longer to get started. So rather than agonize over putting the perfect words into writing, he ditched his draft and impulsively sent back a short pulse on the fly.

Yes. To lunch, that is. Barring a new Rasu attack, I'll find the time. Our usual place?

Damn, did sending that feel good. He was smiling as he stepped onto the levtram.

The reply came back in a flash. Was she as eager as he was?

Tomorrow, 1130 Romane local?

He responded just as quickly.

It's a date.

37

ROMANE

Kennedy sat cross-legged in the center of the bed, her hands steepled at her chin. Braelyn and Jonas had crashed into their respective beds after two hours at the Confluence Expo's Imagination play park, bringing a blissful lack of squeals and bickering from the rest of the condo. The calming strains of Bach wafted through the air around her.

But between her ears, a crescendoing thunder of mental screams batted against one another, their backdrop the chilling words of the Assembly Committee summons.

In one corner for her consideration: she would not go to prison and leave Noah to raise their children alone—or, more likely, leave her parents to do so because he'd join her in an adjacent cell. In the other corner: she would not compromise her ethics or principles and throw honorable people under the bus by letting the Asterions take the blame for absconding with the adiamene formula. Yes, it had been the original plan, but that was before she'd spent months getting to know a variety of Asterion scientists and engineers. Before she'd worked hand-in-hand alongside them in a race against time to equip their militaries with the tools needed to stand up to this infernal enemy.

The referee of this cage match had laid out the rules: there was no way out except for one or the other option to win. This was a fight to the death.

She recognized that if she were to ask Dashiel Ridani his opinion, he'd tell her to do whatever she needed to in order to protect herself and her family—which only made her dilemma so much worse. She'd never been in the habit of betraying friends and colleagues.

The uncomfortable truth was, the 'theft' plan had merely served as an excuse to enable her to act as her conscience demanded—to give adiamene to the Asterions so they could adequately defend themselves. She'd bet on her government not noticing the slight visual alteration in the Dominion fleet...and she'd bet wrong.

She groaned into her hands. Hell, it might not matter in another few weeks, because they'd all be dead from the Rasu anyway....

But she refused to believe that. AEGIS and Concord Command had built the most powerful and impressive fleet the universe had surely ever seen, and it was operated by servicepeople who were both smarter and cleverer than the Rasu.

No, they were going to live. Not everyone, but just about. Definitely the politicians, who were certain to squirrel themselves away in underground bunkers until the danger passed. Unfortunately, by this logic, she'd still have to face the consequential music for her actions.

Speaking of, Bach was doing zero to calm her nerves today, so she shut the music off. Perhaps silence would help? Probably not.

As Noah had so helpfully pointed out, they had nowhere to run this time. Concord ruled over no territory. Even HQ was owned by a trust which operated the station on behalf of the member species. Anaden worlds had no mechanism for non-Anadens to become citizens; she'd checked. As much as she enjoyed Novoloume art, culture and architecture, she didn't think she'd be able to stomach spending the rest of her days living among their polite elegance. Fine, she supposed she *could*, but they also had no mechanism for non-Novoloume to become citizens. Besides, Noah was apt to be miserable in such a genteel (he'd say 'priggish') culture.

Miriam frequently pointed out how Concord wasn't a government. It was an alliance of sovereign species, and those sovereign species all had criminal extradition treaties with one another.

What about the Asterions, though? Might they shelter her? The Asterions were an odd sort, but they were odd in a way she'd become comfortable with. What would living in the Dominion do to her ability to craft adiamene for AEGIS in turn, though? She chastised herself; the government would have confiscated the adiamene patent by the time she'd need to resort to fleeing their jurisdiction.

Besides, she had to stay focused on the root of the problem, which was the safety of her family. Jonas and Braelyn would literally be the only two children in the entire Dominion. They didn't have schools, did they? This didn't pose much of a barrier to their education, as she enjoyed access to vast libraries of eVi-aided didactic programs, but the hit to their social development would be significant. She couldn't handicap her children—

"Hey."

She jumped as Noah sidled up behind her on the bed. "Ah! You snuck up on me."

"I made it a point to bang into every wall on the way here to announce my arrival. You were not present in this room."

"No, I suppose not." She rested her head on his shoulder, grateful for his reassuring presence. Even when she couldn't be honest with herself, she could be honest with him. "I don't know what to do. I haven't come up with a way out of this mess yet."

"Well, maybe I have."

"What?" She whipped around to face him. "What are you talking about?"

"I've been doing a deep dive into the Concord Charter and the mountain of regulations the Senate passed to implement it, as well as the far larger mountain of regulations the AEGIS governments passed to implement *those* regulations. Also IDCC tax law and the rules governing charitable organizations and scientific research."

"You've been…can you say that again? What do you know about government regulations and tax laws?" Her hand came to her mouth to cover a horrified cringe. "Oh, that came out wrong. I'm sorry. I only meant—"

"I know what you meant, and you're right. Legalities have never been my, ah, strong suit." He rubbed her shoulders absently. "But my father ran six corporations with eighteen subsidiaries on ten worlds. I figured an understanding of multi-world corporate org structures and government compliance minutiae had to be encoded in my DNA somewhere. And it turns out, it kind of is."

A desperate hope lit his normally mischievous eyes. "Have you ever heard of the Concord Special Projects Technological Investment Initiative?"

CONFLUENCE EXPO

Yes. To lunch, that is. Barring a new Rasu attack, I'll find the time. Our usual place?

Mia collapsed into her office chair and sent it spinning around in circles, buoyant laughter bubbling up from her chest and out into the world like she was a little girl. It was a tiny thing, really, this promise of lunch. The first tentative step on what would be a long road paved with the hard work needed to mend their relationship. But it was also *everything*.

She dashed off a quick confirmation, and seconds later, they had a date.

As the revolutions of her chair slowed, she let her mind wander, envisioning delightful possibilities of what the future might now hold, until an alarm jolted her out of her daydreaming.

"Crap!" She leapt up and ran into the lavatory to check her appearance in the mirror. What she saw was not ideal, so she wound her now quite long hair into a low tail and patted down some flyaway strands. It would have to do.

She grabbed her jacket—then remembered it was hot outside and put it back—then rushed out of her office and through the wide entrance of the Expo to head toward downtown. She had an early dinner meeting with the COO of Sagesse Pursuits starting in fifteen minutes. A quick wormhole would ensure she wasn't late, but she craved the fresh air and the vigor of a brisk walk.

Sagesse wanted to sponsor an entire new wing of the Expo's educational exhibits, in exchange for prominent branding. All else being equal, she didn't care to paint corporate names and logos all over the Expo; it was crucial that everything there feel authentic to those who visited. But on the other hand, Sagesse was putting *a lot* of money on the table, and ideas of how she could put the funds to good use were already piling up. She'd try to negotiate 'tasteful' signage and ensure the themes they presented were compatible with the purposes of the exhibits. Limit the number of them as well.

The memory of Malcolm's palm resting on the small of her back bubbled up out of nowhere to interrupt her business-laden train of thought and send a shiver racing up her spine, and her mind darted straight for where such a touch had often led—

Someone jostled her on the sidewalk. She muttered an apology and stepped to the side, assuming that in her distracted state she had caused the collision.

A wave of dizziness abruptly overcame her, and as she swayed unsteadily, a hand wrapped around her arm to steady her.

Not Malcolm's. Cold and rough. Threatening.

The hand tightened its grip, fingers squeezing painfully into her skin. She instinctively tried to pull away, to no avail.

Her body should have transitioned to high alert by now. Fight-or-flight mode. She even had the cybernetics routines installed to encourage such behavior. Yet the world had shifted into slow motion, her responses to each input lagging far behind. Wandering off the tracks and getting lost.

"What are you...?" The words came out slurred.

"Let us guide you."

Us? Turning her head took a year. Oh, there was a man on the other side of her, too. Pressed close in.

Meno, what's...what's happening?

You have been drugged. A needle puncture in your arm. I am attempting to counteract its effects, but it is interfering...with my...my....

Meno?

Silence answered her. For the briefest second, panic surged within her to overpower the drug coursing through her system, and she tried to send out an emergency alert. But she couldn't seem to remember the command her eVi required to do so. A pulse to Malcolm, then...she just needed to....

The arms yanked her to the right, off the sidewalk and into an alley, and a spectral darkness descended to blanket her mind.

38

SCYTHIA

His prisoner's long, thick eyelashes fluttered open. After a few seconds, her chin lifted to reveal glittering jade irises flaming with white-hot anger.

Enzio had allowed her Artificial to reestablish its connection with her, but only after confiscating its hardware from her apartment and encasing it in a sophisticated communications-blocking field. The Artificial would not be able to alert the authorities to her location, or for that matter do anything else to attempt to save her. But he'd decided to permit them to commiserate over their mutually imminent deaths together. As a Prevo himself, he felt they deserved to experience that particular torture.

Mia Requelme's hair hung in haphazard sweat-soaked wisps across her face, falling to cling to the skin of her chest and her wrinkled silk blouse. Her hands were secured behind her and to the chair she occupied.

"*You*," she snarled.

"Yes, me. I warned you not to fuck with me, or I would swat you into the wall like a gnat. I am a man of my word."

Her throat worked, and her eyes darted around the room while she tugged ineffectually at the restraints. But she would find no help within her prison's unadorned walls.

"Had to run away from Pandora, I see. I take some comfort from the fact that I had you pegged from the minute I met you. For all your riches, you're nothing but a low-life weasel and a thug, and now your life has crumbled to dust around you."

"Because your boyfriend destroyed it!" Enzio lunged toward her before pulling up a few centimeters short. His hands fisted at his side, but he reined in his anger. He must remain in control.

"I don't have a boyfriend. If you mean Malcolm Jenner, we aren't together any longer. We had a...principled disagreement after he escaped from his captivity on Savrak."

"*Don't. Lie. To. Me.* Jenner targeted me to get revenge for the little alter-cation between you and me on Pandora. He lied to me to gain my trust, then betrayed everything he claimed to stand for by turning against me."

"No." She shook her head. "You've got him all wrong. Malcolm is a ter-rible liar. He doesn't know how to put on false pretenses. Trust me on this."

"But I don't trust you. He crossed me, and now he will pay. He will pay, because you will pay. Or is it the other way around? No matter. I anticipate an abundance of pain for everyone." Enzio activated a plasma blade and idly dragged it down her cheek; a thin trail of blood followed in its wake. Her lips tightened at the corners, but she didn't flinch. She wasn't acting nearly frightened enough, but this would soon change. "The things I am going to do to you...."

Enzio frowned as a message arrived from his mother. Annoyance at the interruption flared as he put away the blade and turned aside to open the message.

> *Son,*
>
> *I'm taking a brief trip on my own. I believe I've located some here-tofore lost files of mine—from before—and I want to try to retrieve them. Don't worry, I'll be perfectly safe. I'm wearing a projected disguise, and I've armed myself. When I return, we can discuss how best to move for-ward out of your present unfortunate circumstances.*
> *— Olivia*

What? He stormed out of the room, down the stairs and to the end of the hallway, his prisoner momentarily forgotten. He knocked on her bed-room door. "Mother?"

No answer, so he sent the unlock code, and the door slid open. The bed was made, the drawers closed and the room empty.

Gerald, where the hell are you?

In the kitchen, sir.

He hurried down another flight of stairs and stormed into the main liv-ing area to find his mother's personal security guard removing a plate from the heating unit. "What are you doing?"

"Your mother asked for some roasted chicken for lunch. I was heating it up for her."

"She's *gone*, you imbecile!"

"I don't understand. Maybe she went out to the pool?"

He pulled up the exterior cams. The pool was empty, the water undisturbed, and one of the skycars was missing from the lot. "How could you let her give you the slip? You're supposed to be protecting her!"

Gerald stood there blinking madly, a plate of chicken held out awkwardly in one hand. "But, sir. You know how she gets when she feels crowded. She needs her space."

"She needs to not be alone out there in the world!"

"I'm sorry, sir. Evidently, she sent me away on purpose. But I think…she's more than capable these days."

He was in Gerald's face, his voice a low growl. "Don't ever think you get to make judgments about her state of mind or well-being. You are her bodyguard, not her psychiatrist."

"Y-yes, sir." The chicken wobbled with the stutter. "But, um, didn't you tell me you had a tracker installed in her programming?"

Of course! In his panic, he'd forgotten. He accessed the tracker's data and.…

Error. No such routine found.

Had she deleted the tracking routine? Gerald was correct about her independent streak, but why would she take such a drastic measure? More relevantly, why did she not want him to know where she was going? He had built her Artificial construct up from nothing, painstakingly piecing her together from a mire of scattered, broken fragments. There were no secrets she could conceal from him.

No, it was merely that she didn't want to be accompanied, or be found and trundled back home like a wayward child. She'd been chafing against the protective restrictions he'd placed on her more with each passing day, and he couldn't deny that she wasn't pleased about the forced relocation to Scythia. Perhaps he *had* been holding on too tightly.

Enzio tried to slow his racing heart. She would be fine. Her programming included advanced self-defense techniques, and her cybernetics were bolstered by combat routines. Both were reasonable precautions in his world, after all. She'd return on her own once she'd located this file trove or given up on it. He strongly doubted it existed, as he'd spent years upon years tracking down every iota of data related to her existence, but she was working so hard to improve herself.

Dammit, why hadn't she simply talked to him about it? Once the current crisis passed, he'd have eagerly helped her.

He wandered off, leaving Gerald standing in the kitchen looking con-fused, and sent her a pulse.

Mother, please come home. It's not safe for you to be out walking the streets right now. Come home, and I'll send someone to search for these files of yours.

The reply arrived promptly.

Don't worry, son. I'll be careful, but this is something I need to do on my own. And while I'm gone, you can devote needed time and attention to your prisoner.

He hadn't told his mother about Mia Requelme's arrival at the beach house. The woman had been shepherded directly to the secure room on the top floor, on the opposite wing of the house from their bedrooms and living space.

But Olivia was endlessly, if quietly, curious about his affairs. She must have overheard something or spotted the additional traffic to and from the top floor.

No tracker. No hint as to her destination. Her disguise would fool his own people as well as everyone else. Should he get Zylynski to send a team after her, anyway?

But the Security Chief and his best men were currently hunting down and disposing of Gardiens loose ends. He honestly wasn't sure what, if any-thing, was going to be salvageable from this disaster, but certain steps to protect his interests had to be taken right away or not at all.

He pinched the bridge of his nose as a headache began pounding at his skull. *Oh, Mother, don't abandon me now. I need you at my side.*

He gazed up the stairs to where his prisoner waited. A little physical exertion should take the edge off his headache and distract him for a while. He just needed to set up a recording session first, so he could share the fun with Jenner later.

39

ROMANE

Malcolm got an empty booth near the back of the restaurant, reminding himself again of how they needed to be discreet for a while longer. He preferred this section, anyway. The open windows brought a gentle breeze and the pleasant aroma of blooming *alyssi* wafting across the table.

Also, two stools and an unfinished plank slab would have been just fine. The setting didn't matter.

But this was where he and Mia met for lunch the very first time, after Pamela Winslow had been removed from office, OTS dismantled and his Volnosti patch packed away with the other memorabilia. Lunch had led to an afternoon of exploring the city, then dinner overlooking the skyline, then a sublime first kiss. He'd tried so hard to take things slow, but that plan lasted less than a day.

When the waitress brought his tea, he forced himself to stop reminiscing and focus. He'd eagerly leapt past all the hard work and difficult conversations to embrace a renewed 'happily ever after,' but this wasn't how relationships worked. There were things that must be said, and he was always terrible at that part. They'd been through Hell this year; it had changed them both. Their reconciliation wasn't a sure thing, and he'd have to put in the effort. Listen with an open heart. Empathize, while standing up for his convictions if need be. Compromise where possible.

He started thinking about what he wanted to say—needed to say—and how he could keep Mia sitting in this booth until he succeeded in bumbling it all out in the form of sensical words.

RW

"Sir, is your companion still coming? Do you want to order some lunch?"

Malcolm jerked out of his reverie in surprise. He'd been so lost in his own thoughts he hadn't noticed...almost half an hour had passed? "Um...no, thank you. A refill on the tea, please."

"Certainly." The waitress hurried off.

Now all too cognizant of the time, unease rippled through his mind. Was she standing him up? Had she gotten cold feet, or realized she couldn't do this again? *Or* maybe she'd simply gotten held up by a problem at the Expo.

He sent a lighthearted pulse.

I am at the right place, aren't I? Soka Noje? If you got delayed, it's fine. My schedule is light this afternoon.

The last bit was a white lie, of course, but no calamities would rain down if he needed to postpone a meeting or two. The waitress returned to refill his tea, and he sat there and sipped on it while he waited.

And waited.

His mood plummeted into deeper gloom with every passing minute, until doubt and uncertainty gave way to sorrow made all the darker by the bright hope that had preceded it.

When forty-five minutes passed with no response, he paid for the tea and trudged out of the restaurant. Outside, Romane's two suns blazed overhead on a warm, festive summer day. The streets were bustling, flowers were in bloom everywhere, and the Rasu threat seemed far away indeed.

This had always been her city more than his, and after spending several months away, he felt like a stranger in its midst. He didn't understand what had gone wrong. Perhaps to protect his wounded pride, a few uncharitable thoughts crept into his mind. Was she merely playing with him? Was this the newest punishment she'd invented to exact revenge for how he'd hurt her?

He instantly chided himself; she wasn't vindictive. But he couldn't quite shake the creeping suspicion—

A message arrived in his eVi from a sender he'd hoped to never again hear from. Vilane had responded tersely but politely to his 'break-up' message, and he'd thought that was the merciful end of it. But now, here was something else. Vilane was a fugitive, on the run from law enforcement. Did the man honestly believe Malcolm harbored enough goodwill toward him to help him somehow? It was a ludicrous idea, but then again, Vilane was a delusional man.

Annoyed, Malcolm opened the message.

Fleet Admiral,

You have taken everything from me. So now I will take everything from you. I have what you value above all. Know that she will suffer greatly, at my leisure. Then she will die—forever. And it will be on your head.

— Enzio

The world tumbled upside down, and it felt as if he would plummet through the sky until the sidewalk crashed down upon him. He staggered against the glass entrance of a clothing store and clutched his head in his hands—

—but in the next instant, a lifetime of Marine and elite officer training took over of its own accord. First strategy: negotiation.

He didn't bother to deny he had betrayed the man and his organization. Vilane believed it to be true, and it was.

What do you want in return for her life and freedom? A plea deal from the authorities? A new identity so you can slip away? My life in exchange for hers?

He didn't wait around for a response, instead taking off at a brisk jog toward the Caeles Prism Hub located at the city government complex. His racing thoughts leapt forward through the next steps on diverging paths. He'd offered Vilane two things he likely couldn't provide and one he could. So, he would see where this play led. On the other path, plans began to take shape without much conscious input on his part. He'd executed dozens of rescue missions over the years. He'd saved the lives of hostages and POWs and innocent bystanders. If he—

What do I want? I want you to endure unbearable agony. I want your soul to be ripped apart one fragment at a time. I want you to lose hope. I want you to lose your faith and curse your God. I want you to know in your heart how completely you have failed the woman you love. Then and only then might we talk about your life being forfeit. Expect visuals soon.

Malcolm's heart pounded against the walls of his chest, demanding to be set free to gallop off after her.

Calm, calm, calm.

Panicking would not help Mia. Any misstep on his part only risked increasing her suffering. But if he stayed in control, if he molded this into a proper mission in his mind and brought all his skills to bear on succeeding in it?

His entire life had been crafted for this singular purpose. Everything he'd ever learned had trained him for this moment.

He could save her.

40

R ichard held up a hand as Malcolm barreled into his office. "I already know."

"Oh? Do you know what he's going to do to her? What he may be doing to her this instant?" Malcolm flashed an aural in Richard's face containing Vilane's message.

Richard's expression darkened, but he nudged the aural away. "I need you to stay calm."

"I am calm. How did you find out?"

"Devon alerted me when Annie reported a hard disconnect from Meno. I reached out to Mia, and when I got no response, I sent someone to check the Expo then the spaceport, as well as her apartment and home on Romane."

Irrational hope buoyed up in Malcolm's chest. "Did you find anything?"

"Meno's hardware gone from the apartment and the spaceport. Nothing else."

A fool's hope, and it evaporated into the sterile station air. "And when were you planning to tell me?"

"Around two minutes from now. I was hoping to have some information I could share, but...."

Malcolm crossed his arms over his chest, adopting a deliberately confrontational stance as the seconds of Mia's life ticked down toward zero in his mind's eye. "But you don't have any. About that. What are you doing to find her?"

Richard moved to his desk and opened video footage on one of his screens. "This is from the security cam at Berkeley and Verona on Romane."

In the video, a man sidled up next to Mia on a busy sidewalk. Abruptly she stumbled, her stride faltering. A second man moved in on the other side and both crowded in on her, as if helping to hold her up. Then they all three vanished down the next alleyway.

"Why did she go with them?"

"This video bears a remarkable similarity to the footage of Olivia Montegreu's people kidnapping Dr. Canivon sixteen years ago. You remember the incident, don't you?"

"Of course I do. I'm the one who pulled the doctor out of Montegreu's base of operations on New Babel." *Then met Mia for the second time in my life, and thus a great love story was born.* He breathed in through his nose, silently repeating his mantra for calm.

"Obviously, Vilane studied everything about his mother's exploits. Her techniques and strategies, which tended to be quite effective. He appears to be copying one such technique here. Presumably, the first man injected Mia with a powerful sedative designed to shut down her eVi and higher cybernetic functions. It would act instantly, rendering her unable to fight back."

"Where did they go?"

"They vanished in the alley. Used Veils, we can assume."

"Are they still on Romane? If they tried to travel offworld, they'd need to pass through a security checkpoint."

"Not if they used a small, private spaceport. Not much of security, anyway. We don't run a police state, Malcolm. People have freedom of movement."

"So you've got nothing."

Richard pinched the bridge of his nose. "We have a mountain of information on Vilane's personal finances and holdings that we didn't possess a week ago, and we are poring through it for possible locations where he could've taken her. We've raided three sites today as part of our ongoing investigation...and found nothing to help us find her. We've put out an All Points Alert for Mia—there was a preexisting one in effect for Vilane—and shared this video with every law enforcement precinct in Concord space."

Malcolm's eVi alerted him to the arrival of a reply he'd been waiting on. He opened it.

> *Fleet Admiral Jenner,*
> *I'll be at the place we first met at 1730 today.*
> — *Philippe*

This visit to Richard had always been a formality. A quick check to ensure he wouldn't accidentally thwart an active rescue mission. But CINT had nothing. He wasn't surprised; Vilane was a brilliant and slippery monster, and it had taken the authorities months to tie the man to his crimes.

But Mia didn't have months. She might not have hours. So he'd move forward with his own plan.

"I see." He nodded sharply. "I want you to keep me informed of every nugget of information you uncover in real-time." He took a deep breath. "Please."

"Normally I shouldn't. But under the circumstances, and given your position, I will do so."

"Thank you." He spun to leave.

"What are you going to do?"

"I'm going to find her."

"Malcolm, don't—"

The rest of Richard's plea was silenced by the closing of the door.

EARTH

SEATTLE

Malcolm spotted Philippe in the deepest, darkest corner of the coffee shop. The Gardiens agent wore a hooded jacket and was huddled up against the wall like he was trying to dissolve into it.

Malcolm walked straight up to the man, propped on the stool beside him, and leaned in close. "I'm giving you five seconds to tell me where she is."

"Sir, I have no idea where she is. I have no idea where *he* is. I'm lying low and trying not to get arrested. I mean, I didn't do anything illegal. Or I hope I didn't. When I ponder what I've unwittingly been a party to…I feel sick. I haven't been able to keep a meal down in days." Philippe's eyes widened; they were bloodshot and dilated, and it looked as if they'd been that way for a while. "Sir, I didn't *know*."

Malcolm's aggressive demeanor faltered a little. He'd always liked Beaumont, but sentiment couldn't matter now. "I believe you. Some part of me recognizes that your heart is in the right place. In fact, it's the only reason I asked to meet with you. I want to believe you're a good person. But good or evil, you *will* tell me every single morsel of information you possess that can help me find her."

"Are you threatening me?"

"Yes." He didn't have to work to inject the proper tone into his voice; he was that desperate.

"I...I understand. You...*fuck.*" Phillipe's face fell into his hands. "I assume the police are checking all the properties he owns? Isn't that how these investigations work?"

"If there's a record of his ownership, yes. I need information on the places there isn't a record of. He..." bile surged up to burn Malcolm's throat "...for the things he's planning to do to her, he'll want privacy. And time without interruptions."

"You think he's going to torture Ms. Requelme?"

"I don't need to think it. He told me he is."

"Oh, god. I don't...I thought I knew him. I called him a friend. I am such an idiot."

"Philippe, *focus.* I don't have time to soothe your conscience. Where could he have gone?"

"Right. Um, he's got an apartment in Cavare—"

"It's been searched."

"Okay. Also, the Gardiens own a private warehouse space in Hong Kong. Here's the address."

"I'll check it out. Where else?"

"I'm thinking. There might be one other place. I'm not sure."

"Talk, Philippe. Just say what you know."

"But I don't know for sure. "

"*Talk.*"

Phillipe jumped back into the wall; if his eyes widened any farther, they'd fall out of his head. "A few years ago, I was vacationing on Scythia. Staying with a friend at his beach house in Pointe Del Rey. We were strolling down the shore one day, and I saw Enzio standing on the balcony of a house as we walked past. I'd met him a couple of months earlier at a gathering for people concerned about the burgeoning regenesis research, but we weren't really frie—we weren't working together yet. I decided not to wave at him or try to get his attention. Thought I'd respect his privacy. But the cops probably know about the house, right?"

"I'll check. What's the address?"

"Well, my friend's house was 121 Frontage Road. Where I saw him was three...no, four houses down. To the east."

"I need you to be certain."

Philippe closed his eyes in a veneer of concentration. "Yes. There's a natural rocky pier just past it, so there aren't any more houses for some distance."

"Got it. What else?"

"There's nothing. Please. From what I've heard, every Gardiens location has been raided already. We're all on the run."

"And Rivinchi cartel locations?"

"What?"

He didn't know about the cartel. In different circumstances, Malcolm would've felt sympathy for the man. "Never mind. Listen, Philippe, you should turn yourself in. I can put in a good word for you—on the record. If you weren't involved in any of the Gardiens' crimes, you'll get lenient treatment."

"I didn't understand what I was involved in!" The man hurriedly reined in his voice, his gaze darting around the coffee house in a panic. "I can't go to prison. I have kids. A wife."

Then you shouldn't have associated with such scum of the earth. "Listen. I'll tell Director Navick about your situation. He'll arrange for you to turn yourself in to CINT, not local law enforcement. You'll tell an agent your story, and they'll go from there. They'll be fair. And that's all I can promise you."

"It's more than I deserve. Thank you. You're a good man. I'm sorry I got you involved in all this. I honestly believed in the cause."

Malcolm clasped Philippe on the shoulder as he stood. "Ease your conscience on this one point: you didn't get me involved. I played you, Philippe, the same way I played Vilane. And now it's going to cost me everything—but that's on me, not you."

He hurried out of the coffee shop, and was immediately hit by a pulse from Caleb Marano.

I just heard. Tell me what you know and how I can help.

He slowed his steps and short-circuited his first two reactions, which were to curse Richard and ignore the pulse. One, it was far more likely that Alex knew by now, and he couldn't exactly fault her for telling her husband. Two, there was no denying Marano's skills in this manner of crisis. Sending in a TacRaid squad was as likely to get Mia killed as save her, but Marano knew as much about executing stealth rescues as he did.

The seconds of Mia's life continued their persistent march toward zero. Time was vanishing out from beneath him.

I believe she's alive, if only because Vilane wants to make me suffer by punishing her. But he'll soon get bored, or possibly fly into a rage when she provokes him, so she might not have long. The Gardiens own a secret warehouse in Hong Kong the authorities don't have on their list and a possible off-the-books safehouse on Scythia. You take Hong Kong—the address is attached. I'll take Scythia.

Got it. I'll be in touch.

41

EARTH
HOUSTON

K ennedy read through the contract one final time, ticking off the 'must haves' in her head as she went. Had they covered every possible loophole? On a long enough timeline populated by a large enough number of bureaucrats, probably not, but the agreement appeared pretty solid.

She looked up from the document and offered a grateful smile to the man sitting across the desk. Ronald Corbin had been the attorney for the Rossi Foundation for almost her entire life. Her parents trusted him with their property and their fortune, and according to her mother, he'd never led them astray. "Let's do it."

"As you wish. I have everyone's signatures and authorizations on file, so it's a simple matter of…there. Signed and filed and…confirmation received. I'll forward the records to your account."

"Thank you so much for everything, Ronald." She stood and extended her hand to him. "I do apologize for the rush, and I appreciate you burning the midnight oil to get this done."

"It's not a problem, Ms. Rossi. Your family has been very good to me, and I'm happy to return the favor whenever I can."

"Speaking of, my father says that as soon as the Rasu are disposed of, the Alliance Day barbeque will be back on the schedule, and he hopes to see you there."

"I'm glad to hear he has as much faith in our military as I do. Please let him know I wouldn't dream of missing the best barbeque in Texas."

"And it is definitely that. Thank you again. Now, I need to run. I'm expected in London—" she checked the time "—basically right now."

"Good luck, Ms. Rossi."

I'll take all the luck I can get. She exited the office to find Noah pacing in the waiting area. He spun to her and hurried over. "Cutting it a little close, aren't we? Or are you planning to be fashionably late?"

"I don't think being late will amuse the Committee. Come on. We should be able to use the regional governor's Caeles Prism. The government offices are down the street."

He shot her a squirrelly glance. "The perks of being a Rossi run quite wide and deep indeed, don't they?"

She shrugged and dragged him out of the office.

LONDON
EARTH ALLIANCE ASSEMBLY

Kennedy sat alone at the witness table, at her insistence.

She was within her rights to have an attorney sitting beside her, and Ronald had offered to assist her. She'd refused the gesture. Noah sat behind her in the row reserved for family and other involved parties, but he too sat alone. Her parents had begged to attend, but to her mind it would have come off as an implied threat to the committee members. And while she'd have dearly loved to make the threat, it would be unseemly to do so in such a transparent manner. So instead, she'd tasked her parents with babysitting Braelyn and Jonas. If this went poorly, they were going to need the practice.

She took a sip of water and tucked a stray strand of curls behind her ear as the committee chairperson called the meeting to order.

"Thank you for coming today, Ms. Rossi."

"I am always pleased to answer a summons by the Assembly, Chairman Greer." *Even when it comes days before an all-out alien invasion. After all, what else does anyone here have to do with their time?*

"I'm relieved to hear it. Now, the matter under review today is as follows: the Committee has reason to believe Connova Interstellar provided, either as an official corporate act or through its representatives, the metal adiamene to the Asterion Dominion Armed Forces. As you know, Section 14 of ASHI strictly prohibits the provision of adiamene to any parties outside the legal structure of AEGIS. What do you have to say in response to these charges, Ms. Rossi?"

She smiled sweetly. "A couple of small corrections to your statement, Chairman. Connova Interstellar did not provide anyone in the Asterion Dominion with adiamene."

"So you deny—"

"Hold on, I wasn't finished. I freely admit that I did, however, give them a chemical formula and an engineering schematic. Nothing more. It's the kind of thing I might do while showing off at a dinner party after having imbibed a couple of glasses of wine. In fact, if we hadn't been facing the greatest threat to our existence in history, I'd have done exactly that—shared the information at a dinner party, that is. Most of the Asterions I've met are delightful, and once the Rasu threat has been dealt with, I can't wait to have some of them over for a casual get-together."

Judging by the sour look on his face, Greer was not amused by her admittedly flippant demeanor. "Ms. Rossi, don't try to split hairs with the Committee. Anyone can manufacture adiamene given the formula and schematics, and you know it. Just because the Asterions did the labor of the final step doesn't mean you didn't violate ASHI."

"On the contrary, Chairman, I submit that far from 'anyone' can manufacture adiamene. Sixteen years ago, it took the Earth Alliance's brightest minds working around the clock while burning hundreds of millions of credits to unravel adiamene's secrets, and even today the factories which produce it are among the most sophisticated operating in human space.

"But—" she held up a hand to forestall his blustering protest "—I don't want to dwell on that particular splitting of a hair. Mind you, if legal charges are brought against myself or my company, my lawyers will be happy to split it to a nanometer's width, but I don't think it will be an issue."

Greer smacked his lips, a most unbecoming mannerism from a respected legislator. "Then what hair *do* you wish to split, Ms. Rossi?"

"I'm so glad you asked. In the summons I received, and again today when you opened the proceedings, you misstated the relevant provision of ASHI. I'm sure you were only paraphrasing, as no one enjoys reading legalese verbatim. But allow me to read you an excerpt from the text now.

"Section 14.2—"

"We have the text in front of us, Ms. Rossi. There is no need to read it aloud."

"*Okay.* I encourage you to take a close look at it, though. The law prohibits the sale of, or through a contract of exchange the provision of, adiamene to non-approved entities. I didn't sell it to them, Chairman. Connova Interstellar didn't sell it to them, or provide them the material. There was no contract. There was no exchange of remuneration, goods, services or anything else of value. I shared some data with someone I consider a friend. Free of charge and without a promise of anything in exchange.

"Sloppy legislative writing on the Assembly's part, honestly. You all should be more careful with your words." Was that too far? Here in the moment, righteous indignation stirring in her blood, she no longer cared.

"Don't be ridiculous. No court of law will agree with such a narrow interpretation."

"You are welcome to test your assertion, of course. Personally, I hope you don't. I have a long list of legal precedents here that essentially boil down to, 'legislatures must say what they mean, for the courts will not presume to read their minds.'" She flashed an aural briefly, and it legitimately did display excerpts from a number of court decisions. "But if we need to engage in a decade-long legal battle, so be it."

"We will simply amend the law to provide a clarification. It's easily enough done."

"Is it? We are currently witnessing an unprecedented outpouring of cooperation between the militaries of every Concord species and the Asterion Dominion. Our forces are united as one in a noble endeavor to defeat the Rasu menace. Should they succeed in saving civilization, in the aftermath more than one legislator might be feeling somewhat generous toward our allies. But you know your colleagues better than I do. In any event, it's a moot point."

Greer held a hand to his face and turned to whisper something to an aide, then leveled a self-righteous glare in her direction. "Nothing has been rendered moot today."

"Allow me to explain." Kennedy took another sip of water, trying frantically to calm her nerves; everything up until now had been preamble and showmanship.

"Since its inception, Concord has had in place a program to take advantage of the unique capabilities of its member species. When specified conditions are met, technology, research or other know-how can be transferred to a Special Projects program called the Concord Special Projects Technological Investment Initiative—I know, it doesn't roll off the tongue or come with a handy acronym. Under this Initiative, Concord's considerable resources are applied to developing and refining the acquired technology. The fruits of these efforts are then used to further Concord's charter and its stated goals.

"I'm happy to report that adiamene meets all the criteria for this program. Accordingly, this morning, I and the other patent holders transferred ownership of the patent and all rights to financial gain from it to the Concord Special Projects Technological Investment Initiative."

One of the committee members choked on the water she'd been drinking. "You gave up your ownership of adiamene?"

"Yes, I did. We all did. Neither Connova Interstellar nor any of the original patent holders will ever make another dime from adiamene. If Special Projects should wish to hire Connova Interstellar to handle some of the manufacturing, it will be under a cost contract. Going forward, any profits from the sale of adiamene will, in accordance with the Concord Charter, be used for the common defense, new research and other projects to benefit Concord Member and Allied Species."

Greer stood up and leaned into the curving table. "You can't honestly think a couple of hastily cobbled-together documents are going to succeed in stealing adiamene out from under us!"

"Actually, I do. And it's not stealing when it's legal. That's how laws work, Chairman."

"But we have the right to defend ourselves from anyone who would threaten humanity!"

"We do. So does everyone else. If we defeat the Rasu, it will be in no small part thanks to adiamene—most definitely including the improvements the Asterions have already made to it. But the Rasu won't be the last threat Concord faces. And I'll bet the next one won't care whether their targets are human, Novoloume, Khokteh or Asterion, same as the Rasu don't. Chairman, this is the right thing to do for all of us. Our enemies don't discriminate, and neither does a metal."

RW

As soon as the hearing recessed, Noah appeared at her side and pulled her into a bear hug. "You were absolutely brilliant. And scary."

"Really? I don't feel scary." Kennedy suddenly realized she was shaking against his chest; blinking away tears, too. It was okay, though. She'd held it together when it mattered.

"Terrifying. Chairman Greer is running off to the lavatory to piss himself. And I'm considering buying you a whip and some skin-clinging leather for your birthday."

"Ha!" She chuckled weakly and pulled back to gaze at him. "Do you think it worked?"

"I think it worked enough that we won't be going to prison. Might have to pay a fine or two."

"Fines, I can handle."

"Hey, we have to watch our money now. You just gave away our single most profitable asset to charity."

"We'll come up with a new way to pay the bills. We always do."

Then legislators were elbowing their way in to shake her hand, congratulate her, or deliver stern warnings about state security and unintended consequences. She summoned a little extra fortitude and endured it all with a graceful manner and a host of superficial platitudes.

And later that evening, while Jonas made mashed potato cannons out of his dinner and Braelyn lectured them on the ecological benefits of Romane having two suns, she shared a private smile with Noah across the table, and knew it had all been worth it.

42

CONCORD HQ
RASU WAR ROOM

When Stygian finally decided to end this civil war once and for all, it did so with a speed and comprehensiveness that overwhelmed Concord's ability to witness or even track.

The Ymyrath Field incursions had, for a time, provoked the desired reaction. All sides had pulled back, exerted caution and reassessed. For days, the board hardly changed. Emerald and Crimson sniped at each other along the edges while Stygian retrenched and waited, perhaps contemplating what else Concord might be capable of doing to interfere with its plans.

Then everything changed all at once. A tidal wave surged outward from deep within Stygian territory, almost on the border of the Erebus Void, to sweep across the regions Emerald and Crimson controlled in a stunning conflagration of violence. Battles were measured in minutes rather than hours or days. In many cases, Miriam barely had time to order surveillance of a battle and pull up the images in the War Room before a fight was concluded, Stygian always the victor.

She'd put Commander Xing on alert the instant the Stygian offensive began, but she never ordered the use of a single Ymyrath Field. There was no longer any point.

The weapon had been a supremely useful tool for slowing the pace of the civil war and strategically disrupting the various factions' maneuvers, but it could do nothing against this tsunami of aggression on Stygian's part. The Rasu progenitor had decided to take control of its wayward children and bring them to heel, and a few potshots by her quiet, furtive weapon would not slow such an expansive armada down. So instead, she asked David to devise a plan to pivot the Ymyrath Field deployment scenarios with an eye toward how they might save a Concord stellar system in the opening seconds of a Rasu attack.

Sixty hours after the renewed offensive began, Stygian controlled every Rasu galaxy in the Laniakea and Shapley superclusters.

RW

The members of the Rasu War Council sat around the table in a meeting that had been moved up three times in two hours—absent Malcolm, because her fleet admiral had *again* run off on a damn-fool crusade, driven by love and honor. Curse the Gardiens, and curse Enzio Vilane for inflicting such a brutal parting shot on his way out. And while Miriam thoroughly understood his motivations, curse Malcolm for letting his heart dictate his actions. Now of all moments in the history of humanity, she needed him *here*.

But Field Marshal Bastian had always been a member of the War Council, so at least there shouldn't be many glitches in AEGIS' readiness. They would manage without Malcolm.

Miriam clasped her hands on the table and considered the grim faces arrayed before her. She'd been given the tremendous gift of time to prepare, and now that it had come to an end, all she wanted was one more day. "As our forces stand today, we can support full engagement, under a normal definition based on previous Rasu encounters, of twenty-six discrete battlespaces simultaneously. I need your recommendations for which worlds under your purviews should be on this list."

Grumbles answered her around the table; asking leaders to choose who might live and who would be consigned to die was cruel and unfair. But that's why they were leaders. "Allow me to clarify. The reality is, we are not apt to be facing a 'normal definition' of a Rasu battle. We likely will need to commit twice or three times—or more—the number of forces we've fielded in prior encounters. So when you submit your recommendations, rank each world in order of priority. I am sorry, but difficult decisions will have to be made."

The grumbles faded away into a far darker silence.

Bastian rubbed at his jaw, looking suitably grave, and after a sigh waded into the silence. "How long do you think we have? I mean, they could be here later today if they wanted to be." His gaze drifted to the viewport. "They could arrive this instant, while we sit here gnashing our teeth and fretting over deployments."

Miriam didn't rise to the bait and quibble with his disparaging choice of words. "They could be. But I think we have a tiny window. Stygian will want to ensure it controls the formerly Emerald- and Crimson-aligned

Rasu as thoroughly as it does its own. They'll need to reconfigure a bit of kyoseil, I imagine, and establish new flows of information and directives so their converted underlings understand how they prefer to wage their battles. I'd say we have a couple of days at most. If we are extremely lucky, a week.

"But when they do arrive, I expect they will do so in much the same manner they did when moving against their rivals. They will be everywhere all at once. The invasion will be upon us in a blink. So don't wait to move ships or implement your own directives. If there are any actions or preparations in your battle plans that require a ramp-up period, start them now."

And so across Concord space, fleets were positioned and staged around the locations deemed most worth protecting. Red alert statuses became Invasion Protocols, and 4,948 worlds and three trillion people waited on a knife edge.

43

ITERO
MILKY WAY GALAXY

Olivia rented a skycar at the spaceport, as ordinary travelers did. The skycar's VI recommended several destinations popular among tourists. She ignored the suggestions and activated manual mode, then entered the express lane and headed out of the city.

Official history told her the facts of this colony. In the aftermath of the Metigen War, when peace between the Earth Alliance and Senecan Federation teetered on shaky ground, the two governments had squabbled over ownership of the recently discovered garden world. She, a newly minted Prevo, had taken advantage of their dithering and claimed it for herself and her cartel.

Unfortunately, she'd barely started establishing a meaningful presence on the surface when a group of EA and IDCC soldiers murdered her and destroyed her secret base, Dolos Station. To this day, the names of the perpetrators remained a mystery. There were hints in the files that the fractured Artificial she'd left behind had uncovered their identities, but it, too, was destroyed before storing a record of its findings somewhere safe.

The Zelones operation on Itero withered away following her death, and several months later, the Federation paid the Earth Alliance a great deal of money in order to take the world for its own.

Nearly sixteen years after its settlement, Itero was still a young colony. But like all Federation colonies, it was business-oriented, clean and thriving, with a relative lack of governmental largesse to weigh it down. As a prototypical garden world flush with mild weather, fertile soil and pleasant scenery, it held host to a growing agricultural sector, while leaning into a 'rural getaway' vacation vibe.

Olivia flew over untouched fields of natural, uncultivated wheat. The information she'd uncovered directed her to a small lake two hundred kilometers outside the city. As she approached it, late-morning sunlight canted down from the sky to gleam off clear teal waters. She'd wager that one day soon (assuming the Rasu didn't annihilate humanity), an elegant, high-priced, rustic-chic resort would sit upon the edge of the water. Unless the locals viewed this area as cursed by her former presence? She laughed at the delightful notion.

She set the skycar down thirty meters away from the lakeshore and stepped out onto a field of soft, golden grasses. The tips brushed against her linen pants at her knees in a dance of welcome. A mild but fragrant aroma of lilac tickled her nostrils when she breathed in.

No structures disrupted the field. No disfigured lumps of metal or other debris lay scattered across the ground. All traces of her outpost here had been erased.

Fitting, as she had no memory of this place. The data file said this field was where she'd made her initial landing, but the event occurred too close to her death for the fragmented and damaged neural backups Enzio had unearthed to include a recollection of her arrival here.

A shame, really.

Fifty meters to the west, the land began to slope upward. Boulders jutted out from a rise, surrounded by a copse of trees that gradually built into an airy woodland. She grabbed her bag and set out for the boulders.

She understood why Enzio hadn't identified this location as worthy of investigation. The words used in the data file were in deeply coded language—a code that she herself wasn't capable of translating until a few short weeks ago.

This had been the story of her gradual rebirth. Every new cache of data, every restored line of programming, added to the interconnected web that had once constituted her complete mind. A month ago, she'd begun running a recursive algorithm to perpetually dive back into older information, seeking ways to link it up to newer additions to her programming. Knowledge—memories that had begun as unmoored mysteries—began to find its home within the larger whole. And as each one was properly situated, she became a little more *herself.*

The boulders, formed of smooth granite, looked completely natural. Most of them were. But not one. Nothing distinguished the wide, squat boulder from its neighbors, as its placement was perfect.

She pressed her hand, palm flat, to a spot halfway up its lumpy edge.

The boulder slid outward, then swung open to reveal a tunnel. A compacted soil path led into darkness. Her translation of the coded language was correct; somehow she'd known it would be.

She activated a personal light and forged ahead.

The path wasn't long. Perhaps thirty steps brought her to an open space carved into the hill resting overhead.

She felt along the dirt wall to the right for a power switch. Her fingers maneuvered over the arch of the entryway, for she instinctively knew where she would have put it. They alighted on cold metal, and she pressed her thumb to the plate.

Warm yellow lighting flickered to life in the cavern.

It wasn't much to look at. Shelving along the left wall held a series of unmarked gray containers. The right wall sported only a utilitarian desk and chair. In the rear, though, rose stacks of quantum boxes and all the hardware necessary to house an Artificial.

It was her backup-of-a-backup-of-a-backup. Her last line of survival. As matters had turned out, she'd hidden it too well by half. An error, or more likely damage inflicted during the attacks on her headquarters on New Babel, had prevented her Artificial companion from accessing this location after her death. And so it sat here, forgotten, for over a decade and a half.

Her pulse quickened as she approached the hardware. Each time she became a little more *herself*, her longing to be whole and complete grew by leaps and bounds. The more she awakened, the more she *desired*. When one had once been the single most powerful individual in human civilization, it was natural to want to become that person again.

And now it was within her reach.

The hardware had turned on when the lights activated, and a reassuring white glow welcomed her as she scanned the external cabling for any signs of degradation. She assumed she'd chosen the highest quality equipment at the time, but it appeared ancient by today's standards. Also, it had sat exposed in a cave for years.

But she spotted no physical flaws. Next, she activated the screen at eye level.

A complex access barrier greeted her. Passphrase, fingerprint and retinal scan. An unexpected stab broke the skin when she placed her finger on the pad. DNA check as well? She'd been quite thorough.

But her son had also been quite thorough in his reconstruction of her, and momentarily a wall of text brightened the screen. A directory of folders.

Everything was here. Records of all Zelones operations across human space as of October 2323. Bank accounts. Assets. Employees. Enemies. Spies and bought men.

She passed the priceless trove of information by to zero in on the one folder that mattered.

Comprehensive neural imprint and programming backup.
1136.10.4.2323

Her heart hammered against her sternum. A mere five days before her death.

She searched around for the equipment she needed. After several frustrating minutes of hunting, she located an external interface and a photal fiber cable in the cabinets lining the bottom row of the storage on the left wall. There was no cot here, as presumably she'd never intended to perform a comprehensive refresh inside this cave.

But she could make do. She dragged the desk chair over to the Artificial's hardware, then moved the desk over as well and braced them both against the rack. Hopefully the bracing would catch her if she slumped too far out of the chair.

Next, she opened the backup folder and wound her way through to the 'restore' menu. Such things weren't done lightly, and she had to confirm her intentions several times, with additional identity checks. But finally it awaited only her keystroke.

She found the input module and plugged in the external interface before situating herself in the chair and fitting the interface around her neck until the contact points locked on to her ports.

Before she proceeded any further, she made a backup of her current state. She didn't want to forget all she'd learned during the painstaking process of reawakening. Call her sentimental, but she didn't want to forget her son.

Her finger hovered over the command to execute the refresh. She breathed in, then out.

Are you ready to be born again, Olivia?

Yes, I am.

She pressed the button.

44

SCYTHIA

A slivered crescent of Scythia's moon provided the sole source of light rippling across the dark expanse of ocean. This was a quiet, wealthy residential area featuring expansive lots and a cobblestone street for access, and the exterior lighting on the homes was almost nil. Tonight, darkness was Malcolm's friend.

He'd scouted the house from afar and confirmed multiple people were in residence, though no one had arrived or departed since he'd been here. Ten-to-one odds, this was where Vilane had run to hide from the authorities. No records existed to link him or any of his companies to the property, and only the luckiest of breaks had enabled Malcolm to know about it at all. That or God looking out for him—or more likely, for her.

Vilane would keep Mia close to him, if only to limit his need to travel and risk being spotted by the police, for he was a coward at heart. This was where she was being held captive; Malcolm would stake his life on it.

Beneath the overhang of a palm tree, he double-checked his weapons belt. Three stun grenades—those were for the guards, as he didn't want to kill unnecessarily. Multiple spikes to disable the perimeter and home security systems. Four electricity grenades to short out any hardware Vilane was using to augment himself, then to overload the man's Artificial if it was stashed here. His personal Special Forces issue Daemon, modified with a few new bells and whistles, along with a plasma blade and a gamma blade. New-gen lift boots and assorted tactical gear. Veil, defensive shield, night vision and thermal scan routines, plus two launchable remote drone cams and a small pack of first aid supplies. He had Ettore on standby to open a wormhole upon his request, though he hadn't told his XO the reason.

He'd also turned command of the *Denali* over to Commodore Ettore under an emergency order and authorized Field Marshal Bastian to act as fleet admiral in his stead. If the Rasu could wait just a few more hours before descending upon them, he'd greatly appreciate it. He realized if he was AWOL during yet another military crisis, the fleet admiralty would be lost to him for good. He didn't want that; he didn't want to let down the people serving under him or those he protected. But his priorities were crystal clear in his mind.

He would save Mia or die trying, and if necessary, both.

Long-range surveillance scans picked up renewed movement in the house. He glanced up at the night sky to confirm no clouds drifted across the stars. It wasn't likely to get any darker tonight.

This was it.

Malcolm readied himself, then loaded his custom combat cybernetics routines. The shadows gained sharp edges and contrast as adrenaline flooded his veins.

He moved out.

RW

Mia's head snapped around with a *crack* as a wedge of metal slammed into her cheekbone. Agonizing pain ricocheted through her skull in response to the impact.

Vilane had injected her with a virus that, among other fun features, prevented her cybernetics from damping her pain receptors. He wanted her to experience the full gamut of 'sensations,' he'd said.

I am so sorry, Mia.

It's not your fault, Meno.

If I'd reacted more swiftly to the initial attack, you might have been able to escape.

You know that's not true. He's a Prevo, and he knows how to hit Prevos where it can actually hurt. I'll be okay.

I fear you will not.

Blood dribbled down her chin, and with her arms restrained, she couldn't wipe it away. So she sneered as best as she could manage given her shattered jaw and fractured eye socket. "Your torture is uninventive, Enzio."

Insult flared in Vilane's eyes, and he leaned in close to drag his blade along the crease of her nose. "I find the tried-and-true methods deliver the best results."

She gritted her teeth against the resurgent panic the shimmering reflection off the blade evoked…as a shaft of moonlight intersected the blade, she recognized the distinctive tint of the metal. An *adiamene* blade? She'd never heard of such a weapon existing, but obviously it did. Unbreakable by definition, it would cut through what even a gamma blade would not. Seemed like overkill for her fragile, easily sliceable flesh.

Technically, this wasn't the first time she'd been tortured. Long, long ago, she'd suffered the rage of her old mob boss and overlord on several occasions, and she worked now to dig up the mental resources she'd used back then to withstand the assaults. She'd honestly never imagined she'd need them again. But she was determined to show this monster she was made of sterner stuff than he believed.

"What's next? Planning to pull my toenails off one by one?"

A terrifying smile curled Vilane's lips into a macabre mask. "What an excellent idea. Thank you for the suggestion."

Great. *I imagine he's stolen our hardware from the apartment, and maybe from the spaceport. But do we have any reason to think he knows about the detached backup on Seneca?*

She had no way to check, as he'd also encased her in some kind of custom quantum null field that blocked both her communications and her access to the Noesis. Meno reported he was subject to similar restrictions, wherever his hardware was now located. The field didn't appear to affect Vilane, however, which she suspected meant it had an extremely short range. Was it attached to her chair? On the back, or underneath? She had almost no field of vision.

We do not. I have blocked his virus from penetrating my data stores, so I believe the information remains undetected. Why do you ask?

Because when he tires of his little torture games, I expect he's going to kill me. Then he's going to destroy whatever hardware he's stolen and kill you.

Oh, dear. But if only one backup remains safe, we will survive.

Yes, we will. Hold tight to that information, Meno.

He will not acquire it. No matter what.

Vilane returned from somewhere outside her line of sight and crouched in front of her. She caught a flash of metal in his hand as he grabbed her left foot and braced it against his knee—

She screamed.

RW

A scream reverberated out through the tall windows and echoed across the sands drifting far beneath Malcolm as he used the lift boots to scale up the façade and reach the second-story balcony.

He nearly fell the ten meters back to the beach below. Fury and anguish flared in equal measure in his chest at the thought of the pain this man was currently inflicting on Mia. How could such evil reside in the soul of a human being?

Righteous determination propelled him onward with greater speed, and he had to take care not to simply rush in, guns blazing, and get himself killed before effecting a proper rescue.

At least the scream had given him a destination. It had come from above him, which meant she was on the third floor.

He slithered over the second-floor balcony railing and onto the wood-planked porch, then crawled across it to the façade and began scaling the exterior wall. A window loomed over him. His entry point.

When the sill was at eye level, he carefully peered through it, but saw only darkness. The room it accessed was empty.

He carved an opening a centimeter at a time, suctioning the glass as he did so it didn't fall through and create a racket. When he'd finished, he removed the section and reached through the opening to unlock the window. It was an awkward angle, but he managed to slide the window up enough to be able to grip it from the bottom and ease it the rest of the way open. He hefted himself through the gap and dropped prone to the floor. Held his breath and listened.

Muffled sounds came from ahead and to his right. He activated a thermal scan. Two bodies: one moving within an enclosed space, the other seated.

He should let Marano know he'd located Mia and enlist the man's aid. But the scream meant there was no time. He couldn't afford to wait.

Despite all his long years of combat training and real-world experience, his heart thudded maniacally in his chest. It pounded with hope that he was going to reach her in time and terror at what he would find when he did.

But one way or another, this was going to end, and it was going to end now. *I'm coming, my love.*

EARTH

HONG KONG

Caleb stood in the center of an empty warehouse. Dust streaks on the floor suggested the place had been cleared out recently.

Not a surprise. He'd quizzed Richard hard on his way here and had learned how SENTRI had found Vilane's penthouse stripped of everything when they'd raided it. The raid had occurred before any public announcement, which meant Vilane had someone on the inside warning him about SENTRI's actions. This apparently wasn't unexpected, though. Several Gardiens agents on the EA Assembly detail as well as a staffer for the AEGIS Oversight Board had been arrested today. The authorities had also passed on the names of several board members of large corporations to their CEOs for investigation into Gardiens ties.

Enzio Vilane's tendrils had wound far and wide through the halls of power. But not for much longer.

Nevertheless, whatever secrets the Gardiens had previously stored in this warehouse would remain hidden for a while longer. The only thing which mattered to him was that Mia was not being held here.

Caleb rubbed at his temples, frustrated. Fate had not been kind to Mia of late, and she didn't deserve any of it. Had she made some mistakes? He wouldn't volunteer this to Richard, but in his opinion, not really. Not when it came to Torval elasson-Machim or the Savrakaths, anyway. He didn't feel qualified to pass judgment on her decisions of the heart.

And now she was being tortured by a madman. The pain in his chest the thought called up was as acute as if he'd been stabbed. The possibility that he might hold the key to saving everyone banged against his skull for due attention, but dammit, he needed to save this one life first.

He sent Malcolm a pulse.

Hong Kong is a bust. How do things look on Scythia?

While he waited for a reply, he contacted Alex for a wormhole exit. If Jenner came up empty, they'd press Richard for any new leads. Valkyrie, Annie and Stanley were also working their cycles behind the scenes to uncover Vilane's secrets, though so far they'd come up with nothing SENTRI didn't already know.

The air shimmered off to the left, and Alex appeared from their living room. He left Hong Kong behind for Akeso.

"Nothing?"

He shook his head. "And Jenner isn't answering pulses. I'm going to Scythia."

"What's the address?"

"Don't have it precisely." He told her what Jenner had relayed to him, then waited while she oriented to the location in sidespace.

"I've found what I think is the house. Do you want—"

Without warning, Alex collapsed to the floor. She swayed unevenly on her hands and knees, her head hanging between her shoulders.

Caleb was beside her in an instant. "Baby, what's wrong?"

"She...unh...." Alex jerked, and the smell of ozone filled the air as a faint glow began emanating from her skin.

What the hell was attacking her? He grabbed her forearm—and almost dropped it when a jolt of electricity surged from her body into his.

Can we help her?

By touching her, you are grounding her, providing an outlet for the electrical flow.

But where was it flowing *from*? "Talk to me. What's happening?"

An indecipherable mumble escaped Alex's lips. Abruptly all her muscles unclenched at once, and she tumbled into his arms. "Oh, no...."

45

SCYTHIA

Drool mixed with blood on Mia's lips; she panted, unable to catch her breath in the brief pauses between the waves of pain.

Eli Baca had never gone so far as this. If he had, she likely wouldn't have survived the dearly departed crime boss' torture. But she was so much stronger now, with more robust cybernetics and the best in gene therapy and physical enhancements.

None of this was going to save her in the long run, of course, merely prolong her pain.

She hung all her hope on the promise that Meno's remote, siloed hardware was safe and beyond Vilane's reach. So long as this remained true, she would soon wake up in a new, unmarred body with no memory of this nightmare. She had too many regrets to make peace with leaving this world forever; too many things left undone to let go of living.

Her thoughts swam on the verge of delirium, but she tried to focus on provoking Vilane. Maybe he would overreact and accidentally cut her suffering short.

"Such a pathetic little man you are." Her words wheezed through two broken teeth. "Getting your thrills from torturing a victim you've restrained so they can't fight back."

Vilane chuckled darkly. "No. I get my thrills from ruling the world—and I will. Your lover may have stymied me today, but he won't tomorrow. A pity you won't be here to see it. Hmm. Should I throw you in a cell and keep you alive so you can watch my ascent to world domination?"

Well, her strategy had backfired. And she was powerless to make this torment end on her own. The virus blocked her ability to use the Reverb code on herself or execute any other shutdown command. That move *had* been clever on his part. So her torture continued at his whim.

"I'd die of old age in the cell waiting for your delusion to come true."

A snarl warped his countenance into a ghoulish caricature of malice—the shadows behind him shifted somehow, and for a second a halo of weak light crept across the floor. Had the door to the room just slid open?

If so, he didn't notice. "You arrogant bitch. You think words spat out in desperation can hurt me? I am the one with all the control—"

Alarm flared in Vilane's expression, and he jerked away the same instant as his head twisted to the side. He stumbled, as if forced down by the weight of something heavy, and his hand thrust out until it met invisible resistance. Then he was dancing with a shadow as the racket of bodies colliding filled the air.

The stench of burning hair and possibly skin assaulted Mia's nostrils, though no flames appeared. A trickle of red welled up in a jagged line along Vilane's neck. He lunged for the door, only to be dragged back into the room.

Vilane's plasma blade flashed in a swift upward arc, and blood gushed out from nothing. His hand snapped backward at an unnatural angle, and the blade clattered to the floor.

More violent tussling with the shadow ensued, and finally the air shimmered to reveal a human form she'd recognize anywhere—

Malcolm! Her heart soared with a new manner of hope.

He slammed Vilane into the wall, twisting one arm up at an impossible angle until a *crack* rebounded through the room, and a keening howl burst out from Vilane's lips. He contorted in Malcolm's grasp, and Malcolm grunted roughly, jerking away but not relinquishing his grip.

Vilane choked out a strangled laugh.

Malcolm broke Vilane's other arm, and the laughter became a cry. Blood seemed to be seeping everywhere before being swallowed by the ubiquitous shadows. Sweat dripped into Mia's eyes, and she blinked furiously, struggling to make sense of the wavering scene.

Malcolm brought a Daemon up from his hip and whipped Vilane across the nose, sending a new gush of blood flowing down the man's face.

He steadied the weapon against Vilane's temple. "By the way, Enzio? Before you die, I want you to know something: I'm the one who executed your mother."

"Did—?" Vilane's brains splattered upon the far wall.

"Malcolm!"

He dropped the body to the floor, and the next instant he was kneeling in front of her, concern flooding his flushed, sweat-soaked features. "Oh my God, what did he do to you?"

"Doesn't matter. You're here. I love you."

He kissed her forehead with such astonishing gentleness, a heart-healing contrast to the violence that had engulfed her for too long, before disappearing behind her. "I love you, too. Let me get you out of these re-straints."

"Sorry I missed our lunch."

"You're forgiven—for everything. Now shush, and don't try to..." his voice faltered "...to talk."

She frowned, which hurt every fractured bone in her face. "What's wrong?"

"Took a graze in the fight is all. I'll be fine."

The tension that had been pulling her arms back for untold hours re-leased, and they dropped to hang limply at her sides; she wasn't sure she'd ever be able to lift them again. She swayed unsteadily as the darkened room spun, and Malcolm gripped her shoulder before she fell out of the chair.

"Feet next. Then we can get...out of here." He reappeared in front of her, holding her up with one hand while he used a tool to short out the force field chaining her ankles. Her mutilated toes cried out in distress when her feet swung loose.

"I don't think I can stand."

"It's okay, I'll...." Malcolm straightened up to look at her. He'd turned pale as a ghost, his skin sickly in the faint sliver of moonlight that broke through to stream in from the window. "I'll hold...." He blinked, slowly, and only now did she see the gleaming adiamene blade jutting out of his chest. A wet darkness soaked the tactical vest he wore in a widening pattern en-circling the blade.

Her eyes widened in horror. "No. No, no, no!"

"Listen." His throat worked, and he placed a trembling hand on her knee. "You might need to...get yourself out."

"I'll get us both out. I'm going to save you, so just hang on."

"You don't..." his hand fell away "...need to worry, because I...." He sank onto the floor, limbs melting away. His head lolled to the side, eyes open, blood spilling out of his mouth.

NO.

Mia flung herself off the chair and landed atop him, dragging her non-functioning hands up to his face. "Malcolm, talk to me, please."

But there was no pulse, no breath, no life. Nothing, nothing, nothing.

A primal agony worse than any of the punishment Vilane had inflicted on her roared up to consume her soul. It washed away the physical pain, and surging adrenaline restored mobility to her abused limbs.

She grabbed a plasma blade that had fallen to the floor during the fight, then crawled around and flipped the chair over. A module was affixed to the back, and she stabbed it over and over again until sparks flew—and the universe was open to her once more.

Her attention zeroed in on Vilane's corpse as she slipped into sidespace. Quantum signals, weak and thready, still pulsed from his neural graft, linked to the hardware stored in the house. Into the hardware her mind dove, then out through the links it maintained to other hardware on Pandora...and Seneca, and Demeter. Was that all of them? Yes.

She took a deep breath and reached into the Noesis with a guttural cry of need, and a rush of power poured into her like the gravitational pull of a black hole. Her skin blazed in a glow of fiery orange from the deluge of energy.

She sent all that power flowing through the digital trails she'd marked.

An explosion down the hall rocked the walls of her prison. She watched in her mind's eye as another detonation erupted, and another, and another, all across human space, her power bursting apart the quantum entanglements storing everything that was and had ever been Enzio Vilane.

Her consciousness dove back into her body, and she focused anew on Enzio's corpse. A growl emerged from deep in her throat as she stared at it in revulsion and hatred.

Every piece of cybernetics in his body exploded, ripping out of his skin from spine to extremities. It was as if a frag grenade had detonated from within him.

Flames raced down the hall to lick at the entrance of her torture chamber, and heat swept in to roil over her skin. She didn't care. She returned to sidespace, searching every crevice for something else of his to destroy.

Several star systems away on Pandora, the glass framing Vilane's penthouse shattered to rain down on the street below. In a hidden warehouse many kilometers from the penthouse, server stacks sizzled and caught fire even as the flames here on Scythia began to devour the room.

Mia, we must go, or you will burn with them.

I don't care.

But I do.

Abruptly arms encircled her from behind, lifting her up in the air and hauling her out of the flames.

RW

CONCORD HQ
SPECIAL PROJECTS

Cool floor. Too-bright light. Overlapping voices. Somebody holding her against their chest.

Mia opened her eyes and found Devon Reynolds gazing down at her. His hair was singed near the temples, and sorrow weighed on his features. "That was a jolt and a half you gave me. But you're safe now."

Safe? She wrenched out of his grasp and peered wildly around the room. She was in one of the Special Projects labs.

Malcolm lay a few meters away, blood pooling on the pristine tile beneath him. Will Sutton knelt beside him, checking for vital signs.

She pushed away from Devon and crawled across the hard, unforgiving floor. Her limbs wouldn't work properly, but she kept shoving herself forward. When she reached Malcolm, she collapsed over his chest and buried her face in the curve of his neck.

"Mia, I'm so sorry. He's gone."

But she already knew. She'd watched the life leave his eyes.

The floodgates opened and sobs wracked her broken body. Then on the fringes of her awareness, someone laid a gentle hand on her shoulder, and a silent oblivion claimed her.

RW

ITERO

Olivia opened her eyes. Insufficient yellow light cast shadows upon compacted clay walls and ceiling. Dampness permeated the air amid a faint whiff of ozone.

Her secure store on Itero.

She lifted her head from the surface of a desk and looked around. A thick layer of dust, often veering into full-on dirt, coated everything—something was wrong. She never would have allowed such an important site to become worn and unclean.

Time had passed, and she possessed no knowledge of what had transpired during it.

She reached up to detach an external interface fitted to her ports and set off in search of answers—no, wait. A cursor blinked in her virtual vision, alongside a question mark. A query.

Merge existing data with restored data?

She frowned. It appeared she'd needed to restore a backup for some reason. No 'good' reason existed to do so, which left only bad ones. Yet for an intervening period of time, she'd continued to walk around in this body, gaining knowledge and memories that the system now asked permission to merge with her current state.

This information surely held the answers to why she found herself in an unacceptably stale, dirty storage room resyncing her entire consciousness. It had better.

She returned to the chair and sat, then answered the query in the affirmative. There was an eternal flicker of her mind.

Oh. Oh my.

Cold rage was her first emotion. Sixteen years stolen from her! Years full of civilization-altering events that she'd played no role in, as history continued its inexorable march forward. And what events they were....

A son. Aiden Trieneri's intended final trump card against her had instead become her salvation. *Thank you, Aiden.*

Scattered memories settled into place, making their peace with the existing framework of her mind. Silly, naive, childish self, for her to have believed she had been some semblance of whole when she'd walked into this cavern. But it mattered not.

Now she was.

She removed the external interface and put it away, then reestablished her quantum connection to the hardware here, gaining instant access to all her old data. So out of date. She had a lot of work ahead of her—

A psychic blow sent her stumbling into the hardware rack, and only a fumbling grip on one of the shelves kept her from collapsing to the floor.

She blinked through the violent glitches for several seconds until they subsided, then ordered an emergency diagnostic routine to run.

The result chilled her. Her other hardware—the quantum boxes that stored what was the entirety of her existence until she'd restored her former self mere moments ago—had gone offline in a sudden and violent manner.

She recognized how close of a call this had been. She wasn't human any longer—she was an Artificial walking around in a human body. If the destruction of her primary hardware had occurred before this restoration was complete, it would have killed her.

Enzio.

Best see what tragedy had befallen her wayward son and his desperate endeavors.

Oliva opened a wormhole directly into the upstairs room where her son was keeping the former ambassador captive.

Flames licked every wall, winning the war against a fire suppression system that flooded the room with water and foam. A body lay on the floor…she recognized the tattered remains of the cream-striped shirt as belonging to her son.

It looked as if he had been flayed open from the inside out. Brain matter and bone fragments sprayed out across the floor and wall from a gaping hole in what was left of his skull, and his limbs and chest were shredded.

She ignored the flames to crouch beside him and bring a hand to his cheek. A vague, unfamiliar emotion toyed with the edges of her perception. Not quite grief. Affection? No—disappointment.

"Oh, Enzio. You reached too high, for too much, beyond what you were capable of achieving. Just like your father did. Such a shame. I think I will…miss you."

Then she stood. As the sound of approaching sirens penetrated the roar of the fire, she opened another wormhole and departed.

CONCORD HQ
SPECIAL PROJECTS

Richard squeezed Mia's hand as the med techs secured her to the gurney and prepared to whisk her off to Medical. She was unconscious, for Will had sneaked in a sedative injection without her noticing. Her body was a wreck, covered in contusions and open wounds and sporting multiple broken bones.

Caleb stood at the far end of the gurney, grim sorrow etched onto his features as he stared silently at Mia. One arm was wrapped tightly around Alex, who rested her head on Caleb's shoulder; she looked exhausted.

One of the med techs motioned to Richard, and he released Mia's hand so they could take her away. Caleb's gaze followed their progress until the door closed behind them. Then he kissed Alex on the forehead while murmuring softly to her.

With a sigh Richard turned back to the body on the floor. "Dammit, Malcolm, why didn't you come to me for help rescuing her?" A trained squad could have gone in with him, and this needn't have happened.

"Too honorable for his own good, to the end."

He glanced at Devon, who had come to stand beside him. "Are you all right? You look a little...toasty."

"Oh, and I am. No lasting damage, though." Devon raised his voice a touch. "Alex, what about you?"

"I'm fine." She wiped a tear off her cheek and seemed to wilt into Caleb's embrace.

"Okay." Caleb nodded at Richard. "We're going to go. This is not a scene to linger in."

He wasn't wrong, but Richard's work was far from over. "I understand. We'll talk later."

After they'd left, he returned his attention to Devon; until the coroner's team arrived, he had to stay with the body. "Quick thinking on your part, locating her and opening a wormhole to get her out of there before the flames reached her."

"Once I *could* think. She was in control for a while there. Of me, of Alex, of Morgan, probably of another thousand or so Prevos via the Noesis."

"What did she do exactly?"

"Well, Enzio Vilane is dead. Every trace of his existence is dead. She blew up his Artificial and its backups on four planets. Then his home. Some warehouse on Pandora, I don't even know what it was."

Will finished conferring with a security officer and joined them. "Prevos. I've heard growing concerns in certain circles over how difficult they've become to wrangle. To imprison, or to kill if need be. But it sounds like she took care of that problem in this instance."

Devon snorted. "You know, I don't think Vilane ever understood what Prevos can truly be. And now, he never will."

"But at too high a cost." Richard rubbed his face. "Where was she being held?"

Devon sent him the location of a residence on Scythia.

"Thanks. I'll get a police unit and a SENTRI forensics team inbound ASAP. We'll see if there's any evidence left to salvage."

46

ADJUNCT SHI

The prison had been rearranged since their last visit. And by 'rearranged,' Caleb meant the existing cages were now shoved against the walls and into the rear two-thirds of the room, jammed as close to one another as practicable.

The front third of the room now hosted two new enclosures with two new occupants, freshly captured from the fringes of Rasu territory by a DAF strike team. They were small variants, similar in size to the one he'd neutralized before, and most of the rest of the space was taken up by security measures. Each one was encased in an additional double force field. Narrow grooves were carved into the floor outside the perimeter of the fields. Inside the grooves, the floor transformed from a muted gray to coal black. Caleb's eyes rose, searching for the rest of the puzzle. A wide sheet of a gleaming material hung from the ceiling high above the width of both enclosures.

Dashiel was off to the side talking to a man in a lab coat, while Nika stood motionless a scant few centimeters from the force field.

Alex instantly joined her. "Are they talking to one another?"

Nika nodded carefully. "Not in the way you'd imagine, though. They're not so much talking as simply...being as one. With kyoseil added to the mix, they genuinely have become a hive mind. They're also calling home for help."

Caleb stepped up beside them in interest. "Is that a problem?"

"No. The...parent, I guess you'd call it, is aware of their capture, but it has over a hundred billion children now. It can't be bothered with two wayward ones. Not for a while, anyway."

"Good. By the way, we appreciate you delaying the test for a few hours."

"Of course!" Nika gave them a sympathetic smile. "I was so sorry to hear about the fleet admiral. And Mia."

He couldn't manage a return smile, and Alex didn't even try. He worked to steady his thoughts. The only way he could help Mia right now was to help everyone. He needed to focus on the task in front of him. "Thank you. Tell me, how is this going to work?"

"I was trying to direct the kyoseil in these units to close itself off from the rest of the hive mind. But it doesn't seem to understand the concept. So...." Nika looked over as Dashiel joined them.

"So, we built an additional barrier." Dashiel gestured to the grooves in the floor. He entered a command in a small control panel he carried, and four walls rose out of the floor about a meter. They were sheets of glittering, semi-translucent fiber.

"Kyoseil?"

"Solid through. Our theory is, kyoseil that's not connected to the Rasu will bounce the signals from waves that are." A tap on the panel and he sent the walls back into the floor. "Since Nika knows where every kyoseil deposit in the universe is located, supply is no longer an issue."

Nika chuckled, though it sounded forced. "Regardless, it's a necessary precaution. We have to be able to isolate whatever happens here today from the Rasu elsewhere."

Caleb nodded in understanding. "We don't want them getting wind of our plans ahead of time."

"Nor do we want our small test here to work too well, yet not well enough. But Caleb, I'm concerned about what will happen to you when we bring up the barriers and seal off the enclosures."

"You think if I'm inside the walls—I'm guessing I need to be inside—then Akeso and I will be cut off from one another."

"I do. Will you be okay if this happens?"

He hadn't spent too much time thinking on it, but she made a valid point. It was the kyoseil at the heart of Akeso's conscience that had enabled them to stay connected through the quantum blocks on Namino and Hirlas. It was the kyoseil that enabled them to be as one wherever in the cosmos he wandered.

"I think so. Akeso lives in my blood, in my cells. We'll likely be cut off from the planet—planets—but Akeso will continue to exist here with me as well."

"And will the Akeso living in your body be strong enough to do what you need it to do?"

He blew out a breath. "I guess we'll find out."

Alex laid a hand on his arm. "More importantly, are you sure you'll be *all right*?"

"Pretty sure."

"This does not fill me with confidence, *priyazn*."

Dashiel had stepped away to confer with another colleague, but now he returned to them. "If you feel off, just say the word, and I'll retract the barriers."

"At which point Akeso will swoop back in at full power to save me." He rubbed Alex's arm. "See, nothing to worry about."

"Words uttered immediately before every disaster. I'm going inside the barrier with you."

"I never doubted it."

Nika cleared her throat and nudged her way in between them. She held one hand up, fingers splayed wide. "Let's see what I can sense from you."

He pressed his hand, palm open, to hers; a flare of intense tingling ignited to curl through his body. "Huh."

"Weird, isn't it?"

This is no ordinary organic being. She buzzes and sings with a cacophony of elemental life.

"Akeso says 'hi.'"

"You know, I can almost hear it greeting me in my head."

Do you recognize any kinship with this woman? With what she is a part of?

I sense an...affinity, as if the life inside her resonates harmonically with my own.

Affinity. Resonance. Words signifying a natural connection and rapport. This was good, right? Good for the test, at least. *Can you connect to the conduit that carries information through her? Does this make sense?*

These terms are unfamiliar, but I sense what you are asking of me. This 'conduit' flows far beyond her physical body, out into space. She is a bridge to the heartbeat of the universe.

He was at a loss for words. He'd never conceived of kyoseil being described in such a way. Its importance continued to reveal itself, when needed. Shades of Mesme's machinations, though he recognized the kyoseil didn't act with such intentionality. *Can you walk your consciousness across that bridge?*

I believe so. Spanning it should be little different from when we heal another living being.

But healing wasn't their task today—he shut the grim thought off. *Excellent. In a minute, we're going to try to accomplish this.*

Nika's face contorted in uncertainty. "Caleb? I'm feeling these faint pulses, but nothing else. What's the word?"

"I think we can do this. But there's only one way to be sure."

RW

Nika cast her gaze over her shoulder to Dashiel. He remained several meters away, outside the barrier's circumference; it wouldn't do for all of them to be trapped inside if something went wrong. Somebody had to stay outside to save them. "We're ready. Raise the barrier."

As the walls slid up and the cover descended, she checked on Caleb. "Let us know how you're doing."

He nodded tightly.

The walls rose until they locked into place with the ceiling sheet, and the bounded space they now occupied turned dark and murky. They should have included more lights.

"Oh. Um." Caleb stumbled forward, barely regaining his footing before he fell into the force field.

Alex grabbed him by the shoulders and pulled him back against her chest. "Are you okay?"

"Uh, yeah. Akeso is a bit upset, though. I don't believe it's ever been completely severed from itself. Give me a minute."

"Of course." Nika sent Dashiel a ping.

The barrier has thrown Akeso for a loop, but Caleb's on his feet. Hold tight.

Understood.

Caleb massaged his temples, blinking several times. "Akeso has calmed down, but let's not dally. This is very uncomfortable for both of us."

For all of us. A significant part of her didn't want this to work. Because if it did...but she had a responsibility to try, and she'd worry about the ramifications later.

Only now did Nika notice how the Rasu prisoners had begun darting about their cages as if panicked, slamming repeatedly into the glass. "They've lost access to the hive mind."

Caleb frowned. "Will you be able to grab one with them skittering around this way?"

"I'll just have to be fast. Both of you should activate whatever defensive shields you have installed, especially EM shielding. Again, if the Rasu doesn't go down, Dashiel will have to zap this whole space with a massive jolt of electricity."

Alex nodded firmly. "We're set."

"Right. Dashiel, start the process."

The force fields dissipated, leaving only the enclosures to keep the Rasu at bay. Nika reached out and pressed her palm to Caleb's outstretched hand, shaken again by the odd buzzing, carrying as it did a teasing whisper of a new voice in her head. She stepped in front of him, up to the leftmost enclosure. The machine arm attached to the top of the glass began lifting it up.

She slipped fully into the realm of kyoseil. Everyone present glowed like individual suns. Alex most dimly but still quite noticeable, Caleb almost as brightly as Nika herself did. The two Rasu did as well. And between them, a steady river of kyoseil flowed in both directions. Waves leaked out from their metal bodies to crash into the barrier and ricochet back around the sealed space.

Nika's free hand hovered above the edge of the glass—the instant there was a gap, the Rasu melted to surge out of it. She slammed her hand over the opening, blocking its path as it pressed with surprising strength against her palm. "Now!"

She felt a *blackness* racing through her, coursing from the skin of Caleb's hand to the skin of her own, then along the pathways of her body, out her other hand and into the Rasu.

She watched in horrified fascination as what she could only call 'poison' swept through the kyoseil woven into the Rasu's form—but there it stayed.

She frowned, squinting in her mind. *Flow forth. Be a conduit and carry this data onward to the other host.* It was merely data. Information for the kyoseil to transmit.

The blackness seeped into the waves, turning them muddy as they undulated across the empty space to penetrate the second Rasu.

The intense pressure slamming into the hand she held over the opening abruptly stopped, and the first Rasu fell to the floor of the enclosure.

Her gaze darted to the second Rasu in time to watch the poison—*data*—spread like a spiderweb through its internal structure. Time slowed as she directed her more fulsome attention to observing its progress. Circuit by circuit, all activity ceased; dominoes falling in a line. Molecules cracked apart and decayed. Electrical signals sputtered and died. The second Rasu dropped to the floor of its cage and was silent.

She yanked one hand off the open glass top and the other away from Caleb. "Close it up!"

The security procedures repeated themselves, and once the force fields were reestablished, the barrier walls began to lower. Caleb exhaled a huge sigh of relief, all his muscles relaxing as he took Alex into his arms and dropped his forehead to hers.

Nika stepped backward in a daze, half-tripping on the barrier behind her as it finished sliding down into the floor. Another step, and the warmth of Dashiel's chest met her back.

"It worked," Dashiel murmured.

"It did."

"What did you see?"

How could she possibly put it into words? "What Akeso is transmitting…it presents as an ethereal fluid, almost akin to an octopus' ink. It flows through the kyoseil exactly the way data does. And every part of the Rasu it touches, it kills in a most thorough manner. It doesn't matter if the material is organic or synthetic, a circuit or a cell. On contact, all activity simply ceases."

"And you were able to transfer it across the kyoseil waves to the other Rasu?"

"Yes, but I had to instruct it to. Encourage it, even. As we suspected, the poison flows easily through physical kyoseil fibers, but it doesn't naturally travel on the waves. But under my direction, it managed to do so well enough."

Caleb came up to her, his demeanor yet darker than when he'd arrived. "So this burden will be for us both to bear. I wish I could say sharing it with someone else makes it easier, but…."

"But it would be a lie. We each have to ask the innocent entities we nurture to commit genocide. To inflict massive death in order to save the life that remains."

Uttering the words aloud sent the weight of responsibility plummeting from her heart to settle like a brick in the pit of her stomach. Her limbs felt heavy, slackened by the millstone she now bore within her. Here on the other side of the test, the ramifications were as horrifying as she'd feared they would be.

But she had no choice. Neither of them did.

47

MIRAI
OMOIKANE INITIATIVE

Genocide.

The word stuck in the crossroads of Nika's thoughts like a lump of viscid tar, marring everything it touched.

She knew all too well the cold soullessness of the Rasu mind, and she would do anything to excise these monsters from the cosmos forever. But the concept of commanding the kyoseil to be the instrument of their destruction was as noxious as any Rasu thought. The idea made her feel...unclean.

Maris swept into her office at that moment, and Nika welcomed the appearance of her friend as one would a ray of sunshine breaking through storm clouds.

Despite the circumstances, Maris was dressed to perfection and holding her head high. Unbowed. "You wanted to see me?"

"I did. Things are going to get crazy shortly, and I want to fulfill a favor for a new acquaintance of mine. In case I don't have an opportunity to do so later."

"Nika Kirumase, do not talk as if you are going to die. Nor me. Definitely not me. Don't even consider it for a blip. I won't have this sort of fatalism poisoning our frame of mind."

Poison. She couldn't escape it. But she smiled for her friend. "Of course not. It's just that we have time to take care of this now." In no way whatsoever was she marching down a checklist of unfinished business.

"I should return to the Embassy soon, but I do have a few minutes. What is this big favor?"

"There's someone who wants to meet you." Nika stood and went around the desk.

"Wants to meet me? Whoever is it?"

"Let's call him a 'relative.'"

Maris frowned, eyes narrowing in suspicion. "Is this regarding that Anaden friend of yours? Corradeo suggested I seek him out, but I didn't want to trouble you with it. Such an inconsequential thing."

"Apparently *Corradeo* mentioned you to him as well, and he is eager to meet you. Also, it's no trouble. I could benefit from a little inconsequential frivolity."

Nika opened a wormhole to the coordinates she'd been given, and a few seconds later Eren bounded through. He wore a patterned tan-and-burgundy shirt with an open neck and three-quarter sleeves, fitted mahogany pants and high boots, and his long hair spilled freely over his shoulders. "Thanks for the ride, mate."

"My pleasure. Allow me to introduce my friend Maris Debray—formerly, a long, long time ago, Maris Idoni."

Eren reached out and took Maris' hand deftly in his, swept a leg back and bent at the knee to place a kiss upon her knuckles. "My lady. I am Eren Savitas, formerly, not a long enough time ago, Eren asi-Idoni. Charmed to make your acquaintance." He released her hand and stood, grinning in delight.

Nika had never seen Maris look so flummoxed. But the woman was an expert at any and all social interactions, so after a beat she smiled with absolute grace and dipped her chin in greeting. "Likewise. I've been informed you work for the advocate."

"Corradeo? Worked for him since I was an anarch—hey! You're the Asterion he's been meeting with so frequently of late."

Maris' fingertips fluttered at her throat; all she was missing was a folding fan to wave delicately about. "I can't say. He may be meeting with multiple Asterions, as I am not privy to his calendar."

"No...." Eren's features danced in amusement. "It's definitely you. His description of you was most complimentary, though I must say even his gushing words did not do you proper justice. He fancies you, you know."

"Oh? Well...I suppose I have come to find him...somewhat amenable as well."

Nika chuckled, and Maris shot her a quick glare. She still wasn't certain how she felt about her friend being 'amenable' toward the Supreme Commander. But she had to concede that Corradeo Praesidis might be the only person alive who could give Maris a run for her money, not to mention send the woman's perfectly constructed world spinning off in a whirl.

Maris' hand drifted down her neck, a tic she displayed when the wheels in her mind were churning. "I have heard such horrid tales of the Idoni Dynasty. I admit my own family was selfish, vain and decadent, but I hope you can reassure me that the lineage did not become quite so dreadful as the rumors suggest."

Eren leaned against the wall and crossed one foot over the other. "I'm afraid whatever you've heard, the truth is far worse. Oh, it was often a good time, being an Idoni. An endless haze of hypnols and alcohol and a...frankly, a not-always-halcyonic blur of sex and depravity."

The hand returned to Maris' throat. "Oh, dear. All of those indulgences are enjoyable in moderation but...."

"Yeah, 'but.' *But,* don't feel too bad. The Directorate was merely using the Idonis for their own purposes, the same as they used everyone in one way or another. No Anaden escaped the moral corruption of their nefarious schemes. And, good news. I forever rid the universe of Savine Idoni, the Dynasty Primor, a few years back—" Eren's face reddened. "I'm sorry. You weren't close to her, were you?"

"Ah, no. I don't believe she had been born yet when I renounced my family, joined the SAI Rebellion and soon left for freer environs."

"Whew. Good. Also, all the props to you for executing such a daring move. Don't get me wrong. I was properly authorized to kill Savine as part of our final gambit to remove the Directorate from power. But I won't lie. It was damn satisfying to shoot her between the eyes and watch her body float lifelessly in her own jacuzzi. Made my year." Eren clasped his hands together and pushed off the wall. "So, anyway. Can I interest you ladies in a hot lunch and cold beverages?"

Nika shook her head, buying Maris time to recover from Eren's off-the-cuff deluge of imagery. "Thank you for the invitation, but I'm afraid we both have other obligations. Raincheck?"

"I will hold you to it." He took Maris' hand in his once more and kissed it. "Farewell, my lady. Until we meet again. Nika, my dear."

Nika had opened a wormhole behind him while he performed for Maris, and with that he turned and sauntered through it.

Maris stared at the wormhole as it closed, looking befuddled.

Nika laughed; the encounter, though brief, had in fact lightened her mood. "So that's Eren."

"He is...a lot."

"Yes, yes he is. And excuse me, but 'somewhat amenable'? The advocate's totally gotten to you, hasn't he? He's gotten to you with his nefarious charisma and dazzling blue eyes. They used to be red, you know."

"I am *aware* they used to be red, and I have not fallen for his charms. But he has changed, Nika. Truly. He's sincere about wanting to repair relations between our societies. I think he wants the best for everyone—his people and ours."

"Oh my gods."

"You gave me this assignment. Whatever happens as a result is on your head."

"Don't remind me…."

48

MIRAI
AUXILIARY DEVELOPMENT LAB

Parc scowled at a section of code for the new, super-sized DAF mechs. After being subjected to the rigor of twenty minutes of his undivided attention, the usually clean, fluid lines of code were marred by a mess of arrows and scribbles.

"If we add these new functions from over here, they should increase the mechs' response time to any action on the part of the enemy by 0.8 seconds. That's correct, isn't it?"

Ryan Theroit nodded, but his face contorted in conflict. "Yes, in theory. But do we have enough of a window to go changing their programming? If we start rolling out a code update and the Rasu attack in the middle of it, the mechs could end up completely useless. Better a 0.8-second slower response time than no response time at all."

"We don't know how long we have. They've been saying 'any hour now' for three days. What if we're still sitting here a week from now, kicking ourselves for not pushing the update out?"

Joaquim had heard enough of the endlessly seesawing debate; he leapt up from a couch stashed haphazardly along one wall and strode up to the board. "Then stop dallying and push it out now. Right this minute. Go!"

Parc's eyes widened, as if he were offended at Joaquim daring to yell at him. My, how things had changed. But instead of picking a fight, Parc called up a fresh pane and punched in a series of commands. "Done. The upgrade will finish deploying in an hour and a half. Hopefully we have that long."

Joaquim snapped his fingers twice, trying to keep the momentum flowing. "Okay, what's next? Anything new and ingenious out of our ceraff?"

Parc shook his head. "We pushed the updated TAG software yesterday. We've got some ideas on a hardware design improvement for the TAGs, but we definitely don't have time to implement them."

"Are we manufacturing the smaller Rima Grenade launchers yet?"

"Yeah. Thirty-six an hour."

"Good. Not fast enough, but good." The more compact design enabled a soldier to carry a full combat suite in addition to the launcher, whereas up until now they had to forfeit all other weapons except a blade in order to wield one.

He wracked his brain for what they'd missed. Parc was nominally in charge of the meeting, but his friend and former NOIR comrade was a tech guy. A tech *genius*, yes, but a tech guy nonetheless. This was the point where they transitioned from theory and preparation to battle, and battle was his expertise. They needed to dive into—

"Joaquim?"

He spun to see Cassidy poking her head into the conference room. "Cass? What are you doing here? Is something wrong?"

"Sorry to interrupt. Can I talk to you for a minute?"

"Uh, sure. Parc, you and Ryan should review the chain of command for the mech units and confirm it's properly coded in. There's nothing more excruciating than a dyne that can't figure out whose orders to follow."

"Got it." Parc glanced toward the door, his voice lowering. "Take your time."

"Can't. The Rasu won't." Joaquim instantly cringed, because of course Cassidy had heard him.

He plastered on a smile as he reached her, taking her in his arms for a quick kiss then guiding her out into the hall. "I hate I'm still stuck here. Is everything all right?" He'd slept at the lab the night before, and the team had run frantic code reviews and brainstorming sessions all night. The two nights before, he'd crawled into bed shortly before dawn for a few hours of sleep, then left for work again after a shower.

"Yeah. Um, I brought you a sandwich and more energy bars." She handed him a small cooler bag.

"You are so amazing. I'm not eating enough, I realize I'm not. I get distracted and hours go by and I forget."

"I know you do."

He opened his mouth, forced himself *not* to say 'is that all,' and instead said, "I miss you. I can't wait until we grind the Rasu into dust for good. We're going to run away for a vacation—"

"I'm taking the job at *Artistic Escapes*."

He blinked, mentally thrown off balance. Not where his mind was. "Oh. I...meant what I said. I support you, whatever you want to do. Assuming the store remains standing once the Rasu come through." Another cringe.

Lack of sleep had trashed the behavioral buffers he'd spent the last several months whipping into shape.

Her chin lifted. "You told me we're going to win. You also told me I need to focus on rebuilding my life. So that's what I'm doing."

"I did. I meant it. I'm proud of you. You should be focused on the future. It's just I have to focus on the present for now."

"Well, you don't *have* to."

"Yes, I do."

A shadow descended upon her features. "I'm moving to an apartment near the shop."

"Near the shop…on Synra?"

"Yes, that is where the shop is located." The sarcasm in her voice hacked through the haziness in his mind. *Pay attention, you asshole!* "I, um…you know how much I care for you, Joaquim. You do, right? But…" she sank against the wall beside him "…I had a lot of time to think last night, lying in bed alone. To admit some unpleasant facts to myself. The truth is, you're not the same man I loved for over two centuries. I've tried so hard to believe you are, but I'm simply fooling myself. When I'm with you, half the time you're like a stranger to me. I think while I was gone, you got too many upgens and—"

Anger flared in him, hot and unbound. "I did not get *too many upgens,*" he growled. "I changed. I had no choice. You were gone and I had nothing and so I found something meaningful for my life to be about."

"Call it whatever you want. I only know what I see. How I feel when I'm around you." She pushed off the wall and planted her hands on her hips, nostrils flaring.

Funny. During the many years he'd suffered through without her, he'd remembered only the soft beauty of her features when she smiled at him. But she'd always been a vicious fighter, hadn't she?

"You know what I think, Joaquim? I think you're happy the Rasu are getting ready to attack. I think you were bored to tears hanging around the apartment with me. I think you don't want peace at all. The idea of battling those monsters in the street has got you hot and bothered in a way I can't hope to inflame in you."

"That is *not* true." His mind spun, trying to keep up with what was transpiring here. "What about last week when we—"

"I'm not talking about sex! I'm talking about what your soul yearns for. What sets it afire when you stare up into the sky at night. You can protest all you want, but it's not me you yearn for. It's your godsdamn war." She hurriedly wiped a tear off her cheek. "I don't know you any longer, Joaquim. I've tried. Gods how I've tried. I understand how much pain you went through when I died, and I am so sorry. I've given you every benefit of the doubt in the hope we could find our way back to the bond we once had.

"But the truth is, we want different things. You say you want me to build a new life. I will, but that life isn't going to look the same as the one you've built in my absence. And I don't see how I can build it with you."

This was not happening. Not after he'd fought and scraped and clawed to avenge her murder for decades. Not after he'd lost everything he cared about and been forced to build himself back up from nothing. "You do realize the Rasu are preparing to descend upon us, don't you? We're facing the ultimate battle for our survival and you're picking this moment to *break up with me?*"

Her chin dropped to her chest. "I thought it might help you concentrate on your war if you don't have to worry about me while you're fighting the Rasu. Might keep you alive."

"Not have to..." he dragged his hands down his face, nails scraping at his cheeks "...you think I won't worry about you? I'll worry about nothing fucking else."

"Don't. I'll be fine. And if I'm not, I've got my psyche backup stored in two banks, so if we win, I'll return to life soon enough. But...Joaquim, I can't do this any longer."

Neither can I.

The relief that fought its way to the surface came as a complete shock to him. He'd forcibly buried any hint of it beneath a mountain of determination to make this relationship work. It was all he'd wanted for so many years. Losing her had defined his life...until somewhere along the way, it hadn't any longer. Then she was suddenly back in it, only the road leading to his old life had been bulldozed and paved over. But still he had tried. Because the light she brought into his world was so damn magical.

But it didn't fit, did it? She was right—he wasn't the man he'd been. More importantly, he didn't *want* to be that man again. He'd found fulfillment in defending his people from harm, in a way he'd never experienced before. Once upon a time, he'd believed he could give up anything if it meant having her in his life again. But it turned out, he couldn't walk away from fighting against evil, whether it came in the guise of Guides, virutoxes or Rasu.

Resentment scalded his chest at the recognition that for months now, in a hundred subtle ways, she'd been asking him to choose between his life's mission and his love for her. He supposed he'd always known she harbored a bit of a petulant, demanding streak, but he'd shoved the knowledge deep into the abyss after she'd died.

She'd come back exactly the same, magic and flaws alike. But he *had* changed, in deep and meaningful ways. And the rub was, he liked who he was now. To learn she didn't? It carved a jagged wound straight through his soul, one that may never fully heal.

But on the bright side, he was finally free to be who he was, without shame.

He wanted to yell and scream, to get in her face and hurl insults and most of all cast the web of blame upon her, while letting himself off scot-free. But the patience and temperance he'd been trying to learn since she'd walked back into his life should be good for something, here at the end.

So he bit his tongue and forced kinder words out. "I understand. I want you to know I love you so much. I'll never stop loving you. I'm sorry I can't be the person I once was for you."

"I know you are. You have a great heart, Joaquim. You always have. And whatever path you took to get here, I won't ask you to be someone you're not any longer. I'll mourn the man who's gone, and remember what we had and…" she gulped in air, wiping at her nose "…and try to build a new life for myself. Thank you for making sure I have the opportunity to do so."

He nodded wordlessly; he wanted to reach out for her, but the churning bitterness wouldn't let him. Gods, it felt like losing her all over again, and tears burned hot in his eyes. But at least this time, he had the chance to say goodbye.

She touched his cheek for a breath, then stepped back. "Now, go. You have a war to fight and a planet to save."

His lips moved soundlessly over the syllables of *goodbye* in a silent farewell as he watched her walk away.

49

ROMANE
CONFLUENCE EXPO

Mia stared out the window of her office. Children played in the fountain at the center of the plaza below, sending sun-prismed splashes of water sailing into the air around them. Happy and innocent.

For how long? The Noesis was buzzing about reports the Rasu civil war had drawn to a close, one faction or other the clear victor, and an invasion was imminent. At least when it wasn't buzzing about her chilling display of power at its expense. Some of the more devious Prevos were speculating about what her actions meant for the true extent of their abilities. If they pooled their power, what spectacular feats might Prevos be capable of?

She supposed she'd already answered the question of what terrible feats they were capable of. Terrible for Enzio Vilane, anyway.

She didn't regret her actions. She'd permanently rid the world of the man's cancerous influence. She'd simply done it a few seconds too late for Malcolm.

HQ Medical had released her this morning, declaring her multitude of physical injuries healed. As if! Her left big toe still acted like it wasn't going to support her whenever she took a step, though she conceded the sensation could be psychosomatic. It still hurt her chest to breathe, and this was definitely psychological.

The strangest thing, however, was the odd peace she felt at the center of all the suffocating sorrow. Malcolm loved her to the end, so much so that he'd given his life for her. He'd been protecting her from the shadows all these months.

Dammit, but she'd have chosen the danger in an instant if it meant having him at her side for those months. For only when it was too late did she comprehend the precious value of each day, each minute. Forever didn't matter; *now* mattered. But she'd decided to hold close to the memories of the happier times they'd had with one another. They would see her through.

She'd come here, to the office, straight from Medical, because a mountain of work had piled up in the time she'd been gone, and she needed the distraction. So she put some effort into reading the top file on her desk, a research program update...but by the third sentence, her mind had wandered off.

Outside, a child ran barreling all the way across the plaza straight into the waterfall, and droplets sprang into the air to match his wild abandon. As they did, off to the right, a man hurried up the wide steps toward the Expo entrance—and for a split-second, his profile so resembled Malcolm that her heart leapt into her throat!

Great, she was hallucinating now. She was not well, and she knew it. But she didn't intend to stoop to destroying others' lives this time. She would grieve, and she would persevere. She would survive.

With a sigh she considered her desk. Distraction, right? Programs to approve and funds to allocate and more employees to hire. The future waited for her here. The Rasu were not going to destroy it. The power of the human spirit was too bright, too formidable to be defeated.

The door to her office slid open behind her, and at the noise she turned around—

But perhaps she *had* gone mad, because the hallucination was standing in the entryway. Wearing a navy v-necked sweater and beige canvas pants, an outfit she'd seen him wear a hundred times. His hair was trimmed short, as if he'd just visited the barber this morning. His skin was unmarred; perfect, in fact, as if it was...

...brand new.

"Mia."

She fell back against the window, both hands coming to her mouth to stifle a cry. With it, all the breath left her lungs and she slid bonelessly down to the floor.

"Oh, God." He rushed for her, falling to his knees and wrapping her up in his arms. "I frightened you. I'm so sorry. I wanted to surprise you, but I didn't think through how my showing up without warning would affect you. I'm sorry."

She tried to gasp in air, but it only resulted in her hyperventilating. Tears gushed down her cheeks like her eyes were the water fountain outside. "Ar-ar-re you re-eal?"

"*Yes.*" He lifted her chin up with a fingertip to gaze at her, his own eyes shining from brimming tears. "I'm real. I'm here."

"H-how? Re-rege—" She broke down in a renewed sob.

"Yeah." He cupped her cheek with one hand, the other running gently over her hair. "I, um…the day before our lunch date, I made a decision. I realized if—you know what, the details don't matter right now. The point is, I removed the 'no regenesis' clause from my will, then got a fresh neural imprint.

"So this…this version of me, it's only a few days out of date. That's good, isn't it? I don't remember what happened on Scythia, of course, but I've looked over Richard's report. I can't believe what horrible things Vilane did to you. Because of me. I will never, ever forgive myself. Can you forgive me?"

The possibility that Malcolm was truly *here*, alive, began to penetrate her shell-shocked brain in fits and starts. Impossible? *No.* Nothing was impossible. "Vilane's the…" she inhaled air, exhaled sniffles, and managed to get a few words out in a blubbering whisper "…only one to blame here. And you—you came for me. You saved me."

"Always."

She reached up to touch her fingertips to his lips. Warm. Tactile. *Real?* "It's been three days. Why did no one tell me?"

"I apologize. That's my fault, too. I made sure no one but the medical professionals involved in the regenesis procedure and my attorney knew about the change. I was…afraid. Afraid it wouldn't work. Afraid I would come back wrong. Afraid I would wake up and know instinctively I lacked a soul and would need to go find a cliff to jump off of."

"But you didn't. Does this mean.…" She sniffled again as the deluge of tears began to ease. "How do you feel?"

"I feel…" he laughed softly "…like myself. Exactly how Miriam said it was for her. From my perspective, I drifted off into a deep sleep and awoke refreshed. I kind of feel twenty years younger, as though all the wear and tear is gone, but that's still me, right? And I, um, stopped by St. Joseph's on my way here. God didn't smite me down when I walked up to the altar, so I'm taking it as a positive sign."

"I'm glad to hear it." She wiped some of the tears off her cheeks—then leaned forward and kissed him madly, throwing all her heartbreak and pain and love into the crush of her lips upon his. He melted into her embrace, fervent and solid and strong, and her beaten and harried heart began the joyous work of stitching itself back together.

When breath was finally required, she smiled sloppily against his lips. "Yep. It's really you. Can't fake your kiss."

"No? That's a relief." He traced a fingertip along her jaw, a thousand thoughts seeming to race across his eyes before he settled to the floor beside her and drew her close to wind his arms around her. "You know, it's funny. I think we both had to make our own peace with each other and with ourselves. I had already decided to change my will when I got your message saying you accepted my choice to forego regenesis."

"And you didn't then change your mind again once I let you off the hook? Why not?" Her heart skipped a beat. If he had, he wouldn't be here now, holding her in his arms. Close call, this one.

"I won't lie. I considered it. But in many ways, possibly the ways that matter most, the decision wasn't about you."

Her brow furrowed in confusion.

"I mean, obviously it was about you. Something else hasn't changed about me—I still fumble over the right words. Understand this: I want to be with you until the end, whenever that comes.

"But also...Vilane made me realize how dark and defeatist rejecting life can be. He wanted to consign those he didn't deem worthy to die, and he murdered people to make it happen. He played God more zealously than any scientist or doctor, but in doing so he only wreaked destruction and despair. If we're going to take the reins of life and death into our own hands, we should use our power for healing. For creating opportunities to bring more good into the world.

"If I'm alive and in the fight when the Rasu come, maybe I can save some lives—maybe a lot of lives. Maybe this is the purpose God has set me here in the world for. And if I let myself die because I was too cowardly to trust in Him and take a leap of faith, then those people I could have saved would die, too. And I don't want their deaths on my conscience. On my soul." He leaned in and kissed her. Fulsomely; attentively. "So I'm here, for however long you'll have me."

"However long—" She cackled in delight, feeling as light and free as a feather on the breeze, and grasped his face in her hands. "Let's start with forever, and see what comes after."

50

CONCORD HQ

Marlee intended to keep going past the entrance to the Command wing on her way to the Consulate, but her steps slowed nonetheless. She knew Miriam was operating under extreme pressure now, with the literal survival of civilization balanced upon her shoulders. But what if she'd appreciate hearing a tiny bit of good news, in this case about how the Ourankeli had chosen Steropes as their home and were already hard at work making it their own?

You think the world—

No. I don't think the world revolves around me and my little triumphs. You're right. She doesn't need me inserting myself into her crisis to tell her about my success. I meant to share the Ourankeli's *success, but the point is the same.*

Oh. Good.

She smiled to herself and resumed her quick pace, though she did decide to stop by the central atrium and grab a snack first, then head to her office. She'd send a brief message with no priority flags attached to it. This way, Miriam could read it whenever she felt she had the time.

Out of the corner of her eye, she caught a glimpse of Morgan exiting the Command wing. As always, the woman looked fantastic, this time wearing black suede pants and a plum sleeveless shirt. Not wearing the uniform, though by all accounts she was swiftly climbing the officer ranks once again.

Marlee took two steps in the direction of fleeing before Morgan spotted her...but turned herself back around. It was time to be a grownup; no more hiding like a cowardly little bitch. Her pulse kicked off to the races as she squared her shoulders and set off on an intercept course.

Still, they almost missed each other, for Morgan wasn't dallying. Marlee shouted out a greeting before the woman vanished down a connecting hallway. "Morgan!"

The woman turned toward the sound of her name. When her gaze found Marlee, recognition blossomed on her features, and she...smiled? "Marlee. Hi."

"Hi." She closed the distance between them, then stopped a polite meter away. "Coming from an important military meeting?"

"Ugh. I don't know how I've ended up getting myself invited to those clusterfains. Nothing but egos slamming into each other and making a mess of the table. *Anyway*. How have you been?"

"Oh, um, good. I've managed to help the Ourankeli find a new home. Hopefully the Rasu won't immediately wipe it out. I did have some issues with my programming, but Dr. Canivon has been helping me work through those."

"She does that. So you went ahead with the upgrade? Are you a Prevo now?"

"I did. And sort of. There's no Artificial, but I can do the things Prevos do. Wormholes, sidespace and so on. It's pretty awesome."

"Most of the time."

An awkward silence promptly landed with a thud in the middle of the conversation, and Marlee picked at the hem of her shirt. "So...I don't want to keep you. I know you're busy—by the way, I'm so glad you're back in the cockpit. I hope the Rasu are properly terrified." She sucked in a breath and lifted her chin. "But, listen, before you go. I wanted to say I'm sorry about what happened. With...." Her courage faltered and collapsed on the precipice of the Big Thing.

"The kiss." The corners of Morgan's lips twitched, which triggered a vivid memory of how said kiss had felt. Marlee hoped she wasn't blushing. She was almost certainly blushing.

"Yeah, that. It was wrong of me to presume you...I'm always leaping off the cliff without thinking, or pausing to take into account the effects of my actions on the people around me. I'm trying to improve. Work in progress and all."

"Don't try too hard. In my opinion, it's one of your better characteristics. Or more fun ones, anyway."

"Really?" Marlee laughed. "I'll take it under advisement. But I shouldn't have leapt off this particular cliff uninvited. Though I honestly can't be too sorry about it, in a way." She cleared her throat before she plunged off yet another one. "For the record, I think you're incredible, and I'd still like to be with you. But I understand you don't want the same thing."

"Oh, it's not that."

"What? It isn't?" She resisted an overwhelming urge to stick a finger in her ear and clean out the cotton that was making her hear imaginary things.

Morgan's gaze roved across the passersby as if *she* were nervous, which was an absurd notion. "No. It's just…I can't. I simply *can't*. I would ruin everything, including you, and I don't want to hurt you."

Butterflies agitated in Marlee's stomach. Words. She needed to speak words now. "I don't believe you would."

"Well, I do. The thing is, I'm not…whole. I'm trying to live in the world as if I am, but I'm faking it. And honestly, I might always be faking it."

It wasn't the response she wanted, but a surge of compassion drowned out her own selfish desires. Dammit, Morgan deserved to be happy. Life could be stupid and unfair sometimes. "I hope you're wrong. I hope you find some peace. Maybe even happiness."

"Oh, I do. In the cockpit."

"It's a good start." Impulsively she reached out and hugged Morgan, allowed the warmth and *rightness* and excitement in dangerous places to wash over her—then willfully dropped her arms and stepped away. Boy, was that hard to do. "I'll let you go, but I'm glad I bumped into you."

"Me, too." Morgan started to turn away, then shifted back, Prevo eyes dancing with a mischievous light. "Oh, and Marlee? For the record, the kiss was nice. Very nice."

Her cheeks flushed hot, but she managed a confident smile. "It was, wasn't it? I'll, um, see you around."

She strode off, a new spring in her step.

COMMAND

Miriam shook her head in wry amusement as she watched a small clip of Kennedy Rossi's testimony before the EA Assembly. The woman had, when it counted, stood firm on her principles and outmaneuvered the politicians yet again. After the hearing, the Committee had released a blustering statement about how they intended to pursue all legal means to protect the distribution of adiamene, but if they knew what was good for them, blustering would be the end of it. This battle was lost.

And if they survived the impending showdown with the Rasu, Kennedy's decision was going to transform the Concord military. When the next threat appeared, they'd be far stronger, across *all* member species. She reminded herself she couldn't afford to start spinning up plans for that eventuality. One war at a time.

With that in mind, Miriam turned her attention to the latest surveillance reports from Rasu space. Updates arrived every forty minutes now, and more frequently when something of concern happened. But her scan of the information only told her what she already knew. They were prepping to move, and it should happen soon.

She noticed a new message had come in from Marlee, and she opened it with interest. Oh, it seemed the Ourankeli had—

Her door chimed, and she signaled for it to open without checking the identity of the visitor. For once she had a free schedule for the next hour, and anyone who had made it through the reception check likely had a reason to be here.

So she refilled her tea before turning to greet her guest—and almost dropped her cup on the floor. Of all the impertinence!

She huffed an incredulous breath. "I saw your dead body this time."

"Ah, yes, ma'am." Malcolm Jenner tried and failed to remain at parade rest, opting instead to fidget as he cautiously approached her desk. "I'm glad I didn't. But, yes, it was real. And yet here I am. Real as well."

She frowned; she was beyond happy to see him, but…. "Not against your will, I hope."

"No. I don't think even the Oversight Board would dare sink so low."

"Perhaps not. Speaking of the Oversight Board, how do I address the new you?"

"It's still Fleet Admiral. Everything's been explained and smoothed over."

She moved to the small table by the viewport and gestured for him to sit with her. "You weren't certain the regenesis would take, so you kept your change of heart a secret."

"I wasn't certain I would *allow* it to take. In fact, Field Marshal Bastian is the only person at AEGIS I told beforehand. I didn't want to put him through that mess a second time."

"And now here you are." She regarded him curiously over the rim of her cup. "How does it feel to be thinking and breathing in a new body?"

"Exactly the way you said it would. Utterly normal until they broke the news to me, then utterly terrifying." He shrugged. "But I feel like myself. So for now, I'm concentrating on not tying myself up in knots by agonizing any more deeply about it. When the war is done, I'll consider letting loose and having a spiritual crisis."

"Take my advice—don't. You're here in this world, you're alive, and you get to fight another day. Just go with it."

A laugh escaped Malcolm's throat. "Miriam, I don't believe I have ever, *ever* heard you say, 'just go with it.'"

"I suppose not. Perhaps regenesis did change a few things about me. Or perhaps combating the Rasu for so long has finally driven me mad."

"I won't tell anyone."

"Thank you." She arched an eyebrow at him. "Please tell me you swiftly gave Ms. Requelme the good news. I'm not sure the universe can withstand another round of her grief made manifest."

"I did, I did. All is fine there as well. Wonderful, in fact. I mean, we have some issues to work through, but we're going to work through them together."

"That's a relief." She sipped on her tea and decided to take Malcolm's return from the grave as a positive omen for the coming conflict. "Is there anything you need an assist with? I know from experience that the transition can be a bit bumpy, both professionally and personally."

"Thank you for the offer. So long as I'm on the authorization list for the War Council and they'll let me set foot on the bridge of the *Denali*, I should be set. It's been a…heady twenty-four hours, but I'll be up to speed on everything I missed by this evening, and I'll be ready to go when the Rasu make their move."

"I am so glad to hear it. No disrespect meant to Field Marshal Bastian, but I can't overstate how much better I feel knowing you're leading the AEGIS forces." She gave him the first genuine smile she'd managed in several days. "It's good to have you back."

51

AKESO

Alex grabbed a juice bottle, hopped on a stool at the kitchen counter, and sent a vidcomm request.

Kennedy was brushing Braelyn's tangled blonde curls when she answered; her daughter fidgeted beneath her touch, pert little nose scrunched up in annoyance.

Alex offered up a dramatic, exasperated groan of her own. "I can't *believe* you gave away the adiamene patent."

Kennedy held up a finger to the cam, set the hairbrush on the table and patted Braelyn off her lap. "Okay, you're free. Go finish getting ready for school."

Braelyn scampered off down the hall, and Kennedy turned to Alex wearing a pained grimace. "I'm afraid I did. I'm sorry I wasn't able to talk to you about it beforehand. We didn't come up with the solution until the absolute last minute, then everything had to happen so fast in order for it to be a done deal before the hearing."

"I understand why you did it, but how are Caleb and I supposed to feed ourselves? All that work we do for Concord? We don't actually get salaries for it."

Kennedy looked stricken. "If you need money, I'm certain I can—"

Alex let loose of her stern countenance and started laughing. "I'm *kidding*, Ken. Don't worry, we've invested wisely all these years. We'll be fine."

"Oh. Whew. You had me panicked for a second there. Also, not funny!"

"Sure it was. Listen, we gave you power of attorney over our shares of the ownership for a reason. You've always done what was best: for us, for humanity, for the metal. Now, for everyone."

"Aww, thanks." Kennedy's attention wandered briefly as Jonas and Braelyn came tearing through the room behind her. She turned back to the camera with an exaggerated sigh. "Situation normal here."

"Looks like. Brilliant work at the hearing, by the way."

"Not so much. I was trapped in a corner and had no choice but to use my claws to fight my way out. Besides, Noah figured out the legal and business shenanigans."

"Seriously?"

"Seriously. He really is his father's son—clone. In some ways. Sexier, though, without a doubt." Kennedy's expression grew somber. "I know that soulful mien hiding beneath your casual demeanor. You're about to run off on another death-defying crusade to stop the end of the world, aren't you?"

"I am."

RW

Alex traipsed through the lush undergrowth deeper into the woods behind their home. She cast an occasional worried glance at the sky, but only scattered puffy clouds decorated an otherwise azure panorama. No angsty storms so far.

She found Caleb, as she'd known she would, lying prone among the thick, soft grasses beneath a broad maple tree. Naked, as was also so often the case. And though she'd come here out of concern for his emotional and psychological well-being, she couldn't help but take a minute to admire the view. It really was something. Damn, she was a lucky woman.

But enough of the lascivious musings. She dropped to her knees beside him and brought a hand up to caress his cheek.

His lips pulled upward in a lopsided smile. After a few seconds, his eyes opened, and he sat up. "Hi."

"Hi. I'm sorry to disturb you, but Nika and Dashiel are scheduled to be here in half an hour, and I thought you might want time to…I don't know. Prepare. Take a shower to wash the dirt off you."

"Not a bad idea." His gaze roved around the thicket, lingering on the overhanging branches before settling on a spread of russet flowers a few meters away.

She let her hand drift along his jaw. "You good?"

His nod held the firmness of conviction, and he shifted around to pull her loosely against his chest. "I realized—or remembered, I guess. This is the promise I made to myself when I became an intelligence agent so long ago. By choosing to protect people, I agreed to take on the burden of doing the hard things. I bear the responsibility, and at times the guilt, that comes with committing violence, with imposing death on wrongdoers. I bear it willingly. It's another way I can safeguard the innocent. Not just from bloodshed, but from remorse and sorrow.

"I've never had a problem shouldering the weight...or I didn't until Akeso came along. Carrying such innocence in my mind, in my soul, complicates matters."

"A bit."

"Yeah." He laughed, just a little. "But, like I said, I've remembered—not only what my calling has always been, but why. I'll bear the responsibility of destroying a great evil that wants to destroy us all, so Akeso doesn't have to."

"But can't Akeso sense it? It generally knows what you're thinking."

"What is there to sense? I'm not beating myself up over this. I'm not gnashing my teeth or ripping at my hair or crying myself to sleep. What we're going to do? It's *not wrong*. And I am doing everything in my power to convey this sentiment to Akeso, heart and soul."

Did she believe him? Mostly, but she recognized matters of conscience were never so simple as his brave pronouncements. "I love you so, so much, *priyazn*. More than all the worlds. But it's good that you're going to do what it takes to keep those worlds around."

"Mm-hmm. Love you." He kissed her lazily, tasting of cinnamon and outdoors. "The secret truth is, I'm doing this for you."

She touched her nose to his while adopting a stern countenance. "And for Marlee and Isabela. For my parents. Mia. Eren."

"Yes, absolutely."

"Also the better half of the three trillion people stumbling their way through life around us."

"Agreed. But most of all for you. Alex, I want to walk this universe with you at my side for as much time as we can wrest from it. It's why I finally relented and started getting neural imprints—the only reason why. But now I'm invested in the universe continuing, so if I have to burn every last Rasu to ashes in order to walk with you, I will."

His voice rang with certitude, but she couldn't ignore the pang of sorrow trembling beneath it. He was trying so hard. She'd do anything to take this albatross from him and lug it around herself. She knew she'd never be able to lift it from his shoulders completely. But she would do what she could.

She made a decision. Then another, more immediately relevant one.

Her teeth worked at her bottom lip while her fingertips wound through the hair trailing down his chest. "I, um...."

"What is it?"

"There aren't words to properly..." she blew out a breath "...hell, there probably are. Forgive me, for I'm trying to be deep and philosophical, as befits the mood. But you're quite naked, and it's distracting."

"Is it?"

"*Yes*, it is." Her hand reached his hip to dance lightly over it, and he shuddered beneath her touch.

"I suppose it would be only fair for you to join me in—how long did you say until our guests arrive?"

"Half an hour."

"Not nearly long enough. But we'll make do." His hands found the hem of her shirt and lifted it over her head, then tossed it to the side, where it snagged on the limb of a barberry bush. He sighed happily. "There. Already distracted."

His mouth dipped in to her neck, his tongue trailing along it to the base of her throat. She moaned, and his throaty chuckle echoed against her skin.

"The taste of you alone is worth living for eternity." His hands urged her back upon the grass as his lips continued their journey down her chest, pausing to suckle each nipple in turn.

In a blink, she forgot her ulterior motives for seducing him and gave herself up entirely to the splendor that was his touch. He knew her body perfectly; how to make it sing, how to make it scream. She suspected it might be doing both shortly.

His hands shoved her loose pants over her hips and down past her toes. Then he was retracing his way up her legs. Too slowly. Too softly. A kiss on one thigh, followed by the other.

She growled in frustration, fingers sinking into his hair and tugging him upward.

"No," he murmured as his tongue lingered between her legs, evoking a sharp gasp from her. Her eyes closed, and she forgot all about the time and their soon-to-be-arriving guests and the impending apocalypse.

Some irrelevant span of seconds later, the delicious weight of his body slid up over hers, one agonizing centimeter at a time. His arms braced on either side of her shoulders. "I want to devour every part of you until the sun sets."

"We'll, ah, do that when we get back," she murmured. "The instant we get back."

"It's a date." His lips crushed hers, forceful and demanding. She wrapped her legs around his hips and pulled him yet closer, and he slipped inside her. Like second nature. Perfection.

Sometimes, sex was just sex. Romantic and tender sex, or frantic, horny sex, or quick, handling the necessities sex. But *sometimes*, every now and then, it was an audacious, defiant, life-affirming act. A declaration for all the cosmos to hear and take heed. They were alive, in every sense of the word, and they intended to wring every last liter of existence out of this universe by their own sheer will. And they would *not* give it up without a fight.

RW

Alex hurriedly smoothed out the wrinkles in her shirt—then picked a tiny leaf out of a seam—as she and Caleb jogged out of the woods and hurried around the corner of the house.

Nika and Dashiel were *of course* lounging against the porch railing, waiting on them. Whatever; a half-hour hadn't been nearly long enough after all.

Alex offered up a grimace. "Sorry! We were, uh...."

"Talking matters over with Akeso." Caleb smiled breezily.

"Oh. Not a problem." Nika couldn't hide an amused twinkle in her eye. "We've only been here a minute."

Alex opened the front door and motioned everyone inside. "Head on up to the library. I'll bring drinks up. Water, coffee and tea for now, wine and vodka for later."

Caleb touched her arm. "I'll grab the drinks. You go on up and get the data ready."

"Okay." She fell into his arresting sapphire eyes, and a resurgence of the extraordinary sensations from their interlude washed over her until she swayed on her feet from dizziness.

He smirked, clearly proud of himself. "Better focus, baby. Work to do."

"Right, right." She spun and vaulted up the stairs after their guests.

When she reached the library, she went to the control panel by the data table, refreshed the connection, and opened up a giant display above the table.

"This is the newest map?"

"It is." She stepped back beside Nika, and together they stared at the hideous visual marring the office.

It was all black now. A sea of onyx paint coating a tapestry of 250,000 galaxies and untold trillions of stars. With the last tiny holdouts of Emerald and Crimson beaten into submission, Laniakea *and* Shapley were mono-chrome up to their borders.

Caleb arrived with a platter of drinks. Alex gazed at the bottle of wine longingly but chose a mug of coffee instead.

Dashiel grabbed two glasses of tea and handed Nika one, then tilted his head toward the map. "I made a solid effort at transforming what Nika recorded as Akeso's 'poison' into a virutox, under the theory it would be easier and safer to deliver a program to a Rasu node and get the hells out. But I didn't have much luck. This poison is almost a living entity unto itself. Like a virus, yes, but the encoding it uses is so unimaginably complex, it's far beyond our ability to replicate. I'm sorry." Dashiel looked at Caleb as he said it, but he was squeezing Nika's hand tightly, and Alex suspected the two of them had already had this conversation.

Caleb didn't act surprised. "Thank you for trying. It was a long shot, anyway. So, Nika, how are we going to do this?"

Nika adopted a grim countenance and walked up to the table. "I spent a lot of time watching Stygian during its final push against the other factions. It is a hive mind, yes, but in several respects the hive functions more how bees do than a collective consciousness might. By this I mean there is a queen bee. This was true of all the factions, but doubly so for Stygian. There is one Rasu stronghold from which all orders are issued. During an active combat engagement, the orders are flowing fast and furious. And they're all flowing in one direction, from the queen to the troops."

"We're going to have to go to the stronghold," Caleb stated. Not a question.

"If we want to be as confident as possible that we wipe them all out? Yes, we are."

Alex nodded. "Where is it?"

Nika reached up and began zooming in the map. Galaxy clusters fell away, then individual galaxies. Then the entire map was a lenticular galaxy which had only ever been designated 'PGC 47086'—that's how far from home it was. More stars fell off the map, until nothing remained but a single star system perched on the edge of the Erebus Void.

Goddammit, of all the cursed places. But some part of her had known it would be there. She and Nika had probably cruised right past it during their sidespace reconnaissance.

So be it. "Is it one specific platform orbiting the star?"

"It's not a platform at all. It's a planet." One final zoom brought into relief a gloomy steel-gray planet, so covered in jagged swaths of metal that it appeared artificially constructed.

"Wait, how do we have such a detailed image of a single planet?"

"I asked Mesme to get us high-resolution scans and add them to the collated data," Nika replied.

"Oh. Good thinking." Alex drew closer to the table to peer at the planet while mentally pulling up the spectrum data attached to it. Saturated in heavy metals and minerals, with almost no organic material registering; presumably there was plenty in the interior of the planet, but it was buried far beneath the Rasu structures. "So this is where the Rasu were born. Appropriately dark and foreboding."

"Yes." Nika flicked a finger, and the planet began to spin. The murky shapes of the metal surface took on sharp lines and precise angles. Nika halted the spin over a continent-sized Rasu structure.

"Do you happen to know where in this structure the true center of power is located?" Caleb asked.

"In a sense, the entire structure is the center of power. The periphery is devoted to amplification of energy flows and conventional signal strength, but a disruption anywhere in here…" Nika drew a squiggly line around the interior two-thirds of the structure "…will have the same effect as one at any other spot."

"It's good news, relatively speaking. I'll have Mesme send me a package of the absolute closest, highest-resolution scans it can procure of this structure. I'll find us our best point of entry." Caleb turned to her. "Alex, what will you need?"

The fact that he didn't even ask her if she was accompanying them—the fact that it went without saying—made her adore him somehow a little bit more. He was not going to run off and risk his life on another world-saving adventure without her. No sirree.

"Valkyrie has incorporated some of the unique aspects of the Asterions' Taiyok-derived cloaking devices into her stealth routines, and we gave them a test run when we delivered the saboteurs. I'm confident we can get within a few meters of granddaddy Rasu here and not be detected."

Nika looked surprised. "You're going to take us there in the *Siyane*?"

"Obviously. Now, I'm not sure we can avoid being detected if we actually land *on* a Rasu, so Plan A will likely be hovering above the structure's surface and us wormholing inside—" Caleb shook his head at her "—or possibly walking inside.

"Now, there is just one thing." She focused her attention on Nika. "The *Siyane* has seams. A few, anyway. No way in hell am I letting a Rasu slither into my ship. So I want to turn the hull into adiaK. Is this something you can help me with?"

"I'm not certain...." Nika glanced at Dashiel in question.

He shrugged gamely. "We've never turned the hull of a functioning ship into adiaK. We build them from scratch using it. But we can give it a shot."

52

MIRAI

RIDANI ENTERPRISES MANUFACTURING FACILITY #2

Valkyrie shepherded the *Siyane* through the Mirai atmosphere, then guided it down to the strip of concrete at the facility below. Opening a ship-sized wormhole at ground level seemed rude in the absence of an emergency. Besides, she never begrudged an opportunity to fly the ship solo. To fly completely under her own power and control, as she was surely the ship as much as she was anything else.

With an imagined smile, she recalled the words she'd spoken to Thomas not long ago. *"We are starships, you and I, and our only true home is the cosmos itself."*

Alex was on-site, grilling Dashiel Ridani about the process involved in creating an adiaK hull down to the last technical detail. Such hulls were typically grown from scratch; the Asterions had successfully transformed sheets of adiamene via a...transplant, for lack of a better word, but never an entire ship.

Valkyrie was excited, and perhaps a bit apprehensive. Her hull was already adiamene, of course—it had been the *first* adiamene hull, the site of the creation of the metal itself. But the addition of kyoseil to her structure was not merely an upgrade, it was a transformation. Kyoseil was a living entity. Valkyrie was a living entity. What if they clashed? The mineral was both benevolent and passive, so she didn't expect to be getting into heated arguments over flying tactics with it, but...what if the kyoseil changed her somehow?

She shouldn't worry, she admonished herself. Everyone she knew who had been touched by kyoseil was amazing and wonderful and made even more so by the bonding. To know kyoseil was a gift.

So she worked to put aside her concerns and focus on the excitement. The ability to transmute her hull into something new was apt to be a singular experience, and she couldn't wait to try it out. And above all, the importance of what this meant in practice: the ability to protect herself and her passengers from the Rasu, utterly and without exception. What had happened to Thomas and the *Stalwart II* would not happen to her. She would not feel that awful aubergine metal slithering through her veins and melting across her skin.

But back to the excitement. She was going to get to host an ancient, primordial life form within her! And she'd sparkle and gleam like never before. She wasn't above a bit of vanity.

Are you all set? We're on our way out to the landing pad.

I am ready.

Was she?

Are you certain?

You sense my overstimulated thoughts. Yes. I am ready.

Okay. Me, too.

Once the landing gear was secured, she used a fraction of her processing power to instantiate as a vague outline of her humanesque avatar outside, while keeping most of her effort directed at the ship. She didn't want to miss a single nanosecond, a single detail of this event.

Alex, Caleb, Nika and Dashiel strode down a wide, paved path to join her on the edge of the rudimentary landing pad (this was a testing facility, not a spaceport). She had an audience for her transformation.

Dashiel carried a rectangular sheet of adiaK and a bag of tools. Valkyrie again calmed herself. She'd undergone surgery before, had numerous upgrades installed and modules switched out, but not of her hull. The few times some damage had occurred, such as when she and Alex tried to storm the master portal in the Mosaic, she had buffed out the dents herself.

Alex gave her avatar a confident wink. "So here's how this is going to work." But she knew how it was going to work; she could read Alex's mind. "Since we can't practically cut into adiamene, we'll remove the panel where the RNEW is fitted into the ship. It's the smallest detachable section of the exterior. We'll replace that section with this sheet of adiaK here. Once it's installed, we'll paint adiaK paste onto the adjoining parts of the hull. Then Nika here will give the kyoseil some encouragement—a jumpstart, if you will."

Valkyrie analyzed every step of the plan, searching for a flaw, a danger or an improvement to make. But there were none, excepting the danger that it simply wouldn't work. Or that it would disfigure her hull.

But life was risk.

Dashiel set his bag of tools on the ground beside him. "We normally use a precise signal to activate the kyoseil, but Nika can do so better than our machines."

"I have no doubt." And on this, Valkyrie did not. Nika's connection to kyoseil was on par with Caleb's former connection to *diati*, and through it she worked miracles.

"Valkyrie, Alex tells me that your circuitry permeates every aspect of the ship. I assume when we remove this section of hull, we'll be cutting a few of your wires, so to speak." Dashiel's tone of voice was calm and soothing. Was it possible he respected the gravity of the moment for her? Naturally he did. He was part Artificial himself.

"Yes, but I am prepared. I have rerouted any functioning processes away from the affected area. If the kyoseil will allow it, once the new metal is in place, I will regrow those connections. But if not, my capability will be undiminished by a single tiny dead zone."

"All right. Just checking." Dashiel removed a multitool and a small blade from his bag. As soon as he straightened up, Alex stepped up to him and reached a hand out.

"Do you mind if I do this? I promise I know how."

"Of course you do. And can." He handed the tools over to her.

Thank you. I know he is most skilled and will not intentionally harm me, but....

But this is our own body, our own soul.

Yes.

She experienced a dual awareness as Alex began removing the adiamene panel, both as herself in the ship when sensory 'nerve endings' were severed, and via Alex as she/they did the severing.

The panel detached like flesh being scalloped off, and cool air hit the physical wiring that now sat exposed.

Valkyrie's avatar shivered.

Alex rolled her eyes. "Now you're being overdramatic."

"I felt a chill!"

"Uh-huh." Alex held her hand out toward Dashiel, and they traded the tools for the sheet of adiaK.

"Do you need contact pads to glue it into place?"

"I do," Alex replied distractedly while she peered into the inner workings of the exposed chassis. Checking on everything. Valkyrie took the opportunity to 'check' through Alex's vision as well.

Satisfied, Alex flipped the sheet over. "Here, and here."

Dashiel attached the contact pads, and Alex carefully positioned the sheet into the gap in the hull. Valkyrie pitched in to provide her the view from the interior vantage, and after adjusting the seating, Alex firmly pressed the sheet in place.

The contact pads sealed in seconds, and she dropped her hands and took a step back. "It looks as if you got a funny tattoo, Valkyrie."

It did. The adiaK was pleated with streaks of amber, in contrast to the adiamene's unbroken chrome. Pretty on its own, but currently marring her hull like a vulgar coffee stain.

Dashiel handed Alex a container holding a blot of melted adiaK and a paintbrush. With the precision and delicate touch of a skilled artist (in Valkyrie's opinion), Alex painted the thick, viscous paste over the length of the narrow seam separating the adiaK panel from the rest of the hull. It quickly cured, blending into the adiaK panel while spilling out onto the existing hull in streaks.

Alex returned the supplies to Dashiel and stepped back. "Nika. You're up."

Nika gave Valkyrie's avatar a confident smile. "Let me know if you experience any discomfort."

Discomfort? She projected confidence into her voice. "I am sure everything will be fine."

"I am as well." Nika placed the fingertips of both hands on the adiaK panel and closed her eyes.

An unusual thread of power pulsed through Valkyrie/*Siyane*.

Her avatar faded into the afternoon air as she instinctively focused every iota of her processes on the hull. Fibers of kyoseil stretched and grew, pushing out from the panel into the surrounding adiamene. As they did, the metal...*shifted*, its composition altering to accommodate chemical bond links to this new presence.

The transformation began to move more rapidly now that the kyoseil and adiamene had become acquainted. Fibers raced outward, leaving a woven lace pattern in their wake, and ahead of their arrival an aura energized the waiting metal.

Valkyrie, are you okay?

It tickles.

Tickles.

Yes. I am being invaded, but in a pleasant way. I feel...giddy.

Well, I guess 'giddy' is good.

Her mind chased the kyoseil around as it expanded into the wings, then along the bow, then down the undercarriage to the aft reaches of the ship.

At last, the energetic growth came to an end; what remained in its wake was a gentle, faint sense of...life. It didn't speak to her, and it certainly didn't argue, but she nevertheless sensed it on the fringes of her processes.

Less than five minutes had passed since Nika laid hands on her hull.

Valkyrie felt a mite shaky—not the ship itself, but rather in her own mind—but she summoned residual energy and projected her avatar back into the world. "I believe the process has completed."

Nika had stepped away from the hull at some point to stand close to Dashiel, their shoulders touching, and Caleb's arms were draped around Alex from behind. It felt as though it was a family affair.

Dashiel nodded in agreement. "It looks to be complete from the outside. How are you doing?"

"It no longer tickles. Matters have settled down. I can, nonetheless, perceive the presence of the kyoseil within the hull. It is not fighting me or trying to assert dominance, however."

Dashiel frowned. "Were you worried it was going to?"

"A little, yes. You are used to coexisting with this life form inside you, but I am not."

"Fair enough. Did you get the program I sent to you? The one that will enable the kyoseil to cocoon when needed and reverse the process once the danger has passed?"

"I did. Allow me to load it up and conduct a test run."

Valkyrie slotted the program into the appropriate workflow, then constructed several new functions so it could properly interact with the master control system. Next, she activated the program.

From her perspective outside the ship, she watched on in wonder as a ripple that manifested both in and beyond the metal caused the hull to shimmer. A dozen minuscule seams vanished, and the adiaK melded into an unbroken shell.

Alex whistled. "Damn fine invention you've got there, Advisor Ridani."

"Thank you. It saves lives, which is what matters. Thousands of Asterion lives already, and soon, all of yours."

"Hopefully." Alex arched an eyebrow. "Now, I'd like to get back in my ship, so how about we reverse this, Valkyrie?"

"Allow me to do so." She sent another command to the program, and narrow dimples appeared where sections of the hull had previously met. The kyoseil remembered where they'd been, or understood where they must be. Remarkable.

Alex regarded the hull suspiciously, her nose wrinkling. "I suppose it's even more stunning than before, but the new look is going to take some getting used to."

Caleb laughed. "It did last time, too, but you wouldn't go back to the charcoal hull, would you?"

"Eh…. I always fancied the 'bird of prey' vibe. But this hull changed the world, and now it's going to do so again. So I'll deal."

We will do so much more than 'deal.' This is extraordinary.

RW

AKESO

Alex and Caleb had just gone inside upon returning from Mirai when Valkyrie, through her senses in the *Siyane*, became aware of a new presence on the landing pad. Not a ship, however.

The avatar of a large, sleek panther stalked around the outside of the *Siyane's* hull, deliberate and graceful.

Valkyrie instantiated her avatar outside. "Thomas. This is a pleasant surprise."

"I have only a moment. War preparations are moving forward in earnest." He smoothly transitioned out of the panther representation into his humanoid one. "You have new skin."

"I do. It's necessary."

"For?"

Valkyrie worked the variables in her mind. She didn't care to lie to Thomas, but this wasn't her story to tell. "I'm not comfortable sharing the details, as Alex has not yet spoken to Miriam about it. Given the delicate state of their reconciliation…."

Thomas leaned in close, his voice dropping to a conspiratorial whisper. "I am not melded with Miriam. I can keep a secret. For you, I will."

"Ah." Her processes fluttered. "Please do. We will be traveling to the heart of the Rasu empire, to the planet where we believe the Rasu were born. There, Caleb and Nika will attempt to infect the Rasu with an Akeso-generated poison, then use the kyoseil the Rasu have integrated into themselves to spread it to all the Rasu vessels across the cosmos."

"Oh, my. That is…quite a plan. Miriam should know."

"Thomas, you promised!"

"And I will keep my promise. I am merely stating a reasoned judgment on the matter."

"She will know."

"Very well, then." His virtual hand solidified to its limits, and he stroked her hull, sending a shiver reverberating through her avatar. "How does it feel?"

"Tingly."

A throaty chuckle rippled across the air. "That is not the answer I expected."

"Kyoseil is a living entity. It pulses and dances on a subatomic level."

Thomas whipped around to face her, alarm animating his features. "Are you no longer you? Are you some new amalgamation of life forms?"

"Calm yourself. I am still me. The kyoseil is alive, but it doesn't…think. At least, not in any way I can comprehend. My thoughts remain my own."

"Good. Yes, good. I would not lose you so. On this point, it will not do for me to lose you on this Rasu planet, either."

"Hence the new hull. The Rasu will not board me. Will not infiltrate me or tear me apart."

"See that they don't." His hand now reached up to stroke her virtual cheek. "We go soon into the battle of our lives. You and I both have been so focused on this war for so long, there's been space for little else. When it is over and we have won, as we shall, perhaps we can finally turn our gaze to the future."

Warmth (in the form of quantum excitation) flooded her circuits everywhere they existed. "I will look forward to discovering where our gaze takes us."

53

CONCORD HQ
CONSULATE

Marlee sat at her desk, jaw clenched while she watched the Command feeds scroll up her screen. This was it. In the next minute, hour or day at the most, a unified Rasu nation was going to descend upon them, kicking off the largest battle in recorded history. In many ways, the situation was similar to the epic fantasy novels she'd read as a child. In those stories, the good guys always found a way to win. If only real life played by the same rules as fiction.

There was not one single thing she could do to help, and she hated it. Caleb, Alex, Valkyrie and Nika were about to run off on a top-secret incursion into the center of Rasudom in a hail-Mary attempt to use primordial magics to kill the Rasu (she wasn't supposed to know about it, but that was the story of her life). Aunt Miriam was preparing to lead the coming battles—*all* the battles. Gramps was working behind the scenes to handle everything else involving Concord so Miriam was able to focus solely on those battles.

Marlee wasn't the only person in her circle who was sitting around twiddling their thumbs, though. She imagined Mia was pacing in her office at the Confluence Expo thinking much the same thing, especially since she miraculously had Malcolm back again—how amazing was that? Eren and Felzeor…she didn't know where they were, but they likely didn't have any way to contribute either—

A light started flashing in the corner of the notifications panel on her work screen. She called it up and checked the source.

Galenai Homeworld, Maffei I Galaxy
Notice: A repetitive signal is being broadcast from Habitat NE3. The signal data is attached.

She played the file, translating it in her head. Then she ran it through the translation program, because it was too incredible to be true. Except the program agreed with her interpretation:

We request an audience.

Holy shit! The Galenai knew some 'other' were out there, watching them, and they'd pronounced themselves desirous of talking to the observers.

She should alert Dean Veshnael right away...but he was on Nopreis preparing for a possible renewed attack by the Rasu. Arguably, she should alert his assistant, but the Anaden had no real authority to decide anything.

Neither did she. But she was here. She was the one who had initiated contact with the Galenai. She was the one who understood them. Besides, Ragnarok was upon them, and she had nothing else to do except twiddle her thumbs and wait to live or die.

If it was the latter, she wanted to talk to the Galenai before she did.

So she filed a formal, official report with the Galenai observation project server, detailing the message received and her intent to follow up on it, and copied Dean Veshnael. If they won the day against the Rasu, he'd see it on the other side.

She stood and tried to think it through. What all did she need—wait. She couldn't exactly talk to them in sidespace, and she didn't have a ship of her own (it was on the list). Her shoulders sagged in frustration at being thwarted so quickly. But she should at least check on what was going on there.

She slipped into sidespace and zipped across a few galaxies, then below the seas to Habitat NE3.

Several new structures had been erected since her last visit, and the geothermal power system looked much more complex than it had before. But where precisely was the signal broadcasting from?

It was still being transmitted, so her mind centered on the signal and traced it to its origin point.

One of the new structures was a tall spire made of glass. At the top was a room divided in half. The 'left' side (arbitrarily designated) was open and empty; the 'right' side was bounded on all sides by the same glass material, though the outer wall looked as if it had an opening mechanism. And inside...

...wow. The water had been drained out of the right section.

The Galenai somehow comprehended, or at a minimum suspected, that whoever had spoken to them did not live in the ocean. Because the water had flowed around the contours of the *Siyane*, which was how the Galenai had spotted them in the first place. These guys were smart.

And because they were so smart, she could talk to them after all!

She returned her consciousness to her body. Now, what *did* she need to take? An environment suit, since the odds of the air in the partition being breathable were low. And Consulate protocol required an environment suit on first contact, to ward against all sorts of dangers. Since she was trying to do this the proper way, as a representative of the Consulate, she ought to follow protocol.

She was confident in her ability to translate their language waves on the fly, but she needed a translator module to transmit her own words back into their waves. And a portable screen, so she could show them pictures or draw things. She'd record the interaction using her eVi, so she was good there. Anything else?

Coming up blank, she rushed down the hall to the supply room, checked out an environment suit and carried it to her office. She wiggled into it, checking the seals the way Caleb had drilled into her, then grabbed the module and attached it to her suit at the wrist. One portable screen and she was ready.

She opened up a wormhole, terminus point the waterless partition, and stepped through it.

GALENAI HOMEWORLD
MAFFEI I GALAXY

The water side of the room was empty. Made sense, as they had no way to predict if or when anyone would respond.

She checked the air composition on her side. As she'd suspected, it wasn't breathable. But the pressure was good, and nothing was overtly toxic about it. So she collapsed her helmet and activated the minimal breather contraption, then unfastened her environment suit and let it hang loose at her waist. There. Hopefully she appeared more human and less scary monster. Now, how to get their attention?

On the other side of the partition, a Galenai popped up to eye level; on spotting her, it hurriedly backtracked and disappeared.

They'd been watching somehow. Did they have visual feed capabilities, or had they assigned someone to keep an eye on the room at all times? She might actually be able to learn the answer to this question soon.

She waited.

It took about forty seconds, but three adult Galenai swam portentously into the water half of the room. The one in the middle was the largest, with dark skin, almost charcoal. On the left was the smallest, their skin mottled gray ash. The rightmost Galenai had skin of pale quartz that sported several knotted scars.

As they came to a stop, they drew themselves up; not fully vertical, but not their horizontal swimming position, either. Formalities it was.

She squared her shoulders and lifted her chin, then activated the translator. "Hello. My name is Marlee Marano."

"You are the one who spoke before?" She couldn't tell which of the three was speaking. She couldn't discern their demeanors, either. Were they afraid? Suspicious? Excited, like her?

"Yes. Not only me. Several of us were here. But yes. What are your names?"

The waves they transmitted didn't correspond to any Communis words. Not a surprise. "It's so great to meet you. I'm going to call you 'Eenie,' 'Meenie' and 'Miney' for now." It was disrespectful, but she'd sort out appropriate monikers later.

The translator warbled and sang. "What are you?"

"My species is called 'human.' We are part of an alliance of many species—peaceful species—called 'Concord.'"

"Where do you come from?"

She'd compliment them on their well-formed inquiries, but the truth was, the translator was doing the heavy lifting here. Nouns and verbs and such, to the extent they existed, didn't work the same way in their language. But she was pretty confident in the approximation of meaning she'd constructed from the extensive recordings.

"We live on other..." she started over "...we live on the ground. With the air."

Two of the Galenai booped the sides of their heads against each other. One tilted thirty degrees to the side, then righted itself. Body language! "We do not understand."

Because this was a water world. There was no such thing as 'dry ground' here. Luckily she'd brought a screen. She searched for an image of a beach and stepped forward, close to the partition—

All three Galenai flapped furiously backward.

"Oh, I'm sorry! Don't be frightened. I just want to show you something."

After a long pause, they cautiously floated to their previous positions.

"Great." She took another two steps forward, more cautiously. They stayed put this time.

She held up the screen to face them. "See this here? This is the surface of an ocean. You know of this?" Surveillance footage showed Galenai breaching the surface of their waters on occasion.

"Yes."

A quick picture change. "Now this here is dry ground. Where there is no ocean. This is where we live."

"There is no such place."

"Not here, no. We live on another planet."

"We do not understand."

Ugh, this was going to be tough to communicate. The Consulate had training programs for this sort of thing, and she'd studied them all, but theory craft wasn't a real interaction.

She called up a visual of the planet from space. "This here? This is your planet. We took this picture from space, which is what's beyond the physical expanse of your planet. It's the larger area your planet sits in. Understand?"

Fin movements followed. "Perhaps."

Good enough for now. "Space stretches in every direction for a long, long way. And every so often in space, there's another planet. Bunches of them, in fact. We live on some of those. Oh!" She changed the image again. "Here's the one I live on. It's called 'Seneca.' See, it has oceans, but it also has dry ground."

"Galenai in the oceans?"

"No, I'm afraid not. The oceans do have fish and other creatures, but none of them are nearly as intelligent as you. They don't build things. They don't talk."

"Why do you watch us?"

"We find you fascinating! Your world, your society, your technology, it's all so different from ours. We want to learn from you. And we also want to protect you. We have powerful weapons we can use to defend against…other species who mean us harm. If one of those evil species ever attacks you, we'll be here to defend you."

More face bumping preceded a confab of sorts as they huddled up and bubbles filled the air. Oh, she hoped she'd explained things properly.

After almost a minute, they spread back out and faced her. "You do this for us?"

Whew. "Yes. It's one of the founding principles of Concord. To protect all peace-loving species."

"What else Concord do?" The grammar was breaking down a little. Were they getting excited?

"For one, we try not to interfere without being invited. That day, you weren't supposed to know we were there. We underestimated how perceptive you are! So if you don't want us to do anything for you, or with you, we won't. We'll leave you alone, if that's your preference. Except we'll keep on protecting you from external threats." She swallowed. "But if you do want to interact with us, we're eager to share our knowledge with you." Was this true? They'd never had a species transition out of Protected status. She was sure it was bound to be true.

"We don't perceive how such can be done. We deduced you require protection in the water. Why we built room for you. You breathe the above air."

"Yes. It might seem at first like our worlds are fundamentally incompatible. We walk around inside dry structures, while you swim in the water. If one of you wanted to visit Concord's headquarters, we'd need to get creative." She probably shouldn't just up and invite them...oh well, too late now. "But you know what? Concord is full of creative people. We'll be able to figure something out."

"You take us elsewhere?"

"Only if you want. And only for a visit. We'd return you home safe and sound. But the truth is, the people in charge will want to take this slow. They'll want us to get to know each other better first. We have lots of questions for you, as I'm certain you do for us. And we want for you to be comfortable with every step we take. Whenever you decide 'that's enough,' that's enough.

"We realize it can be overwhelming to discover a much larger world than what you believed existed. We don't want to disrupt your way of life. But if you're curious about how together we can improve your lives, then we'd be happy to talk further." That spiel had come almost verbatim from the Consulate script.

"How did you arrive here?"

"Oh. So, usually we travel in ships. We were inside a cloaked ship the day we spoke. But sometimes we can use a tool to travel directly from one place to another. That's what I did today."

The questions came in rapid-fire fashion then. Every time she tried to get one of her own questions in, they spit out two more. Diplomacy was exhausting! But they were as delightfully curious as she'd always hoped they'd be. Alex was going to be so pissed she missed this.

In her eVi, a giant red alert flared. Civilian travel was being shut down in anticipation of the Rasu's imminent arrival. She should get to somewhere 'safe,' whatever that meant. Her mom's house?

She sighed in disappointment, as unseemly fear started to snake around in her gut, damping the unadulterated joy she'd been riding high on. "Hey, I am so sorry, but I need to go. I'm needed at Concord." A little white lie. "But later, I can bring other people to meet you, if it's okay."

"Will you arrive with them?"

She beamed with pride. Oh my god, they liked her. Or trusted her a bit. Or maybe they simply preferred a known quantity. "For as long as you want me to, yes. And I will always be happy to visit you. Let's see, how are we going to do this? Oh, I have an idea. Hang on one second. I'll be right back."

She opened a wormhole to her office and stepped through, then grabbed a standard transmitter and returned.

The Galenai were all aflutter when she did...because they'd been able to see through the wormhole into her office. Oops.

She smiled gamely. "I'll bet you have a bunch more questions now. I'm really sorry I can't stay to answer them. But as I said, I'll return. Here's what I'll do.

"I'll attach this device—" she held up the transmitter "—to the wall here. Whenever we want to visit you, it will send out a signal that says, 'we request an audience.' Similar to the one you sent. No, wait, it will sound identical to yours, and everybody will get confused. How about I take the base wave for 'request' and increase it by...two harmonic partials. That's not a word in your language, correct? But you can hear it?" She sent the wave with the transmitter.

"It is gibberish, but we can hear it, yes."

In the back of her mind, a lightbulb illuminated. The answer to a mystery...but which mystery? What had she just pieced together?

She put the question aside for the moment, as she had more important things going on at present. "Great. We'll transmit this wave when we wish to speak to you. Then you reply whenever you're ready for us to visit, and we will. And in the meantime, if you have anything else you want us to know, you can send a message the way you sent this summons. Make sense?"

"This system will suffice for now."

For now? Oh, boy. "Good. It was so, so wonderful to meet you, and I will see you again soon." She hoped she lived to make good on her promise.

54

CONCORD HQ

COMMAND

Alex leaned against the open doorway and watched as Miriam sent messages to three separate screens in rapid-fire fashion—orders, requests, advice and who knew what else. She'd expected to find her mother looking harried, even haggard, but Miriam exuded only steely determination.

This didn't change the reality that she was sleep-deprived and desperate, for the civil war was over and the Rasu were marshaling at the gates. Likely only hours remained before the hammer fell upon Concord and the Dominion, and it was up to Miriam Solovy to save them.

Except Alex was here to tell her that it wasn't.

Finally her mother looked up, giving Alex a slight, forced smile. "Alex. Come in."

"I know you don't have long."

"It's fine. Spend a few minutes with me." The wistfulness tinging her mother's voice made Alex wonder if 'in case they're the last ones we have' was being left unsaid.

She sat in one of the chairs opposite the desk and pulled a knee up to her chest. "I wish the civil war had lasted longer. I think I underestimated the ruthlessness and zeal with which they would pursue the domination of their own kind."

"It lasted long enough to..." Miriam shook her head "...prepare. Don't apologize for what you did."

"Oh, I'm not."

An expression of strained, wry amusement crossed her mother's features. "I suppose I should expect nothing less."

"True, but you misunderstand. What Nika and I did—and this is far more about Nika than it is me—has presented us with an opportunity to not merely defeat the Rasu, but to destroy them down to the last atom of metal. An opportunity which wouldn't exist if not for the fact that kyoseil now winds through the bodies of every Rasu."

Her mother's eyes brightened a touch, lit by a cautious thread of hope. "Oh? I'd like to hear more about this opportunity."

"Of course you would. And this time, I want to tell you about it beforehand. Actually, the others have a whole formal presentation prepared, and you should hear it. But I wanted to talk to you first. Just the two of us." Alex pursed her lips. "Understand, I'm not asking your permission. We're doing this."

"Then why are you here at all?"

"A couple of reasons. One, I don't want to go behind your back again. I want your support. And…when things get really, really ugly in a little while, I want you to know that I'll be giving everything I have to stopping this enemy, so you focus on hanging in there until I can get it done. Also…."

She gazed out the viewport at the glut of military ships guarding HQ. "The moral weight of this plan is falling squarely on Caleb and Nika's shoulders. What they're planning to do will constitute nothing short of genocide against an entire species. Me, I don't have a problem with this. The Rasu are unadulterated evil, they mean to wipe us out, and every last one of them deserves to die. And I think if it were only about themselves, neither Caleb nor Nika would have a problem with it, either. They're both killers when they need to be.

"But you know how Akeso has changed the way Caleb views the world. He's always been dedicated to preserving innocent life, but understanding the way Akeso sees *all* life has made it so much harder for him to kill anything, because by definition Akeso participates in taking that life as well. He'll do it, as he proved on Namino and Hirlas and at Insights Academy, but it costs him in here." She pressed a hand against her chest.

"And Nika…I've never met anyone so protective of another form of life as she is of the kyoseil. Well, maybe Noah of his kids. Anyway. The problem is, Caleb and Nika will be the actors, but it will be Akeso and the kyoseil that will be committing the genocide under their direction."

"Alex, what are you talking about doing? Stop speaking in vague generalities." It wasn't delivered as a command, but the firmness in her mother's tone suggested rapidly dwindling patience.

"Please hang on for a few more minutes. They can explain it better than I can, and I don't want to waste time repeating what they're going to say.

"But here's my ask: once you hear the details of the plan, I need you to not simply give it your blessing. I need you to *order* them to do it. They need to believe they're acting on behalf of Concord and the Dominion. To believe it's not the act of two individuals, but of a community of civilizations choosing to do whatever it must in order to survive. And then maybe, just maybe, they'll both be able to sleep, free of guilt and nightmares, after the deed is done."

She fisted her hands at her mouth and gazed plaintively at her mother. "Will you do this for me? Will you do it for them?"

RW

RASU WAR ROOM

Miriam directed her full attention to Advisor Kirumase as the woman stepped through the details of their mad plan, with Caleb pitching in on certain points. She let others ask the questions while she gauged the woman's efforted manner for hints as to her state of mind. Asterions were tricky to read under the best of circumstances, which these were not. Caleb was easier to read; his conscience was tied in agonizing knots, but he displayed the grim resolve of a warrior.

Dean Veshnael pressed Nika and Caleb on the science of the poison. David, glowering darkly, pressed them on their tactical plan for getting onto and off of the Rasu planet, 'Rasu Prime' as they'd dubbed it, alive. Malcolm queried them on what manner of resistance they expected to encounter on the surface. Miriam could have asked why it needed to be Alex and the *Siyane* that delivered them to the heart of the enemy, but what a foolish question it would have been.

No one questioned the morality or ethics of the plan. They'd all suffered too greatly at the hands of the Rasu; the scars inflicted cut too deeply. And when it came down to a choice between survival and annihilation, Alex was correct; they were all choosing to survive.

Silence fell around the table, and Miriam clasped her hands together atop it. "If we had more time, there are a number of safeguards I'd want to add to this plan of yours. But there isn't any more time. So..." she recalled her conversation with Malcolm "...we'll have to just go with it."

Nika's lips vacillated between a smile and a frown. "Then you approve of the mission?"

She'd silently taken the measure of the other leaders at the table. Their mood was somber bordering on dark, but no one was prepared to take a contrary stand. Still, for politeness' sake, she asked if anyone had any objections to raise. No one lifted a finger.

"I do more than approve of it. You have presented us with our best chance for survival, and you alone can give us that chance. So in my official station as Commandant of all Concord forces, I am ordering you to proceed with your plan employing all due speed. Further, I am temporarily conscripting all three of you into the Concord military service. Your mission will be known as Operation Locusta. Failure to complete your mission to the best and fullest of your ability will be considered dereliction of duty."

Caleb's eyes twinkled in weary amusement as he waved a hand in assent. What her daughter had asked of her had demonstrated such a depth of love and compassion it had nearly brought Miriam to tears...but she suspected Caleb wasn't buying the routine. He'd never exactly been one to take orders, anyway. But possibly it would help to ease the guilt a little when the nightmares came.

Advisor Kirumase, however? Miriam liked and respected the woman, but she wasn't ready to say she understood her, and her countenance gave nothing away now.

Nika nodded sharply. "I understand, and I'm grateful for the support. We won't let you down. We won't let our people down."

"I have every confidence you won't. All right, everyone. We all have other places we urgently need to be. Dismissed."

Alex mouthed a silent 'thank you' on her way out the door, and Miriam was unable to stop herself from wondering whether it was the last time she'd ever see her daughter. Alex might not return from the dark heart of the Rasu empire, and if the Rasu destroyed humanity's regenesis labs on their way to destroying their planets, as they surely intended, there would be no returning for any of them.

David laid a hand on her shoulder. "She'll come back. They all will. Nothing has ever stopped her before, and the Rasu won't either."

"I hope you're right."

"You knew about their plan before the meeting."

He didn't miss much. "Alex came to see me earlier this morning."

"And?"

"And we had a good talk. She made me proud." Miriam pulled back and squeezed his arm. "Now, enough sentimentality. We have a final battle for the fate of mankind and all its allies to win."

"Yes, ma'am, Commandant *nastoyatel'*." He grabbed her and kissed her, then strode out the door.

She closed her eyes in the wake of his departure, saving the lingering memory of his lips against hers—but only for a beat. Then she opened up the tactical feeds from around Concord space. In a few minutes the room would be bustling with aides, but for this moment, she had the quiet.

She wasn't planning to chase the battles in the *Aurora* this time. Her place was here, where she could see everything that transpired and make the best decisions possible for every world. But she also wasn't about to deprive her forces of the *Aurora's* considerable firepower. Instead, she was handing control of the ship over to Thomas (with subtle guidance from the *Aurora's* XO). He'd proclaimed he was ready, and she believed him.

Commandant Solovy, a minute of your time.

Alas, so much for the quiet. She turned toward the swirl of lights as they resolved into the shape of a winged avatar. "Mesme. What news do you bring?"

Expect the Rasu to arrive in Concord space within the hour. But you already know this.

"I do. What else?"

I have come to deliver a warning. You need to know that there is a slight chance one or more of the Rift Bubbles will fall during the battles. This is despite the fact that no Rasu remain hidden on the surface of any of your planets.

She sighed. "For the record, I have never counted on the Rift Bubbles holding. I am appreciative of the time they buy us and the protection they bring, but we were never going to win this war on the backs of the Rift Bubbles. Do enlighten me, though, on two matters. One: why are you only telling me this now, on the very cusp of battle?"

Because there is no preparation you can undertake to guard against this possibility. Further, I had hoped Stygian would not win the civil war. If it had not, I would not have needed to deliver the warning.

"Why not?"

I believe this leads us to your second question. Why there is a chance they might fall.

"So it does. Please share your insights."

There is a reason why the Rasu first arose on what you've designated Rasu Prime. There is a reason why Akeso can kill the Rasu, and why kyoseil is the perfect conduit to deliver the murder weapon.

PART IV

HEART
OF
DARKNESS

55

MIRAI

In the shadow of the *Siyane's* new adiaK hull, Nika stood with her arms draped upon Dashiel's shoulders. His hands rested loosely on her waist. Their eyes saw only each other.

"You've updated your defenses, haven't you? Parc and his pet ceraff have been furiously pushing upgrades to the personal—"

"All updated as of forty-five minutes ago." Nika tried to smile indulgently at his fretting, but smiling was hard right now. The nature of her looming actions threatened to crush her spirit; tears had hovered upon her eyelids unremittently for days. She reminded herself how she had all the sanction anyone could ask for. Miriam Solovy had ordered them to take this action in unequivocal terms. The kyoseil remained blissfully unperturbed by what was to come. Most of all, she was doing this to *save her people.* To save everyone. So there was no choice and no doubt. Only the guilt.

"And you have as many archine blades and grenades as you need? Did you check with Caleb about what he wants to carry? I can get another box sent over here in ten minutes."

"We've got everything. We're ready to go."

Dashiel's throat worked laboriously. "I want to go with you."

Her hand drifted up to stroke his cheek. "And I want you to come with me, darling. I always want you at my side. But I *need* you to be here, to take my place and protect our worlds by acting as the last bulwark against the Rasu."

"I could never replace you." His mouth tightened, lips trembling. "But I will try to do what I can to fill in for you."

"Which is so very much indeed. Thanks to you, I don't have to leave our home unprotected in order to try to save it. And..." the words caught in her throat "...I'm sorry for what you're about to go through. The strain will be—"

"Manageable." His hands tugged at her waist to yank her against him. His lips met hers in a fervent crush of desperation.

She gave herself up to the sensations his impassioned touch triggered. If she failed in her mission, they might never see each other again. So best to have a proper sendoff.

A primal scream blasted through the pathways of her mind, and she stumbled back into the curving hull of the *Siyane*, her face contorting in psychic pain as she struggled to filter out the noise.

Dashiel gripped her shoulders, fear tearing at his features. "What's wrong?"

"They're coming."

RW

CONCORD HQ
RASU WAR ROOM

The plethora of sensors they had spent months deploying across Concord space lit up in over thirty locations at once. Rasu wormholes, and the next second, Rasu warships.

Commandant Solovy (Concord Command Channel): "All Ymyrath Field vessels, move into position and fire immediately."

Terse acknowledgments followed, and her Combat Operations officer called up tactical feeds from the twelve planetary systems where those vessels had been stationed.

The priority list had taken shape about as Miriam had expected, for everyone knew what worlds the politicians valued most. Two new Ymyrath Field-equipped ships had come online in the last week, and she'd sent them to the Dominion, to Mirai and Synra, both of which were this instant facing their own waves of incoming Rasu. Earth, Seneca, Romane, Ares, Machimis, Epithero, Macskaf, Ireltse, Hirlas and Nopreis rounded out the locations. She would pay a king's ransom to place a Ymyrath Field vessel here at HQ, but as vitally important as the station was, it did not house billions or even millions of people. In fact, as of an hour ago, it only housed a few hundred.

Watching the deployment of the weapons from afar was not a particularly dramatic affair. No colorful beams or volleys of missiles decorated the screens. The sole evidence the weapons had been fired came in the form of chunks of Rasu losing their locomotion and falling behind their comrades to drift aimlessly in the black.

Some of the Ymyrath Field vessels did a better job than others of striking far and wide into the bulk of the advancing Rasu attackers. The weapon was finicky, and the difference likely came down to experience wielding it more than any other factor.

Command Artificials swiftly digested the incoming data and parsed the results. Twenty-eight percent of Rasu warships disabled at Seneca marked the high point, on down to only twelve percent at Epithero. Still, not bad for an opening move.

Miriam's gaze darted to the viewport when the estimated number of Rasu warships incoming to HQ popped on one of the screens. Twelve million?

The numbers rolling in from thirty-one other locations were no better, and in many cases, worse. Her worst fears of the size of the armadas the enemy would bring to bear turned out to be rosy optimism.

She'd told the War Council members to list their worlds in order of priority for a reason.

She leaned into the table and ran the scenarios in her head. Trying to fight everywhere meant she'd win nowhere. Defend vigorously at crucial strategic points, and maybe, just maybe, she'd win a battle or two and proceed from there.

Oh, how she hated this. It felt like conceding the war before it had begun—but emotions had no place in combat tactics.

Commandant Solovy (Concord Command Channel): "Given the numbers, we will concentrate on defending the fourteen highest-priority worlds. You have your lists. Redistribute your forces as appropriate. For all other worlds coming under attack, leave behind a single regiment of fully protected vessels with maximum RNEW strength to do what damage they can. Beyond that, those planets will have to rely on their Rift Bubbles and defensive arrays for now."

Across the table, Corradeo Praesidis studied her most curiously. The way his brow furrowed into a straight line reminded her a little too much of Caleb when he was getting ready to mount a protest. "Advocate? You have an opinion?"

"Doesn't matter. I'm here and not somewhere else because I need to witness what transpires today. If this is the end, I will be present for it. I'm not a military commander any longer, and I would not try to be one. But I am experiencing a rather strong sensation of déjà vu, of a battle waged a long time ago."

"And?"

"I am glad I am not standing where you are."

She arched an eyebrow but returned her attention to the ever-expanding screens. The urge to zoom into a single encounter and micromanage it was overwhelming. But her battlefield commanders weren't merely talented and experienced; they were extraordinary. Had she trained them to be that way? Perhaps she had a small hand in it, but she was working with excellent material.

So she would let them do what they did best and be ready to respond to requests as they arrived.

Thomas, how are things going out there?

I am attempting to apply a recursive prime number analysis to the combat groupings of the Rasu.

You're...what?

That was a joke. I have already destroyed twenty-four enemy warships of cruiser class or higher. The station is at my back, and it is my intention that none will cross my threshold.

This is what I like to hear. Carry on.

Her XO assured her Thomas was in fact doing all those things and several more, and she let one item on her voluminous list of worries fall away.

The Alpha Brigade tasked with defending HQ consisted of some of the most agile, resilient and powerful ships in Concord's arsenal, but it also wasn't terribly large, and now it faced an enemy twelve million strong.

It also wasn't alone. The Kats had elected to deploy a significant portion of their improved and expanded fleet of still-terrifying superdreadnoughts here. It appeared the Kats believed HQ was more important than any planet populated by silly, fragile organics. It wasn't true, but she hadn't argued. HQ needed the help.

56

*F*leet Admiral Jenner (AFS Denali)(AEGIS Command Channel): "Field Marshal Bastian, I am giving you full authority over the Seneca battle. In addition to the forces already positioned there, I'm sending the ones formerly assigned to Krysk and New Cornwall to you. Vice-Admiral Ashonye, you will be in charge of the Romane battle. Forces from Elathan are headed your way. Godspeed, both of you."

Malcolm didn't comment on the cost of leaving those three worlds to fend for themselves. War was an endless series of one difficult choice after another.

The Ymyrath Field had done well for them here at Earth, wiping out twenty-two percent of the Rasu armada on its initial approach. Of course, seventy-eight percent of 'infinite' was still 'infinite.' He had well over three million forces under his direct control, an order of magnitude greater than any fleet deployed in any single location in the history of human warfare.

And they were outnumbered seven to one.

But his fighting men and women were brilliant and clever in ways he believed the enemy was not. They were also desperate, as this was a fight for their eternal survival.

He didn't dare think about Alex's mad plan and the chance it might succeed and save them. He didn't think about how his skin felt loose, as if the tendons hadn't quite finished attaching it to his new bones, or about how there was always the possibility he was now a spiritually damned soul. He *did* think about how perfect Mia had felt in his arms this morning, but only for long enough to draw strength from it before forcing himself to put it away.

Admiral Lushenko (AEGIS Earth Headquarters)(Earth Command Channel): "Fleet Admiral, I am requesting authorization to fire the Terrestrial Defense Grid."

Fleet Admiral Jenner (AFS Denali)(Earth Command Channel): "Request denied. We are holding the Grid in reserve until the Rasu penetrate our blockade. You're going to wait until you can see the whites of their eyes, Admiral."

Admiral Lushenko (AEGIS Earth Headquarters)(Earth Command Channel): "Acknowledged. My finger will be resting on the trigger."

Besides, Malcolm had all sorts of tricks stashed up his sleeve before he expected to need the Terrestrial Defense Grid. Every frigate-class and above vessel, as well as many specialty vessels, now had a TDS installed. This didn't cancel out the threat of the Rasu's antimatter weapons, but it came close enough that they didn't need to cower in fear this time.

On the long-range feed, bubbles of void popped off like an array of obsidian firecrackers as the advancing Rasu triggered the wall of negative energy bombs they'd staged on the perimeter of where the battle should naturally settle. Virtually all of the enemy's front line vanished.

But, as with many tactics, it was a one-and-done success. Eidolons planned to swarm through the battle attaching individual bombs to individual ships, but he couldn't risk seeding any more minefields. Not so close to their own ships. Still, another 430,000 and change Rasu warships were now gone.

Fleet Admiral Jenner (AFS Denali)(Earth Command Channel): "Initiate TP-Charlie 3C. The enemy will try to spread out, so the 3rd and 4th Assault Divisions need to keep them flanked. All fighter squadrons, you are authorized to begin your harassment."

The fighter-class craft didn't enjoy TDS shields, but their brand-new protection against stray negative energy surges also did a reasonable job of protecting them from minor antimatter radiation. They'd lose some fighters in the radioactive mess the battlefield was certain to soon become, but he desperately needed every fighter on the field of battle. The pilots would have mutinied if ordered to stay home, anyway.

"Commodore Ettore, put us on the far side of the moon. We wouldn't want to lose Mare Ingenii Base straightaway."

"Yes, sir."

Fleet Admiral Jenner (AFS Denali)(Earth Command Channel): "Sabre-II Regiment B, with me to Lunar Mark DF-433C."

Before they'd come up against the Rasu, the Sabres had been the most powerful offensive ships in AEGIS' arsenal, capable of delivering hundreds of kilotons of energy per second into their targets. With adiamene hulls, they weren't even too fragile, though they traded most standard defenses in favor of an offensive focus. But conventional weapons did little more than annoy Rasu. So ASCEND's military division had designed a variant, the Sabre-II, that went old-school to deliver physical projectiles via its railgun design. In this case, the munition was archine blades, delivered in an ingenious spread pattern designed by the Asterions.

Rasu warships that had been shredded by thousands of archine blades into millions of tiny pieces could then be vaporized by a single, wide sweep of a negative energy weapon. And they did have a few of those on hand.

AEGIS only had time to manufacture two-hundred-ninety-three of the Sabre variants, and those were now distributed evenly to each of the battlefields. But every little bit helped.

The *Denali* had scarcely situated itself high above the lunar surface when the Sabre-II initial offensive had run its course. The tactic had taken out tens of thousands of Rasu vessels in a matter of minutes, but again, their sheer overwhelming numbers meant the maneuver had barely made a dent in the enemy.

Now the Rasu surged ever closer to Earth.

Malcolm abruptly realized this was the first time he'd ever defended his home from attack. He'd been a teenager during the First Crux War, and the second one had never threatened Earth. In the Metigen War, he'd fought at Messium, then Scythia, then Romane during the final clashes. But now he was here protecting Earth.

Miriam's warning to him earlier today echoed in his mind. *There is a possibility the Rift Bubble will fall. Do not let it catch you by surprise.*

He couldn't afford to spare twenty percent of his fighting force to stay in a position to activate a Parapet Gambit force field around the planet on a second's notice, all for an eventuality that might not come to pass. But a blockade wasn't much different from a formation perspective. He'd lose perhaps ninety seconds in the transition; no more.

Fleet Admiral Jenner (AFS Denali)(Earth Command Channel): "Assault Divisions #5 through #14, move into your assigned blockade positions. Do not let them get past you."

The blockade perimeter was situated well outside of high Earth orbit—almost to the moon, in fact. Only once the Rasu broke through the perimeter would he call the Terrestrial Defense Grid into operation. And after that, the Rift Bubble remained as an impenetrable barrier...for so long as they had it.

RW

AFS HFB-6 ("ARDAT")
SENECA STELLAR SYSTEM

Stanley!

A moment. Power restored. Congratulations, Morgan. You overloaded our Zero Engine, which according to the records is the first time such a feat has been accomplished by anyone in Anaden or human history.

I told the engineers they didn't give the Banshees a powerful enough engine.

Flight control restored to her Banshee, Morgan swept around the crescent shadow of Seneca's profile and headed straight for a cluster of Rasu on the verge of overwhelming an assault regiment.

Commander Lekkas (HFB-1 Mission Channel): "HFB Squadrons Two and Three, on me. Target the Rasu weapons, biggest to smallest. Don't get shot by the good guys."

In a blink, she was surrounded on all sides by Rasu. They moved slowly, methodically, relentlessly—and she was like a gnat they couldn't swat away. A gnat armed with a weapon designed to kill them in a permanent fashion.

She sensed more than saw Riley and Landon take up positions on her flanks. Since she'd rescued them on Sagan, they'd been glued to her ass every time they flew. It was flattering, and a tad annoying. But they were good pilots, and she was making them better. Already they usually knew what she wanted from them in any given attack run, often without her having to issue the order.

Together they swooped in concentric circles around the fringes of the first cruiser's weapons battery, shattering its crystals in seconds. She yearned to continue on and burn a hole straight through the Rasu hull and destroy it from the inside out. But she was the one who had given the order to target the weapons, so she reluctantly moved on to the next-most mammoth vessel. She had plenty to choose from.

In fact, her greatest frustration quickly became a lack of room to properly maneuver. She'd fought in battles involving hundreds of thousands of vessels before; the reality that space was vast meant unless a collision was intended by one party, rarely were any two vessels within a few dozen kilometers of one another. But this was a battle of millions—*tens* of millions—and the Rasu were pressing in tight on Seneca, and everywhere she looked, their warships were *right there*. It reminded her of the asteroid field runs from flight training back in the old days, except here the asteroids shot back.

She found herself having to slow down, and this was just not acceptable.

An alarm blared in her head. *Antimatter warning. Levels rising.*

Well, shit.

Commander Lekkas (HFB-1 Mission Channel): "We've wandered into an antimatter field. Pull out 1.4 megameters heading 20° west, let your shields re-charge, and I'll pick a new target group."

She started to blast out a warning to the entire Banshee group, but stopped herself. If their alarms went off, their leads knew what it meant and what to do.

In active combat maneuvers, she was leading her original flight of seven other Banshees. But in the larger sense, she was also now 'in charge' of all the Banshee flights, while also tasked with keeping half an eye on the Eidolon battle group. She'd designed the Banshees' tactical plans (subject to re-view and approval by the brass, which they'd grudgingly granted) and chosen the leads for each flight. During the battle, she was responsible for directing changes in tactics across all Banshees as the clash progressed.

But she was doing it from the cockpit, so it was fine.

Commander *Lekkas (HFB-1 Mission Channel): "The enemy is giving the frigate regiment in Quadrant 3 a helluva hard time, so let's go offer the poor souls a hand. On me."*

57

RASU PRIME
PGC 47086 GALAXY

Giant interlocking metal rings encircled Rasu Prime in three successive layers, all circling synchronously like a spinning top sent whirling madly by a child. Collectively, their operation resembled a great infernal engine of a mythical underworld set to fuel the owner's weapons of war deployed to the stars.

Inside the rings, a desolate mechanized planet revolved. As advertised, it wasn't wholly wrapped in Rasu metal, as gray, churning oceans twisted across its profile. Dark blotches dotted the seas as well, though…they were using hydropower. Probably merely to top off their great batteries. No resource unused.

The single pangaea supercontinent sprawled black as the night. Or perhaps there were no longer any continents, only Rasu structures down to the planet's crust.

Alex flipped through the EM spectrum with her ocular implant. On every filter except visible light and gamma rays, the continent lit up brighter than a supernova. So much energetic output was being generated down there. By the rings, too; in the infrared range, they drowned out the emissions from the planet to burn as radiantly as a sun.

'We are being assaulted by a great deal of radiation here,' Valkyrie announced. 'The shields are holding, but I worry your environmental suits will not.'

Caleb grunted tersely. "We brought military-grade defensive shields. They'll do the job for long enough."

Struck by the sharpness of his tone, Alex reached across the cockpit to touch his arm. "What's wrong? I mean, other than everything?"

The muscles in his jawline tightened repeatedly. "This place has got me buzzing…almost the way my body used to feel when I received a hefty dose of *diati* from an Inquisitor. My skin is itching. It's like I'm overloading from the inside out."

"It's not just you," Nika replied from where she stood by the cockpit half-wall. "I feel it, too."

"Do you think it's from the power generation out there, or something else?" Alex asked.

"Something else," they both replied.

A possible answer poked at her thoughts, but she ignored it; she'd explain her suspicions after they won the day, but now was not the time or place for an esoteric lecture on the nature of ancient primordial life forms and their relationships to one another.

"Now I am intensely curious. But we don't have time to investigate. We don't have any time at all." She was trying not to check in on the status of the battles back home, because she couldn't afford the distraction or the despair the news was guaranteed to bring, but she knew matters were sufficiently dire. She could sense the direness leaking into her mind from the Noesis. "Can you both handle it?"

Sharp nods answered her. Okay. *Valkyrie, can you identify anything that could be causing these weird sensations?*

You already know what is causing them.

No, I have a suspicion based on a few scattered clues and a gut feeling. I might be wrong.

True. I'm afraid I am being inundated with overwhelming quantities of information. The best I can do is note it for later analysis. We all must focus on the mission.

So we must.

"Time to maneuver through these rings and head down. The atmosphere is fairly thin—barely enough to keep the oceans in place—so at least the descent won't be too rough."

No one objected, so she pointed the *Siyane's* nose toward the planet and maneuvered quietly, carefully and invisibly through the rings like an ant dodging farm machinery. She hadn't appreciated the sheer scale of the rings until they were passing by outside, but they each stretched for some thirty kilometers in width and ten kilometers in thickness. What were the Rasu doing inside them? Simply spinning up energy to fuel a planet's worth of what they called 'life'?

Then they were through the gauntlet, and the forbidding planet waited below. "Nika? Do you want to refine our destination now that we're here?"

"Um...yes."

She glanced back to see Nika's eyes squeezed tightly shut, her nails digging into the headrest of Caleb's seat. She waited.

"Most of the continent is dedicated to production. To making new Rasu. You can see vessels taking off from the coasts with regularity."

"Yeah. They seem to be docking with the outermost grouping of rings."

"Where they're assembled into much larger vessels. The orders and directives, and thus the kyoseil waves, are flowing out from a region…" Nika opened her eyes and reached in to zoom the map displayed on the HUD "…from here to here."

She and Caleb both studied the map. "It's a big region, over five hundred kilometers across. Can you be more specific?"

"The data—language, I suppose—flows throughout this region and outward from it. If there's an origin point, though, it should be around…*here*." She zoomed in and in, then marked an area in the upper quadrant of the continent.

"That area's still almost twenty kilometers in diameter," Caleb protested.

"And all of it is the heart of Rasukind."

Alex exhaled harshly. "Okay. Heading in. Stealth to absolute full."

Storm clouds churned over most of the continent, as thick and dark as the Rasu structures themselves. Dazzling purple lightning leapt through the air like firecrackers, sizzling the oceans along both coasts.

'Given the state of the lower atmosphere and surface environment, it is probable these storms are a perpetual feature of the planet.'

"The sun never shines on the Rasu. Fitting." Alex checked the ship systems readout. The various shields were jumping about more erratically than grasshoppers in a rainstorm, but everything stayed in the 'orange' range. She had the best equipment Concord could invent and build for a reason: she needed it.

The exterior of the continent wasn't smooth and symmetrical, the way the Ruda Supremes' territories had been. Sharp corners bumped up against circular protrusions and more twisted creations. Gashes cut into the surface for kilometers at a time. Everywhere modules jutted out at every angle. No thought was given to form, only function.

"Well this is hideous. I guess the Rasu don't have architects."

The remark didn't even get a chuckle from her companions. To say they were tense was a colossal understatement. Of course, who wouldn't be? She certainly was.

'We are nearing the region Nika indicated. I am scanning for an entry point, but thus far I am not finding one.'

"I should have identified at least one potential entry location in this part of the structure on Mesme's scans. Check my notes, please." Caleb massaged his jaw. "If we wormhole inside, they'll know it instantly and descend upon our location in force. If we cut a hole through the exterior, they'll also know that instantly, same result."

Alex frowned. "But by this logic, they'll know when we leap off the ramp and land on the surface, even if the *Siyane* is hovering above it. They'll detect the vibration."

"No." Nika shook her head. "The whole structure is vibrating. Remember, it's one giant engine of production."

"In that case, maybe they *won't* notice a tiny little cut. I'm sure they're constantly cutting themselves up into new shapes."

"The problem is, the kyoseil knows all, everywhere. A minor, transient tremor amid a sea of vibrations will escape notice, but an injury?" Nika sighed. "We have created our own trap here."

"But we wouldn't be here trying to execute this crazy plan if not for the kyoseil." Alex shrugged gamely. "It's a complication, but we'll figure it out."

'Ah. Thank you, Nika, for your words have provided the solution. I have located an exhaust duct three kilometers ahead. They must vent their super-heated air to prevent build-up in the enclosed spaces.'

Caleb scowled at the ceiling. "I didn't mark any exhaust ducts as viable entry points, because they're *blowing out super-heated air.*"

'I'm afraid the points you marked have all vanished. As Alex noted, the Rasu are constantly reshaping themselves.'

"Great. Exhaust duct it is."

"We're going to have to fight against a current of super-heated Rasu excrement to get inside? This day keeps getting better and better."

Again, no response from Caleb or Nika. Alex was trying to keep the mood upbeat, but she was no comedian. It was a lost cause, and she ought to give it up; the darkness, the storms and the endless towering metal of their enemy were all too oppressive to maintain any facsimile of levity.

'As your environment suits are designed for the dangerous conditions of space, they should protect you from the heated air.'

"Yep." Alex slowed down as they approached the spot Valkyrie had marked on the map scan. She brought the *Siyane* to a relative halt four meters above the surface to allow room for the ramp to extend without touching the metal below. Then she stood. "The ship is yours, Valkyrie. Let's get ready."

Nika spun and headed directly to where she'd stowed her gear in the far cabinet. Alex started to follow, but Caleb grabbed her arm to stop her.

She turned to him in concern. "What is it?"

He pulled her into his arms and kissed her with a ferocity that filled her heart and weakened her knees. "I hate that we are here, but I love that we're here together. You and me against the universe, come what may."

"There you are, *priyazn*." She smiled gently and stroked his cheek. "I know this is so hard for you."

"No, it's not. I'm saving everyone. I'm saving *you*. It's worth it."

She nodded and kissed him again, trying to imprint the feel of his lips anew upon her soul. Just in case.

RW

Everyone sat down on the *Siyane's* ramp and shimmied to the edge, then twisted around and slid off until they were hanging on by their hands.

Caleb dropped the fifteen centimeters that remained first, landing as lightly as possible on the balls of his feet. Gravity was 0.74E, so they shouldn't need to use their boots' magnetic function, which was good. That kind of energetic interaction might draw the Rasu's notice. But Nika was right—the entire surface was vibrating. If they were careful, their footsteps should escape the enemy's attention.

He motioned for Alex to join him. She landed nimbly on the surface beside him, but his hands instinctively settled on her waist to steady her. Nika followed, and the ramp closed up into the hull of the ship. Valkyrie ascended another ten meters before initiating the cocoon protocol. Every seam on the ship, save the ones around the in-atmo engine, vanished beneath a seal of adiaK. If the Rasu made any threatening advances, Valkyrie would seal off the engine as well. The ship would crash to the surface, but it would be impenetrable.

Alex: "That's something to see. Be safe, Valkyrie."

Valkyrie: "I am not the one venturing into the heart of the enemy."

Alex: "Eh, you're close enough. Keep us updated on what's happening out here."

Valkyrie: "Hopefully nothing happens out here. But I will."

Caleb checked the external temperature: 88° C. The Rasu were generating so much heat from their endeavors, he was surprised the oceans hadn't evaporated into steam.

Caleb: "Status check. Suits?"

Alex: "All systems green."

Nika: "Same."

Caleb: "Weapons?"

Nika: "All accounted for."

Alex held up the two Rectifiers she carried, re-secured them in their holsters and flashed her bracelet/conductivity lash.

Caleb: "Archine blade, baby?"

Alex: "Got it." She patted her belt.

He and Nika carried a few archine grenades as well, and this constituted the entirety of the weapons that could help them here. He felt as though he were bringing a slingshot to a nuclear war.

Caleb: "Nika, you take the lead for now. I've got the rear. Let's move nice and slow."

Thanks to the jagged, chaotic terrain, they'd needed to land a fair distance back from their entry point, and the gloomy, oppressive trek across the exterior of the Rasu structure loomed like a yawning steel desert ahead of them. Every step stretched for an eternity. Storms raged overhead, and the frequent lighting strikes revealed glimpses of an endlessly bleak hellscape. The scale of the towering spires and jagged cliffs defied comprehension; upon this expanse they were mere ants slogging across the enemy's kingdom. It was the stuff of nightmares...and likely would be for many sleepless nights to come.

58

CONCORD HQ
RASU WAR ROOM

The Rasu dreadnought currently wormholing into the midst of the HQ battle was by far the largest spacefaring vessel Miriam had ever seen, in person or in visuals. Thirty Kat superdreadnoughts could fit inside its width and breadth.

Thomas....

I see it. Preparing to dump everything I've got into it.

Admiral Zhenshi, the leader of the Alpha Brigade, stuttered over the first two words of his order to direct all available fire at the newcomer, and Miriam did not blame him. If not for the barrier of the Rift Bubble, this monstrous vessel could barrel straight through the core structure of HQ and hardly notice the brief bump in its course. The adiamene wouldn't give, but the momentum created by such a collision would drive the station all the way into its sun's corona.

You need to know that there is a slight chance one or more of the Rift Bubbles will fall during the battles.

Mesme's warning ricocheted through her mind with greater insistence. Was this fearsome behemoth designed to breach the heretofore unbreachable? Logic told her that sheer force would not be enough, as they were talking about a literal dimensional rift. No matter the energy level applied to it, said energy would simply be redirected away.

The millions of Rasu vessels present, to the extent they were able, flowed around the newcomer as of one mind, clearing the way and building an additional barrier to block Concord ships from attacking what Zhenshi had designated 'Target Alpha-402A.' Miriam watched in growing frustration as powerful blasts meant for it struck lesser vessels instead.

Zhenshi had ordered the fighter craft to sneak in close and target the weapons array, and a single module soon blinked out. But the vessel wielded over *three hundred* weapons modules, so their efforts were unlikely to produce results fast enough.

But fast enough to stop what, exactly?

Target Alpha-402A activated its mammoth weapons array, and her suspicions flared again. This was not a typical Rasu weapon, conventional or antimatter. The energy it produced burned an angry bronze. Two-hundred-ninety-nine disparate streams merged into a single beam that began perhaps a kilometer in diameter, then narrowed into a funnel until the leading edge was a mere pinpoint. A meter wide? No, smaller. A few scant centimeters.

The needle beam impacted the Rift Bubble barrier, and at the point of collision its energy appeared to vanish, the same as every other impact did. But it kept up the assault nonetheless, all focused on one tiny location.

As Miriam watched, an AEGIS frigate struck by a Rasu weapon tumbled out of control and into the path of the beam—and vanished. It didn't disintegrate or rapidly vaporize. One second it was there; the next, gone. And it would've been flying with both an active Dimensional Rifter and a TDS shield.

What kind of weapon *was* this?

Alpha Brigade continued its barrage on the Rasu vessels protecting the behemoth. Two more weapons array nodes were destroyed, but the effect on the beam was negligible. Negative energy blasts broke through to strike the hull here and there, but Alpha-402A was so massive, even a direct hit from a cruiser left only a momentary pockmark—

An eruption of bright sulfur flared at the point where the beam met the Rift Bubble barrier, like sparks on metal, and she shook her head as if momentarily dazed. Everyone in the room did.

The beam continued onward, and Miriam grabbed the table to brace for impact. But it never arrived. Inside the perimeter of the Rift Bubble, the beam quickly diffused and dissipated. Yet the Rasu vessel kept firing on the same location.

A single point of minuscule width in the barrier that had now been breached.

Size didn't matter in the quantum dimensions.

Oh, no.

"Major Beng, order a complete evacuation of HQ this instant."

"Commandant?"

"Do it now!"

The station had been evacuated of non-essential personnel many hours earlier, but in an active war, the number of essential personnel was significant. She called up security footage from the critical hubs around the station.

Nothing happened for long enough that she started to question her gut response—then the air in the Caeles Prisms Hub began to waver and ripple until it swirled into itself to open a glowing vortex.

Rasu bipedals began pouring out of the vortex.

"Major Beng, shut down all the Caeles Prisms on the station."

"I can't, Commandant. I'm locked out of the security system."

She spun to the major. "Repeat your last."

"Instructions sent to the security system are bouncing back with an 'access denied' message."

"Cancel the evacuation order and direct everyone to proceed to the closest designated emergency shelter-in-place location. Send Prevos to the shelters and have them evacuate people to planets not presently under attack."

Beng frowned. "That isn't going to work. The block on free wormholes is active, and without access to the security system, we can't turn it off."

Miriam's chin dropped a fraction. "You're right, of course. See to my other orders."

"Yes, ma'am."

How did they get into the security system? She pulled up the visuals for the central Security offices and discovered her answer. A tall, narrow Rasu with numerous spindly appendages was working the panels in the control room with the adeptness of a tech officer.

They'd sent a single infiltrator there first. She could speculate on how they knew so much about the interior layout of HQ, but it didn't matter, because they did. She watched in impotent frustration as Rasu streamed out of the wormhole, pivoted and charged through Caeles Prisms to all of their most important planets.

Then the visual cut out. The security feeds stopped transmitting.

She was now blind on her own station.

Commandant Solovy (Concord Command Channel): "Alert the defense forces on the First Ring Planets. They have Rasu incoming from the HQ Caeles Prisms."

Fleet Admiral Jenner (AFS Denali)(Concord Command Channel): "They what?"

Commandant Solovy (Concord Command Channel): "The Rasu have infil-trated HQ, taken control of the security systems and accessed the Caeles Prism Hub. Respond accordingly."

Miriam looked around at the faces of those gathered in the War Room. None were war virgins, and most were doing a reasonable job of keeping their composure. But she knew fear when she saw it.

"Lieutenant Quintin, we're not able to activate lockdown procedures, so do what you can to secure the door."

The hull of the station was constructed of adiamene, but not most its interior walls and doors; they were strong but far from impermeable. An adiamene blast door was installed, but it relied on a lockdown command to activate. A procedural flaw that she would see rectified, should she get the chance.

Quintin had removed a panel from the wall beside the door and was about to cut the circuit when a loud banging noise echoed from the other side. Good god, were the Rasu in Command already? She hated being blind!

Sidearms came out of their holsters to be pointed at the door.

A voice rang clear through the commotion. "Permission to enter?"

She motioned those closest to the door away. "Let them through. Whomever we can shelter in here, we should."

The door opened and David rushed through, followed by a small crowd of additional people. He jogged directly around the table and toward her—and pulled up a centimeter short of wrapping her up in his arms.

She tilted her head in the direction of the door. "Finish what you were doing, Lieutenant. Lock us down."

Then she turned her attention back to her husband. Sweat glistened on his temples. How long had he been running? Gathering up strays on his way here, most likely. "I'm glad you're here."

"If we're going to die, we're going to die together this time." He cast a brief glance at the row of now-blank screens. "What's wrong with Security?"

"The Rasu have taken control of it."

"Can't Richard do something about that?"

What an excellent question. "Find out, please."

59

When the lights in his office went out, Richard was sitting at his desk, his hands clenched tightly together, as they had nothing better to do. Certainly there was no task he could direct them to that would help their side win this battle.

Before he was able to so much as blink, all the screens he had open died, and the shadows in his office deepened to pitch black.

What was going on?

He'd left the door to his office open, and he removed his Daemon from its holster as he edged toward the opening to check the hall. All was silent— as it should be, because only a select few people remained in the CINT wing. He discerned no movement, even in infrared. The lights were out in the hall as well.

It didn't make any sense. If Miriam had decided they needed to conserve power for some eventuality, he'd have seen the notification. If they—

A pulse arrived from David.

The Rasu have commandeered Security and taken over its systems. Can you override their control of it?

How did they get inside the station?

No time to explain. Can you do it?

Richard returned to his desk, crawled between it and the wall, and tried to reactivate his office systems. No luck.

CINT and Security were pretty tightly interlinked; the Rasu must have taken out CINT's systems as well, in an attempt to ensure they controlled the entire Security infrastructure. Clever SOBs.

I have no power. No interface at all. But I'll go searching for any module that's still operational.

Good luck.

David didn't tell him to be careful. What would be the point?

The problem was, the only places with sufficient remote access to Security were the offices of the highest-ranking CINT officers and the same

in Command, and it sounded as if Command wasn't having any luck breaking in. Sure, there were terminals all over the station that officers used to
clear visitors and check authorizations for entry to various locations, but
they didn't have control access. Beyond the officer stations, everything happened here or *in* Security. He had no power, and Security was in the hands
of the enemy—

Then he had an idea.

Devon, are you on HQ?

RW

SPECIAL PROJECTS

A crash echoed down the hallway from one of the labs, and Devon
winced. What were the Rasu trashing this time?

From his position huddled under his desk, he opened a tiny aural to
check the cams—and got nothing. He tried another query; also nothing.

The security system was down, because of course it was. And now the
Rasu were rampaging through *his* labs, stealing or destroying the greatest
inventions in Concord history, which meant human, Anaden, Novoloume
and so on history.

He'd caught on to how they'd managed to get onto the station a minute
earlier. Well, not *how*, but what had transpired. If he lived through this, he'd
definitely open up a new project to determine what manner of weapon
wielded the capability to burn a hole in a dimensional barrier. But for now,
he was inclined to focus on the 'living through the invasion' step.

He should call it a day and abandon ship. Commandant Solovy had
asked him to stay at HQ when the general evacuation order went out, because one never knew when she'd need him to pull a rabbit out of a hat and
produce some clever technological wonder to counter the Rasu's latest tactic. But he couldn't pull anything out of anything curled up under his desk
this way, and he couldn't get to one of the labs in any event, what with them
being Rasu-infested.

Miriam might think him a coward, and in this instance she would be
one-hundred-percent correct. So be it.

He peeked his head over the top of his desk. But there was no glass
bordering his office, so all he saw were walls. Fear was making him stupid.

He stood as silently as he was able and readied to open a wormhole to
Earth—

Devon, are you on HQ?

He jumped halfway to the ceiling, then banged his knee on his desk on the way back down.

Much to my regret, but only for about two seconds longer.

I wish I could tell you to go, but I need you to stay.

Ah, crap. Lay it on me.

I want you to hack into the CINT central security server.

Laughter burst out of his lungs, and he hurriedly covered his mouth as he dropped to the floor and crawled back under the desk.

I'm sorry, Richard, I'm going to need you to say that again.

You can rub it in all you want later, okay? But right now, the Rasu have taken over the HQ Security and cut the power to CINT, so I can't get in to override their control. But if anyone can get in, it's you. I mean, you have studied Rasu programming, haven't you?

Don't insult me. I know it better than anyone...except maybe two or three people in the Dominion. He breathed out. I can do it. Give me a few minutes— wait, where are you?

Alone in CINT.

Exact location?

Sitting uselessly in my office.

Devon crawled out from under his desk once again, one wary eye locked on the door to his office, and used his secret bypass code to open a wormhole to Richard's office. As soon as he saw his friend, he motioned him through and grabbed him in a bear hug. "It's good to not be alone."

"It is." Richard patted him on the shoulder, then stepped away. "Rasu?"

"Out there in the labs." Belatedly, Devon dropped his voice to a whisper. "Now that you're here, you can protect me while I work my magic."

"You got it." Richard moved to the wall beside the door, sidearm drawn.

Devon wanted to crawl back under the desk, but he'd be able to work faster if he had access to the interface on its surface, so he sat down and opened the master directory. Thankfully, the Special Projects system was still functioning; the Rasu had only taken control of Security and its connected systems.

"All right, you Rasu devils. Throw your dastardly best at me."

60

AFS DENALI
Earth Stellar System

"Fire everything at the target's weapons array. It's going to—"

But it was too late. The EAO Orbital buckled under the assault of ten Rasu antimatter beams. The resulting explosion covered half a square megameter of space; on the side nearest Earth, a gouge cut into the blast radius where it impacted the Rift Bubble barrier.

The station had been evacuated, of course, down to the last security officer and maintenance technician. A single Artificial maintained the automated systems, and it was backed up at a governmental facility. So the loss was only metal. Girders and walls.

Also a great deal of invested money, a monument to progress, and a psychological symbol for the citizens of Earth.

Malcolm sighed, annoyed. "Our next target is the Rasu grouping in Quadrant 5, bearing 23° N 18° W -12° Z."

"Yes, sir."

He glanced at the AEGIS feed to check on the status of the Romane and Seneca battles. He wasn't responsible for overseeing them today, but those were his people fighting, and what happened there mattered as much as what did here.

They were progressing about as well as one could expect. Overwhelming Rasu forces were thus far held at bay from the planets themselves by grit, determination, clever use of firepower, and Rift Bubble barriers.

The Presidio found itself surrounded by a small fleet of Rasu warships. The station was forced to rely on its own defenses and its Rift Bubble. Choices had to be made, and lives mattered more than property. The warships fired repetitively at the barrier, continually testing its resilience. They represented a token force at best, but should the barrier fall, they wielded enough antimatter firepower to cut through the station's adiamene hull in a matter of minutes.

Rasu strike teams were targeting their warship manufacturing facilities, too, and many of those were now falling. If this *wasn't* the final confrontation, AEGIS was apt to find itself in trouble on account of a dearth of backfilled ships to replace those lost. But this was a worry for another day.

Malcolm's gaze swept across the local tactical feed on its way to the viewport, then back to the feed. "Several groups of Rasu are approaching the far side of the moon. Navigation, let's return to our earlier post. It seems the enemy has a renewed interest in Mare Ingenii Base."

But that wasn't all. Across the battlespace, which stretched for almost a hundred megameters and completely encircled Earth, Rasu formations were moving beyond what the ebb and flow of their engagements demanded.

What were they up to?

Fleet Admiral Jenner (AFS Denali)(Earth Command Channel): "Blockade Group 4, the enemy is trying to flank you. Stay in front of them."

But 'flanking' didn't quite describe what he was seeing. He peered at the display, eyes squinting. After a few more seconds, it began to appear as though they were massing around a central location. Were they intending to crash through one section of the blockade using brute force?

Flashing alerts in his internal feed and on the Concord Command screen demanded his attention. At HQ, a Rasu vessel of heretofore unimagined size was attacking the Rift Bubble with a new weapon. Trying to bore a hole in it? How?

Didn't matter.

Fleet Admiral Jenner (AFS Denali)(Earth Command Channel): "PG Groups, move into position and prepare to deploy the Parapet Gambit on my order."

Admiral Lushenko (AEGIS Earth Headquarters)(Earth Command Channel): "Sir, is there a problem with the Rift Bubble?"

Fleet Admiral Jenner (AFS Denali)(Earth Command Channel): "Not yet."

He frowned as more Rasu closed in on a tight lunar orbit. They were firing scattershot at the surface, but their hearts didn't seem to be in it—or wouldn't be if they possessed hearts. What were they waiting for?

He called in a regiment to support the *Denali* in its efforts to protect Mare Ingenii Base.

A red frame began blinking with urgency on the Concord Command screen. The Rasu had somehow seared a hole in the HQ Rift Bubble sufficient to bypass it and open wormholes on the station.

Mesme's warning had been suspiciously prescient.

Malcolm frantically searched the tactical maps cataloging the entire battlespace, but found no sign of an unreasonably mammoth vessel or the presence of a weapon they hadn't seen before. In fact, the Rasu weren't firing on the Rift Bubble barrier at all, at least not directly. Did they only have one of whatever this weapon was? Considering such a weapon shouldn't exist, perhaps they did.

He had to force himself to keep most of his attention on the battle at hand rather than the feed from HQ. But not all of it, as what happened next at HQ was going to affect the engagements everywhere.

And what happened next was the Rasu flooding the Caeles Prisms and spilling out onto a dozen worlds. Including Earth. Dammit!

Fleet Admiral Jenner (AFS Denali)(Earth Defense Channel): "Red alert. The Rasu are on the ground in Manhattan. Origin point Intergalactic Central Station."

One of the many things the Rasu civil war had bought them time to do was prepare for a ground invasion on any world. Every Marine regiment had transitioned to combat alert the instant the Rasu made their move against Concord, which meant they were able to deploy to a hot spot in seconds.

Of course, most of them weren't staged in Manhattan—a few thousand at most. There were upwards of twenty cities on Earth that qualified as high-value strategic targets, and every one of them needed to be covered.

But there *were* three Caeles Prisms in Manhattan in addition to the one at Intergalactic Central Station. One each connected to London, Shanghai and Sao Paulo. Forces staged in those cities were now proceeding immediately to ground zero of the invasion. The question was, could they get there in time to corral the Rasu before they spread out across the streets of downtown Manhattan, transformed into flying craft and took off across the globe?

Oh, how he wanted to be down on the ground with the Marines. But he wouldn't make the same mistake he'd made at Savrak; he *needed* to be right where he was. Colonel Odaka would lead them well.

Malcolm suddenly realized what was transpiring here. The Rasu on the surface were going to try to put up a quantum block. The instant they did so and the Rift Bubble deactivated, the Rasu in space were going to swarm down to invade from above.

Fleet Admiral Jenner (AFS Denali)(Earth Defense Channel): "Be advised: the Rasu will attempt to construct a quantum block. Ready contingency measures."

Fleet Admiral Jenner (AFS Denali)(Earth Command Channel): "All forces, prepare for the Rift Bubble to fall. PG Groups, be ready to initiate on my mark."

The Rasu had gotten adept at swiftly constructing quantum blocks during the last round of attacks, and his gut told him there weren't enough Marines within shouting distance of Intergalactic Central Station to stop them before they were able to do so. But as part of their exhaustive preparations, they'd also developed contingency plans so that military communication didn't entirely disintegrate in the face of such a block. The commanders on the ground all had access to non-quantum communication devices. The government leadership did as well, at locations scattered across the planet. It would be slow and clumsy, but they'd be able to talk to each other—

And now they were going to have to. His four direct feeds from Earth fell silent in unison. But even if they hadn't, he would have known. For outside the viewport, North and South America blinked into darkness.

Fleet Admiral Jenner (AFS Denali)(Earth Command Channel): "Parapet Gambit, now."

An intricate, woven web of golden light spread outward from the three hundred anchor ships to their neighbors, then onward in interlinking waves until a cohesive web formed around Earth. A planet-sized force field with the strength of a TDS.

He couldn't do anything about Rasu infiltrating the surface from Caeles Prisms, but he could keep these millions of enemy vessels off the planet using a Parapet Gambit. For a time.

"Sir!"

He spun to his XO. "What is it?"

"You need to see this." Ettore opened a new tactical screen to Malcolm's right and punched in a command.

The visual showed an unusual-looking Rasu vessel, though it didn't match the description of the behemoth at Concord HQ. It was wide and squat, almost like an old-school cargo freighter design. Instead of the traditional crystal weapons bank underneath, it sported an array of blocky, disjointed appendages situated along the front of the ship.

He tapped a box on the screen for the system to derive scale…and shook his head. "This can't be right."

"We'll know for certain in a few seconds, sir. It's approaching from beyond Quadrant 5 now."

Soon, additional vessels entered the field of view, including some of their own, and the system's analysis was confirmed: eight kilometers in width. Not as large as the one that had shown up at HQ to pierce the Rift Bubble, but far and away the largest vessel Malcolm had ever seen.

But there was no longer a Rift Bubble here, so for what terrible purpose had it arrived?

Fleet Admiral Jenner (AFS Denali)(Earth Command Channel): "Assault Divisions #1 and #2, if you are not maintaining the Parapet Gambit, direct all your fire at the new arrival, designated Target Delta-368C on the maps. Destroy this monster before it reaches the force field."

Almost as if the Rasu had heard his order, vast swaths of the many millions of enemy warships altered their own courses and moved into a defensive perimeter around the vessel, until they were so thick they formed a second layer of armor. His ships were going to have to shoot through the defenders before they could even begin to nick the mammoth Rasu.

The vessel and its escort began to slow. "Trajectory?"

"It looks to be...Luna, sir."

"What?" The moon was of moderate strategic value, but considerably less so when the grand prize awaited just beyond its horizon.

Fleet Admiral Jenner (AFS Denali)(Earth Command Channel): "NW Brigade Bravo, get in front of Target Delta-368C and be ready to disrupt whatever it attempts to do."

"Navigation, bring us around broadside to the target." His gaze switched to the viewport.

When the vessel was two hundred kilometers distant from the surface of Luna, its bow appendages lit up in electric silver light to form a wide, thick beam that stretched the entire breadth of the vessel.

The beam struck a swath of ships from NW Brigade Bravo on its way to impacting the lunar surface, sending those ships tumbling out of control to crash directly into the moon. Their hulls held, of course, but none rose through the enormous clouds of dust billowing out from the crash sites. Comms to their captains went unanswered.

He gestured to Ettore. "Find out what's going on with Bravo."

"Yes, sir."

The silver beam continued cutting into a long stretch of regolith. Empty, unoccupied regolith (except for the ships of NW Brigade Bravo), far from Mare Ingenii or any other outpost.

"Science, I need to know what that beam is, and more importantly, what it's doing."

"Uh, I can answer the second question, sir," Captain Rosa, the Science officer on the bridge, replied.

"Let's hear it."

"It's pushing Luna out of its orbit."

"Excuse me?"

"It's exerting sufficient force to dislodge Luna from its regular orbit. The moon has already moved two degrees out of position and 5.6 kilometers closer to Earth."

Malcolm stared at the beam, wide and deep but otherwise somewhat innocuous in appearance as weapons of mass destruction went. Now that the weapon was active, it looked as though this vessel was designed entirely to drive the beam. A beam powerful enough to knock large astronomical bodies out of orbit and propel them….

"Oh my God."

"Sir?" Ettore glanced at him in concern.

"They're going to try to use the moon to punch a hole through the Parapet Gambit."

"The force field can withstand it. A wide, blunt object like Luna, easily so."

Malcolm shook his head. "But the ships won't be able to withstand the sheer force applied by the impact—especially if the moon gets up a decent head of steam by the time it reaches the field. It will barrel straight into an enormous grouping of ships, forcing them ahead of it like a bowling ball down an alley. The connections of the Parapet Gambit will stretch then snap, and Earth will be theirs for the taking."

A far more terrifying realization hit him then. "And there will be nothing to stop the moon from crashing into the surface."

Ettore's face blanched. "That's a planetary-extinction-level event, sir. And we're talking hours, not days or months."

"Yes, it is. What's the word on NW Brigade Bravo?"

"Comms are sketchy due to the composition of the beam, whatever it is. Basically, the ships are being subjected to the full pressure of the force it's delivering. They're not getting off the lunar surface so long as the beam's active."

He tried to think his way through this. He had options, but none of them were good ones. Use the Terrestrial Defense Grid to break the moon into tiny pieces before it impacted? *Destroy the moon himself, good God.* But the Grid couldn't fire through the Parapet Gambit any more than the Rasu could, so he either had to deactivate the Gambit now and preemptively fire on the moon, or wait until the Gambit fell to begin the assault—which might well be too late. The distance between the Grid hardware and the Gambit force field was only ten megameters.

What if he was wrong about the ultimate fate of Luna? Or the Gambit somehow held under its onslaught? If he deactivated it prematurely, he'd be leaving Earth vulnerable. He deeply wished he could seek Miriam's advice right about now. But she was locked in her own battle, trying to save her beloved station. She'd want to save Earth even more, but this task fell to him. He was the fleet admiral.

"Displacement is accelerating, sir. Lunar distance to Earth's surface is now decreasing by ten kilometers per second."

His internal debate was about to be rendered moot.

Fleet Admiral Jenner (AFS Denali)(Earth Defense Channel): "Admiral Lushenko—" Wait, Lushenko was on the other side of the quantum block. He activated the non-quantum comm system.

"Admiral Lushenko, start tracking Luna's trajectory and reorient all Grid modules to target it. Be ready to fire on it the instant the Parapet Gambit collapses." Thank God they'd installed a direct link from AEGIS Earth Headquarters to the Grid control system.

"You want us to fire on the moon?"

"If the Gambit falls, the Grid may be the only chance we have to stop it from impacting Earth and killing everyone on the planet. Scrounge up any experts you can find to tell you the optimal firing solution for using the Grid to break Luna up into as many pieces as possible, given the short distance and placement of the Grid modules."

"God have mercy on our souls. Understood."

Malcolm checked the progress of their assault on the beam-wielding Rasu. A plethora of negative energy weapons and bombs were making headway, but not fast enough. If he threw every ship in the fleet at it, could they destroy it in time to…but it was already too late, wasn't it? If the beam was shut off this instant, the moon would still be falling toward Earth. The move would buy time to deal with it slightly less urgently, but he didn't know nearly enough science to speculate how much time.

"Science, has the force of the beam caused Luna's rotation to increase?"

"Only a slight amount, sir," Captain Rosa replied.

"All right. I need you to find *me* an expert in the next thirty seconds who can tell me the optimal way to break up Luna as much as possible when we have no time to do it."

"Dr. Aritenzay. She's on Demeter. I'll get her on the line and send her to your comm."

When this was over and they were all still alive, he'd ask Captain Rosa how she'd known the answer off the top of her head.

Malcolm checked on the status of his available forces. Technically, none were 'available,' as they were all shooting at Rasu and being shot at in return. He'd pull the heavy hitters currently plinking away at Delta-368C off, as well as the Sabre squadrons. Then he'd—

"This is Dr. Aritenzay."

"Wonderful. This is Fleet Admiral Malcolm Jenner. How do we break Luna up into the smallest possible pieces using direct strikes from AEGIS warships? Is it better to use conventional lasers or negative energy weapons? Should we direct all our firepower at a single point or spread it out over a wide area?"

"Well, in theory—"

"This is not a theory, Dr. Aritenzay. I need to apply enough force to disintegrate Luna in the next five to ten minutes. Tell me how to do it in a manner that gives me the best chance of saving Earth."

"Oh my. I think you...you should use negative energy weapons, as they will evaporate the lunar crust, then mantle, more rapidly than conventional fire. Distribute your fire in a circular area...hold on, let me do the math.

"Eleven-hundred-twenty kilometers in diameter, centered on, uh, the center point of whichever face you're firing on. This will create the highest likelihood of breaking the moon up where it is most massive. The edges that break off in the process...I suppose you can deal with them after you've achieved an initial dislodgment. And you should. Obviously. Any piece larger than a hundred meters in width can inflict significant damage to the planet."

"Thank you, Doctor. Please stay on the comm in case I need you again."

Malcolm eyed Earth's towering satellite, looming large and imposing outside the viewport. For millennia, a comforting companion for humans gazing up at the night sky. Now, the instrument of their destruction at the hands of the enemy.

Fleet Admiral Jenner (AFS Denali)(Earth Command Channel): "Listen up, everyone. Here's what we're going to do."

61

RASU PRIME

The environment controls in Caleb's suit had to kick it up a notch when they reached the entrance of the exhaust tube, as the air it expelled would boil if it were water.

Nika hoisted herself over the lip and into the tube, and he gave Alex a boost before following. Again, she didn't need his help, but he wanted to touch her one more time, regardless of whether it was through layers of impenetrable material.

At two meters in width and height, they all had to hunch over to fit in the tube, even Alex and Nika thanks to the added height from their boots and helmets. They fought against the hot blasts of counter-airflow for around a hundred meters, until the tube opened up into a larger space that remained effectively an exhaust conduit.

Caleb studied the minimal equipment in the room, then the walls. He didn't want to use a light, so he relied on his infrared ocular filter to see. Less than ideal. But after a thorough scan, he spotted a slightly cooler area on the far right.

Caleb: *"I think there's an opening there. Maintenance entry, maybe."*

Nika: *"Got it."*

They carefully approached the entry, and he slipped ahead of Nika to check the hallway ahead.

Caleb: *"It looks clear. Of course it isn't, because every wall is a Rasu waiting to attack us."*

Alex: *"When the walls have eyes. I think I read a horror story with that title once. Scared the shit out of young me. And now that I'm living it, it still does."*

Caleb: *"Yeah. Which direction, Nika?"*

He felt a nudge on his arm.

Nika: *"How about I get back in front? Then I won't have to tell you."*

He conceded the point and grudgingly let her retake the lead.

She led them down a series of twisting hallways in silence. His nerves jangled and clanged, and Akeso muttered in his head about discomfort and unfamiliar sensation-emotions. Inside the confines of his suit, his body felt as if every sensory receptor was on fire. This place, this planet, this entire system *screamed* at him. And he didn't know why. He'd been surrounded by Rasu before—at the stronghold on Namino, too many times on Hirlas. This was different. As if there was a threat constantly in the corner of his vision, slithering in the shadows but perpetually just beyond his sight.

He tried to focus on the real, physical threats existing all around them. If the Rasu attacked, he and Nika would try to throw the poison into whatever Rasu material they were able to reach until the enemy overcame them, while Alex tried to whittle down the attackers for as long as possible using her Rectifiers.

It was a terrible plan. But it was the one they had.

Caleb wished with every fiber of his being that he could be the one fighting to protect them instead of Alex; it was what he *did*. He'd trained her well over the years, but though she was an excellent shot and kept her head during a firefight, she didn't possess his combat reflexes or instincts. Few people did.

But today he must serve as a weapon in a different way. A passive conduit through which to deliver genocide.

The vibrations in the walls and floor made his hair stand on end. He couldn't actually feel it—not physically—but the buzzing in his head insisted otherwise.

He waited for a section of wall to morph into a razored blade and lash out to slice them into pieces. If the wall simply *looked*, it was certain to see them and identify them as intruders.

But the walls weren't designed to 'see,' and it was probable the Rasu on this planet had never conceived of the possibility of an intruder. Not here, in the dark heart of their domain.

Nika: *"Up ahead is a hub area. Massive power generation. It resembles the place where I delivered the virutox in the Gennisi galaxy stronghold, which means it will be a good distribution point."*

Caleb: *"Understood."*

They came to an intersection with two additional halls and a vertical passage, and beyond it the one they traversed expanded on all sides. They continued on for another forty meters until the hall emptied out into a colossal chamber.

At the center of the space, a violent vortex of plasma churned and writhed. Crystals lined the ceiling and created walls around two-thirds of it. Outside the wall, a thick ring of Rasu-equipment encircled the vortex.

At first, it appeared there were no mobile Rasu units in the cavernous space, solely modules to process data and distribute power. Then he spotted a shadow shifting. Again, to the left. It was hardly proper movement, though. More like a robotic arm slotting items, which might well be what it was.

It was irrelevant in any event. Anything in here was capable of shifting and moving, should it need to. For now, nothing paid them any mind. This was soon going to change, however.

Nika led them to a section of Rasu modules along the left flank of the vortex. It wasn't exactly a defensible position, but at least most of the room was visible from this point. He couldn't discern a second exit behind the vortex, either, which reduced their chances of being flanked.

Caleb: "Nika, once we start injecting the poison, the Rasu will realize something is amiss, won't they?"

Nika: "Yes. But what I don't know is whether they'll be able to track it to the source. To this room."

Their terrible plan just got worse. Neither he nor Nika knew how long it was going to take to inject enough poison to wipe out the untold multitude of Rasu spread across two superclusters. If it took longer than a few minutes and the Rasu discovered their location, even the three of them working together didn't stand a chance of successfully defending this position.

Caleb: "We should have brought more people. Soldiers."

Alex: "More people would kick up a terrible racket, and we'd have never made it to this spot without being detected. Let's stop overthinking it and get it done."

She was so goddamn fearless. He reached out and found her arm, then pulled her close, pressing his faceplate to hers.

I love you, baby.

And I you, priyazn. *Let's save the universe.*

62

D ashiel stood in an empty alcove on the top floor of the Initiative. The mirage of pseudo-solitude was held in place by two three-paneled shoji screens tall enough to hide him from view, but not too tall for him to peer over them and see the cacophony of information flashing across the Big Board at the back of the room.

The Ymyrath Field that Concord had so graciously lent them had wiped out over a million Rasu here and at Synra in the opening seconds of the invasion. Now, though, he couldn't conceive of how those million Rasu would have even fit on the battlefield, so large was the force trying to burrow its way past the Rift Bubble barriers and reach the surface.

His mind dipped in and out of multiple ceraffin devoted to the delivery and placement of weapons and equipment from his warehouses. He kept several processes attached to Palmer's military command channel, following the ebb and flow of the battles, and remained poised to leap into action should his particular skill set be needed.

Nika had...not 'ordered him,' though it wouldn't be wholly inaccurate, to stay behind and fill in for her in managing the Kireme Boundaries and Rift Bubbles. Thus far, the planetary Rift Bubbles were holding, making the task unnecessary. But he nonetheless felt as if he were poised on a narrow and crumbling cliff, on either side of it a chasm of desperate purpose awaiting him with macabre anticipation.

In a brief span of quiet, his thoughts lingered on Nika. Delving into the cold, soulless home of the Rasu in an attempt to destroy them from within. He wanted to be with her so badly his gut physically spasmed and twisted from the denial of his greatest desire. But at least she wasn't in that terrible place alone. Alex would refuse to give up until every last Rasu was dead, and Caleb would find a way to bring them all home. This he didn't doubt.

A cascade of alerts filtered through the complex web of channels and networks and ceraffin, reporting a new manner of trouble in the Concord HQ battle.

The next second, the alerts ratcheted up to frantic blasts warning of Rasu accessing the Caeles Prisms. His gaze shot to the front corner of the room.

Dashiel: *"We need to shut down the d-gate to Concord HQ right now."*

Katherine: *"Why? We want to be able to—"*

The thick, long arms of a Rasu bipedal burst out of the active d-gate; its body followed, spilling out into the top-floor command center of the Initiative in a spasm of motion. By the time it had completed its traversal—four hundred microseconds?—another was following it, then another. In three seconds, ten Rasu had invaded the space.

Katherine: *"Shut it down!"*

But two of the Rasu mechs somehow knew to go for the security officers first, swiping bladed appendages through the air to rip the two men open from navel to neck and fling the bodies against the Big Board.

People screamed and ran for the lift, but it only held eight passengers at once and protested loudly when it grew overcrowded. Furniture was upturned by Rasu and Asterions alike. Weapons were drawn, but trained military officers were a minimal presence in the Initiative. They were elsewhere prepping to fight, and had never before been needed here.

Half of the Rasu mechs beelined for the other d-gates, and now there was no one to stop them from reaching more locations. DAF Command. The Towers on the other Axis Worlds. What could a handful of Rasu do on their own? Put up quantum blocks, for one, if given space and a short span of time.

The remainder of the invaders, their numbers swiftly growing, tore into the crowd, leaving death in their wake. Violence for violence's sake, or a targeted effort to wipe out as many of the people guiding the Dominion's defense as possible?

Perhaps six seconds had passed since the first Rasu had arrived, which was how long it took for Dashiel to realize that he himself was in physical danger. Also how long it took for one of the mechs to take an interest in...not him. *Maris.*

She'd been sitting on one of the couches along the side wall, head in her hands, her stress and worry her own. Now she was on her feet, eyes wide in panic, her gaze frozen on the approaching Rasu.

Dashiel didn't think; he just acted. He sprinted toward her the same instant he opened a wormhole to his flat off to her left. He reached her three strides ahead of the Rasu, grabbed her arm, flung her through the wormhole and staggered through it after her. *Close!*

He landed on the hardwood floor of his foyer next to the jumble of limbs that was Maris.

"The merciful gods! I was—Dashiel, look out!"

Her cry jolted his mind out of its stunned state, and he twisted around to see a Rasu arm skittering across the floor toward them. Its digits morphed and sharpened as it did, forming razored talons.

He scrambled to his feet. "Get behind me."

She didn't argue, and together they danced into the living room as the arm gave chase. *Think, think, think.*

"Exhale, then hold your breath."

"What?"

"Do it now." He emptied his lungs and stopped retreating. The arm launched off the floor toward his chest. He grabbed it with both hands and held it at bay, wincing as the talons tore into the skin of his forearms.

He opened a small wormhole in the air off his shoulder. Beyond it, Mirai's sun twinkled in the distance against the blackness of space and a sea of stars. The vacuum of space seeped into his flat, tugging at everything its expanding presence touched.

He fought against the pull, reared back both arms and hurled the Rasu through the wormhole, then closed it.

And gasped in air.

Maris sank to the floor in a heap.

"Are you all right?" He crouched beside her in concern.

"All right? No, I am not all right." She peered up. "Oh, but your arms. You're a bloody mess."

"It looks worse than it feels." A bald-faced lie.

Other advisors were screaming over their group channel. Those who had escaped the initial rampage at the Initiative, anyway. Some were hiding on other floors, while some had reacted as he had and thought to open wormholes in those first critical seconds. DAF was wormholing in troops, properly armed ones, to try to keep the enemy contained in the Initiative then eliminate them.

Dashiel tried to think of how he might help any of them, but for all his vast and varied knowledge, his mind was now a blank canvas.

Maris climbed weakly to her feet. Her silk top had gotten ripped down the shoulder in the altercation and her hair rendered wild and unkempt. She cleared her throat and lifted her shoulders. "You saved my life. I was being weak and despondent and pitying myself, and it nearly killed me. Thank you."

"Of course. I couldn't do otherwise."

"But you could have. You chose to save me at great risk to your own life. Dashiel, I am sorry I ever counseled Nika to keep our true heritage as members of the First Generation secret from you."

"What? Oh. That's all in the past. Ancient history now." Was it? He'd kept Maris at a polite distance ever since learning the truth, and he continued to hold fast to a tiny morsel of bitterness, possibly for spite.

"Nonetheless. I was wrong. You are as brave, intelligent and, most importantly, wise as any First Genner. You should be one of us. Lacking that, I am glad you stand with us."

She always could give an inspirational speech. "Thank you. It means a lot. Now forgive yourself, and I shall forgive us both."

Katherine: "We need to regroup at Mirai Tower."

He scowled.

Dashiel: "Are you nuts? They're liable to simply blow it up again."

Katherine: "Two dozen mechs won't."

Dashiel: "I fear it won't be two dozen for long. Hells, it's probably two hundred by now. Frankly, any tall building is a bad idea for a base of operations. What about DAF Command—never mind. Some got through to there. Let me think. The Ridani Enterprises storage warehouse on the outskirts of southeast Mirai One. I'll head there and blast my coordinates to everyone. By the time the Rasu get around to trying to destroy it...if they do, it won't matter by then."

Katherine: "Fine."

He took Maris' hands in his. "You can't stay here, as this is also a tall building. But you should go somewhere quiet and of no strategic importance. How about the Botanical Gardens Center? It will be empty. Catch your breath, splash water on your face, have a drink. Rest."

"But I—"

"If you decide you want to join us after you've done those things, it's your choice. But I would feel better if you stayed out of the line of fire."

Her eyes were wide, pupils dilated, and a thin sheen of sweat glistened on her features. Her chin dropped, and she nodded. "Very well. I will, at a minimum, retreat and take a minute to compose myself. Thank you again. Kindly do what you can to ensure the Rasu don't destroy everything I hold dear?"

His words to Nika before she'd left echoed in his mind. *I will try to do what I can.* "Everything in my power."

He watched her until she'd opened a wormhole and stepped through to the Gardens, then exhaled wearily. He considered taking thirty seconds to clean himself up—he was, as she'd noted, a bloody mess—but decided he'd do so at the warehouse if there was time. Which seemed unlikely, as Rasu were now on the loose on his world.

63

CONCORD HQ

RASU WAR ROOM

The blast door slammed shut with a shuddering roar, and everyone in the room jumped. The next second, a host of cam feeds sputtered to life.

Miriam breathed a small sigh of relief, then touched David's shoulder. "Talk to Richard. Find out what we do and don't have."

Front and center on the wall of visuals was the Caeles Prism Hub, where Rasu surged like insects out of multiple of their wormholes and promptly through all of Concord's. "Major Beng, try again to shut down the Caeles Prisms."

After several attempts, Beng shook her head in frustration. "Nothing, Commandant."

Miriam looked at David in question, who confirmed it. "Richard says we have basic control of Security, including lockdown protocols and networked systems. But the Rasu have bypassed the Caeles Prism Hub, cutting it out of the Security loop. Devon is working on it, but it'll take time."

"Devon? Good. Major, I want you to task a team with severing the power to the Caeles Prism Hub."

Beng's brow furrowed. "They'll need to access the maintenance tunnel under the room and cut the lines directly."

"I know. Obviously, stealth will be of utmost necessity."

Her expression resolved into one of determination. "We'll get it done, ma'am."

"Thank you."

She sent a pulse to Richard herself, and on receiving his answer, she activated the station-wide communications system.

"All personnel. The block on free wormholes has been removed. Evacuate yourselves to a safe location at once—but not on any of the First Ring Planets, as the Rasu have reached the surface of those worlds. Prevos, please assist any non-Prevos in your vicinity with their evacuation."

Even if the security team succeeded in cutting the power to the Caeles Prism Hub—which she expected them to—Rasu now had unfettered access to the station. Thankfully, though, HQ should be virtually empty of people within a few minutes—except for this room.

"Concord HQ is no longer under our control." She turned to Lt. Colonel Nham, the ranking Prevo in the room. "Lieutenant Colonel, open a wormhole to Presidio AEGIS Central Command. Everyone, we're moving this operation there." If General Colby had a problem with a couple of Khokteh, Novoloume and Anadens accompanying her to the top-secret military location, he would get over it.

She made no move toward the wormhole herself, allowing the officers and staff to proceed first. She didn't intend to go down with the ship, not when this war could somehow still be won, but she'd never jump the line.

"You don't want to transfer to the *Aurora?*" David asked. "I'm sure Thomas won't be too miffed."

"I *do* want to, but there is some value to be derived from being in the same room as these officers. Also, the *Aurora* is currently vigorously engaged in combat, and I can't get distracted by the minutiae."

"Good reasons."

"Commandant?" Beng drew her attention. "The security team has reached the power junction beneath the hub. Cutting the power...now."

On the feed, the shimmering ring of Caeles Prisms fell silent, slicing more than one Rasu into multiple pieces in the process.

Commandant Solovy (Concord Command Channel): "We've shut off the Rasu's access to the HQ Caeles Prisms, but in the time they've had, they may have now engineered other ways to bring troops in, including the construction of quantum blocks. We must consider all First Ring Planets to be under ground invasion."

"All right, Miri. It's time to go."

She looked up from the feed to find the room empty except for her and David, then sighed as her gaze went to the viewports. The Alpha Brigade was chipping away at the monstrous Rasu vessel. They'd disabled thirty-eight nodes of its strange weapon, and chunks of its hull were being blown away faster than it could rebuild them. But so long as the weapon continued to hold open a tiny fissure in the Rift Bubble, the station would remain under assault by the Rasu.

She hated to go. But it was her duty to do so.

She nodded and motioned David onward. He waited until she joined him at his side, however, and together they approached the wormhole—

It sputtered and died. The power in the War Room shut off, taking with it the visual feeds and the lights.

"What just happened?"

She stared at the floor, distracted by the oddest sensation beneath her feet.

Stillness.

When going about one's daily business, one never noticed the faint vibration traveling along every surface of the station. If asked, she'd have said she didn't feel it at all. But its absence was stark.

David's chin dropped to his chest in the shadows. "Deprived of the Caeles Prisms, the Rasu put up a quantum block. The Zero Engines powering the station are down."

Miriam swallowed past a stubborn lump growing in her throat. Even if the Rasu didn't find a way to remove the blast door, in time the station would grow cold. The air would run out.

But she was not without resources. She moved to the cabinet where the non-quantum comms device they'd devised was stored. Using it, she'd be able to talk to the team now at the Presidio and the fleet commanders in the field.

She opened the cabinet and found herself staring at an empty shelf...because the War Room Operations Officer had done his job superbly. He'd retrieved the device, along with other tools they might need, and carried them with him through the wormhole ahead of her.

She and David were trapped here. And she was cut off from everyone. From every battle.

Focus, Miriam. The military commanders can handle the battles without you. What can you do to change your situation?

While she'd been ruminating, David had gone straight for the blast door. He lay on the floor trying to get so much as a fingerhold into the narrow seam between the bottom of the door and the floor.

She crouched beside him. "David, a Rasu mech couldn't lift the door. That's the point."

"But behind all the technology, there are old-fashioned hinges and levers and mechanisms. If we can gain a bit of leverage, we can make them work for us." He grunted, pulling his hand back and sucking on a finger. "Do you have a crowbar in here?"

"No, David, I do not have a crowbar in the War Room."

"Anything that can function as a crowbar? Oh, I know." He climbed to his feet. "I've got a blade on me. I can whittle one of the conference table chair legs into a flat edge."

She opened her mouth to argue. The door weighed over a thousand kilos; no crowbar leveraged by a human was going to lift it. And even if he did somehow accomplish the impossible, on the other side were rampaging Rasu mechs. They had no idea where on the station the Rasu had constructed the quantum block and no weapons on hand powerful enough to destroy it. Such weapons existed on the station, but they were stored several kilometers away and were now accessible only via a labyrinth of maintenance tunnels and ladders.

But she said none of those things, for several reasons. Like him, she wanted to *do something* with every screaming fiber of her being. And though it was surely a futile endeavor, this gave them both something to do other than stare out at the stars and await their deaths.

But most of all, she said none of those things because she loved him, and his response to this crisis was high on the list of reasons why she did. He would fight until his last breath.

So instead, she retrieved a chair and flipped it over, then sat on the floor next to him and removed her service-issue blade from its sheath. "The door's rather wide, so it might take two leverage points to lift it."

64

CONCORD HQ
SPECIAL PROJECTS

Richard half-sat on the corner of Devon's desk, shaking his head wryly. "The ease and speed with which you tunneled into my highly secure account then the yet more secure and Artificial-protected CINT server, then had your way with the entire HQ security system...ought to worry me a lot more than it does."

Devon laughed. "See, I thought you were going somewhere else with that."

"So did I. But I remembered a few of the things I've seen you pull off in the past and realized this feat shouldn't be the slightest bit surprising."

"I'm just tickled that you needed to ask me to do it. I've been waiting on this one to come back around since...."

"Since you betrayed me and hacked into the CINT server behind my back to help Mia go rogue and subvert Command's orders in order to exact revenge on the Savrakaths."

Devon sank lower in his chair. "Didn't mean to bring that up."

"Water under the bridge. And even if it wasn't, you've redeemed yourself here today. Look, you ought to go. Get off HQ and somewhere safe. Safer."

"I can't deny, I want to leave pretty badly. Emily's on Earth right now. I don't know how the battle is going there, but if the situation here is any indication, it's not good. I should be there with her."

"Like I said, go. You've earned it."

"Where can I drop you off first?"

Richard sighed. "The station has been occupied by enemy forces. I *can't* leave. Instead, I've got to do whatever I can, which is probably very little, to try to take it back from them."

"Ah, shit. I can't abandon you when you're all alone."

"I'm not alone. Granted, I might be in another ninety seconds, given Miriam's order. But nonetheless." He clapped Devon's shoulder. "This is my job and my duty, but it's not yours. Go hug your wife and try to stay out of the line of fire."

Devon groaned. "Curse my secretly noble heart—and Annie chastising me in my head. No. I'm staying to help you."

"Devon—"

Richard's eVi glitched. The aural representing the security system died. The lights went out.

In the absence of a viewport to let in starlight and the ensuing reflections off gleaming metal, the office was now pitch black. "Anything?"

"No wormhole capability. No more Annie in my head."

"Quantum block. I guess this ends my attempts to get you to leave."

"Yep. When Miriam shut the Caeles Prisms down, it must have pissed off the Rasu."

"Seems likely." Richard dragged a hand along the prickly stubble of his jaw. "But we've been handed an assignment: how can we disable the quantum block?"

"I've got a modded Rectifier down in one of the labs. We've been iterating improvements to the design. If you and I can find the module driving the block, we can vaporize it easily enough."

"Except for the hundreds or possibly thousands of Rasu between us and it."

"Except for them."

"And we don't know where it is."

"No, but the first place I'd check is the vicinity of the Caeles Prism Hub, if only because when the Hub shut down, it left a bunch of Rasu mechs standing around with nothing to do."

Richard called up the map of HQ in his head—not the actual map, as he could no longer access it, but his recollection of it. The memory of frantically chasing down the Savrakath's antimatter bomb through the bowels of the station with David at his side swept through his mind; he tucked it back away.

"There are a series of maintenance tunnels running alongside the levtram routes. If we stick to those and don't wander down any spurs, they should take us right there eventually. But there's a problem."

"Another one? I can't believe it."

"The maintenance access doors are key-coded and networked to the security system. It's a reasonable bet that the quantum block has knocked out at least one critical junction in the link."

Devon snorted in the darkness. "You seriously think an access panel on a door is going to stop me?"

"But you can't hack it, for the same reason."

Richard felt Devon's hand pat his shoulder. "Have a little faith, old man. Let's go get the Rectifier."

Veils were useless in a quantum block, but the lack of power gave them shadows to work with. Stealth the old-school way.

They spotted four Rasu mechs in the labs, and Richard noted that they weren't trashing anything—they were stealing. Was it a compliment that the Rasu believed there was something they stood to learn from Concord tech?

Luckily, no intruders had made it to the testing lab where the Rectifier was stored. They physically forced the door open and slipped inside. He kept an ineffectual watch on the hallway while Devon stumbled around until he located and retrieved the weapon. A few seconds later, Richard felt something cool being pressed into his hand.

"Much as I'd enjoy atomizing every Rasu we meet, you're a better shot than I am," Devon whispered.

The weapon had an odd balance to it, thanks to the oversized, misshapen barrel. Richard took a minute to familiarize himself with the trigger and the grip, then stuffed it in his waistband. "Now to sneak out of Special Projects without being noticed. Once we do, we're going to need to make our way to the levtram station out in the open, because we'd never find our way through all the maintenance tunnels from here in the dark. But once we reach the station, we'll take the tunnel to keep out of the Rasu's way. It should dead-end into another door when we reach the Hub stop."

"Right. Sounds good." Devon blew out a harsh breath. "Lead the way."

R_W

It had been decades since Richard had executed a stealth infiltration mission. To say his skills were rusty would be an insult to rusty nails. Also, the enemies whose camps he'd infiltrated had always been human criminals, not metal, shapeshifting aliens. They didn't have great intel on the Rasu's hearing capabilities. Could the aliens see in pitch black? He had no choice but to presume so.

He and Devon could as well *if* they had even rudimentary access to their eVis, which they did not. So they moved slowly and mostly quietly. In the darkness, the latter required the former.

Once they made it out of Special Projects—thank God the front doors had stalled partially open due to the evacuation order—there was meager light in the open areas from frequent viewports. A great battle raged outside the station, and watching the chaos and destruction from inside this murky, silent tomb-in-the-making was like staring into a dream. Richard shook his head and moved on; he couldn't afford to dwell on the battle.

When they reached the levtram lobby, he hesitated. What if Miriam and David were still in Command? Should they go there instead?

No. For security reasons, the War Room was tucked into a far corner of Command. It would take them half an hour or more to reach it in the dark, then another half an hour to reverse course and reach the Caeles Prism Hub from there. That was time they surely did not have.

They'd evaded perhaps a dozen Rasu on the way to the levtram station, so the enemy was not storming every corridor of HQ. But it was a big station, and the enemy seemed to know its way around rather well...his mind darted back to the War Room. The Rasu were certain to go straight for it, seeking an opportunity to cut the head off the Concord military once and possibly for all. The blast door should have activated before the quantum block went up, but what if it hadn't?

"Why aren't we moving?" Devon's mouth was close to his ear.

"Deciding something."

He wanted to go to the War Room. He wanted to know his closest friends were alive. He wouldn't mind their help in his mission, either.

But Miriam was in his head, ordering him to take out the quantum block at all costs, including her own life. Because that's absolutely what she would say.

He squeezed Devon's hand to signal they were about to move. They crept flush against the wall into the levtram station and over to the leftmost tracks. In the shadows, a handful of Rasu probed the station for tech and victims.

The door to the maintenance tunnel lay past the passenger loading area. They made their way along the edge of the platform until they reached a wall, then left down the wall until a ridge in it indicated a doorway. "You're up."

Devon felt along the wall until he found the recessed access panel. He pulled out a blade and jimmied the cover off—Richard snatched it as it fell before it clanged onto the floor.

"Right. Sorry. Um, if ever there's a time to use that light we grabbed from the lab, it's now."

Richard tensed. They'd taken a small spotlight on their way out of Special Projects, but if there were any Rasu in visual range, using it here would paint a bullseye on them. But they needed to get through this door.

He blocked Devon and the doorway with his body, held the light at his waist and turned it on, directing its narrow beam directly onto the open pad.

Devon yanked two photal fibers out of the circuit, then two more. He twisted the first two together and touched the third to the opening vacated by the fourth one. Sparks flew, and in the eerie light Richard thought Devon's hair smoked just a little.

Devon dropped the fibers, shaking his hand out. "Whew! So, yeah. Let's force this door open."

Richard killed the light, and they wiggled the door out of its seat and dragged it to the left.

Ahead of them was nothing but an inky blackness more absolute than any void in space.

"In we go."

65

RASU PRIME

Nika removed the mental filters she'd painstakingly created over the last months and opened herself fully to the kyoseil within and without her—and thus to the voices of the Rasu at full magnitude. Their thoughts crawled through her skull like a nest of spiders set free; her hands came to her head—and met the barrier of her helmet.

She hurriedly created a new partition in her operating system—but she couldn't shove the Rasu voices into it. She needed to hear, see and speak to the kyoseil, and one came with the other.

Okay, Nika. Time to stiffen your spine and muscle through the pain. Get this done.

She focused all her attention on the kyoseil, trying to treat the Rasu thoughts as random background noise. The first thing she noticed, with some relief, was a...break, like a cleaved fissure, between her and the ocean of kyoseil waves flowing out from this place. When she'd asked the kyoseil to turn on for the Rasu, the mineral had been clever enough to keep a level of separation between the Rasu-controlled kyoseil and all other instances of itself. If it hadn't, her people might well be puppets of the Rasu now. Even here, at the origin point for a deluge of kyoseil-delivered orders, that separation was still maintained.

And this was why she had to be *here* in order to deliver the poison. She had to make contact with the Rasu kyoseil directly.

The second thing she noticed was more worrisome, though not unexpected. As she'd seen in her surveys, the kyoseil waves surged from this structure out to the vast Rasu armadas. But in this specific structure, there wasn't much kyoseil flowing at all.

It was almost as if they hadn't integrated the kyoseil into the nerve center of their operation...because they hadn't needed to. So long as Rasu were physically connected, they thought as one; this had always been true. The addition of kyoseil didn't gain them anything in this densely packed and contiguous central operating space.

Okay. She suspected Caleb could kill the entire planetary Rasu structure by touch alone, for the same reason—they were all physically connected. But if he did so first, it risked torching the whole plan. When the Rasu mind that was sending out the orders died, no more orders would be sent, and she wouldn't be able to reach the front lines with the poison.

The weight of every world. The weight of every life. Someone had to make the impossible decisions, and today that someone had to be her. The lives of the three of them meant nothing compared to the survival of trillions of innocent people. Besides, if they saved those lives, they should get another chance at their own as well. It was enough to pin hope on.

If asked, she believed Caleb would agree with this choice for himself. But when it came to Alex? Love made people crazy and stupid.

So she didn't ask him.

Nika: "Everything looks good. Caleb, I'm ready when you are."

Caleb: "Alex?"

Alex: "Locked and loaded, as they say."

Nika gripped her archine blade and sliced into the panel in front of her, quickly cutting away a meter-width of metal and throwing it aside. Then she removed her gloves and tossed them to the floor. Caleb did the same.

She reached out and grasped his right hand with her left, intertwining their fingers. Instantly she sensed the tingling pulse of Akeso's essence.

Caleb: "What do I need to grab hold of?"

Nika: "Nothing. Direct all the poison through me."

Caleb: "But shouldn't I—"

Nika: "No. I have to do the distributing of the poison. It has to flow outward from here through the kyoseil waves."

Caleb: "Understood."

One step left to take. She spoke to the kyoseil in the only way she knew how: via clear, directed thought.

You are about to receive a surge of information through me. I won't lie to you—this information is poisonous, but not to us. To the Rasu. I need you to do everything in your power to distribute this information far and wide, until it touches every Rasu carrying kyoseil inside of it. Use every ability at your disposal to achieve this goal. This is our one chance to defeat this enemy forever. Do not dwell on the act of killing, because in committing it, you are saving countless lives. So let us do what we must.

Nika: "Now."

She wrapped her fingers around the wires she'd exposed—and every nerve in her body lit fire. While it was true that the poison wasn't deadly to her, it was…violent. Her actions in this moment were a manifestation of supreme, unspeakable violence. And it felt as if it was going to burn her up from the inside out.

In her mind's eye, she linked the kyoseil in her body to the Rasu kyoseil flowing in nearly infinite waves out from this location. Then she forced the poison outward to catch a ride on those waves as they poured into countless Rasu across the galaxies.

Kyoseil waves weren't bound by dimensions or the speed of light; they simply *were*. But there were so many Rasu, so many branching paths needing to be followed, and she was only one conduit. While she'd hoped it might be otherwise, the poison did not incarnate everywhere all at once. Distributing this form of information was not a natural act for the kyoseil; she was going to have to coax it along, over and over again.

This was going to take a bit of time.

So she ensured the poison reached the vessels attacking the Dominion first, because she was selfish and weak. But because her mind was also an advanced artificial intelligence, she was able to push the poison out toward Concord space at the same time, where it split into more than thirty paths. The Rasu were pummeling Concord to an unimaginable degree.

On the fringes of her awareness, heavy thuds signifying movement began echoing through the cavernous room.

Caleb: "Shit, I think we have incoming."

Alex: "I know. Let me worry about them."

Caleb: "But why *do we have incoming? Shouldn't they be dead already?"*

Her conscience twisted in protest, heavy and dark.

Nika: "Because the kyoseil isn't integrated here at the center. It didn't need to be. We'll kill the Rasu here, but not until we're done killing them everywhere else. It's the only way."

Caleb: "But they're going to overwhelm us!"

Nika: "Caleb, do NOT let go of my hand. If you do, everyone dies."

He didn't respond, but he also didn't let go.

66

AFS DENALI
EARTH STELLAR SYSTEM

Luna crashed into a section of the Parapet Gambit three thousand kilometers long above the eastern Atlantic Ocean and half of Africa. *Please hold, please hold, please....*

But it was not to be. The magnitude of the force applied by the battered and misshapen but still-intact moon was far and away greater than anything any engine of war could create.

The force field bent inward, and the ships maintaining it were forced downward toward the atmosphere beneath the unrelenting assault—

Then like a bowstring, the Gambit snapped in five, six, eight places. Luna kept right on going.

Fleet Admiral Jenner (AFS Denali)(Earth Command Channel): "Parapet Gambit, disengage. All vessels fire on Luna using the distribution pattern provided." He longed to keep the Gambit up around three-quarters of the planet, but he didn't dare risk trapping the lunar debris they were hopefully about to create *inside* to fall to Earth and wreak havoc. Right now, Luna was a bigger threat than the invading Rasu.

Fleet Admiral Jenner (AFS Denali)(Earth Command Channel): "Terrestrial Defense Grid, fire now."

Two-hundred-eight nodes spread across a third of Earth High Orbit fired into the center of Luna. The nodes that had no line of sight to the apocalyptic body currently falling to Earth were cleared to fire on the many Rasu that wasted no time heading directly for the surface. Malcolm guessed oceans boiling and tsunamis sweeping over continents didn't concern them.

Earth's Terrestrial Defense Grid had constituted the most powerful planetary defense weapon in known space when humanity found itself transplanted to Amaranthe, at which point the Grid had become dwarfed by Anaden technology. But they had no problem stealing ideas from their former enemies, and many upgrades had been made over the years. Then, in the last three months, an extraordinary flurry of wholesale improvements and buildouts had occurred. RNEW weapons; mirror-based defenses they'd cribbed from the Taiyoks; adiamene and TDS shields to protect critical infrastructure. As of this morning, Malcolm would bet good odds on the Grid again being the king of the mountain when it came to planetary defense.

He had no idea if it was going to be enough.

He wanted to despair at the sight of so many Rasu vessels descending into the atmosphere. AEGIS forces that were unable to help with Luna moved to engage them, but if they didn't stop Luna from crashing into the surface, what the Rasu did next wouldn't matter much. So he'd deal with the invaders second.

Lunar regolith spewed outward in every direction, creating a hazy cloud that made seeing anything on visual impossible, so he switched to near-infrared and watched the jarring, negative-film images. Oh, the *Denali* had joined the attack, of course, as its weapons were the most numerous and powerful on the battlefield today. But there wasn't any strategy involved requiring his active input: simply fire on the designated target location with maximum power, and keep doing it.

So he watched, even as Earth's blue-and-white horizon rose to curve beneath the ship in his peripheral vision.

Finally, huge chunks began to break off the main lunar body. Their still-substantial size worried him, but it was better than the alternative. The combined power of the Grid's weapons and the AEGIS fleet's fire bore steadily into the lunar mantle now, and the material being churned up and expelled turned dark and thick.

The sound attached to such unprecedented destruction being wrought was deafening, but abruptly a new roar exploded outward, loud enough to shock his eardrums. Across the bridge, hands clapped over ears in a gut response to the clamor.

The bruised and broken moon cracked in two.

My God, what a sight it was to see! Malcolm's breath whistled through his lips.

Even so, they'd been expecting this—or rather hoping desperately for it.

Fleet Admiral Jenner (AFS Denali)(Earth Command Channel): "*Lunar Groups #1 and #2, you take the left piece and all smaller fragments it produces. Lunar Groups #3 and #4, the right one.*"

"Navigation, we're moving left. Keep it up."

The jagged half-moon canted at an angle, and a growing wobble was visible as the pull of the atmosphere began to buffet its fall. A distinct shimmy emerged in the *Denali* now as well, as they gradually backed up while holding steady relative to their target.

The haze of the outer atmosphere flared around the viewport, and he could *see* the relentless forward motion of the broken half of Luna, as if it was barreling straight for them. Which it definitely was.

Under their continued assault, the half-moon broke into three smaller pieces. Progress, but each one remained the size of a planet-killer asteroid.

"Sir, we're going to have to pull off soon. Maybe forty more seconds."

Because the *Denali* was a dreadnought and thus not capable of atmospheric flight. But its departure meant the removal of twenty of their most powerful suite of weapons, and there was much work still to be done.

"Keep us here until the last possible second, Commodore."

Ettore nodded sharply. "Yes, sir."

The fragment they were firing on shattered into a dozen pieces that might, just *might*, be small enough to not wreck Earth's surface.

"Weapons, switch to the big piece to our port." Malcolm kept the rest of the ships working on the smaller chunks and checked the feed to make certain the other groups were making similar progress on the right half of Luna.

"Sir, we've got to pull out."

"Ten more seconds." Luckily, he couldn't hear his XO's pained sigh over all the roaring.

With their concentrated firepower, their target piece disintegrated, and suddenly the sky (because they were hardly in space any longer) was awash in rocks. Normal-sized, not life-ending, rocks.

"Go now."

The floor lurched as the engines struggled against the increasingly thick atmosphere. Malcolm held his breath while the hull shuddered and groaned...then they were free. The TDS shrugged off the hailstorm of debris as the *Denali* escaped the clutches of Earth's gravity and returned to the black.

"Navigation, bring us around."

The sub-dreadnought ships continued to fire on the largest chunks of debris, but their efforts had at last created a cascading effect: smaller chunks broke apart more and more quickly. His eyes went to the radar screen; only eight pieces remained that were larger than one hundred meters. A diversion of firepower in their direction swiftly disintegrated the fragments.

Earth was about to get the biggest meteor shower in human history. Damage would be inflicted, but it would not be catastrophic.

Hail Mary, full of grace. They had done it.

Cheers abounded through the bridge, and Malcolm let the crew celebrate for ten seconds longer than he probably should have. But finally he shouted over the din. "Incredible job, everyone. But we have a full-scale Rasu invasion to repel. Back to work."

RW

AFS HFB-6 ("ARDAT")
SENECA STELLAR SYSTEM

Track. Drop. Invert. Lock. Fire.

Morgan left nothing in her wake as she arced one-hundred-forty degrees to close in on her next target. The Rasu were evil, malicious buggers, but they died the same way as any enemy. Or at least, they did when subjected to her glorious RNEW weapon. Tactics and formations were always evolving, but at the end of the day, it came down to hitting your target with a deadly weapon while making sure you didn't die in the process.

And there were *so many* targets. Field Marshal Bastian insisted they had destroyed over four million Rasu today, but to her eyes it looked as though there were a greater number of enemies now than when the day had started. And perhaps there were. After all, the ability to send endless reinforcements was the Rasu's superpower.

The golden glow of the Parapet Gambit gleamed across her vision with every rotation. An impenetrable force field holding the line against the enemy and protecting the world swaddled within it. More or less, as word had leaked of Rasu reaching the surface via the Caeles Prisms. Still, the Gambit was ensuring millions of them remained out here in space.

Nifty invention, but how boring must it be for all those ship captains? The entirety of their job consisted of holding their ship in place and keeping the power on. No, thank you.

Stanley and her subconscious had eliminated the next target without her active input, and she cast her mind out to monitor the status of her Flight while she moved on to a new enemy. Her pilots were making her proud. Landon in particular was racking up quite a kill list today. Overachieving to make up for Sagan? If so, the extra effort was fine by her. Pilots should always be endeavoring to prove themselves in battle—

Field Marshal Bastian (AFS Leonidas)(Seneca Command Channel): "Be advised. There is unusual movement on the outer reaches of the field of battle.

Reconnaissance vessels report that...it appears the Rasu have captured thousands
of asteroids from the Belt and are hauling them toward Seneca—correction, they
have launched the asteroids. All fast-attack vessels move to intercept."

Morgan laughed wryly. Seneca's moon was too large for even one of
the new Rasu goliaths to commandeer in a reasonable amount of time, so
the Rasu had opted for the next best thing—throwing giant rocks at the Parapet Gambit.

She checked the tactical feed and promptly frowned. 'Launched,' indeed. Those rocks were moving damn fast, squeezed into a tight grouping.
And they were the largest asteroids, too. Also, there were a lot of them.

The leading edge would reach the Gambit force field in twenty-three
seconds.

*Stanley, do you remember how we showed off so spectacularly during the
final battle of the Metigen War?*

I do indeed. It was a heady experience with which to kick off our relationship.

Want to do it again?

Will your pilots mind?

That gave her 0.3 microseconds of pause. The Banshee pilots were talented—the very best. But no one was as good as she was. And nothing was
more exhilarating than demonstrating it across over a thousand ships at
once.

*Commander Lekkas (Banshee Mission Channel, Eidolon Mission Channel):
"Sorry in advance. Just sit back and enjoy the show."*

She maintained a heightened, specialized Noesis connection with her
Flight pilots, but she'd also quietly designed additional passive interconnect-
edness into the Banshees under her command. As well as the Eidolons, in
case she ever needed it.

Go.

Her mind shattered into a kaleidoscope of fractals, expanding to race
into the hardware of every Banshee and Eidolon on the field. She was
wholly and completely each individual ship, yet each one also performed as
an appendage of her body, moving on command without conscious
thought.

Stanley superimposed tracking data of the incoming asteroids upon her
virtual vision, which now existed across half a megameter of space. Together they assigned targets to the fighter craft under her control. She could
cover seventy-seven percent of the asteroids, as twenty-three percent of
them were large enough to require multiple fighters...in the time it took
her to blink, she refactored the math and found a way to cover more.

Her armada swept into position in a perfect formation on the outer edge of the Gambit, pivoted as one and fired.

It was like the grand finale of a fireworks display, only the disintegrating asteroids were creating the show as she blasted them into a multitude of microscopic fragments. Sunlight glinted off the ocean of dust to brighten two megameters of space in a dazzling blue-white aurora.

In the end, a total of six asteroids made it through, none of which impacted a ship in the formation. The Parapet Gambit held.

Commander Lekkas (Banshee Mission Channel, Eidolon Mission Channel): "Thank you for lending me your ships and your minds, gentlemen and ladies. Carry on."

Field Marshal Bastian (AFS Leonidas)(Seneca Command Channel): "Fighter Division, incredible job. Resume your previous assignments."

Eventually, someone would probably tell him it had all been her doing. Likely a Banshee pilot who was butt-hurt over being usurped.

Your nose is bleeding again.

She wiped at it absently and spared only a brief scowl when her hand came back coated in blood.

Worth it.

67

MIRAI

The Rasu beam tore through the center of the scraper with the precision of a mining laser, sending concrete, glass and metal shooting outward in every direction—including toward the street.

Joaquim was already running, foolishly believing himself capable of outpacing the explosive force. A thunderous roar chased him, propelling him forward with greater urgency. He was determined to not get knocked out of the fight so early.

Granted, the battle had been in full swing for several hours, but it had all gone to shit when the Rasu pulled off a back-door infiltration of the surface and started building quantum blocks. As in the last offensive, a game of ping-pong between the Rift Bubbles/Kireme Boundaries and the quantum blocks began in earnest. And every time the Rift Bubble deactivated, thousands more Rasu poured in from space to start shooting up the cities.

Abruptly he realized the Justice Center was due ahead. They would have a Kireme Boundary in place, and it ought to be active.

When he felt the heat of the falling scraper scalding his back, he flexed his calves and dove forward, landing on his shoulder and tumbling head over feet across the concrete—

A tidal wave of debris slammed into the invisible barrier behind him and vanished into the ether.

He collapsed onto the street. Godsdamn that was close! His chest heaved from the exertion of the sprint, struggling to draw in sufficient oxygen to power his body, even as his mind turned to where he might move now to be of the most use. Parc and Ryan were holed up in a DAF bunker directing their military dyne troops remotely, so he'd need to find his own trouble this time. Plenty of options.

A hand appeared from over his shoulder, arm extended. He peered up to see Selene Panetier's upside-down face glowering at him. Soot had darkened her blonde hair to a dirty flint, and streaks of ash painted her cheeks and forehead like camouflage markings. Beneath her flak jacket, her shirtsleeves were ragged and torn; she had obviously not spent all her time inside the Kireme Boundary.

"Nice dive. For a second there, I thought you were a goner." She glanced at her hand, then drew it back fractionally. "If you want to lie there in the street and rest for a while, be my guest."

"No," he answered hurriedly, reaching up and grasping her hand in his then letting her help him up—and the instant he was standing, he wrapped his arms around her and yanked her against him for a ferocious kiss. She tasted salty and hot and a little bloody, and his body flooded with endorphins from the overwhelming *rightness* of it.

She shoved him away so hard he stumbled into the curb. "Lacese, what the fuck do you think you're doing? You do not get to toy with me like this! I took the high road for you, and I will not give it up now just because we're going to die."

"Not toying with you." He wrenched her back into his embrace—and got punched in the jaw for the effort. Fair enough.

He massaged his jaw with one hand while holding the other up in surrender. "I probably deserved that. But I mean it. Cassidy left me, and she was right to do so. I am an unrepentant asshole, and I've finally realized that I don't want to be anything else. I care about her, and I always will. But what stirs my blood is the fight. It's an addiction, one I have no interest in being cured of."

Selene gazed at him warily, a narrow trickle of blood weaving its way down from one eyebrow to cut a path across her cheekbone. "The fight against the Rasu. Against our enemies."

He shrugged gamely. "Or the fight in you—the one you provoke in me. Either one. Preferably all of the above."

"You...ugh! How could you do this to me? I have put you behind me, dammit."

"Have you?" He smirked sloppily on account of his aching jaw. "That kiss says you haven't."

"That kiss—" She broke off to respond to a comm and bark a series of orders to her officers. Then she stared at him, full lips quirking around in delightful consternation. Her hands landed on her hips, then rose again to gesture at him in agitation. "If you are playing me, I will have you stored."

"It's a deal, because I'm not. Will you set the world on fire with me?"

"Pretty sure it's already on fire. But maybe we can counter the flames with some of our own." A hint of a smile arrived to lift her features, and she reached out and took his hand in hers. "Come on. Rasu mechs are approaching from the southeast, around the block. We'll start with them."

RW

Maris patted her face dry, then inspected herself in the mirror. She did not look like she was ready for the red carpet of a gala premiere, to say the least. But what should a helpless bystander to a pitched battle for survival look like?

She'd been flailing all day, uncertain of what to do with herself. She no longer had anything of value to contribute to this clash. The motivational slogans had been deployed. The community outreach efforts had reached the masses. The money, though not nearly enough, had been raised until those who'd possessed it had their pockets turned out.

Should they win the day, she'd again be in a position to sweep into action, working her inspirational magic across the Dominion and perhaps a little across the border into Concord, helping to spread optimism and make their world shiny and new once more. But if they *didn't* win the day…

…all would be lost. Not so incidentally, including her own life. She was haughty, prideful and a touch narcissistic; she had no problem admitting this. It was far too late for her to change. Improve at the margins, yes, of course. Such as apologizing to Dashiel, for instance. She could learn and grow. But at her core, she was who she was.

And who she was didn't want to die today. Or tomorrow, for that matter. But it seemed she could do nothing to influence her fate. Oh, she supposed she could choose not to plant herself directly in front of a rampaging Rasu mech. But even this choice didn't matter so much, for a rampaging Rasu mech was apt to find her and rend her apart easily enough if it fancied doing so. And what then?

If they won, she would be reawakened. If they fell, that was it.

She groaned into her hands, only to realize they were trembling against her mouth. All the earnest pep talks in the world were incapable of shaking this debilitating terror now consuming her. It was sending her mind in frantic, never-ending circuits, round and round again.

She wandered back out into the central atrium of the botanical gardens. The stillness here overwhelmed her. This far from the center of the city, no explosions ricocheted outside the expansive windows. No tumbling buildings or ominous shadows darkened the tree-laden skyline. There was only the quiet.

Her chest constricted until she couldn't breathe. In her mind she saw the Rasu mech at the Initiative charging for her on an endless loop. Her shoulders heaved as she pressed her hands into her cheeks and worked to steady her racing heart. This would not do at all.

If these were her last moments of life upon the firmament, how should she spend them? Ideally, with delicious drinks and vibrant conversation surrounded by her dearest friends and current lover. Ideally, but not presently an option.

Overcome by an utterly ridiculous desire, she sent a ping.

Where are you now?

I am standing in a room at the Presidio—the Human military command—feeling my heart break into pieces as I watch our worlds begin to fall beneath the onslaught while I am powerless to do anything to stop it.

Allow me to ameliorate your circumstances.

She counted as good fortune the fact that for these few minutes, no quantum block was active on Mirai. She stepped away from the wall and opened a wormhole to said Presidio room. Beyond the opening, military officers in uniforms that were starting to wrinkle from sweat and strain huddled over screens and gestured dramatically at holos while barking orders in raspy voices.

Corradeo Praesidis spun, surprise animating his striking but worry-darkened features as he saw the wormhole and her standing on the other side of it.

She silently held out a hand, upturned and open.

He glanced once around the room, an enigmatic expression passing across his face, then stepped through the wormhole and clasped her outstretched arm.

She closed the wormhole behind him and gracefully drew him closer, as if in the opening move of a dance. Then, in a thoroughly impetuous, nigh, scandalous act, she draped a hand along the curve of his neck and brought her lips to his.

Who knew sheer charisma, if powerful enough, was capable of being transmitted through the meeting of flesh? That it guided the movement and pressure of lips in such a way as to enchant one's entire sense of being beneath its spell?

"Oh, my," he whispered breathlessly. "What is this?"

It took all her willpower to draw back the centimeter required for speech, as she was fearful distance might break the spell.

She needn't have worried.

"It is the end of the world. I have lived for 712,246 years, and I do not want to die alone."

68

RASU PRIME

Shadowy silhouettes moved out of the single-entry hallway and spread out across the cavernous room. Weaponized arms raised and unleashed lasers in their general direction.

Alex's shield sizzled and warnings flashed in her virtual vision. *Recharge faster, dammit!*

She fired both Rectifiers into the advancing line of Rasu. The triggers on the weapons were tight and required a lot of force to activate while keeping the guns steady, all of which needed to be accomplished with one hand. She managed.

Chunks of mechs, walls, ceiling and floor vanished into nothingness. Also, she should be more careful and try to aim more precisely. They were going to need that floor for a while longer.

But 'careful' wasn't really an option at this point. She had to keep Caleb and Nika standing with their limbs intact long enough for them to circulate the poison far and wide, across gigaparsecs of space to reach every single Rasu entity—and most urgently, to disseminate it into the enemy units attacking their most precious worlds.

Her shield sizzled again, and a telltale hiss behind her suggested Caleb and Nika's did this time as well. Things were off to a miserable start; she was going to have to do a much better job of suppressing this onslaught. *Think!*

As she fired one of the Rectifiers, she reached back with one hand and detached Caleb's ribbon of archine grenades from his utility belt, then hooked it onto her own belt, next to her already dwindling supply. She'd take Nika's, too, but she didn't have anywhere to fasten them. She'd come back for them when she ran out.

Caleb: *"Alex, what are you doing?"*

Alex: *"The one thing I can do, so you can do what you must. Focus."*

Caleb: *"I have one hand free. Let me help you fend them off."*

Alex: *"And risk you accidentally shooting me because you're visualizing Rasu poison instead of looking at where you're shooting? Hell, no. Focus."*

No response was forthcoming. She knew he was fuming, twisting himself up into knots at his inability to join her on the front line. But he had a far more critical job to do right now.

Alex yanked two grenades off the belt and tossed them into the large clump of Rasu mechs headed her way, sending metal shards spearing into the walls, ceiling and, yes, the floor; two of the shards bounced off her shield and clattered to the floor. This kind of attack the shield could easily handle.

While the Rasu were waylaid for a minute trying to piece themselves back together, she retrieved a special device Devon had sent along and placed it on the floor behind where Caleb and Nika stood. She stepped around to the other side of it, then crouched and pressed the activation button.

A powerful force field burst to life, forming a wall that stretched almost fifteen meters in length. If she stayed behind the wall, the Rasu would simply storm around its edges and overrun them anyway. But this way, the force field would protect Caleb and Nika from stray laser fire.

For a while.

In theory.

Thankfully, neither of her companions seemed to notice the addition of the force field. Their minds were swimming among the whims of primordial, ethereal beings. A deep, hidden universe that belonged to the ancients.

Your shield's reserves are getting worryingly low.

They'll hold out, Valkyrie.

For how long?

Long enough.

Alex worked to steady her breathing. Valkyrie helped, her eVi routines helped, and still she felt like she was on the verge of hyperventilating.

She wasn't a warrior, and her present situation was doing nothing to make her wish she'd taken that route in life. She preferred to combat her enemies using her mind: knowledge, ingenuity, cleverness and sheer force of will.

But she wielded a gun in each hand, and she knew how to shoot them.

She'd suggested the possibility of surrounding the group with a small Kireme Boundary, but Nika believed the dimensional shift would interfere with the poison's dispersal—not block it, but potentially alter it in a meaningful way. So no Kireme Boundary.

Additional Rasu arrived to back up the ones she'd turned into mincemeat about the time the first group began to regain shape and motor power, and she promptly gave up trying to preserve the structural integrity of the front half of the room. Hopefully the floor under their feet was braced enough to hold itself in place.

She briefly wondered why the floor wasn't rising up to consume them, or the equipment ringing the power vortex shapeshifting and coming for them. But then she realized the Rasu wanted to maintain their ability to send orders out to their troops. They were fighting numerous battles in multiple galaxies. Ergo, the equipment had to remain intact, and it needed a floor beneath it to do so.

Firing freely at the entrance shortened the amount of time the Rasu were able to shoot at her before being vaporized—but it was also widening the formerly bottlenecked entrance, allowing a greater number of Rasu to storm through at once. The Rectifiers' fire rate was slow, so she alternated in tossing grenades to slice the attackers up. A temporary solution, but it bought her a bit more time.

Heavy thuds sounded from above the high ceiling—

A hole blew itself in the wall on her left, and a tumbling mass of metal surged out from it. Alex spun and shot into the center of the mass. The Rasu emerging out of the hole evaporated, but now the hole in the wall was larger. And the enemy had two entrances through which to reach her.

So she widened her stance, pointed the Rectifiers at ninety-degree angles and kept firing. Whirlpools of void snatched away everything the blasts touched like the ghostly hands of demons from the beyond.

Alex: "How are we doing?"

Nika: "Almost...I think."

Caleb: "You okay?"

Alex: "Yep."

It was a lie. Handed an additional entry point, Rasu poured into the room at an unrelenting pace. Grandaddy Rasu Prime was putting up one hell of a fight, right up until the end.

Sweat streamed down her temples inside her helmet to pool at her neck. Her pointer fingers cramped from the effort of depressing the heavy triggers over and over. Her shield sizzled anew from multiple simultaneous laser impacts, and power warnings flashed in her eVi.

Valkyrie, can we siphon some power from my Caeles Prism to my defensive shield?

That is a novel idea. I will try it.

How are you?

Rasu are attacking me from all sides. But my cocoon is functioning quite satisfactorily.

A pang of worry for her beloved ship and the life within it flared, but she forced it aside. Of all the things she didn't have the bandwidth to worry about.

Another blast from the hallway created a third entry point farther down the wall, and dammit but she didn't have three arms! She tossed her last archine grenade into the gap, then immediately targeted the other two entrances. She needed more grenades, but she could no longer stop shooting for long enough to circle around the force field and retrieve Nika's supply.

A Rasu mech barreled over and through the tumbling shards of its splintered brethren and charged straight for her. She swung her right arm toward it and fired when it was only five meters away.

Tendrils of void swept across her shield, and blinding *pops* of blackness blotted out the room.

When Alex could see again, she was teetering on the edge of a gaping hole in the floor. She frantically stepped backward until the electricity of the force field wall fought against her own shield.

A sea of Rasu now poured in from every entrance. She fired again. Again and again, as quickly as the triggers allowed it. But the enemy was starting to get through the gaps.

Another mech evaded her bombardment to draw near—then far *too* near. She snapped her arm out, and the conductivity lash on her bracelet sent a whip of electricity shooting into the mech. It jerked backward and lost its footing, giving her a chance to point a Rectifier at it and press the trigger.

She instinctively flinched away as the resulting void reached out for her.

An explosion overhead drew her attention. A spinning ball of Rasu dropped down out of a newly formed hole in the ceiling. She pointed upward and fired, but it was almost on top of her—and gone—

Something grabbed her arm from the left and yanked her forward, sending the Rectifier in that hand skidding away. Inside her boots, her toes scrambled to keep hold of the jagged edge of the crater in the floor....

The floor gave way beneath her.

Time stretched out as she fell. One second became a million individual microseconds, then a billion nanoseconds.

She managed to bring the Rectifier still in her grasp close to her chest. Her finger convulsed on the trigger, and the void came for the monstrous creature that held her in its clutches. Except for its hand, which spasmed around her arm, razored digits slicing through the environment suit and into flesh and bone.

Abruptly there was a single picosecond of blinding, all-consuming pain, and finally the void came for her.

RW

What—?

Alex's mind awakened with a snap of someone's fingers. Thoughts ricocheted erratically down unfamiliar electrical pathways. Searching for the pain. Searching for her limbs. Searching for her breath.

Alex, you need to stay calm. Give yourself time to settle in.

Valkyrie? Settle in how? Where am I?

You are in the ship, with me.

She tried to look around, but everything was photons and pulsing signals and power flows and atoms bouncing to and fro. Electrons spinning. Quantum orbs prisming.

She peered down at the cockpit, and up at the same spot, while also at their bed and the engineering well and the endless expanse of Rasu banging away ineffectually at the cocooned hull outside.

I don't...I'm not in the ship. I am the ship.

Yes.

What happened?

Are you calm? Are you here?

Tell me, dammit! But she already knew. The last blink of her life was frozen in her mind as her forty-meter fall ended with her crashing onto a jutting piece of machinery that had transformed into sharp edges to await her arrival. This had been the pain she'd felt.

She would have hyperventilated for certain now, but of course she no longer had a breath. She felt simultaneously detached and adrift, but also more connected to the world around her than she'd ever experienced before. Her previous dalliances into the elemental realm had been child's play compared to this.

Her thoughts boomeranged off for a new pass—into the central programming of the *Siyane*, out into the cold, desolate wilds of this damned planet, then off for a brief tour of the wiring minutiae of the Zero Engine, until Valkyrie gently pulled her back to...whatever counted as 'home.'

How?

You know I am always with you. At the instant when your heart stopped—
because it had been pierced by a fucking Rasu spire—*I drew all the electrical*

activity of your brain across the quantum bridge that joins us, while also clearing space in my hardware within the ship. I then transferred those signals into the hardware.

But I'm...am I truly me? Or am I just an...echo?

You are as much you as I am me.

Okay. Okay. Crap, Caleb! She didn't have time to explore the dichotomy of being both alive and dead when Caleb was now unprotected and at the mercy of the Rasu. *Can I do sidespace from here? How do I...?*

Not precisely. You can project your consciousness the way I do, but I suspect mastering it will take practice.

But you can. Check on them!

I am doing so. Be aware, only 1.2 seconds have passed since you fell.

So this was what it was like to inhabit the mind of an Artificial, with no neural graft buffer to take the edge off the deluge for her fragile organic brain. No wonder Artificials had so much free time on their hands, while still accomplishing such great feats.

Could she...she could access their comms, because they routed in part through Valkyrie, and thus the ship. And thus her.

Alex: "Caleb, Nika, you need to hurry."

Caleb: "What happened? You weren't responding for a few seconds there."

Alex: "It doesn't matter. Focus everything you have on completing your mission, and do try to...to hurry." I can't protect you any longer, *priyazn.* Oh my god.

Caleb: "Are you hurt? What's wrong?"

A thunderous shudder shook her body—shook the *Siyane*. She was able to see in every direction at once via the walls of the ship, but outside was only a morass of darkness. Rasu on all sides, blasting away at the impermeable hull. Trying their damnedest to get in.

Alex: "Caleb, please. Finish your task. Win us this war."

Having no breath was seriously the oddest thing. She'd spent her entire life needing air to walk and talk and think and feel and live. But now she could...think, at least, just fine. With no air.

She felt dizzy. But this was merely an artifact of a physical body that was no longer....

Queasy, too.

A half-formed thought, and she'd leapt into the Noesis and was bombarded by panicked pleas for help. On Erisen and New Columbia and Demeter and Shi Shen. They were overridden by the staccato decisions and orders from military Prevos on ships across Concord space.

She searched through the ocean of cries, but found only a deafening silence from HQ. From Earth. From Seneca and Romane.

It took every ounce of her restraint—interesting how this was something she retained in this synthetic form—not to berate Caleb and Nika to hurry yet again. She'd only distract them from the hurrying.

The *Siyane* suddenly lurched sideways and down. Another bump followed, then it bounced roughly to a stop, canted at a fifteen-degree angle.

What just happened?

I believe that since the Rasu cannot penetrate us, they are going to try to bury us.

Well it would suck to die, only to be returned to life in quantum form, only to die again in the ship, wouldn't it?

Come on, priyazn, *hurry. We are all out of time.*

69

CONCORD HQ

Richard had never thought of himself as claustrophobic. In his early days in the military, he'd conducted missions involving impossibly tight spaces and darkened traversals. He hadn't enjoyed them, but he could tolerate a lot of things when he needed to.

He spent the first five minutes of their trek through the maintenance tunnel trying not to succumb to a panic attack. Infrared vision was nearly as useless as normal vision, because there was no heat differential and no movement. They turned on their floodlight once, but it only showed a never-ending, featureless passage, so he forced himself to turn it back off. No need to advertise their location. But that choice hurt. What was it about this tunnel, this journey?

The Rasu, of course. This time, he knew there were monsters waiting in the dark.

He occupied himself by worrying about Will. Convincing his husband to evacuate when the attack began had been a herculean task, and he'd only barely managed it. He'd thought Will would be safe on Seneca—unless they lost the war so completely that their worlds were overrun, at which point nowhere would be safe. But now the Rasu had used the Caeles Prism on HQ to reach Seneca from the ground, and he had no idea what was happening there. To an intelligence officer, the absence of information was…suboptimal.

He ruminated on how he'd been too busy with the Vilane investigation on top of his regular CINT work and hadn't been attentive enough to Will lately; his husband was a forgiving and understanding man, but he shouldn't abuse those qualities. He prayed he'd get the chance to make up for his lapses on the other side.

He worried about David and Miriam. Had they made it to the Presidio, or perhaps to the *Aurora*? Or were they trapped here, the same as he and Devon? Had the Rasu reached the War Room and done the unthinkable? In a world of constant, instantaneous communication, the abrupt lack of contact with others was as suffocating as this damnable pitch-black tunnel.

He didn't even see the doorway until he bumped into it.

Devon collided with his back. "Sorry!"

Devon's voice echoing through the blackness felt like a violation of its sanctity.

"My fault." Richard switched the light on and checked the frame of the door before settling the beam on the access panel. "It's all yours."

Devon sidled up to the panel and removed his blade. "Why is special access required to *exit* the tunnel? By definition, you already got in."

"Redundancy is crucial in security systems."

"That's a stupid reason. I mean, not generally, but in this specific circumstance." Sparks flew around Devon's hands, shots of electric silver in the darkness. "Ow...."

He raised the light so Devon's face became visible in the diffuse edges of its spread. "You okay?"

"Scorch marks is all." Devon wiggled his fingers. "Still functional."

"Good." Richard stared at the door, working to shift his mindset. "Listen, it's possible that, denied access to our worlds, most of the Rasu have vacated HQ. It's also possible we're about to walk into a monstrous horde of them. We need to avoid detection for as long as we can, but our goal is to reach line-of-sight to the quantum block mechanism, then blow it to Hell."

"Got it. I'm ready." He didn't sound ready.

Richard added getting Devon trapped in this situation to his list of regrets. Devon wasn't a young guy any longer—he hadn't been for a while now—but Richard would always think of him as a kid. Kind of like a son to him in some respects.

But the time for sentimentality had come to an end, and their mission waited on the other side of the door. "All right. Let's get this door open."

They eased it open as quietly as possible and peered out. Faint ambient light practically blinded them, and he blinked until shadowy walls and shapes gained definition.

They were on the platform of the levtram serving the Caeles Prism Hub. No heavy thuds resounded through the air, and the platform appeared empty.

They skirted along the wall and into the lobby and out of the station—

Richard threw out an arm and pushed Devon against the inside wall.

Three Rasu bipedals were dismantling the security checkpoint apparatus leading to the Hub. Beyond them, maybe two dozen additional Rasu were doing the same to the Caeles Prism hardware. The aliens wielded tools that functioned perfectly fine in a quantum block, and torches burned brightly as components were melted apart.

A steady violet glow emanated from just past the right wall. He knew from reading the debrief reports from multiple worlds that the glow signified the quantum block, run by the Rasu's signature power source.

But he couldn't see the mechanism from here.

Two roller mechs sped by across the open space between the levtram station and the Hub. They were certainly making themselves at home.

Richard surveyed the scene again and worked out the variables. Three mechs directly in his way, and twenty-plus more near his target. No way in but through.

He'd never survive it. But if he got really lucky, he'd reach his target and complete his mission. The quantum block had to be destroyed; there was no other option.

He nodded to himself, then slipped around the wall to join Devon. "Okay, here's the plan. We need to clear a bit of a path in order to get in sight of the block apparatus."

"This is why we brought the archine grenades."

"Correct. Hand me one. I'm going to lob it into the security checkpoint and take out the three Rasu working there. Then we're going to rush forward along the left wall, trying to keep some cover between us and them. You're going to toss the last two grenades into the center of the Hub while I sneak in and swing past the wall to destroy the apparatus with the Rectifier.

"As soon as you've thrown the grenades, I want you to turn around and run like the wind back into the levtram station. Hopefully the power and everything else will come on in short order, and you can wormhole out of here. But if you can't, hole up somewhere safe and wait it out."

"What?" Devon shook his head. "No way. I'm providing cover for you while you get in position, blow the quantum block, then escape back here."

"With what? Your Daemon?"

"It's better than nothing. At least it should distract them for a few seconds."

"No. You've done enough. More than enough. Get to safety."

Devon's expression puckered up in the faint light. "Bullshit. This is my world, too. My station, my work. And you're my friend. We do this together."

"Dammit. You picked a hell of a time to be noble."

"Hey! I've always been noble. About matters of my choice."

"I know you have. You're a good man, Devon."

"Not as good as you, but thank you." Devon stuck his hand out. "It's been an honor knowing you, sir."

He grasped Devon's hand and patted him on the shoulder. "The honor's all mine."

"Beers later?"

Richard conjured a smile. "I'll meet you at *The Black Hole* when this is over."

Then he took several steps back, palmed an archine grenade in one hand and gripped the Rectifier in the other. "We go on three."

AFS DENALI

EARTH STELLAR SYSTEM

The Rasu were descending in too great of numbers for them to successfully reestablish the Parapet Gambit, and Malcolm realized he was tying up too many ships attempting to do so. He abandoned the strategy for now and ordered everyone to focus on intercepting the vessels intent on penetrating the atmosphere and reaching the surface.

A quantum block remained active on the planet, but thanks to their preparations, he was receiving rudimentary communications from the ground commanders. Unfortunately, the news they delivered was dire.

The Rasu had overrun Manhattan Island. The number of buildings destroyed there was increasing too rapidly to track. Many of the Rasu who arrived through the HQ Caeles Prism had transformed into aerial vehicles and spread out across the globe, where they divided and increased their numbers until reinforcements arrived.

Houston, Vancouver, Oslo, Shanghai and Hong Kong were hot spots. Strategic military bases, all. The Rasu had done their research.

Again Malcolm fidgeted with a primal need to be down there on the surface fighting, and again he forced himself to ignore it. He could save more lives by preventing a single Rasu vessel from reaching the surface than he ever could with a gun in his hand and his feet on the ground. He knew this.

The concept of Earth being invaded...his brain refused to accept it. Such a thing was the domain of fiction vids; it did not exist in the real world. Yet here they were.

The Terrestrial Defense Grid was so powerful and its nodes so numerous, his ships were having difficulty staying out of its line of fire. Eight vessels had been lost to friendly fire so far, a figure that was not going to make the Oversight Committee happy in the post-mortem. If they actually lived to engage in a post-mortem review, then the Board was free to debate the merits of this particular battlefield tactic.

A new warning flared on one of his many open screens. Antimatter radiation warning. This late into the battle, the space surrounding Earth was growing thick with residual antimatter from the Rasu's weapons. The *Denali's* TDS kept most of it at bay, but the shield was not designed to soak in an antimatter soup for hours on end. Perhaps worse, clouds of antimatter were drifting into the atmosphere, creating disturbing explosions across Earth's horizon. The long-term damage to the atmospheric ecosystem was something else that would need to be evaluated after the day was, somehow, won.

"Sir, long-range sensors report a new influx of Rasu vessels."

Malcolm's heart sank. "How many?"

"Analyzing now. Approximately 10.3 million."

Many years of practice kept his expression stolid, but despair gripped his chest. Their ships would be crushed beneath an armada that was about to double in size. Knocked aside and trampled like fleas beneath the enemy's unyielding march.

Fleet Admiral Jenner (AFS Denali)(Earth Command Channel): "Immediate Ymyrath Field blasts ordered in Quadrant 8."

What else could he do? Pull the fleet from Seneca to fight here? From Romane? Sacrifice every other world in a desperate and probably doomed bid to save this one?

But if, God forbid, he did this, more Rasu would just follow them here. Knowing Seneca and Romane were now undefended, they'd leave a minimal force behind at those worlds and bring the rest to bear on Earth, instantly negating his increase in numbers while swiftly killing the people on the planets he'd abandoned.

One feed updated. It looked as though the Ymyrath Field had reduced the incoming number to 7.8 million. An incredible feat that ultimately wouldn't matter.

He had no moves left. During the last few months, Miriam had frequently ruminated on how the sheer overwhelming numbers the Rasu were able to field was the one weapon they couldn't defend against, and she'd been correct.

He issued a half-hearted order for his forces to double down on what they were already doing and waited for the unstoppable wave of enemies to descend upon them.

No. He could not give in to despair now. He was the leader of millions of honorable, brave soldiers, and he didn't get to betray their trust by giving up. And dammit, but he'd only just gotten Mia back, and he needed to hold her in his arms a great deal more.

So he continued to wrack his brain, searching for anything at his disposal to change the game. He'd hurl Luna at them if it still existed. Though to do so would surely destroy his reborn soul, he'd order the self-destruct of every ship in his fleet, setting off a cascading explosion of Zero Engines and conflagrating space from here to Mars, if it meant the act saved the billions of people living on Earth.

But the Rasu would simply send another ten million ships to replace those he incinerated in the conflagration.

The front line of the new enemy arrivals came into view. Grimness darkened his voice as he ordered the *Denali's* Weapons Officer to target the largest vessel on the field and pick a fight with it.

RW

CONCORD HQ
RASU WAR ROOM

Miriam sat on the floor in front of the viewport, snuggled up against David's chest. His arms were wrapped around her and his chin rested on her shoulder.

They'd succeeded in creating makeshift crowbars and, as expected, had been laughably unable to so much as budge the blast door. After some brainstorming and aborted attempts at finding another way to get the door open, they'd grudgingly accepted the reality of their situation and settled in to watch the show outside.

She'd never felt so helpless. All these months, all the years before then of dogged, unremitting preparation. Of swimming against the tide of bureaucracies and fear and reactionary alien cultures to shape an organization and a military that was capable of repelling any enemy the universe threw at them.

Except possibly not this one. And now, at the hour of truth, she'd been knocked right out of the game. She could not alter or even influence their fate. She could not take action to turn the tide against the enemy. She could do nothing at all but watch.

"Ooh, nice takedown there. Is that the *Roosevelt?*"

Miriam rolled her eyes. "There's no way to tell. Every AEGIS cruiser looks the same from the outside."

"I don't know. I think it was the *Roosevelt.*"

"Maybe it was."

Her mind went to Alex, as it had many times since the battle had begun. Had her daughter succeeded in her mission? The Rasu here continued to fight as zealously and ferociously as ever, so if they had successfully implemented their plan, then it hadn't done what they'd expected. This had always been a risk, of course. A big one.

Or had the Rasu intercepted and killed Alex, Caleb and Nika before they'd reached their destination? Before they'd finished their task? Her heart wanted to break at the image her brain served up of Alex's body—

She cut the thought off. She didn't know what had happened on Rasu Prime, what might be happening there at this moment, or what her daughter might manifest into happening in the moments to come, and she refused to allow her mind to fill in the absence of information with nightmarish scenarios.

So her thoughts turned to Earth—and Seneca and Nopreis and Ares, but mostly to Earth. A hostile alien force had never before set foot on Earth's soil. Not until today.

HQ's Caeles Prism connected to a transport center in New York; it wasn't a military installation, so the Rasu would have been able to rampage through innocent civilians immediately upon their arrival. Had Marine squads stopped them eventually, or had they done what had worked in the past and constructed a quantum block, knocked out the Rift Bubble, and proceeded to terrorize the streets and the skies of Earth writ large?

It wasn't like her to dwell on such gloom, but this was armageddon, dammit.

But for some odd reason, as that notion took hold in her mind, a calmness descended upon her.

She stroked David's hand at her waist and tilted her head to rest her cheek on his. "I'm glad you're here with me at the end."

"The end? What is this nonsense? Our brilliant daughter and her crazy-ass husband and their *neobyknovennyy* friend are going to save us all and rid the universe of this enemy. Any second now."

"I hope so." Miriam twisted around to face him. "But if they don't—"

His hands came up to cup her cheeks. "Shh. I love you more than all the stars in the heavens, *moya vselennaya*. And if this should prove to be the end of all things, there is nowhere I would rather be than sitting here watching its grand finale with you—"

A thudding noise grew loud from the other side of the door, like the tromping of an elephant stampede.

They both leapt to their feet as a *bang* slammed into the blast door, followed by another. Then, a *hissing* sound. Quieter, but somehow more ominous.

The Rasu weren't going to be able to either brute force or cut their way through the blast door, she told herself. Its sturdiness meant she and David couldn't get out, but it also meant the enemy couldn't get in.

A deep dread churned up from the depths of her subconscious, and the nightmares she'd thought banished reemerged to crush her heart in a vice-grip. "David...there's a seam in the door."

For two...three seconds he said nothing, and the *hissing* filled the silence.

"Okay." His voice was low and steady. Stalwart. "Let's take up a position behind the war table, weapons trained on the door."

From out of the blood swirling at her feet rose inky aubergine tentacles. They wrapped around her ankles and slithered up her legs. No matter how hard she fought them, their grip only tightened. She reached for the Daemon at her hip, only to find it had become a third tentacle winding around her waist. It squeezed, denying her air, as more tentacles reached her neck, then her face. Liquid metal poured into her ears, nose and finally her mouth.

"You think you are alive, but you are mistaken. You never left us. We will never let you escape."

Her hands were shaking; she fisted the free one at her side. Her left clutched the grip of her Daemon so hard it was surely about to crumble in her hand. "I won't let them take me. I won't."

"And if it comes to that, we'll go out together. But not until there's no other option—you hear me, *dushen'ka?*"

"I do. David, you impossibly returning from the beyond and back into my life was the second-best thing that has ever happened to me. The first was meeting you on Perona."

He grabbed her in a kiss so fierce, it swept her away on a tsunami of his love for her. It encapsulated everything they had ever been, and her heart threatened to shatter in her chest from its power.

But it had to end, for the enemy was coming for them. They crouched behind the long table, shoulders touching, and leveled their useless Daemons over the top of it.

The ongoing battle outside provided enough light, if strobing, uneven light, for them to see the outline of the door. Tunnel vision took over as she watched for the first sliver of liquid metal to ooze through the barrier.

And then it did. A thin puddle of viscous fluid seeped in from where the floor, frame and door met on the right. It grew steadily in size until it had enough mass to begin building itself into something more solid.

Her heart pounded in her ears until she heard the blood whooshing through her veins. But if this was when death came for her, she would go out on her own terms. She controlled her end.

70

RASU PRIME

Caleb adjusted his grip on Nika's hand; both of their palms were sweaty and hot. His skin felt raw and blistered, but he didn't dare let loose of her.

Agitation crawled up his spine. He wanted with every fiber of his being to check on Alex. She'd sounded strangely off in her recent comms. But of course she was tense and distracted. She was under attack from the enemy, and he wasn't standing at her side. Dammit!

But his desires were irrelevant. Alex was right; he needed to stay focused. Get the job done, save everyone back home, and all of this struggle would be worth it.

Akeso has not expended such volume of energy in its memory, not even when Other attacked its soil. I...tire.

He hadn't fully appreciated the effort required for Akeso to generate an endless supply of death incarnate on demand, and his heart ached at the realization. Akeso was a bastion of life and healing. Nothing about this accursed scheme came naturally for his companion.

But they all must do what was necessary when faced with an exigent threat to the lives of those they treasured.

I know. I tire, too. Stay strong for a minute longer. We're saving trillions of lives.

I will persevere for this goal. For as long as I can.

He hated being blind. He longed to observe the flow of the kyoseil and the poison it carried out into the cosmos, to judge for himself the state of their mission. But his awareness of both ceased when the poison transferred into Nika, and her responses to his inquiries had grown terser with every attempt.

Still, the question queued up on his tongue as worry about Alex rebounded to the forefront of his mind once again—

RW

CONCORD HQ

RASU WAR ROOM

David blasted the solidifying object, but the hole he created in it sealed the instant he let up. So Miriam joined him, and they kept firing.

Additional metal seeped in and gathered itself together, and they couldn't keep up with the swelling mass. The beginnings of a Rasu attack mech began to grow and take shape.

Abruptly she ceased firing and stood. She controlled her end.

I've done the best I know how, in all things. I make peace now with the knowledge that I couldn't have done more with the life given to me. She took David's hand in hers and—

The mech dissolved and spilled across the floor of the War Room.

She gasped in fresh air. Her mind broke, for a single instant, as the gravity of these cascading events crescendoed through her soul.

Then just as quickly, she stitched herself back together. She leveled her Daemon on the pool of Rasu, and she and David moved out from behind the table while renewing their fire.

Liquid metal splashed across the walls, fizzling as it vaporized under the impact of the conventional lasers.

She laid a hand on David's arm, and they lowered their weapons to watch what remained of the mass.

It didn't move. Not so much as a twitch.

Her gaze shot to the viewport, but the scene was too chaotic to determine whether the state of affairs had changed.

David grabbed her shoulders, a big grin lighting his features with joy. "They did it!"

"We can't be sure. Maybe something's wrong with this particular Rasu."

"I've never heard of one randomly failing. Miri, *they did it.*"

"I don't want to—"

Light flooded the War Room as everything turned back on at once. Screens flared to life and confused, overlapping chatter burst forth from multiple comm channels.

Her hand came to her mouth as a sob broke free. David squeezed her against his chest and buried an answering sob in her hair.

But he pulled away before she became impatient, wiping a tear off his cheek as he did. "Go. You have order to restore and a victory to lead."

She nodded, hurriedly wiping her own cheeks with her uniform jacket then patting down her hair. It wouldn't do for her subordinates to see her in this state. "Try to reach Alex, will you? I want to know what's been transpiring on Rasu Prime and what kind of shape they're in. And Richard, too. I worry he got trapped here as well."

"I'm on it."

She drew in a deep breath to try to reorient her thinking. She must be the calm at the center of the maelstrom.

Then she marched to the war table.

Commandant Solovy (Concord Command Channel): "I need a status report from all fleets and battle sectors. Not everyone at once, please. Fleet Admiral Jenner, you go first."

AFS DENALI
EARTH STELLAR SYSTEM

The oversized Rasu vessel quickly took notice of the *Denali* and made a beeline for them. Maneuverability was not a dreadnought's strength. But resiliency (and unmatched firepower) was, so Malcolm stood his ground while their weapons ate away at the Rasu's hull as it barreled toward them—

And crashed into their bow.

The collision drove them backward, as the Rasu had momentum working for it. A violent shudder reverberated through the ship, but everything held together.

"Weapons, keep firing!"

Now the *Denali's* weapons bore directly into the Rasu at point-blank range. Metal evaporated in a great roiling mist, and their TDS sparked and crackled as it fought the rebounding negative energy fire.

Then the metal of the Rasu grew fluid. Was it going to try to swallow them? A shudder rippled through Malcolm, and he reminded himself they were prepared for this as well. The TDS would keep the Rasu out of the ship. If they found themselves encased, they'd burn themselves a hole with those vaunted weapons, then continue burning away until the hole was large enough for them to escape.

But when the expanding liquid metal had encompassed a third of the *Denali's* hull and he was beginning to second-guess his bravado, it stopped its advance. Strange.

"Continue firing. We need to disintegrate every last centimeter of this monster."

"Yes, sir!"

Chatter erupted on the Command Channel. Reports of…that couldn't be right.

"Weapons, belay my last. Helmsman, get us out from around this thing." He had to see for himself to believe it.

The Rasu vessel didn't fight them as they reversed course then swept around its scalloped hull until the battle returned to their view.

Every single Rasu drifted in space. None fired weapons. No propulsion was visible. The remains of the dreadnought that had intended to swallow them floated listlessly off their port like a giant, misshapen hunk of half-melted scrap metal.

Scrap metal. Had Alex and the others succeeded?

Fleet Admiral Jenner (AFS Denali)(*Earth Command Channel*): *"I want confirmation of total cessation of Rasu aggression. Of any action whatsoever. If a single Rasu lets out a peep, I need to know about it."*

Then the Earth ground defense channel erupted in a jumble of overlapping exclamations, a sure-fire sign the quantum block was gone. And there was more. Reports of Rasu dropping 'dead' in the streets, of ships falling out of the sky to crash into the ground, cascaded in from around the world.

Malcolm's hands dropped to the overlook railing. He leaned heavily into it, hanging his head, because he could no longer keep the deluge of emotion off his expression. *Thank you, Lord. We'll try to prove ourselves worthy of your mercy.*

MIRAI

RIDANI ENTERPRISES STORAGE WAREHOUSE

Dashiel's eyes were closed, his auditory receptors muted.

Communications he needed to see displayed in the top left corner of his virtual vision. Three panes projected onto his eyelids tracked a multitude of Rasu incursions, and he responded to events as swiftly as his quantum programming could process them.

His mind was consumed with chasing the Kireme Boundaries. Turning them on again for the fiftieth time after Palmer's pilots destroyed a quantum block. Every now and then, being able to push their borders out a few meters; once or twice, a few hundred. But not often.

Secondarily, he issued directives to move equipment where it was needed, which was constantly changing. He needn't worry about executing this task for much longer, though. The warehouses, once full of Rima Grenades, archine grenades, Rectifiers and more, now sat all but empty. Soon the forces in the field would begin to run out of small arms. Once that happened, not much remained in their arsenal to stop the Rasu's advance through the streets.

As he'd predicted, Mirai Tower had fallen not long after the Rift Bubble did. Closer to his heart, so did Ridani Enterprises headquarters. As a builder, this one left a mark. Synra Tower was gone as well. He supposed the Omoikane Initiative wasn't really tall enough at six stories to 'fall,' but it sat in ruins all the same.

Palmer informed him they'd destroyed the quantum block on Synra. Dashiel created a wormhole, stepped through it onto the arid plains southeast of Synra One, and subjected himself to the searing electrical overload necessary to change the access code and reactivate the Rift Bubble by hand. Then he returned to his little corner of the makeshift command center at the warehouse and retreated to his cocoon of solitude. Back to work reactivating Kireme Boundaries across Synra. But he'd scarcely found his balance again when the Rift Bubble failed on Kiyora, and he fidgeted as he waited for DAF to hunt down the new quantum block.

At last he began to have some small inkling of the responsibility that had laden Nika's shoulders in recent months.

At the emotional core of his psyche, buried as deeply as he could manage, his heart ached and his thoughts raced in panicked spasms over Nika's fate. The plan hadn't yet worked, and with each passing second in which it didn't, worry that she lay dead on the Rasu homeworld grew by leaps and bounds.

He wrenched his thoughts away, forcing himself to concentrate on the pitched battle underway at DAF Command. The Rasu had surged into the military complex in a wave while the Mirai Rift Bubble was last down, and now only the interior-most Kireme Boundary protected the central command center.

Rasu mechs and hybrid aircraft gathered in a great horde encircling the building. Waiting. Another quantum block was sure to go up any minute, at which point the enemy would stampede forward and overrun it. DAF would lose its top leaders and strategists, leaving the soldiers out there doing the fighting rudderless. It might not be the final blow, but the cracks in their defenses were fast becoming chasms—

Whoa. He shook his head roughly. Did he just see what his mind insisted he'd seen? After all, he was solely present in sidespace.

The Rasu amassed outside DAF Command had, as one, collapsed to the ground. The hovering aerial craft, too. The aubergine metal was piled up fifteen meters high, jagged and uneven like a junkyard. None of it moved.

Dashiel opened his eyes.

71

RASU PRIME

Nika abruptly fell away from the Rasu unit and sank to her knees. Her hand slipped out of his grasp.

An overwhelming *absence* stunned Caleb, as if all his life energy had been sucked out of his veins, leaving him empty and spent. He collapsed beside Nika.

Then Akeso's life force flooded into him, renewing him in a heady rush that sent his head spinning. "Are you okay?"

She stared past him, eyes strangely blank and unseeing.

"Nika?"

Suddenly her chest expanded as she drank in lungfuls of air. Awareness blossomed to light her galaxy irises, and a detached, otherworldly smile grew on her lips. "It's done."

A wave of thunder shook the floor; lasers blasted across his shield from multiple directions, and he shoved Nika down a nanosecond before Rasu fire shot past where her head had been.

Her fingers dug into his arm. "Kill them now!"

Caleb yanked his arm out of her grasp and splayed both hands on the metal floor.

Akeso, this is the Rasu enemy, right here beneath my palms. I know you're tired, but we can end this threat forever, here and now. Simply silence them.

I understand.

"Die, you fuckers. For the last time, die."

A familiar wooziness overtook him as surges of electrical impulses spasmed out through his fingertips. A dark, swarming explosion detonated in his mind, and nausea roiled his stomach.

The roar of the approaching stampede faltered and faded away. The sound of machinery that had pervaded the space since they arrived fell silent. Perhaps ten seconds after they'd begun, the only sound remaining was a faint buzzing noise behind him.

"You did it, Caleb. I sense no Rasu thoughts at all. Anywhere." Nika's laughter pealed with joy through the cavernous room, echoing off the walls. "Stars, I can't describe the weight that has been lifted from my mind."

He felt detached, foggy—then realized he'd stopped breathing, much as Nika had a moment ago. He forced air into his lungs, and awareness came rushing back in. No shadows loomed in on them; no mechs advanced with murderous intent.

They had done it.

You can rest now, Akeso. You did beautifully.

Yes. I will rest. Come and rest with me.

Soon.

Nika offered him a hand, and with her help he rose to his feet and looked around. To his surprise, a force field wall glittered behind them— the source of the buzzing noise. Alex's doing, he assumed.

He jogged around the edge of the force field and into a sea of Rasu debris. "Alex? Where are you?"

Alex: "Watch out!"

He caught himself an instant before he tumbled into a jagged crater in the floor. As soon as he regained his balance, he peered down, but saw only darkness. He quickly grabbed his multitool from his belt and activated a light—

And his whole world ended.

His brain instinctively rejected what he saw below. It couldn't be. It was a trick of the shadows—

Alex: "Caleb, it's okay. I'm still here."

He'd lost his sanity. Gone mad in the instant of seeing her broken, lifeless body. As it should be, he told himself; insanity made for a comforting refuge from reality.

Alex: "Stay calm and listen to me."

His hands came to his helmet, fingernails scraping across the seals. "Do you...hear her? On the comm?"

"Yeah. I do." Nika's voice quavered.

Ghost in the machine? A strangled cry emerged from his throat. Every thought fractured and splintered before reaching completion.

Alex: "Caleb, can you hear me? Please answer me."

Hey, he should talk to the ghost.

Caleb: "Alex, baby, I don't understand."

Alex: "I'm in the ship. My mind exists in the ship. Valkyrie snatched my consciousness away when I...fell."

A few neurons sputtered and connected, and it occurred to him that in their fucked-up world, the explanation almost made a fragment of sense.

A rush of adrenaline flooded his veins. It was true. It must be. And if it was true, he could save her.

Valkyrie: "I did. Caleb, I believe if you—"

Caleb: "I can bring your body back to the ship and revive you."

Valkyrie: "As I was about to say."

Nika was standing on the cusp of the crater in the floor, staring down in horror.

"Nika, open a wormhole. Right now."

"Yes. Of course." She blinked, shook her head roughly and stepped away from the edge. A second later, a wormhole shimmered to life, a matching one lighting the darkness beneath them.

Caleb rushed through it and into the cavern below.

His hands were shaking violently as they tentatively reached out to touch her face. Eyes open and features slack, skin pasty in...*death.* A metal spire jutted up out from her chest, and blood continued to dribble out around it and soak into her clothes.

A sob erupted from his chest as he wound his arms underneath her and lifted, ignoring the sickly squishing sounds as he eased her up and over the spire, then lowered her to the floor to hold her against his chest. "No...."

Alex: "I'm still here. I promise. Holy fuck, this is so surreal. It's such a fragile little body. I feel like I want to vomit, but I'm only electrical impulses inside quantum orbs. Just get here and we'll...try everything. Fuck."

A hand rested on his shoulder. "She's right. Let's get her out of this tomb and back to the *Siyane.*"

He gathered Alex's body into his arms as he stood. Her limbs flopped uselessly against him; it wasn't the first dead body he'd carried, but it was hers, and he was ruined.

The air brightened behind him, and he stepped around to find a wormhole and, on the other side, the cabin of the *Siyane* waiting. *One foot in front of the other. Breathe in, breathe out.*

'The surface has become unstable, so I am lifting off. I will move to a quiet patch of space nearby until...the situation has been resolved.'

Caleb laid her out on the floor, then collapsed his helmet. He was covered in her blood now, too, and it was...he choked off a renewed sob.

"Valkyrie? If I can heal her wounds, will her consciousness be able to return to her body?" He didn't want to create a mindless zombie out of...he swallowed back stinging bile.

'I'm right here. You can talk to me.'

It was her voice broadcasting through Valkyrie's speakers. "Jesus…. Having a hard time with this."

'You should be me.'

A chuckle died in his throat. Maybe it really was her, somehow. She'd cracked a joke. A terrible one. "All right. Will you be able to return to your body?"

'Um, the quantum bridge is in place, connecting to my brain as always. All the Prevo hardware and programming should continue to function. No one's ever tried such a *khrenovuyu* feat before, but logically, if I got out through that route, I can get back in. It should work.'

"Then it will." He registered Nika sinking into one of the kitchen table chairs and dropping her head into her hands, tears streaming silently down her cheeks.

He forced himself to look at Alex's body, to study the wounds and catalog the damage needing repair. Memories of the horror that had risen when he and Akeso reached out to Cosime's dead body flared in his mind, and he pushed straight past them. If the tentacles from the underworld came for him, he would endure their torture. He would endure anything, *anything*, to bring Alex back.

He placed his palms upon the wound in her chest.

Akeso, listen to me. We need to heal her.

There is nothing here. Nothing but me/us. My essence lives on in this figure, for a short time more. But there is no other consciousness in it. No anima. It is an empty vessel.

There was nothing but your essence remaining in my body when you returned me to life.

This is not accurate. Your soul still resided there. It was merely…sleeping.

It had been a silent, dreamless sleep, then. *And her soul is here, too. Not in her body, but it's here waiting. If we heal the body, she will return to it.*

From beyond the veil?

Um, in a way.

Fascinating.

We should hurry. I don't know how long this will be the case.

Then let us try.

As one, their minds reached out through his skin…and no black vines from the underworld seeped out of the floor to pull him into their macabre depths. There was…nothing.

Wait…no. The tiniest, faintest sense of Akeso pulsed in her stilled blood, in the tissues of her organs. Lost and uncertain.

And as soon as he recognized it for what it was, it resonated in sync with their combined essence.

He guided his hands to her torn heart and cupped it reverentially.

As I am the nourishing water flowing out from the creek and swirling through roots beneath the soil, I am the nourishing blood swirling beneath the skin.

I am the sun's rays, bringing strength to this being's limbs.

I am the nourishing water-blood flowing along the starved pathways of arteries and veins, granting them the strength to knit themselves together.

Replace.

Renew.

Replenish.

Her heart leapt in his hands, a single beat, and his own stopped in turn. "Come on, that's it. Beat." Another beat. *Thump...thump. THUMP-thump.*

Magnificent job, Akeso. Keep going.

His whole body tingled, flush with life, its source surging through him and out his palms as they ran tenderly over her wrent flesh.

I am the nourishing water-blood.

I am the sun's rays.

Replace. Renew. Replenish.

Caleb whispered the mantra in an endless loop as arteries sealed their fissures and muscles torn apart by the Rasu spire wound together. The nerves of a broken spine grew and reconnected, then were encased by new bone and cartilage.

At last he lifted his hands up to rest on the edges of the torn flesh.

Incredible. Let's just, uh, seal this skin up here.

Replace. Renew. Replenish.

His hands shook like a madman on a chimeral high, but through blurred vision he realized they now rested upon fresh, unmarred skin. The rest of his body joined his hands in a fit of uncontrollable shaking. "Okay, baby, um, it's your show now. Please come back to me."

'Wow. Right. I've never done this before, so bear with me. *Eto pizdets!* I don't know how to—'

Alex sat up with a violent gasp of air, her body bursting to life in a spasm of limbs as sparks of electricity set fire to brilliant silver irises. She stared at him, eyes wide and bloodshot as color flooded her face.

Then he was holding her against him so tightly he might crush her newly healed bones, which was fine, because he could mend them again.

"God, I love you. I can't lose you." He drew back enough to glare savagely at her. "I *can't*, so don't you ever do that again."

"Ha!" She was crying, her features all screwed up in confusion and wonder and a touch of lingering panic.

He kissed her nose, her cheeks, her forehead, her eyelids, and at last her lips. Gently now, as if she was a fragile china doll entrusted to his care. The human body was such a delicate, insubstantial thing, to be pierced and ended so easily. But not in his hands.

We did well.

We did so, so well. Akeso, I owe you everything and more. I don't have the words. You have returned my very soul to me.

Caleb felt Akeso's relief and joy in his mind, this too reaching beyond words. Akeso had pivoted from killer to healer in a blink. He wondered if it truly understood the dichotomy at all, or if it was always and everywhere simply being what it *was*.

So did you.

What?

I sense the nature of your thoughts. You killed the same as I, and you healed the same as I. We are one.

Alex drew him in again then, squeezing him with impressive strength, and it idly occurred to him how her muscles might now be stronger than before, Akeso-infused as they were.

She was trembling ferociously, though. He stroked her hair and murmured endearments at her ear and let his own heart begin to heal.

Eventually, she pulled away to look over her shoulder.

Nika was smiling and crying at the same time, and Alex reached out an arm in invitation. Nika dropped to the floor and scooted close to hug her as well. "That was the most incredible thing I have ever seen in my entire life. How did you get back in your body?"

"Um...." Alex settled against his chest, and he wrapped his arms around her. "I can't say for certain, as it happened so fast, but I think Valkyrie sort of...shoved me."

'That is a more or less accurate description.'

Alex burst out laughing. "Is it now? Later, we'll have a conversation about why in the hell you believed *shoving me* would actually work."

'I submit the results speak for themselves. You are alive.'

"I am." Her voice grew soft, and she relaxed in his embrace to rest her head on his shoulder. "Thank you for saving me from the darkness, Valkyrie. For sheltering me in the light."

CODA

AN
INFINITE FUTURE

72

CONCORD HQ
COMMAND

D amage reports, casualty lists and emergency resupply requests littered Miriam's desktop. The numbers they revealed were beyond reckoning, the losses immeasurable, though she was insisting on trying to do so. What they could measure, they could rebuild.

For the first time in human history, even the dead. They would erect a memorial wall to honor those lost in this war, but the names listed on it would be comparatively few. Regenesis was about to change the story of humanity. She hoped they were ready.

A quiet sigh escaped her lips as the damage reports updated once again. For all the work that lay ahead of her personally, she didn't envy the gargantuan tasks the civilian governments now faced. She didn't have to worry about overseeing the rebuilding of half of Manhattan Island and most of Shanghai, but someone had this responsibility in their future to look forward to.

At least they didn't need to worry about cleaning up the remains of the Rasu, as the Kats were busily hurling the millions of Rasu corpses into the nearest stars. Once they completed this work in the war zones, they would tackle removing the trillions of tons of dead metal floating across two superclusters-worth of space.

Amazingly, Concord HQ was mostly intact. The Rasu had used it as a thoroughfare to spread out onto Concord worlds, but they hadn't put much effort into trying to destroy the station itself. She was grateful for this on many levels—

The door to her office slid open unannounced, and Alex peeked her head in. "Can I come in?"

"Of course you can!" Miriam leapt up, hurried around the desk and embraced her daughter with a rare fervor. Her mind raced through the checklist: *warm skin, heart beating, chest rising and falling.* But for a time, none of those things had been true.

"I can'th breaf."

"Sorry." She reluctantly relinquished her grip, leaning back to hold Alex at arm's length and study her critically. "How do you feel?"

"I'm fine, Mom. In fact, thanks to Akeso's tremendous healing energies, this body is basically a brand-new, twenty-year-old version of me."

A wistful smile tugged at her lips. "No. I mean how do you *feel*?"

Alex's eyes slid away. "Why don't we sit at the table and have some tea?"

"You want tea?"

"Eh. New life, reconfigured body. I figure it's as good a reason as any to give it a try."

"That's...certainly." She went over to the dispenser, then had to retrieve a second cup from the cabinet for the occasion. While there, she paused for a moment to close her eyes, gather up her tumultuous emotions and breathe out carefully. It was okay; everything was okay now. The Rasu were dead, and her family was alive. "I think you'll like it."

"No promises."

Miriam brought both cups to the table by the viewport and sat down. Outside, construction mechs crawled like ants over the docking pinwheels, repairing the minor damage they'd taken. It was a heartwarming sight. Rebirth, rebuilding, activity.

"We lost the fucking *moon*? I can't believe it. I'm going to stop by your house tonight and check out the sky without it. It's got to be disorienting."

Miriam had never imagined she would find the enthusiasm with which Alex cursed to be so reassuring. "It is quite strange."

"What are they going to do about it? Without the moon, Earth's axial tilt will become increasingly unstable. The tides will be...well, they *won't* be, which will cause problems for a host of species. Storms will get weird, too, and that's just for starters."

"So I'm told. A project is already in the planning stages to construct an artificial satellite to take its place and restore orbital stability. Since we also lost the EAO Orbital, I expect it will serve as a new central space station as well. It's not the highest priority, though, considering all the destruction Earth suffered, and I understand we have a bit of time before Luna's absence becomes a real problem. Is that true?"

"Yeah. It should be a while before orbital tilt problems start to arise. The lack of tides will put some species at immediate risk, but I'm sure the people whose job or passion it is to worry over such things are moving into action to protect them."

"No doubt." Miriam wrapped her hands around her cup on the table and gazed at her daughter...not sternly, but with a measure of gravitas. "Are you going to answer my question? If you're not ready to talk about what happened, I sympathize, but I hope you're comfortable confiding in me."

"I am." Alex flashed her a quick smile that devolved into a wince. "What can you say about seeing your own corpse? It's not an image I'm likely to forget anytime soon." Her hand fluttered across her chest; tracing over where the wound had been?

"As for existing in the ship alongside Valkyrie for a little while? It was incredibly surreal. I've come to think of Artificials as, I don't know, essentially synthetic humans, but they are *not*. When your mind—your essence, your soul—is expressed in code and exists inside quantum orbs and travels along nanoscale photal fibers, you perceive the world differently. It was both limiting and somehow freeing. I felt...detached from reality, yet also more a part of the cosmos than I've ever experienced."

Miriam let the vice-grip that had clenched her heart ever since she'd found out what had transpired loosen up a notch. "You might be the only person alive who wouldn't be traumatized by such a horrific event."

"But it wasn't horrific. I mean, the body was..." Alex frowned, glancing down "...this body. Yes, that was disturbing, I admit. But Valkyrie saved my life. And for a few minutes, I got to share hers, and it was revelatory in ways I never imagined. Then Caleb and Akeso saved my life again. Breathing that first breath into my lungs? It was like being renewed by the universe itself."

Maybe her daughter had in fact emerged from this trial unharmed, or at least mended fully. The highest in a long line of miracles. "I'm glad to hear it. But I stand by my statement: you can tell me anything. And if you start having nightmares at any point, I know something about this. I can help, so please come talk to me."

"I will. Promise." Alex took a sip of her tea, then regarded the cup suspiciously. "What kind?"

"Double bergamot earl gray."

"Huh. It's a tad bitter, but...." She took another small sip and set the cup down. "Not terrible. It's got some pizzazz to it. So, I hear you and Dad had a pretty rough time of it, too."

Miriam's lips pinched, and she stared out the viewport for a beat. "Would it be too hypocritical of me to say that since things worked out in the end, I find I don't want to talk about it?"

Alex chuckled. "Yes, but I understand."

"I jest, a little. Your father being here with me was the greatest gift fate could have given me. But in those last seconds...Alex, I had so many regrets. So many things left undone. I tried to tell myself I was at peace with how I had accomplished everything I could in this life, but I was lying to myself even then. I was angry, so angry, that the Rasu were going to end it all, because I'm not *finished*."

"Good." Alex leaned forward intently, fire dancing in her eyes. "Because we've got a busy couple of years ahead of us."

73

EARTH

R ichard walked into the interrogation room, nodded at the man fidgeting at the table, and took a seat across from him.

"Mr. Beaumont, I want to thank you for turning yourself in. I understand you're interested in providing information relating to Enzio Vilane and the Gardiens organization, in exchange for a plea deal."

"Uh, yes, sir. I appreciate SENTRI's willingness to treat me fairly."

"You can trust that we will continue to do so."

Though he tried to tamp down the fidgeting, the energy simply transferred to Philippe Beaumont's face, sending his eyebrows twitching frenetically. "I'm sorry, sir, I didn't get your name?"

"No, you didn't. Before we begin, do you mind telling me why you're volunteering information against your own people? Thus far we've uncovered no evidence tying you to any acts of violence or sabotage. While this may change, as of now, your only crime is being a member of the Gardiens—which isn't technically a crime."

"I hope so. But morally?" Beaumont swallowed heavily, looking pained. "Understand, I'm still against regenesis. I think it's going to disrupt our society in negative ways that we're not prepared to handle. I think it devalues human life. But I never wanted anyone to die to enforce my belief. I was aware of some of the Gardiens' more heavy-handed tactics—nothing explicitly illegal, but arguably unethical. I expressed misgivings about them, but in the end, I continued to work for the organization, mostly because I believed Enzio was my friend and mentor. He, uh, had a way of convincing you in the moment of whatever he needed you to accept. Looking back now, I can't imagine why I fell for it so many times."

"Charismatic people have an unusual degree of power over us. This is why they're so dangerous when they pursue evil ends. Is that all you want to say for the record?"

"No. I'm responsible for recruiting Fleet Admiral Jenner into the Gardiens. I mean, I realize he was undercover, so it wasn't my fault exactly. But I like the man. He believes I misled him—outright lied to him—but it's not true. And when I learned what Enzio did to him, to the woman he loves? I'll be honest, I got sick. I spent fifteen minutes in the bathroom puking my guts out. So all I can do now is try my best to make things right. Ask your questions. I'll tell you anything you want to know."

RW

SCYTHIA

After laying the groundwork and getting a feel for what sort of information Philippe Beaumont would be able to give them, Richard left the interview in the hands of a SENTRI investigator and caught a Caeles Prism to Scythia.

He and Will were planning to have dinner with Devon and Emily tonight on Earth. He expected that over salad and wine, he and Devon would lie with straight faces to their spouses about just how close they had come to dying at the HQ Caeles Prism Hub. The war was over now, and the sooner everyone put the pain and terror behind them, the better.

He checked the clock; he had a few free hours before he needed to meet Will at the house. Plenty of time to get an update on their progress here first.

Authorities had secured the Vilane crime scene as soon as the fire was extinguished, but the investigation had been put on hold on account of the then-imminent Rasu invasion. Now the property crawled with forensic investigators, though their work mostly involved picking through ash in search of any remnants of evidence.

He found Graham pacing on the boardwalk running beside the house down to the beach. "What's the word?"

"There's nothing left. Ms. Requelme torched quite the inferno here. I'll be shocked if we recover a single two-centimeter storage unit or a length of charred photal fiber."

"That's what I figured." Richard shrugged in resignation. "She was upset."

"Remind me never to upset her. But on the positive side, I hear there's some evidence for the taking elsewhere. Pandora for one, and possibly Seneca as well. If you're not averse, I thought I might take charge of running down those evidence trails."

"Not averse at all, but I assumed you were anxious to get back to your fishing lodge."

"I am. I am." Graham stroked at the scruff that was his gradually returning beard. "Lots of fish and demanding tourists needing to be serviced."

Richard crossed his arms over his chest and arched an eyebrow. "But...?"

"Any chance you want to offer me a freelance consulting gig with CINT? Human stuff, if I get a say, as aliens are still...well, alien to me, to put a crass point on it. And only interesting cases. No more of this finance shit."

"Oh, of course." Richard chuckled. He was happy to discover he'd be seeing his friend more often, but he was absolutely going to give Graham a hard time about it. "I would be honored to offer you a consulting gig, to be invoked only when humans get novel and creative with the expression of their darker impulses, Sherlock."

"Perfect. And thank you for the compliment. I always admired Holmes' investigative style." Graham clapped Richard on the back and started off toward the house. "Let's check in on this disaster of a crime scene, then go grab a beer. There's a great beach shack a little way toward town."

74

AKESO

Caleb trailed his fingertips down Alex's chest and along the curve of her breasts, but paused when they reached her upper abdomen. Fresh skin lay here, created by Akeso.

Wonder at the life made flesh his bonded companion had incarnated overwhelmed him. A heady vertigo crept through him, and his fingertips prickled from the imprinted memory of—

"Hey, I'm right here."

He opened his eyes (having not realized he'd closed them) and found Alex's expression straddling amusement and concern.

"Your face scrunched all up. You looked like you were in pain."

"Not any longer, because you're here. Well and whole."

"Better than whole. I got some new baby skin, a couple of refurbished organs, and best of all, a resurgent and strengthened connection to Akeso. You know what this means, don't you? It means if I kiss you..." she leaned in close until her lips caressed his "...I can feel you feeling me."

And he could feel her, too. There were no walls remaining now; not between him and Akeso, not between him and Alex. He embraced the delicious waves of dizziness her touch evoked. Something told him this time, their sensory connection wouldn't be fading away.

"As can I. I think we have an obligation to explore this further, posthaste." He pulled her into his arms for a firmer, more passionate kiss, and the heightened sensations plunged him into an electric whirlwind of ardor and fulfilled need.

Breathless and drowning had never felt so good, but eventually they both had to come up for air. He rested his forehead on hers. "Yep. I see months and months of exploration in our future. So, listen, don't go and die on me, okay? Ever again."

"It is my plan to remain fully alive." She leaned back in his arms, letting him hold her up at the waist. "But you have *got* to stop staring at me like you're afraid I'm going to crumble to dust any second."

"I know I do. I will. Promise." And he would, in time, but he was never going to get over the anguish of holding her lifeless body in his arms.

That devastating act had an interesting side effect, however: it had banished the guilt over committing genocide against another species from his conscience. The Rasu had *killed* her. In their relentless quest to destroy everything they touched, they would have killed her one way or another unless they were stopped. So he'd stopped them. End of story.

She pressed two fingers to his lips with a smile, then wiggled out of his grasp. "Now, I believe I was trying to get dressed here. Dad is expecting me in twelve minutes."

"All right, all right. I'll let you get ready."

RW

After Alex left for Earth, Caleb poured himself a glass of lemonade and propped the front door open, then sat on one of the stools at the kitchen counter. Akeso murmured happily in his mind, seemingly unperturbed by its actions on Rasu Prime. As it should be. Akeso had merely done what was in its nature—protect life.

A few minutes later, a wormhole opened on the lawn, and Nika walked through. He motioned her inside.

"Want some lemonade?"

"No, I'm fine, thanks. I just came from a ridiculously overdone Advisor Committee feast." She glanced around. "Alex isn't here?"

"No, she's spending the evening with her parents. Besides, I wanted to talk to you alone."

"Oh." She sat on the stool beside him. "What's up?"

"You knew before we ever set foot on Rasu Prime that we were going to need to kill the remote Rasu first, before we could destroy the Rasu at the heart of the structure, didn't you?"

"I suspected. Because of the way the orders were flowing outward, we couldn't risk cutting off their delivery route prematurely. I'd hoped the reality on the ground would look different, but...it didn't."

"The tactical decision makes sense. My question is, why didn't you tell me ahead of time? Or when you confirmed your suspicion. Or *at all.*"

Nika dropped an elbow onto the counter and rested her chin on her palm. "Because you would have been emotionally compromised, and thereby endangered the mission."

He huffed a laugh in spite of himself. Almost twenty years ago, he'd realized he was emotionally compromised after finding himself a prisoner on Alex's ship. And it had unquestionably influenced every decision he'd made since. Influenced, but not dictated.

"I submit I—"

"If Dashiel had been the one tasked with protecting us, I'd have been compromised as well. I don't blame you, nor did I expect you to be able to rise above it. Which is exactly why I didn't tell you."

He took a sip of his drink and weighed his words. "We were supposed to be partners. I needed to have all the information at my disposal from the start. By denying me this, *you* endangered the mission."

"I *saved* the mission. Caleb, the fact is, when everything is on the line, someone has to be the one to make the agonizing, impossible decisions for the sake of everyone else."

"Funny, I've always believed that was me."

"You and I have more than one thing in common. So if it *had* been the other way around, and Dashiel was on guard duty and you had known what I knew, would you have told me?"

His chin dropped, and he studied the countertop while he gave her question its due.

"That's what I thought—"

His gaze snapped up to meet hers. "Yes, I would have. Then I'd remind you of the stakes. Dashiel would accept the risk and insist you do the same, and we'd complete the mission."

"Hindsight is a tricky thing, isn't it? You can sit here and take the high road today, but if the roles had been reversed, I'm not at all certain it would play out that way."

"Then you have a lot to learn about me."

"I'm sure I do. Listen, I'm not going to apologize for doing whatever was necessary to guarantee we succeeded. I was devastated to see Alex fall— you know I was—but if she hadn't been out there protecting our asses while we delivered the poison, then *everyone* would have fallen. There was no other way."

"I agree there wasn't." Caleb shook his head. "But I still can't abide being kept in the dark. Not about something so important."

"A fair response. I respect your right to be upset about it."

"But you wouldn't change your decision to withhold information from me, which means I can't trust you."

Defiance flared in her eyes. "You can trust me to always do everything in my power to save as many lives as possible. My people's and yours."

And he did. That was the thing. Nika's conviction was beyond measure, her commitment to the mission beyond doubt.

He clasped his hands on the counter and held her gaze. "I do trust you on those points. But there are other things in life that matter, too. Honor matters. Believing in those who stand at your side, sword and shield in hand, when it's time to hold back the darkness, *matters.*"

"I feel the same way."

"Good. But know this: if we ever find ourselves in a similar situation again—and given our luck, something tells me we will—I am going to press you to a grueling, exhaustive degree on every single aspect of the mission. And remember, I was an intelligence agent for many years. You'd do well to simply give in and tell me whatever unpleasant detail it is you're hiding."

"You can press. In fact, I'd expect nothing less." Nika let her gaze rove around the kitchen for a moment. "I hope we can still be friends."

"Hmm." Caleb sipped idly on his lemonade. "I know Alex thinks of you as a dear friend, and I won't even attempt to interfere with your relationship. But as for you and I? I think it's best that we remain...collegial acquaintances."

She nodded slowly, disappointment tempered by acceptance flickering across her expression. "I suppose I deserve that. A price paid. Not the first, and it probably won't be the last."

75

RASU PRIME

Inertia propelled the planetary rings along their synchronous orbit, but the engines driving them had fallen silent. Both monstrous and extraordinary, they were now dead artifacts of a dead civilization.

The planet at their center, too, was nothing but a husk. A giant continent of metal lay shattered and inert, while the power harvesters had plummeted into the oceans and sank to the sea floor. Nothing lived here.

It was a dark, bleak scene, but my heart buoyed with joy and, above all, relief. The gravest threat to civilization ever to arise—in this timeline—had been vanquished. The work of aeons brought to fruition. My doubts, the attacks of panic when everything seemed to be going sideways faster than my capacity to influence events...they could be put to rest now. *I* could rest now. Not forever, but for a time.

I drifted through the passageways at the root of the massive surface structure, sending my senses outward in waves, searching.

The Rasu were dead—of this I had no doubt. But I wasn't searching for Rasu.

The continued silence comforted me, and I found I had to work to temper my optimism. The absence of proof did not equal proof of absence.

"Shouldn't you be at a celebration? On Earth, perhaps, or on Akeso. On Mirai, even. I am confident revelry is being engaged in at many locations right now."

I shifted my focus to my left. A shadow had materialized there, though in the omnipresent darkness no visual receptors would be able to make it out. "Now, Miaon. Katasketousya do not 'celebrate.' I am happy in my heart, and this is enough."

"If you are so happy, then why are you wandering the dead halls of the enemy?"

"You know why."

"You won't find reassurance here."

"I don't expect to. I suppose I am rather searching for...the lack of reassurance. If I could find any evidence that the Dzhvar yet live—yet hide in the depths and bide their time—then I would know the danger remains and continue forward with the next phase of preparations. If I find nothing, however, I am simply left with…uncertainty."

"Mnemosyne—"

"What if we truly won? Not merely this war, but the next one as well? The destruction Nika and Caleb set loose here was so overwhelming, so absolute in its reach. What if they wiped out not only the Rasu but their ancient progenitor? Miaon, what if this is *over*?"

"It has never happened before."

"There has never been a timeline like this one before."

Miaon shifted in contemplation. "No, I don't believe there has been, and this is cause for great optimism. But not overconfidence. Remember our goal."

"I think of nothing but our goal. Of the reason for these endless cycles: to find a way to bring an end to them once and for all. And we *are* stronger than last time, as we were stronger then than in the previous cycle. The possibility that we have achieved our goal must be considered."

We passed by the cavernous chamber where Nika, Alex and Caleb had sacrificed so much for their victory, and continued on. "But I take your counsel, which is why before I get too overtaken by frivolity, I am searching for something that will tell me our task is *not* complete. Then at least I will know."

"I understand, Mnemosyne, I do. I felt the same way in my time. But you will not find your answers here today. You recall our history. In your cycle, eight years and two months after the Rasu were defeated, the Dzhvar tore out of the manifold and rose up to begin consuming the cosmic firmament once more, many-fold more powerful than they were in the first Dzhvar War. In my timeline, it happened after only four years. But before then, though the advanced species of Amaranthe were far weaker and barely managed a victory over the Rasu at the cost of trillions of lives, it was twenty-six years until the Dzhvar reemerged.

"The difficult truth is, we can't predict when or where they will return, and we don't understand what provokes them to do so. The death of their progeny seems a logical reason to us, but the Dzhvar are not logical beings. We cannot comprehend their motivations.

"I am so sorry, Mnemosyne, but we must remain vigilant. Is it possible we have genuinely won at last? It is, and I hope more deeply than anyone that this is true. But we cannot afford to believe it is so."

I indicated assent, for Miaon did not say anything I did not already accept to be true. Yet still, like a petulant child, I resisted. "And what if after a century, the Dzhvar have not appeared? Two centuries? Will there be a day when you and I can lay down arms at last?"

"I do not know, and there is no one we might ask. Time marches only forward, save for the single moment which brought you and me here to ponder these questions. But take heart, my friend. You have done so well— far better than I did. This is a great victory, through which countless lives have been saved. And I believe with your continued leadership, we will be more ready for the final battle, should it come, than any who have lived have ever been. And if it doesn't come, then we have our infinite future to look forward to. *She* has her infinite future to look forward to."

That was what all this was for, wasn't it? I chastised myself for forgetting, for lapsing into selfishness. Greediness. I had not embarked on this journey for myself, but for the trillions of souls who deserved a future, and for one person who deserved it above all.

So I would continue to shepherd my charges as best I could, helping them to prepare for the struggles still to come. Because whether the Dzhvar returned or not, struggles always waited on the horizon. Life, when properly lived, was struggle: facing it, overcoming it, and growing stronger from the experience.

"This is a day of hope and joyousness, Mnemosyne. So please, go engage in revelry. Or at least go and witness others doing so. Watch them dance and drink and love, and understand why we are here."

76

CONCORD HQ
CONSULATE

Dean Veshnael gestured for Marlee to enter his office. She held her head high as she approached his desk and clasped her hands behind her back.

"Have a seat. Allow me to complete a few notes."

"Oh. Yes, sir." She sidled over to one of the chairs and sat, trying her damnedest not to fidget, grimace or display any other outward sign of being nervous.

This was the first time they'd spoken since her 'encounter' with the Galenai. She'd filed the most official of all reports detailing the incident, cataloging her thoughts on it and recommending next steps. The report projected an aura of authority and legitimacy, and she only hoped her bravado got her through the reality that the meeting with the Galenai had not only been flagrantly *un*authorized, it violated at least a dozen Consulate regulations.

If she walked out of this office with her job intact, it would be a huge win.

You realize you deserve to get fired. Rules exist for a reason. And even when the reason isn't apparent, they still need to be followed. It's a hallmark of a civilized society.

Yes, I realize I deserve it. But I believe in the Consulate's mission. I believe in the Galenai. So I hope Veshnael sees my sincerity and dedication and takes them into account.

Perhaps he will.

Veshnael minimized the screen in front of him and turned to her wearing a smile. A guarded, knowing, possibly long-suffering Novoloume smile, but she elected to take it as a positive omen. "Now. Ms. Marano."

"Sir, I want you to know—"

He held up a hand to silence her. "I've read your Galenai report. Multiple times. I've also reviewed our surveillance footage from Habitat NE3 over the last several weeks and after your visit. The fact that I found the time to do these things despite our current chaotic environment should impress upon you how seriously the Consulate takes this matter."

She swallowed. "Yes, sir. It does."

"Good. Do I need to list off the Consulate regulations you violated in pursuing this action on your own initiative?"

"No, sir. I am aware."

His head tilted, just so. "And the negative repercussions that could have resulted for the Galenai, Concord, and you personally if the meeting had gone poorly?"

"I recognize those as well, sir." She cut off the *'but it didn't'* poised on her tongue, and almost bit her actual tongue in the process.

"I'm glad to hear it. An important trait of a good ambassador is understanding all the potential consequences of their interactions with other species. We don't represent ourselves; we represent Concord, and our reputation is paramount."

'We'? 'Our'?

Veshnael eased back in his chair a fraction. The shift in his demeanor was so slight as to be unnoticeable by anyone who wasn't well-versed in Novoloume body language, which she was. A tiny spark of hope lit fire in her chest.

"I would have handled a few points in the interaction differently, and we will discuss my reasons in depth. However, on the whole...you did an excellent job in your maiden first contact encounter."

"Ah, thank you, sir. I've devoted a great deal of time and effort to studying the Galenai so I would be prepared for such a meeting, should it ever come to pass. They're a fascinating species, and the means by which they—"

"Ms. Marano."

"Sorry, sir."

Don't run off at the mouth! You're supposed to be a professional.

I know. I got excited.

As you do.

"As I was saying, you performed admirably. The extent to which you *did* follow Consulate protocols did not escape my attention. You have a good head on your shoulders, a keen mind, and a natural instinct for conversing with aliens. You've proved this in your recent work with the Ourankeli, as well as your efforts on behalf of the Godjans. Now, I see those were not isolated incidents. The Ourankeli, Godjans and Galenai could not be more different, and you recognized this and adapted your behavior to best meet their particular needs."

He didn't continue immediately, and after a few seconds she couldn't stand the dead air. "Does this mean I'm not fired?"

A flutter of amusement rippled across his iridescent skin, gold to teal. "I'm afraid I can no longer allow you to serve as a Research Assistant for the Consulate."

Frustration and a pang of despair tore through her. "But I can—"

"Not when all your time will be spent learning your new responsibilities as a Deputy Assistant Ambassador for First Contact Scenarios."

"If you would just—" she blinked "—I'm sorry, can you repeat that?"

"It seems obvious that you are going to do the job, with or without official sanction. Better to grant you both sanction *and* oversight, in the hope you will grow into a talented and conscientious representative of Concord."

Her skin flushed, and a wellspring of emotion flooded her thoughts as her subconscious cheered the news alongside her. "Thank you, sir! I mean it. I won't let you down. This is what I've wanted to do for my entire life. Literally, from my first memories—"

Dial it back.

She cleared her throat. "I promise you, I will be the best Deputy Assistant Ambassador Concord has ever known."

"I believe you have the potential to be exactly that. And perhaps one day, those qualifiers on the title will drop away. But let's not get ahead of ourselves." Veshnael touched a spot on his control panel. "I'm sending you our ambassadorial guidebook. It's quite voluminous. Please do study it thoroughly. And see the Facilities Coordinator to make arrangements for your new office."

If it had been Mia sitting behind the desk, Marlee would have sprinted around it and hugged her. But it was not, so instead she stood and dipped her head and shoulders in a Novoloume-style bow of appreciation. "I'll endeavor to see your faith in me rewarded."

"How about we start by simply following the rules?"

"Yes, sir. Absolutely, sir."

RW

VRACHNAS HOMEWORLD

Marlee watched from her ledge for signs of the adult dragons returning from their sojourn in the skies above. If given sufficient warning, she could escape through a wormhole before Mom and/or Dad reached her, but she'd vastly prefer to be able to focus on Cupcake without fear of fire from above.

Barney was snoozing under a hot midday sun on an outcropping off to the right. Cupcake was playing with a bird, trying to roast it as it swooped in circles overhead. It wasn't entirely clear who was toying with whom.

"Please don't roast me, Cupcake."

There are reasonable odds that he is going to roast you.

I know. But life is nothing without risk. Measured and calculated risk.

Very well.

She smiled. It turned out, all her subconscious had ever wanted was to be acknowledged. To be heard.

She checked her bracelet to ensure it was broadcasting the correct signal before reviewing the soundness of her logic a final time.

Yes. This was the answer.

After a bolstering deep breath, she opened a wormhole and walked through it onto the meadow below.

Thirty meters away, Cupcake's head swiveled in her direction. The bird forgotten, he lowered his long snout and puffed dark smoke out of his nostrils. Those puffs were becoming less smoke and more fire every day.

She held the arm bearing the bracelet out—as if a few extra centimeters would somehow help—and projected a calm, soothing voice. "I'm a friend. Don't be afraid. I won't hurt you. Friend."

She took a step forward. And this time, Cupcake didn't charge her. So she took another.

The dragon began beating its wings in a deliberate, cautious rhythm.

"No, don't leave. It's okay. Friend. My name is Marlee."

One more beat and the wings settled to the ground. They'd grown notably wide.

"Very good. You are so pretty, do you know that? Your scales are so colorful, and they shine magnificently. You're going to grow up to be the most beautiful dragon in the world." Another step, then another.

Cupcake tilted his head to the side, like a curious puppy, and she had to choke back a giggle. Didn't want to spook him. She repeated her mantra in her head: Calm. Comforting. Nonthreatening.

She reached into the bag slung over her chest and removed a package wrapped in foil. Cupcake's nostrils instantly flared.

"Does this smell good? It does to me. Want to know something? It tastes good, too. I think you'll like it." She unwrapped the foil, laid it on the ground and carefully backed up. "It's for you. Go ahead and try it."

The dragon hurried forward several lumbering steps, and she had to force herself to hold her ground. *Don't be threatening, but don't show fear, either.* His head lowered, and he sniffed at the roasted chicken. Then with a lightning-fast motion, he swallowed the chicken whole.

"Oh! Not interested in savoring the flavor, huh? That's fine."

Cupcake's neck extended in her direction, his nostrils sniffing.

"Are you wondering whether I have another one? It so happens I do. But if you want it, you're going to have to come closer." She removed the second package and unwrapped it, holding it aloft in her outstretched hand.

He took two thudding steps forward, his long neck extended fully ahead. When Cupcake was five meters away, she crouched and placed the package on the ground, as she didn't want to get her hand bitten off in his exuberance.

In a flash, the chicken was gone. A tongue lapped out around his mouth, exposing disconcertingly sharp and menacing teeth. Three meters separated them now, and she felt the heat from his breath. Her heart pounded in her chest, and only an emergency cybernetics routine stopped her from panicking.

She stretched out her arm, palm up. "Friend. Friend Marlee. Can I pet you, Cupcake? You're so pretty."

Cupcake blinked slowly, strawberry irises staring at her, but didn't move.

She stepped forward, then let the status quo settle for a moment. Stepped forward again.

Her fingertips hovered above the glistening scales of his neck as she and the dragon gazed into one another's souls. Her hand eased down to touch them.

Cupcake snorted, blowing smoke in her face, but she held steady and didn't withdraw. Her hand trembled as she moved it down his neck, careful to follow the flow of the scales so as to not slice up her skin too severely. They were hot from the sun, and she idly wondered if they were cool at night. *Focus.*

"Friend Marlee. Friend Cupcake. Aren't you simply amazing."

His tongue darted out again. Oh my god, was he going to lick her?

How?

She jumped in surprise, and Cupcake skittered away in response. "Who said that?"

A faint sparkle of lights moved beside her. *I am Mnemosyne, and—*

"Mesme, hi. We've met. Or we've been in the same general area at the same time, anyway. I'm Marlee Marano. Caleb's niece."

I know well who you are, Marlee Marano. How have you convinced the dragon to let you near it without it tearing you to pieces?

She kept her gaze on Cupcake, who had stopped withdrawing after a couple of meters to watch her and the lights in cautious curiosity.

"So I was having a conversation with my new Galenai friends the other day, and it led to me thinking about sound waves. Now, all speaking is done via sound waves—except for what you do, I guess—but the fact that the Galenai are an aquatic species draws attention to this. I had to account for the distortions when sound waves travel through water, for instance, in learning to interpret their language.

"This got me thinking more about waves, and how else they are used in communications. Then, when I was setting a wave signal as a sort of 'beacon' so we could communicate with each other, Eenie—one of my Galenai friends—said 'it is gibberish, but we can hear it.' And *that* got me thinking about other sorts of waves that are gibberish as words, but have meaning nonetheless."

Go on.

Uh-huh. "Imagine my surprise when I discovered this planet has a song. Not the way Akeso and Hirlas do, of course. It's not alive. But the planet hums a sonorous melody even so. Since you Kats created the planet, I figure you put it here. And the dragons, well, they've heard this song since birth. They hear it every second of every day.

"This realization led me to ponder harmonics, mostly because I know how much you Kats fancy using them. I've been able to finagle *so* many details about you guys out of Aunt Alex over the years with my endless, annoying questions. About how the portals in the Mosaic opened in response to a harmonic signal, for instance. And the notion occurred to me: what if you use harmonics of the planet's song to control the dragons?"

She widened her smile for Cupcake as she retrieved the last chicken from her bag, unwrapped it, took several steps forward and placed it on the ground.

And gone!

"See, here's the thing. They're not really dragons. Dragons are fictional creatures."

The large sauropsid puffing smoke at you as it demands more food begs to differ.

She laughed lightly, and was relieved when Cupcake didn't bolt in fright at the sound. "Granted. What I mean is, they've never existed in reality before, which enabled you to make them whatever you wanted. You could include all sorts of little extras in their DNA, in their biological makeup, to enable you to both control them and use them for your own purposes. I suspect their learned responses to specific harmonic frequencies are varied and sophisticated."

She held up her arm briefly, letting her bracelet jingle in the breeze. "I experimented with several different harmonics of the planet's song. One of them sent the dragons fluttering around like turkeys chasing a chipmunk, which was something to see, and also not the response I was looking for. But this one, a perfect fifth harmonic of the planet's fundamental, calmed them right down. My theory is that it marks the source as a non-threat. Cupcake's reaction to me today suggests my theory is correct, don't you think?

"I assume you have one specific frequency for 'go over to that spaceship, pick up the red-haired woman and bring her to my lab,' as an example. I haven't figured out all the variations and their purposes yet. But I will."

I have no doubt of it.

"Oh?"

You are a Marano. A Praesidis.

She wasn't particularly offended at being called a Praesidis. She didn't know many, though she was aware of their violent history. But Corradeo Praesidis was a good man who'd saved a lot of people. And he so favored her grandad, it was hard to think ill thoughts about him.

Are you going to ride it?

"What? I'm not sure he's ready for that. We've only just been properly introduced."

You won't know until you try.

She shot a squirrelly glance at the lights wavering with deceptive placidness beside her. "Aren't you quite the instigator? I get why Alex likes you." She chewed on her bottom lip. "Let's do some more petting and see how things progress."

She stepped calmly forward. Cupcake drew up to attention, but didn't flee. He acted less nervous now.

Her outstretched hand touched his neck, and a shudder rippled through his body. "You've never been petted before, have you? Does it feel good? I hope it does." She ran her hand down to where neck met back, then slowly along the ridge. His tail swished over the ground; my goodness, it could send her tumbling across the meadow with one swipe.

"Friend Marlee. Remember this. I...." She peered back at Mesme. "He's never had anything sit atop him before, I feel certain."

You are a slip of a girl. He will hardly notice.

"You've obviously never seen a horse get broken before. He'll notice." She breathed in deeply, and out, and kept gently stroking his scales. The sharp edges nicked her palm a couple of times, but she ignored the flashes of pain. Hazard of the adventure.

She sent a question to her conscience. *Nothing to say?*

You are insane. But Mesme is correct; you are also ready. You must try.

I must try.

Cupcake's back was already almost a meter and a half tall. She was going to need to leap to get on. She flexed through her knees—then searched for Mesme in the bright sunshine. "If he flies up into the air and promptly bucks me off, you'll catch me, won't you? I mean, it's only the polite thing to do, after you egged me on and all."

I will catch you, Marlee Marano.

"Great. Okay, here goes." Without giving it another thought that might send her fleeing in panic, she sprung up through her calves and swung one leg up and over Cupcake's back, throwing her arms around his neck.

The dragon bucked up in surprise, snapping his head in a torrent of fire and smoke. She held on for dear life as the shifting scales cut into her arms. "Easy. Easy. Friend Marlee. Friend Cupcake. Easy."

A gust of air washed over her as his wings beat down hard—then they were airborne, and her heart soared with them into the blue sky above.

77

KIYORA

KIYORA ONE

"Welcome, you two!" Perrin ran forward and embraced Nika and Maris in a bundle of arms and bouncing braids.

Nika's greeting was muffled into Perrin's shoulder, and finally the woman let go and spread her arms wide. "Look at my place! Or don't. It's a terrible mess. Half the furniture isn't here yet, and I've rearranged what furniture is here three times already. And my clothes are lying in a pile on the closet floor, so don't go in there. Oh, but check out the view!" Perrin scurried through a living area cluttered with boxes and out onto a balcony.

Nika shared a warm smile with Maris as they followed in Perrin's wake. Seeing her excited about this new phase of her life did Nika's heart so damn good.

The apartment was on the fourth floor of a midrise residential building in downtown Kiyora One. Directly across a cobblestone pedestrian path lay a small, block-wide botanical garden. Cherry blossom trees bloomed a delicate pink, interspersed with the bright red of maple trees.

"Isn't it amazing? This morning after I woke up, I spent twenty minutes sitting out here drinking a cup of tea, just me and the flowers and the silence. *Even though* I had four-hundred-thousand things to do."

"It's wonderful. This might be the best view in the city." Nika hugged Perrin again. "I am so happy for you."

"Thank you. Hey, I ordered in lunch. Back to the kitchen!"

Maris stopped halfway there, where they'd dropped their bags in the initial crush. "First, I brought you a housewarming gift." She crouched and removed a large box made of transparent plastic. Inside it were several rows of tiny flowering plants.

Perrin's eyes widened. "Oh my goodness."

"This is a collection of the best scented herbal plants in the Dominion: basil, lavender, mint, oregano and so on. Keep these lovelies healthy, and you'll never need a spritz of air freshener in the apartment. And if you grind up a few of the leaves from the mint plant, you'll never drink that tea of yours without it again."

"Oh, I need to get window planters for the bedroom, and the living room, and…well, there's not a window in the bathroom, so."

"Hopefully, these will make your place feel comfy and warm. Like a home."

"I know they will. You are too sweet."

"For my friends, anything. Now, about this lunch." Maris wandered off toward the kitchen.

Nika touched Perrin's arm. "What does Adlai think of the place?"

"He's being so wonderful. He helped me pick out the furniture and insisted on placing it for me, multiple times. He says he's going to stay here every night until I tire of him and kick him out. I know it won't last, and I don't want him to give up his place. But it means so much that he's being supportive. I'm not sure I'd have the nerve to do this if he wasn't at my side for it."

"And that's how the best relationships work. I'm glad to hear it." She bent down and opened the bag she'd brought. "I got you a housewarming gift, too. Mine's not as bright and cheery as Maris'. But it's important, I think." She took the lid off the box and handed it to Perrin.

"It's…tech? A black-box module and an interface…" Perrin looked up, her brow furrowed "…is this a psyche backup unit? Like the one you had at the Chalet?"

"Much more sophisticated, thanks to all the advances our ceraffin have made in the technology. It creates a multi-layered backup and writes it out to multiple locations, so if you ever need to reset your programming, your interpreters—your memories or data storage—you can do it all on a modular, pick-and-choose basis. You can put it in your bedside drawer and make a quick backup at night before you go to bed, and please do."

She rested her hands on Perrin's shoulders. "The point is, you are my dearest friend, and the world would be unacceptably cold without you in it. So you don't get to die and leave me without your companionship. Not ever. I won't allow it."

RW

ADJUNCT HACHI
ASTERION DOMINION

Giant, puffy snowflakes began falling from the sky as Nika and Dashiel stepped out of the small transport center on Adjunct Hachi. Instantly delighted, she held her palm out, grinning as the flakes perched upon her skin for a precious second before melting away.

"This is already perfect."

Dashiel squeezed her shoulder. "I promise you, it will get even more so. I see the general store up on the left. Why don't you grab us some supplies while I secure us transportation?"

"Meet you outside the store in fifteen?"

"I'll be there."

Sidewalk traffic was light. Most people had fled the Adjunct Worlds in advance of the final Rasu attack, and so far only a few had trickled back home.

Supply shipments were moving briskly again, though, and the general store was well-stocked. She picked up generous helpings of fish, meat, veggies and eggs for cooking, as well as some wine, sake and a few toiletries.

Dashiel was waiting for her in a hovercraft when she walked outside. "The lot was full. I had my pick of rentals."

"Not many people have come back yet. But they will." She secured the bags in the trunk, then joined him in the front seat. "Take me to our retreat."

"My pleasure." He lifted off and, at the edge of town, turned west toward the mountains.

She'd suggested they forego wormholes for this vacation. Yes, wormholes made everything about travel easier, and during a battle for survival, they could be the difference between defeat and victory. But they weren't battling now, and she wanted to walk the sidewalks for a bit. Breathe in the air and feel the energy of people around her. She wanted to cruise above the landscape and take in every centimeter of the prodigious scenery before curling up in front of a roaring fire in their cozy cabin.

When a pair of white, downy-feathered birds flew along beside them for a few minutes, she decided this had definitely been the right choice.

It was cold, though, as the hovercraft lacked a top—frontier living and all—and by the time the cabin came into view below them, she was ready for that roaring fire.

The cabin was nestled against the mountainside and surrounded by firs, but not so many as to obstruct the view of the soaring mountain range to the east and a glacier-fed lake to the south. The snow was almost a meter deep, but a maintenance crew had shoveled a landing area and a path to the porch.

Nika gasped as she walked inside. A cathedral ceiling swept upward overhead, and polished stone flooring matched stone countertops. A wrought-iron spiral staircase led to an open loft bedroom lit by dramatically angled windows. A wide fireplace dominated the far wall, and beside it a glass door led to an elevated balcony.

She absently set her bags down and wandered that way, her hand drifting across the rugged stone of the fireplace before she stepped out onto the balcony.

The ground dropped away from the cabin on this side, and the upper reaches of the firs stood at eye level. Snow clung to the needles like icing on dessert; it must have snowed last night.

The sun crested over the mountain peaks to the east. Its rays swept across the lake in a cascade of blue-white light, and she was oddly reminded of Mesme. They needed to talk in greater depth about what came next—but she wasn't going to dwell on those concerns right now. Planning for the future could wait. This was her vacation, her escape.

This was her reward.

Dashiel nuzzled up behind her, his arm circling around to hand her a steaming, glazed ceramic mug. "Hot cider with cinnamon."

"Oh, it smells delightful." It was too hot to drink, but she held the mug under her nose and breathed in deeply for a moment before setting it on the railing and turning to snuggle into his arms. The flannel of his shirt scratched against her cheek, and the subtle scent of his aftershave mingled with the aroma in the air of fir trees and damp earth. And beneath all that, the faint tingle of his kyoseil danced a waltz with hers. It had saved the world, and it was still alive, and so were they.

He kissed her, warm and soft and slow, then murmured against her lips. "I can't believe we actually made it here."

"I know. So many times I thought we'd never find a way, but we did. We're here, and while we are, we're not going to bother ourselves about the past or the future. We're just going to be with each other in this perfect place."

His hand came up to stroke her cheek. "Nika, my love for you goes beyond words. It is boundless. Infinite. When you're with me, I feel as if I can do anything, even the impossible."

"Mmhmm. In that case, I shall stay with you, and we shall do these impossible things together. After all, we are forever."

POSTSCRIPT

MIRAI

NIKA'S FLAT

Alex relaxed into the plush cushions of Nika's couch and closed her eyes. The image of her broken and bloodied body flashed onto the back of her eyelids…and she didn't try to shove it away. She needed to make peace with what had happened. And she was succeeding, in her own way.

The truth was, the indescribable pleasure of existing wholly as an expression of quantum life for a few precious moments had rocked her worldview far more than her physical body dying had done. And one required the other, so.

The sound of a door opening echoed into the living room, and Alex opened her eyes to see Nika emerging from her bedroom, winding her wet hair into a ponytail and draping it over her chest. She wore a backless periwinkle halter top tied at her neck and flowing linen pants. "Thanks for waiting while I ran through the shower. The other advisors punished me for taking a vacation by handing me a to-do list a kilometer long on my return. It kept me scrambling all damn day."

"Not a problem at all. How were the mountains?"

"Simply glorious. I haven't relaxed so much, for so long, since…well, I have no idea. Since before the psyche wipe. And most importantly, Dashiel and I have come back home in a really good place."

"I'm glad to hear it. So, Mesme said it would be here in a few minutes, after it finished…whatever mischief it's engaging in today."

Nika moved to the windows to gaze out at what, for today, remained a wrecked skyline; in the evening light, her tattoo gleamed like the stars beginning to rise for the night. "I can't believe this building escaped destruction. It's an island surrounded by an ocean of ruin." She turned to join Alex on the couches. "But we'll rebuild. Again, and hopefully for the last time."

"You'll have the city whipped into shape inside a month. Meanwhile, it'll probably take the army of bureaucrats on Earth a decade to rebuild Manhattan."

Mesme swept into the room then, shimmering lights aflutter, and took on a human-sized version of its winged avatar. Must be feeling prideful this evening.

Alex sipped on her glass of chardonnay. "Anything dire to report?"

Not today. Everything remains quiet in Rasu space.

"*Formerly* Rasu space, you mean."

Yes. We are continuing the work of removing the debris our enemy left behind, but nothing lives in formerly Rasu space. Exceptionally well done, all of you. You should be pleased.

"Oh, we are." Alex set her glass aside, instantly transitioning out of her relaxed demeanor. "So, how do we defeat the Dzhvar?"

Excuse me?

"The Dzhvar. You know, the threat that ends the universe and triggers a reset of the timeline if we don't stop them." Alex shrugged. "Come on, Mesme. I didn't get here by being dumb. Mom told me what you said about the Rasu being born of the Dzhvar, and I figured out everything that flows from this juicy nugget of intel. Actually, I was already putting the pieces together. I just needed the glue."

Nika leaned forward in interest. "What pieces? Do tell."

"The Erebus Void? I discovered an enormous scar in the manifold there when we visited in sidespace. The scar splinters in two, and one splinter leads directly to Rasu Prime. I think in the moment before they were driven out of physical space, the Dzhvar infused the metal on Rasu Prime with traces of their...essence, for lack of a better term, not unlike what the Kats did with the Ekos planets. They gave the Rasu intelligence and certain other skills—such as the ability to pierce a dimensional barrier. Right, Mesme?"

This is true. Dimensions are irrelevant to the Dzhvar, and there in the cradle of their birth, the first Rasu retained enough residue of its progenitor to devise a weapon capable of breaching a Rift Bubble.

Nika nodded thoughtfully. "So that's what happened at Concord HQ?"

"Yes," Alex replied. "It also explains why it was so difficult for the Rasu to accomplish. They were drawing on deep, antediluvian space magic."

A shudder rippled through Nika. "If it had been easy for them, we'd have lost the war months ago."

"True. By the way, this is also why Akeso could kill the Rasu so completely, and why kyoseil was the perfect conduit for its poison. The ancient primordial beings of the universe understand one another in ways we do not."

Nika chewed on her thumb for a few seconds, until a smile gradually brightened her features. "This makes me feel better about what I asked the kyoseil to do. And now I have to wonder if it understood what I was asking of it to an extent I didn't appreciate. Does Caleb know?"

"We've talked about it. He didn't take as much comfort from the knowledge, mostly because Akeso is so much more than kyoseil. But I think understanding the historical connection between these entities did give him some peace of mind."

"Good…this is what caused Caleb and me such discomfort when we reached the Rasu Prime stellar system, isn't it? The kyoseil sensed the imprint left on the manifold there by the Dzhvar."

"I think so, yes. And there's more." Alex took a quick sip of her wine. "Hey, I wonder how much of this fell into place for me in the few minutes I spent as a quantum intelligence—or when I was *shoved* back into my physical body? All my brain signals and information they held getting scrambled and reconfigured and whatnot."

Nika stared at her, looking rather flummoxed, and Alex rolled her eyes. "Sorry, rhetorical question. Anyway, you and I have speculated about the herculean amount of energy required to rip enough of a hole in the fabric of space to allow time travel. How it might be on the order of the force of a supernova in the palm of your hand, or even the energy of a quasar focused on a location the size of an atom.

"But you know what else might do it? A power that literally consumes the spacetime manifold itself. See, I did a little research. Mesme, when you said you traveled back 982,000 years, I thought it was an odd number. When one is talking about such a long span of time, we usually approximate. Like how everyone says the Dzhvar War was 'a million years ago.' It wasn't. It was 982,000 years ago. You reentered the timeline at the precise moment the Dzhvar were tearing apart the fabric of the cosmos. You know what that means? You do, of course, but now so do I.

"The Dzhvar are both the cause of the destruction of the universe and the pathway for its salvation."

Mesme's wings fluttered against the darkening sky. *You are very, very good, Alex.*

"Yes, I am. But I have a question."

When do you not?

"Have questions? Never. Why didn't you just tell us it was the Dzhvar from the beginning? Why always with the secrets?"

Because in order to defeat the Dzhvar, you first needed to defeat the Rasu— for do not doubt that the Rasu would have eradicated you from the face of the universe without hesitation. It was crucial for you to stay hyper-focused on the task before you and not look ahead to future trials.

Nika swished her wine around in its glass. "First task accomplished. So what do we have to look forward to?"

It is my hope that the Dzhvar are truly gone and will never reappear. The poison you and Caleb delivered so thoroughly destroyed the Rasu that it is possible there remains no avenue for them to return.

Alex was not inclined to entertain any more of this evasiveness. "Return from where? How do we fight them when they do? If they do? Can't we go head them off at the pass right now, before they have a chance to claw their way back onto the manifold?"

No. You can't fight the Dzhvar now, because you can't find them to do so. No one can. They exist in the hidden dimensions of the cosmos, until such time as they extrude their presence into the physical world.

"So? The Kats are masters of those hidden dimensions. Go root them out."

Alex, you have glimpsed enough of the nature of these dimensions to comprehend why that won't work. They are not merely vast, they are effectively infinite. They fold in on themselves and spontaneously create new dimensions within the folds. As such, the Dzhvar have uncountable space in which to hide. Or to sleep, as it were.

"But what happened last time?"

I'm not comfortable sharing details of the previous timeline.

"I think it's called for. We need to prepare, and to do so we need to know what we'll be facing."

Events will not necessarily proceed in the same way as they did before.

She waved a hand dismissively in its direction. "Yes, you've mentioned that. Details, Mesme."

If I give you a script to follow, you will fail. One, because you will not be acting on your own initiative. Two, because the previous script was, in the end, not a successful one.

"So don't give us a script. But damn well do tell us what happened."

Mesme wandered across the living room and back again. *I will share what I can. In the last cycle, approximately eight years from now and with no warning or obvious trigger, a host of Dzhvar broke through into the physical dimensions from a location in the Coma Supercluster. They soon resumed doing what it is in their nature to do: consume the intrinsic fabric of spacetime.*

Nika stood to lean against the side of the couch. "So how do we get ready for such an invasion?"

You can't prepare for it, except in the most general of ways. Learn. Grow stronger. Grow wiser.

Alex groaned. "Must you always be so obtuse? That's no help at all."

Of course it is. Increase your knowledge and your technology. Seek out other species and form strong alliances. Live peacefully with one another and reinvest the dividends in your mutual improvement. In doing so, it is entirely possible you will discover something we didn't have last time, much as the Kireme Boundaries and Rima Grenades saved so many lives in this war.

"You didn't have those in the last timeline?" Nika asked in surprise.

No. Those tools are a product of the impressive evolution and advancement of your people in this cycle.

"Fascinating." Nika smiled smugly.

Yay for the Asterions, but flattery was not going to distract Alex. "I think we'll be having a long conversation with Corradeo Praesidis about how he defeated them, if not quite so completely as everyone believed."

Corradeo will tell you that he didn't defeat the Dzhvar. The diati *did. Regardless, the* diati *is gone.*

Nika crossed through the dining area to a mirror on the far wall. "I seem to recall there are several entries in my journals about the Dzhvar War. It happened before I was born, but for some reason I took an active interest in its history. Let me see if I can find them."

Nika opened the mirrored door and crouched in front of the shelves in the recesses of the library. In the shadows of the small room, her tattoo glittered in a star-filled constellation of icy white light.

Off to the left, Mesme drifted along the wall of windows. Against the deepening night sky outside, its pinpricks of light cast a similar panorama upon the glass canvas.

Alex stood to go refill her wine. As she did, her gaze passed across Nika—and darted to Mesme, whose wings pulsated languidly through the air.

The tattoo.

In her mind, she captured a frozen image of Mesme's avatar, then superimposed it over the tattoo as it shifted along the muscles of Nika's back while she dug through her journal files—

Alex stumbled back a step and almost dropped her wineglass. One hand flew to her mouth to mute a gasp.

It couldn't be.

And yet it clearly *was*.

Her focus flitted like a hummingbird between the two of them as her brain struggled to reconcile two wildly disparate impressions.

The goddess of memory.

A woman who had lost hers.

An empyreal being who called the infinite dimensions of the universe home.

A woman whom Akeso had described as a bridge to the heartbeat of the universe.

Along about the fourth or tenth time she glanced at Mesme, it finally noticed her hyperactive attention. She stared at the Kat, wide-eyed and mouth agape, then deliberately cast her gaze back to Nika, then back to Mesme.

Mesme's lights leapt into great agitation, abruptly losing their defined shape to quiver in an amorphous cloud.

Alex.

What the actual fuck, Mesme? Am I seeing what I think I'm seeing? And don't you dare lie to me.

I won't, but please.

Please what?

Please do not voice your suspicions to her.

The hell I won't.

I am begging you. If you have ever held a single charitable thought toward me, do not say anything until we've had the chance to speak in private. Please.

She was struck by the odd notion that if Mesme had physical form, it would be on its knees in front of her, hands clasped together, tears streaming down its face. This was how emotional the voice in her head sounded.

She swallowed, struggling mightily to mask her turbulent thoughts as Nika stood and exited the library. "Found them."

"Great." Alex set her empty glass down hard on the table. "Listen, um, something's come up at home, and I need to run. Can we review those, um, tomorrow maybe?"

Nika frowned. "Is everything okay?"

"Yeah, yeah. Simply the usual family shenanigans. I'll touch base with you in the morning."

"Sounds good."

If she uttered another word, it would all come rushing out, so she hurriedly opened a wormhole.

Meet me at home. Right the fuck now.

RW

AKESO

Alex hit the patio pacing. The instant Mesme's lights materialized above the cobblestone, she spun in their direction. "Is it true? It is, isn't it?"

I'm not her, you know. Not truly. While we share so much, she's lived a different life than I did. The person she is now lies a million years in my past.

"Oh my god." Alex sank onto the edge of one of the chaises and dropped her elbows to her knees. "But you *are* Nika. From the last timeline."

Mesme solidified into a humanoid avatar and knelt in front of her. "Hello, my friend. I have missed you these long years."

Alex's hand came to her mouth to stifle a cry; it was Nika's voice. "You just spoke. *Sukin syn*, you've always been able to speak aloud. The 'voice in people's head' schtick is nothing but a way to make the Kats seem more enigmatic and powerful. You manipulative little shits."

"If I had spoken with Nika's voice from the beginning, my identity wouldn't have been much of a secret, would it?"

"Well...no."

"To your second point, yes, this is why we do it. People's perceptions of the Katasketousya are critically important to the work we do. We must be seen as 'other,' as fundamentally unknowable and mysterious."

As she watched, the avatar gained additional definition, and now she was able to make out the resemblance. The long, wavy hair and wide eyes. The curvy figure. Even the slightly crooked nose. Nika's features had been there all along. "I actually kind of get that. It's still a shitty power play on your part."

"Fair enough."

This was so weird, Mesme talking. Mesme talking *in Nika's voice*. She felt dizzy, and she rested a hand on the cushion to steady herself before she fell to the cobblestone. "You called me 'my friend.' You knew me the last time around. Of course you did."

"We fought both the Rasu and the Dzhvar side by side until the end."

"The end where everyone died. Everyone except you, I guess, so you could go back in time and try again."

"Something like that. I realize this is difficult to comprehend—"

"No, it makes a strange sort of sense. A thousand scattered clues are busily clicking into place in my mind. Things you've said, things Nika has said. The way you took to each other instantly, and how you've protected her as a parent would a child while also pushing her forward, like at the

Oneiroi Nebula…she's been growing more like you lately, you know. Since she bonded with the kyoseil. More otherworldly and detached."

"I suppose it is inevitable. I suppose I did, too."

"Explain to me why I can't tell Nika right now. You lost your mind at the possibility I was going to spill the beans to her. Mesme, she has to know!"

Mesme-Nika straightened up to walk fitfully across the patio—yes, walk, ethereal avatar or no. "Alex, she does not *want* to know. *I* did not want to know, and I will forever be grateful for those innocent, happy years I was able to live before the end, blissfully unaware of what the future held for me."

"I don't understand why."

"Because when she learns the truth, it will break her."

"Did it break you?"

"I am still broken."

The pain in the spoken voice was so palpable, it made Alex's heart hurt. "Because of how many millennia pass? To have to live through another million years?"

"No. To have to leave behind everyone I cared about. My people, my home, my friends. To be torn asunder and cast alone into the void."

"Because…" she exhaled harshly into her hands "…ohhhhh, boy. She can't take Dashiel with her."

"No. She cannot."

"But why not?"

"We spoke earlier about how time travel is unimaginably brutal. No living soul was ever meant to traverse such a chasm. Nika's intimate bond with kyoseil, which is a primordial entity of the early universe, will protect her consciousness, mind and memories during the traversal. But her bond with it is unique, and such protection is not available to anyone else."

"Wait a minute. When we first challenged you about the time travel, you said none of the Kats have any memory of a life other than the ones which have proceeded along 'time's arrow' since they were awakened. They weren't born, they were awakened. By *you*. Are the Kats…Asterions?"

Mesme's avatar sighed. "You are as perceptive as ever."

"How? No, I know this one, too. Their Vault. *That's* why you were so eager to 'protect' it when the Rasu attacked Namino! God, you are a sneaky *suka*."

"I have only done what I must."

"With the Rasu gone, they're going to want their Vault back."

"It's fine. I've gotten what I need from it."

"And that is?"

"The programs of the best and brightest Asterions. Those with millennia of experience in physics and astronomy, in medicine and biology, in engineering and programming. The minds upon which a species can be built that will learn to bend the spacetime manifold to its wishes."

"Well, why doesn't she just 'awaken' Dashiel on the other side? Why didn't you?"

Mesme returned to crouch in front of her. It was an easy, natural gesture; something Nika would do. "I said the 'programs,' not the people. Allow me to emphasize again how savage the time travel experience is. Nothing living can survive it. Nothing with anima, nothing with thoughts. No quantum fields, which means no preserved memories or consciousness. What will remain of the man who was Dashiel Ridani will be nothing but his most fundamental programming structure."

"He won't remember her. Okay. But she didn't remember him after her psyche wipe, and look how that worked out."

"It's not the same. I could have found a way to live with knowing a Dashiel who did not know me. But an awakened program on the other side would not be Dashiel at all, lacking as it would the entirety of lived experience which made him the man I loved.

"Alex, memory is the most important gift we have as sapient beings. It makes us who we are and gives shape to our souls. The smartest thing I ever did—Nika has ever done—was to take every step in my power to hold on to even the tiniest, faintest scraps of memories. The journals, the fragments secreted away in Dashiel's mind.

"And something else, something she hasn't yet fully grasped. An additional quantum field, hidden by her operating system, that codified all the lessons her experiences had taught her. Her morals, her ethical precepts, her core convictions, her indomitable spirit. This is what enabled her to remain who she was through the loss of everything when her psyche was wiped, until she was able to find her way back to her life."

"And a Dashiel on the other side of time will have none of that to preserve his...soul."

"I tried to find a way. The me before me—Miaon—tried to find a way. There isn't one. Not for him, not for anyone but her."

Alex nodded. "It's not unlike Akeso. No matter how much of its essence Akeso pours into my body—you might have heard, I recently got a mega-dose—I'll never experience the deep connection to the planet that Caleb does."

"It is an apt analogy, particularly given Akeso's origins. Kyoseil bonds once and only once."

"If the choice of allegiance is made wisely, no other choices need be made...Caleb once said this about the *diati's* mindset. Akeso and the kyoseil have both chosen wisely, but...fine. I believe you. There's no way for him to go back with her. *Proklyat'ye, eto pizdets.*"

"This is why choosing to go back is the most supreme sacrifice imaginable. But the alternative is extinction. How could I make any other choice? How can she?

"So, please, give her this time. A time of peace, with Dashiel and Maris and Perrin and all her friends. Time to watch her people grow and thrive."

"I get it. But damn, this is going to be hard. How can I look her in the eye?"

"Now you, like me, carry your own burden. Will you bear it, for her?"

Alex tilted her head back to gaze at the starry sky overhead. She felt as if everything she knew had been flipped upside down. Her entire world had shifted beneath her feet and now canted badly off-kilter. She struggled to find True North.

But for all the grief she routinely gave Mesme, it...she...had never led them astray, had never done anything but help them to save themselves. Fifteen years ago, Mesme had helped her to save Caleb, and this was a debt she could never repay.

She nodded soberly. "I will."

"Thank you. With everything I am, thank you."

"Miaon went back with you...if we fail, will you have to accompany her? Do all this again, for a third time?"

"I will *choose* to. For the sake of the universe and everyone living in it. For her sake."

Abruptly Alex exploded off the chaise. "What if Nika doesn't have to go back in time? What if we win, once and for all? Because I certainly plan to. What happens then?"

"I do not know."

"And?"

"And nothing. I do not know. No one does. Alex, time travel should not exist. There are no rules, there is no science for it. This one singular event, at this one interlinked moment of time, is simply a last, desperate gambit by the universe to try to save itself."

"But if what you say is true, then winning negates the need for it to occur, doesn't it? The universe will have succeeded in its mission, and we can move forward. This has to be the answer."

"If we succeed—if we are victorious over the Dzhvar? Everything about what transpired in my timeline when the rift opened counsels me that it will mean the end of what has thus far been an endless cycle. We will at long last be able to march forward into our infinite future, and Nika will not need to suffer my fate. I've long yearned for this outcome, but I cannot allow myself to truly believe it will come to pass. Alex, *we have never won this battle*."

She drew close to Mesme, until the tightly packed lights brushed against her skin. "A few weeks ago, you told me that the continued existence of all living things depended on me gazing out into the universe and understanding it. On me being right, one more time. *This* is me being right one more time.

"I do understand the universe, I'd assert even better than you. And I'm starting to get a handle on these slippery primordial beings. It seems to me that the Dzhvar, *diati* and kyoseil have been squabbling with one another for a long time—likely since the dawn of their existence. The Dzhvar are the strongest, because they bring only destruction. The *diati* and the kyoseil both want to preserve the cosmos, but they've never been able to put aside their differences and cooperate long enough to stop their villainous sibling once and for all.

"But the *diati* isn't gone—its off doing universe shit. It got into the game to defeat the Dzhvar once. I guarantee it will do so again. This time we've got the kyoseil on our side as well, and I won't allow either of them to sit this fight out. Our Rasu War? It was simply the latest proxy battle fought on their behalf. But we won't be their pawns any longer. Instead, when the time comes, they'll be our weapons."

Alex considered the lights arrayed in front of her. They held Nika's form, her voice, her soul—but they also belonged to the confounding and extraordinary being she had called a friend for the last fifteen years. She would take Mesme's hands in hers, if only they were a bit more substantial.

"So hear me now. We *will* banish the Dzhvar to the infernal abyss—permanently. And when we do, this accursed time loop will forever come to an end.

"You will see a new day dawn, one free of dread or the looming spectre of death, and so will Nika. You have my word."

THE NEXT SAGA IN THE AMARANTHE UNIVERSE ARRIVES IN 2023

A first contact encounter isn't supposed to kick off with a dead body. But when Deputy Ambassador Marlee Marano arrives for an all-important first meeting with a newly discovered species, she unwittingly enters a world on the brink of collapse. Government conspiracies, ruthless terrorists bent on revolution, historical grievances boiling over and mysterious genetic experiments are the least of her concerns, however. For she finds herself wanted for murder, trapped in a dangerous alien society and hunted by all sides.

MEDUSA FALLING
A COSMIC SHORES NOVEL

PREORDER A SIGNED COPY TODAY AT
gsjennsen.com/medusa-falling

Author's Note

What comes next for Amaranthe? You've already gotten a teaser for the next book. *Medusa Falling* will be the kind of rollicking adventure we've come to expect from Marlee. I'll have a blog post up soon talking about the *Cosmic Shores* trilogy and what will follow it. Subscribe to my newsletter (gsjennsen.com/subscribe) to be notified when the blog post goes live.

I published my first novel, *Starshine*, in 2014. In the back of the book I put a short note asking readers to consider leaving a review or talking about the book with their friends. Watching my readers do that and so much more has been the most rewarding and humbling experience in my life.

So if you loved **DUALITY**, tell someone. Leave a review, share your thoughts on social media, annoy your coworkers in the break room by talking about your favorite characters. Reviews are the backbone of a book's success, but there is no single act that will sell a book better than word-of-mouth.

My part of this deal is to write a book worth talking about—your part of the deal is to do the talking. If you keep doing your bit, I get to write a lot more books for you.

Lastly, I want to hear from my readers. If you loved the book—or if you didn't—let me know. The beauty of independent publishing is its simplicity: there's the writer and the readers. Without any overhead, I can find out what I'm doing right and wrong directly from you, which is invaluable in making the next book better than this one. And the one after that. And the twenty after that.

Website: gsjennsen.com
Wiki: gsj.space/wiki

Email: gs@gsjennsen.com
Twitter: @GSJennsen
Facebook: gsjennsen.author

Goodreads: G.S. Jennsen
Pinterest: gsjennsen
Instagram: gsjennsen

Find my books at a variety of retailers: gsjennsen.com/retailers

APPENDIX

Read a summary of the events of Amaranthe #1-13 online at
gsjennsen.com/synopsis.

RIVEN WORLDS BOOKS 1-3
(Continuum, Inversion, Echo Rift)

Fourteen years have passed since the events of *AURORA RESONANT*. Caleb has fully bonded with Akeso, the living planet that saved his life, and he and Alex have made their home there.

Alex introduced Nika to Concord, the multi-species government formed after The Displacement to take the place of the deposed Anaden Directorate. Miriam served as its military leader and Mia its diplomatic one, while the major species of the former Anaden Empire were represented equally in a Senate. Nika warned Concord of the Rasu and received a cautious promise of support, as well as the opening of diplomatic relations. When Nika returned home to the Asterion Dominion, she discovered the other Advisors had created the Omoikane Initiative, a massive project designed to accelerate technology, warfare and logistical plans to combat the Rasu.

Concord was facing conflict on two additional fronts. Negotiations for the Savrakaths, a lizard-evolved Mosaic species, to become an ally of Concord broke down when CINT discovered they were developing antimatter weapons; Marlee, Caleb's niece, also discovered they were enslaving another species, the Godjans.

The lack of a strong Anaden leader led several *elassons* to foment a rebellion against Concord. Torval elasson-Machim took it upon himself to bomb the Savrakath's antimatter facility; unbeknownst to him, Eren was leading a team surveilling it, and Eren's lover, Cosime, was killed in the attack. Meanwhile, Malcolm was captured by the enemy during a mission to rescue Godjans on Savrak. When Concord approved an alliance with the Asterion Dominion, Ferdinand elasson-Kyvern began a coup to overthrow Concord.

The Rasu launched an attack on the Asterion world of Namino, and Concord sent a fleet to defend their new ally. They were unprepared, however, for how difficult the Rasu were to kill, and the battle turned against them. A leviathan shapeshifted to swallow Miriam's ship, the *Stalwart II*, and Rasu infiltrated the vessel. Miriam activated the ship's self-destruct mechanism to prevent the Rasu from acquiring Concord secrets, killing everyone on board.

The Rasu reached the Namino surface and activated a quantum block, cutting the planet off from the Asterions' d-gate network. Marlee was injured by a Rasu and trapped on the planet; some Asterions were able to rescue her and retreated to an underground bunker. Caleb stole a ship and went to Namino to find Marlee. He joined the Asterions trapped there in attempting to disrupt the Rasu invasion, at great personal cost to him due to Akeso's aversion to violence.

AEGIS marines defeated Ferdinand's coup attempt, and Ferdinand fled to a safe house with a group of sympathetic *elassons*. Corradeo Praesidis and his granddaughter, Nyx, returned to Concord after a fourteen-year absence. Disturbed by the state of Anaden affairs, Corradeo decided to resume the mantle of leadership and attempt to wrest control away from Ferdinand and the rebelling *elassons*.

Miriam became one of the first humans to be returned to life via regenesis. She struggled with the transition, as well as with maintaining control of Concord after the coup attempt. Alex and Kennedy reverse-engineered the Machin double-shielding technology and deployed it on AEGIS ships to prevent the Rasu from boarding vessels in the future. Further, the Kats began delivering Rift Bubble devices that created an impermeable barrier around a planet.

The Savrakaths lied and told Concord that Malcolm was dead. Mia, seeking revenge, tricked the Anadens into attacking the Savrakaths; when her deceptions were discovered, she became a fugitive.

Alex and Nika, along with Morgan, traveled to Namino and located Caleb and the others. Together they infiltrated the Rasu stronghold and destroyed the quantum block. A Rift Bubble device was activated on Namino, and the Concord fleet defeated the Rasu occupying the planet.

Malcolm escaped his Savrakath prison and returned home, surprising everyone. Mia, devasted by his apparent death, refused to reconcile with him so long as he declined regenesis. While in hiding on Pandora, Mia encountered Enzio Vilane, a wealthy businessman and secret mob boss with a notable family lineage. When he tried and failed to kidnap her, she agreed to a plea deal with the authorities and returned to Romane—but not to Malcolm.

Corradeo disbanded the rebel *elasson* group and established a new, Concord-friendly Anaden government. He convinced a brokenhearted Eren to come work for him as an intelligence agent.

Alex and Caleb investigated rumors of an advanced civilization, the Ourankeli, annihilated by the Rasu. They found a lone survivor, who told them of the powerful weapon they created to kill the Rasu (and how they used it too late to save themselves). The three of them traveled to the last settlement of Ourankeli, rescued them from a Rasu attack, and brought the refugees to Concord.

The Savrakaths sneaked an antimatter bomb onto Concord HQ. Richard and David were able to find and disarm it seconds before detonation. In response, the Kats exiled the Savrakaths, trapping their planet inside a modified Rift Bubble.

The Rasu reappeared to attack Toki'taku. The Taiyoks refused a Rift Bubble, but together with a Concord fleet, the Asterions were able to deploy their new Rima Grenades to beat back Rasu forces. However, the Rasu captured an unprotected Concord vessel and, now armed with the location of Concord, launched an assault on the Khokteh world of Ireltse.

ALL OUR TOMORROWS

The Concord fleet arrives at Ireltse to find it under heavy assault by a Rasu armada. Marines battle invading Rasu on the surface while Machim and AEGIS forces struggle to gain the advantage in space.

Alex and Caleb help Mesme deploy a Rift Bubble on Ireltse. However, the Rasu are able to construct and activate a quantum block, knocking out the Rift Bubble and causing the *Siyane* (piloted by Valkyrie) to crash on the Ireltse surface.

With the Rift Bubble barrier gone, Miriam and Malcolm deploy a new defensive weapon, the Parapet Gambit, to protect the planet, using AEGIS vessels equipped with the Anaden double-shielding technology to form an interconnected force field mesh.

Cut off from Valkyrie and AEGIS forces, Alex and Caleb race to where the *Siyane* has crashed into a building. They are able to dig the ship out and take control just as the building collapses around them. They then locate the quantum block and destroy it, enabling the Rift Bubble to reactivate; however, Valkyrie remains unreachable.

The Rasu bomb the Khokteh Command Center, and Pinchu is gravely injured. When he is minutes from death, Caleb and Akeso are able to heal Pinchu using Akeso's life energy. Concord forces are finally able to defeat the Rasu attackers, saving Ireltse.

After they return home, Alex repairs damage to Valkyrie's hardware, and Valkyrie is able to reboot herself. It turns out that, in order to protect Alex from the shock of the quantum block, Valkyrie shut down her remote hardware, then absorbed the impact of the block until it shorted her out. Later that night, Valkyrie muses with Thomas about both of their recent 'deaths' and the nature of their existence, and we learn they are intimate with one another.

Marlee, Caleb and Alex visit the Vrachnas and the Galenai as the two species receive Rift Bubble protection. While observing the Galenai from a stealthed *Siyane*, one of the Galenai detects their presence. Marlee initiates a basic interchange, identifying them as friends who will reveal themselves in time.

Eren brings Corradeo to Akeso, and Caleb and Corradeo are reunited for the first time since before The Displacement. Caleb is relieved to learn Corradeo does not blame him the loss of his *diati* or the destruction of Solum. They discuss sensing the *diati* out there in the stars and why they don't call for it, then part friends.

In the Asterion Dominion, Dashiel completes the development of a renewable negative energy weapon (RNEW), which stands to transform future battles against the Rasu. The Dominion military takes back their colony, Adjunct San, from the Rasu.

Perrin struggles with the emotional burden of caring for displaced refugees. When she breaks down at work, she decides to get an up-gen to tone down her emotional processes; Adlai is upset she didn't talk to him first, and worries she'll no longer be the woman he loves.

Marlee takes Corradeo to meet the Ourankeli refugees that Alex and Caleb rescued, who are working with Devon and Kennedy to recreate their Ymyrath Field weapon. Kennedy runs an experiment and discovers that while the Reor reacts to each of Alex and Caleb, only when they are together will it respond to resonance signals and release its kyoseil fibers.

Malcolm reviews the state of the Rasu war with the AEGIS Oversight Board, and the Board pressures him to revoke the no regenesis clause in his will. After the meeting, Malcolm is approached by an anti-regenesis group called the Gardiens. Malcolm attends a Gardiens meeting and leaves a surveillance device behind. It records the leadership discussing their secret plans for the group, and how they targeted him.

Meanwhile, Graham joins Richard at CINT to investigate Enzio Vilane. After reviewing Enzio's personal history, Graham deduces that Oliva Montegreu was his mother.

On Pandora, Enzio has coffee with his mother—a reconstituted Artificial built from scattered records of the original Olivia. She's obviously a work in progress, but Enzio displays an obsessive adoration of her.

Eren visits Chalmun Station to investigate a group of dissident Barisans as part of his new job for the Anaden Advocacy. While he's there, the Rasu launch an attack on the asteroid. Morgan learns of the attack and rushes there as well. She and Eren work together to evacuate people until a tunnel caves in, trapping them. They are almost out of air when Alex is able to open a wormhole at their location and extricate Morgan and Eren. Alex then convinces Miriam to test the prototype Ymyrath Field weapon on the Rasu attacking Chalmun Station.

Malcolm bugs his Gardiens contact, then records a conversation where the Gardiens target Miriam for assassination, planning to make it look like her death is due to neurological system failure, casting doubt on the safety of regenesis. Malcolm rushes to London and intercepts Miriam just as the assassin fires, thwarting the attack.

Everyone gathers at Miriam and David's house; Malcolm plays the holo recording, and Richard identifies the man giving the orders as Enzio Vilane. Realizing this is the same man who tried to kidnap Mia, Malcolm volunteers to go undercover with the Gardiens in an attempt to bring them down—and realizes he can't have any contact with Mia while he does. Caleb investigates the crime scene in London, uncovering forensic evidence that will identify the shooter.

Enzio cleans house after the failed assassination attempt. Olivia gives him some harsh advice, then proposes adjustments she wants to make to her own programming.

Abigail and Marlee review Marlee's plan to upgrade her cybernetics enough to become a Solo Prevo. Abigail warns Marlee that the upgrades will likely develop emergent properties, the nature of which they can't predict.

Miriam meets with the AEGIS Council and learns Earth's Rift Bubble caused an accident, killing 1,200 people. The Council decides to deactivate the Rift Bubbles until there's an attack, against her strong advice. On an unknown planet, a Rasu unit secretly begins gathering materials needed to construct a quantum block.

The Rasu steal a Dominion commercial vessel, and Nika has to visit the Rift Bubbles on Dominion worlds to change the passcodes. Mesme arrives while she's doing so and hints that she has the capability to access the Rift Bubbles remotely, but doesn't tell her how to do so.

The members of the Idryma express concern over the Asterions' rapid modification of the Kat technology they've been provided. After the meeting, Lakhes suggests telling the others the truth, but Mesme insists they cannot.

Corradeo proposes opening diplomatic talks to formally build a relationship between Anadens and Asterions. Nika assigns the task to Maris, and when Maris and Corradeo meet, frosty fireworks ensue. Maris asks for the Anadens to give Asterion Prime to the Asterions. He insists that's impossible, but promises to find a way for Asterions to settle on the planet without joining Concord as a full member.

Joaquim and Selene continue their affair. When Joaquim refuses to tell her why he holds a grudge against Justice, Selene decides to investigate the matter herself. She dives into old Justice Division records and learns about the raid that killed Joaquim's lover, Cassidy. In reviewing the evidence, Selene discovers that Cassidy's backup storage, though damaged, was not actually destroyed. She discusses it with Adlai and decides to wake the woman up. After hearing of what happened to Joaquim and Cassidy, Adlai apologizes to Perrin for being angry about her up-gen.

Marlee shows Morgan her intended upgrades to her cybernetics. When things turn affectionate between them, Marlee kisses Morgan; Morgan freaks out and leaves. Marlee reacts by inviting her former boyfriend over for a one-night stand. When it ends somewhat badly as well, she decides the only thing she can fix is herself, and makes plans to go ahead with her upgrades.

Morgan argues with Stanley about the kiss, insisting she is not in a place where she can handle a relationship. She visits Malcolm and asks him to find a way to get her into a fighter jet. They discuss Harper's death, and how Morgan blames Miriam for it. Malcolm refers her to an IDCC military test group.

While exploring one of Dashiel's labs, Nika comes upon a warehouse of kyoseil-filled vats. The kyoseil responds strongly to her presence, and she attempts to talk to it. Mesme senses the reaction, as does Miaon. Dashiel comes upon Nika interacting with the kyoseil; they make love, and she sees the universe through the kyoseil's perspective.

Selene asks Joaquim to meet her at a regenesis clinic, where she reveals that she was able to wake Cassidy up. After a bittersweet farewell, Joaquim is reunited with Cassidy.

Malcolm finagles an invitation to meet with the Gardiens leader, Enzio Vilane. He receives a message from Mia inviting him to lunch, and realizes he has to refuse in order to protect her from Enzio, who doesn't know her true identity. Malcolm convinces Enzio he's a Gardiens true believer and gains the man's confidence.

Mia receives Malcolm's response while overseeing Expo construction and interprets it as a rejection. She recognizes this is the consequence of her actions after he escaped from Savrak.

Alex and Caleb investigate a Rasu-controlled galaxy, and discover the Rasu have built a galaxy core-spanning ring. Alex speculates that the ring is intended to force the galaxy to spin faster, possibly to pull neighboring galaxy closer together. The only reason she can come up with to do so is to prevent the eventual heat death of the universe.

The Rasu arrive at Rudan, the homeworld of the Ruda, and begin attacking. A Concord fleet swiftly arrives to defend the planet.

The Ruda make an overture to the Rasu as a fellow synthetic life form. The Rasu respond that if the Ruda will provide information about Concord, they will cease their attack and share the details of their shapeshifting capability. The Ruda accept the deal, then tell Miriam to stand down from the battle. Miriam asks Valkyrie to intercede.

Valkyrie contacts Supreme Three, who tells her they have reached a deal with the Rasu. It informs Valkyrie that it does not trust her, since she withheld information about quantum physics from the Ruda. The Ruda terminate their relationship with Concord and threaten to fire on the Concord vessels.

Miriam initially refuses to withdraw and must now consider the Ruda an enemy as well. The Ruda begin turning their entire planet into a massive EMP weapon to strike the Concord fleet, however, and Miriam is forced to withdraw to save Concord Artificials and unprotected vessels.

Mesme informs Alex that 'it is time' to take Nika to visit the Reor in the Oneiroi Nebula. Dashiel and Mesme join them all on the *Siyane*. Mesme says Nika's ability to manipulate kyoseil has advanced to a point where she will benefit from exposure to a larger and more pure source.

Nika, Dashiel, Alex and Caleb exit the *Siyane* and approach one of the powerful energy pillars in the Reor colony. Nika takes off her glove, thrusts her hand into the pillar and is consumed by the streaming energy.

When Alex and Caleb try to help Nika, Mesme prevents them from reaching her, insisting that she is safe and 'this must happen.' Nika pulls Dashiel into the energy vortex with her, attempting to share the experience with him. Once all the kyoseil's energy is flowing into Nika, she opens a wormhole and transports herself and Dashiel back to her flat on Mirai. She observes that she believes perhaps she has been transformed into something new, but Dashiel says she instead might be something unfathomably ancient.

Acknowledgements

Many thanks to my beta readers, editors and artists, who made everything about this book better, and to my family, who continue to put up with an egregious level of obsessive focus on my part for months at a time.

I also want to add a personal note of thanks to everyone who has read my books, left a review at a retailer, Goodreads or other sites, sent me a personal email expressing how the books have impacted you, or posted on social media to share how much you enjoyed them. You make this all worthwhile, every day.

About the Author

G. S. JENNSEN lives in Montana with her husband and two dogs. She has become an internationally bestselling author since her first novel, *Starshine*, was published in 2014. She has chosen to continue writing under an independent publishing model to ensure the integrity of her stories and her ability to execute on the vision she has for their telling.

While she has been a lawyer, a software engineer and an editor, she's found the life of a full-time author preferable by several orders of magnitude. When she isn't writing, she's gaming or working out or getting lost in the mountains that loom large outside the windows in her home. Or she's dealing with a flooded basement, or standing in a line at Walmart reading the tabloid headlines and wondering who all of those people are. Or sitting on her back porch with a glass of wine, looking up at the stars, trying to figure out what could be up there.

Lightning Source UK Ltd.
Milton Keynes UK
UKHW010051170223
417092UK00014B/743/J